MANIFEST DESTINY

Books by Brian Garfield:

Nonfiction:

THE THOUSAND-MILE WAR: *World War II in Alaska and the Aleutians*
I, WITNESS: *True Personal Encounters with Crime* (editor)
WESTERN FILMS: *A Complete Guide*

Fiction:

THE ARIZONANS
THE LAWBRINGERS
SEVEN BRAVE MEN
VULTURES IN THE SUN
APACHE CANYON
THE VANQUISHED
THE LAST BRIDGE
BUGLE AND SPUR
WAR WHOOP AND BATTLE CRY (editor)
ARIZONA
THE VILLIERS TOUCH
VALLEY OF THE SHADOW
SLIPHAMMER
THE HIT
THE LAST HARD MEN (aka GUN DOWN)
WHAT OF TERRY CONNISTON?
SWEENY'S HONOR
DEEP COVER
RELENTLESS
DEATH WISH
LINE OF SUCCESSION
TRIPWIRE
GANGWAY! (in collaboration with Donald E. Westlake)
KOLCHAK'S GOLD
THE THREEPERSONS HUNT
THE ROMANOV SUCCESSION
HOPSCOTCH
TARGET MANHATTAN (pen-name: Drew Mallory)
DEATH SENTENCE
RECOIL
FEAR IN A HANDFUL OF DUST
THE MARCHAND WOMAN (pen-name: John Ives)
WILD TIMES
THE PALADIN (in collaboration with "Christopher Creighton")
CHECKPOINT CHARLIE
THE CRIME OF MY LIFE (editor)
NECESSITY
MANIFEST DESTINY

MANIFEST DESTINY

Brian Garfield

PENZLER BOOKS • NEW YORK

Penzler Books, 129 West 56th Street, New York, N.Y. 10019

Printed in the United States of America

Library of Congress Cataloging-in-Publication Data

Garfield, Brian, 1939–
Manifest destiny / by Brian Garfield.
p. cm.
Bibliography: p.
ISBN 0-89296-382-4
1. Roosevelt, Theodore, 1858–1919, in fiction, drama, poetry, etc.
I. Title.
PS3557.A715M36 1989
813′.54—dc20 89-9253
CIP

For Jane and Thomas
in memory of John

MANIFEST DESTINY

A Note

"All the historical books which contain no lies are extremely tedious."

—Anatole France

"Some events do not occur at the right time, and others do not occur at all. It is the proper function of the historian to correct these faults."

—Herodotus

Let me take you into my confidence.

This book is a novel about real people and real events. It relates a true story—by Herodotus's rules.

All the characters lived; virtually all the significant events took place. The tale is based largely on the recollections and writings of actual participants. But in the attempt to put history in tidier order, I have oversimplified and rearranged.

Every person who is named in the book was real, except for a hotel guest whose stolen watch is a fictitious invention; a few characters, however, are composites of more than one real person—

and several people who played important roles in reality have been left out altogether. I beg the forgiveness of their partisans. For similar reasons of economy the book fails to mention various places and institutions (including one of Theodore Roosevelt's two Dakota ranches).

Some of the dialogue derives from actual words spoken or written by these people; much of it, naturally, is fictitious but most speeches and items from newspapers are abridged from real ones (with occasional revisions designed to fit the narrative) and much of the trial testimony and vituperation are quoted directly from the records. The letter from the Marquis De Morès, challenging Theodore Roosevelt to a duel, is genuine, as are Roosevelt's reply and choice of weapons.

The novel compresses an actual five-year span into a fictitious two years. Some incidents are not related in the sequence in which they actually occurred, but as a general rule all the events, confrontations and adventures of consequence actually took place, although the knowledgeable reader will see that some have been repopulated and reorganized for dramatic purposes.

If an incident or character in the novel seems particularly outlandish, it probably existed in reality. (E.g., the menacing two-gun man who disrupted Roosevelt's 1903 speaking tour of the West, and the curious character called "The Lunatic," are not my creations; they are described in Theodore Roosevelt's *Autobiography*.)

With a cheerful sort of recklessness I have tried to impose dramatic coherence on an assortment of events that took place a century ago in ragged haphazard fashion. I have also been merrily willing to accept versions of a few events from sources of dubious veracity when their accounts seemed both entertaining and at least plausibly conceivable.

In sum, I have no ambition to mislead: this novel aims to be a dramatized homage to history rather than an unblemished factual record. If it goads the reader's curiosity, facts that are uncorrupted by my imagination can be found by consulting nonfiction sources such as the works listed in the bibliography at the end of the book.

—Brian Garfield
Los Angeles, 1989

Prologue

June 1903

Apprehensive, Arthur Packard stepped off the Northern Pacific Flyer onto the platform. He carried his valise through dwindling coal-ash smoke to the near corner of the weathered wood depot and peered past it at the town below the weedy embankment.

No one stirred in the twilight. Empty buildings sprawled like a hand of cards dealt hastily. Heat contraction brought echoes from broad rusting metal rooftops beneath the spire of the old abattoir's great brick smokestack that loomed against Bad Lands bluffs and the broad darkening Dakota sky. A little dust devil turned a dainty pirouette along a street the name of which he could not remember.

He was startled by the voice of the porter who spoke from the train behind him: "Sir, I don't see nobody. You sure you wants to get off here?"

Arthur Packard fluttered a hand at hip level to waive the porter's concerns and absolve the railroad. He heard a train door slam—chuff of steam, jostle of couplings and wheels; he set his valise down on the platform and caught a glimpse of his own reflection in the unbroken half of a window—tall, bearded, Lincolnesque—and heard the train clatter across the bridge. He made a face at his reflection and looked back across the river in time to see the caboose disappear around the long bend in deep silver shadows at the foot of Graveyard Butte.

The wind was a gentle ruffle against his ear. Otherwise there was no sound. No life. His stare lifted to the terrace alongside the butte—to the big house that loomed southwest of him, overlooking the river valley and the town.

Château De Morès. It stirred uneasy memories. Against the fading evening sky there was some sort of trick of reflection, for it appeared as if there were a light in one of the downstairs windows.

He put his back to that, picked up the valise and stepped off the platform and walked down off the embankment, kicking up little misty whorls that tickled his nostrils with a scent that invoked remembrance.

Irritated by the weakness of such sentimentality he looked down and saw, with a sort of gratification, that the powder dust had instantly obscured the polish on his boots. So much for remembered charms.

The embankment did not seem different; no more weeds than ever. It ran straight across the flats from one set of bluffs to the other like a military earthwork, interrupted midway by the flatiron bridge that spanned the fitful surges of the Little Missouri River. Pack walked down the flats on the northerly side of the embankment amid false fronts and weathered boardwalks: except for a fading of paint the ghost town appeared eerily unchanged from its glory days. Evidently there had been no fires since the blaze that had destroyed his newspaper nearly two decades ago. He walked slowly, memories stirred by the little brick church that the beautiful Madame la Marquise had built, the sagging shops his friends had occupied, the saloons that had seen as much commotion as conviviality, the great mass of the abattoir with its towering brick smokestack, the open field where they had chased baseballs in those days long before it had become the national game, the jail shack they had called the Bastille: with an audible grunt of quiet laughter he remembered the time a dozen drunken cowboys, determined to bust a friend out, had tied lassos around the building, hitched it to an unsuspecting train, and watched aghast as the departing train towed the entire sturdy little structure all the way down to the river's edge before the ropes had snapped—and all of it without a scratch of visible damage to the Bastille. Pack remembered the horror with which he had put the key in the padlock and dragged open the heavy door (it, like the rest of the Bastille, was constructed of railroad ties) only to find the occupant unharmed if you didn't count his inebriated bewilderment: "My God, boys, wasn't that one hell of a earthquake!"

Now Pack looked around the town and it seemed the only things missing were the people, the animals, the noise of uncivil civilization—and the stink of slaughter.

Remarkable.

In an abasing dusk on the porch of the general store he propped himself beneath the false-fronted sign that was still more or less legible: JOE FERRIS GENERAL MERCHANDISE. In a moment he would go inside to take shelter from the Western night. Just now he leaned against the wall to rest his legs and contemplate the scorched plot across the way where his own establishment had stood.

He was like that, picking a tooth with a fingernail, when the sudden loud scrape of a door made him wheel in heart-suspended fear.

A walrus of a man came through the doorway; one arm, brawny as a side of beef, held the door away. His squint of irritation became a peculiar scowl of surprise followed by dubious delight. "—Look what we got here, then."

Uncertain at first in the poor light, Arthur Packard squinted at him. It was the voice, finally, that gave it away. "Joe Ferris." He laughed. "Must be prosperity. You have sure as hell filled out."

"You haven't. Still too damn skinny to live." The unexpectedly stout Joe Ferris beamed and pumped his hand. "Be that as it may. Pack, Pack. Now this is fine. Oh, Pack, I've missed you. Letters every three, four Christmases just don't cut the mustard."

Pack's glance tipped up toward the signboard with Joe's name on it. "You don't still own this . . . ?"

There was a grunt of aspersion. "See anybody around here to sell goods to? I've got my big store over in Montana. One's enough."

"Then I assume we're both here for the same reason. But the President's not due till tomorrow—you're a day early."

"May be. So are you."

Pack said, "I wanted to get here before the crowd."

"Me too. Came in on the eastbound this morning. Tramped the whole town today. Nothing to see—unless you count recollections."

In the flowing shadows color died out of the world. Joe Ferris continued to hold the door. "Come upstairs. We'll light a fire. You can tell me things. You're newspapering in Chicago—that's all I know, and it ain't enough."

Pack followed his old friend inside. Joe struck a match and put it to the stub of a candle from his pocket. The big room was empty—shelves, counters and hardware being too valuable to leave behind—but implausibly there lingered a faint familiar redolence of leather, kerosene, linseed oil, licorice.

"Remember when I had to fort up in here with a shotgun to keep Jerry Paddock from robbing all my stocks?"

"Now in fact I remember before that. I remember when Swede owned this place."

"And Jerry Paddock ran him off. Wonder what ever came of Swede?"

"How old are you, Joe?"

"Forty-eight."

"I'm forty-three," said Pack. "Listen to us. Like old men—chewing over the past so long ago it's history."

Joe started up the stairs. "Does seem a hell of a long time ago, doesn't it. I wasn't a Republican then. Hell, I wasn't even a citizen."

"Another age—another century. You realize Roosevelt's only forty-four?"

"Tell the truth I never could enumerate whether he's too young or too old," Joe Ferris said. "Either he was born an old man or he's a bright little kid that never grew up at all."

"I thought you were his man, Joe, body and soul."

"And I thought you were against him. What are you doing here?"

"I'm a newspaperman," Pack said evasively. "He's news."

On the upstairs hearth a fire had been laid; Joe ignited it with his candle. A blanket-roll lay against the wall. Joe began to unpack it—a bottle of whiskey, fold-handle frypan, airtights of peaches and pork-and-beans.

Most of the windows had been papered over. One still had its glass. Pack went to it and looked out. That definitely was lamplight in a downstairs window of the château up on the bluff. "Somebody's up there. Squatter? Pilgrim taking shelter for the night?"

Joe Ferris took a look. "More likely caretaker. Madame De Morès still owns it, I hear. Had somebody looking after it, case she ever comes back."

"Not much chance of that after all these years." Pack set his valise down. "Now I remember how your great man took one look at that woman and all of a sudden it was as if a locomotive had hit him in the face. Which is not surprising, I suppose, when a man finds himself face to face with a woman who ought to be against the law."

"That was all in your head, Pack. Don't you know that yet? She never had an eye for anybody but her husband. That was her big mistake, you ask me."

Pack had learned years ago there was no point arguing that particular matter with Joe Ferris, no matter how obvious the real facts might have been. He changed the subject. "Now it's odd—I was going to camp up here tonight. Right here." He turned a full circle on his heels. "He stayed up here that day, on his way out to face De Morès."

Joe said shrewdly, "You remember that, do you?"

"It was a ridiculous thing to do. You've got to admit that."

"No," Joe said. "I sure as hell don't have to admit that." He was working the cork out of the whiskey bottle. "He did the right thing that day. He usually does."

"Hell it was ridiculous. He pictured himself in some Wild West dime novel. But then he's always been ridiculous. That act he puts on—big words and bravado. The bully big stick and the pompous moralizing. You know what he is, Joe? He's a *character*."

"Aeah," Joe Ferris agreed. "Pretty good one, too. Otherwise you wouldn't be here today—and he wouldn't be President." He offered the bottle. "Let's drink to the pretty good character."

Pack hesitated. Then he reached for the bottle. "Well all right."

In the morning three men came riding in, each leading three or four saddled horses.

Pack watched from the porch as they emerged from their own dust cloud. He couldn't quite make them out yet. "Look like first-class horses. Who's that?"

"A.C. Huidekoper," Joe Ferris said. "Say he's still got a horse ranch on the river here. Looks like he's brought visitors."

"Why that's Howard Eaton—and Johnny Goodall."

The horseman dismounted in a swirl. There were shouts of delight and bone-crushing handshakes. Pack hadn't seen any of them in years. He hadn't known Huidekoper was still hereabouts. He knew the other two came from far ranges—Howard Eaton from his famous ranch in Wyoming, Johnny Goodall all the way from his native Texas.

Howard Eaton, who was something of a celebrity—he and his brothers were known all over the world for having founded the dude-ranch industry—said to Joe Ferris, "You weighed in at a lot less, last time I saw you." He turned to Pack. "Well I have come home to Medora to see the great Rough Rider—the first citizen of the world." Eaton aimed his friendly crinkled outdoor eyes east toward the gap where the rails descended from the plateau. "When's the train due, then?"

"Nine o'clock if it's on time," Joe Ferris replied.

Pack said, "It wouldn't dare be late."

Joe Ferris said, "Who're the horses for?"

"Yourselves," said A.C. Huidekoper in his precise Pennsylvania voice, "which is to say the President and whoever he wants to bring with him. We'll have to get out there and back in twenty-four hours."

Pack said, "He's a little on the beefy side for a sixty-five-mile round-trip ride, isn't he?" The thought made him glance at his friend Joe Ferris. "Not to mention certain present company I wouldn't care to name out loud."

Joe said, "I can still ride rings around you on a horse, Pack, any time I'm a mind to."

"I seem to recall you never were a mind to. Never could stand riding a horse if sitting in a chair would get the job done."

Joe flashed a grin that brought back all his old boyishness. "I don't mind going outdoors nowadays. Just so long as I don't have to make my living at it. As for Mr. Roosevelt, I remember when he rode a hundred miles without a break and I haven't heard anybody say he's slowed down any. They say he runs around the White House grounds every day. That beef you're talking about is muscle."

A.C. Huidekoper was looking around at the buildings of the town with a look that struck Pack as somewhat prideful: almost proprietary. Not that there was anything wrong with that; Huidekoper was the only one of them who still lived hereabouts so he had a right to think of the town as home if he was a mind to.

Huidekoper said, "Tomorrow he'll make a speech right here—it's what he wants. There'll be crowds coming in from Dickinson and Bismarck and Helena too, I would venture to guess. But nobody knows he's stopping here today. Today it's just us. The old friends." Huidekoper swept off his big hat, exposing his bald cranium to the sun. "We were privileged, I perceive, to be witness to the making of an American hero. I'm pleased to take note that a few of us were aware of it at the time."

Joe Ferris looked pointedly at Pack: "And a few of us were not."

"He's a famous man now and that colors a lot of memories," Pack said. He felt cross with them all. "The plain fact of the matter is he was a ridiculous dude in the Wild West. He was a wretch and I marvel he survived at all. Sickly young fool and half the population trying to kill him to gain favor with the Marquis."

A.C. Huidekoper said, "It was this country made a man of him."

"No sir," said Joe Ferris. "He always had it in him. It took some longer than others to see that."

"Possible," Howard Eaton conceded. "But the Bad Lands brought it out. The Bad Lands and the Stranglers. They were enough to put gristle on any young man."

Joe Ferris said, "I'll differ with that. Thing about it is, the Stranglers didn't harden him. The first time you see a man hanging by the neck it's horrible. The second time it's not so bad. By the fourth or fifth time most folks become indifferent. But *he* never got that way."

Pack was unable to compose a further retort before Johnny Goodall ranged forward amid the crowd of horses and drawled greetings: Johnny the Tall Texan—a good man, kind and fair, who had put the lie to the myth that if you got down with dogs you had to get up with fleas. Johnny had been the Marquis De Morès's range foreman but no one had held it against him—not even Theodore Roosevelt.

Waiting for the Presidential train the five men stood clustered in eager impatience, telling stories and waiting to tell stories, until suddenly there was a racket of steady angry explosive barks that froze them in sudden confusion.

Pack remembered that sound. Knew it.

Gunshots. Not far away at all.

Nine . . . ten . . .

Johnny Goodall said, "Forty-five hog legs. Two-gun man. Far side of the embankment." His voice left no aperture for dispute; Johnny didn't say much but when he did, only a fool would argue with him. Johnny generally knew what he was talking about.

A.C. Huidekoper bristled. "What kind of fool would disturb the peace out here at a time like this?"

The unseen shooter started up again with a steady banging rhythm: ten shots, evenly spaced. Echoes spanged back from the bluffs.

"Target practice," Joe Ferris observed. "Let's take a look."

They swarmed awkwardly up the weedy pitch of the Northern Pacific rampart. Pack's boots skidded under him and he had to scramble to keep from losing his balance.

At the top Huidekoper continued to scowl. It made Pack recall how the bald little Pennsylvanian's indignations always had lingered near the surface. "There's the rascal—there he is."

It took Pack a moment to find the object of Huidekoper's glare—he saw the saddled horse first, ground-hitched and waiting; then the man farther away, tall and gaunt in a long dusty black coat, fifty yards south of here along the riverbank, standing in a clutter of volcanic boulders, peppering away with steady deliberation at a pile of tin cans that individually leaped and bounced like carousing fleas. When the right-hand revolver was finished the left-hand one began with no interruption in the metronomic rhythm; there was something awful about it—as inhuman and indifferent as a machine.

Having emptied his third pair of cylinder-loads with baneful effectiveness the two-gun man paused to plug out his empties and refill the chambers from coat pockets that bulged with a weight of ammunition. Then he holstered both weapons and turned toward his horse. He put one foot in the stirrup, lifted himself aboard and adjusted the reins in his grip. Then he looked up. That was when he discovered Pack and the other four. Under the flat black hatbrim his face shot forward with an atavistic suspicion.

It was a blade-narrow face upon which two features were remarkable even at this distance: great jagged eyebrows and the drooping Mandarin-style mustache—silver-hued now, but twenty years ago they had been deep glistening raven black: as singular then as now. For there was no mistaking that Ichabod Crane angularity, the poised stance, the belligerent thrust of jaw. Even at this remove, Pack identified the villain instantly, as if the intervening years had been erased.

Joe Ferris said, in a voice soft with revulsion, "Jerry Paddock. Didn't know he was still alive."

"He wouldn't be, if justice had been left to me," said Howard Eaton.

Johnny Goodall said, "Never mind, sir. I expect you're just as satisfied you never took occasion to lynch anybody."

"Speak for yourself," Eaton growled, but Pack knew Johnny Goodall had told the truth of the matter.

The villain couldn't have heard the words at that distance but he lifted his reins as if in response, swept the five men with one final withering stare, wheeled the horse expertly on its hind legs and broke away in an immediate canter, riding off upriver with leisurely insolence.

A.C. Huidekoper said, "I put forward the suggestion we consider what might bring that vile carrion here to this place on this particular day."

Howard Eaton chopped the blade of one hand into the other palm. "I brought my hunting rifle, in case it's the President's pleasure."

Huidekoper was squinting cheerlessly toward the river bend to the south where the departing horseman continued to dwindle. "I wouldn't care to begin to count the number of times Jerry Paddock made threats upon Roosevelt's life."

"Not to mention the time Theodore got the better of him barehanded against both revolvers," Eaton added.

Pack said, "I wonder if those are the same two Colts."

Eaton went on: "It must have been the kind of humiliation that would have galled a far less arrogant man than Paddock. You were there that time, weren't you, Joe?"

Joe Ferris said, "I was, and I don't think Jerry Paddock's forgot it either. Be a good idea if we all stand close around Mr. Roosevelt today—and keep both eyes peeled on the horizons. Those of us, that is," he added with a dry glance toward Pack, "who give a damn about the life and good health of the President."

"Now Joe, that's hardly fair," Pack complained. "I'll keep as sharp an eye as any man here, and you're a hell of a friend if you think any different."

"I was only pulling your leg there," Joe Ferris said. "Let's not all get even more tetchy than we need to."

No one else had heard any signal yet—certainly Pack hadn't noticed anything—but when Johnny Goodall said, "Here comes the train," nobody doubted him for an instant. They all turned and marched toward the platform.

By the time they had reached it and Pack had bent to sweep some of the dust off the knees of his trousers, the train was in sight, coming down out of the cut between the eastern bluffs.

Watching the advance of the heavy steam locomotive, Pack felt his heart race with an unexpected thrill—and at the same time his eyes swiveled fearfully toward the trees upriver where the evil horseman had disappeared.

The run to the Elkhorn that day became a flickering confusion in Pack's mind; later when he thought back on it there was little he remembered of the thirty-mile ride downriver except for the heat, the gritty dust in his teeth and the general sweaty discomfort of it.

The train came in on time and there was a crowd of men with the President: Westerners, most of them—Roosevelt's avid Colorado and Wyoming boosters from the Rough Rider regiment, but strangers to Pack. Right from the outset Pack felt himself pushed to the back of things; there was no chance to get close, and in any event he felt a troublesome responsibility to watch the horizons for any hint of Jerry Paddock.

He was not able to get close to the President during most of the day, especially at the beginning; he was not even in earshot when he saw Roosevelt jump down off the train and climb onto the horse Huidekoper provided. Pack watched as the President, attired in rough riding clothes and a near-shapeless narrow-brim hat, adjusted his feet in the stirrups, gathered the reins and led the parade through town.

After that it was all Pack could do to keep up; Roosevelt made a thundering race of it.

Half an hour downriver the President slowed the pace to breathe the horses. They dismounted and led the animals. Someone said something that brought out Roosevelt's peculiar chattering bark of laughter. "We'll send half a dozen gunboats and the Colombians won't know the difference. It takes four weeks on muleback to reach their capital—and in any event they're in the midst of what appears to be an interminable and perpetual civil war, with the result that it's impossible to know whom to treat with. Only one solution, by George. The Panamanians will declare their independence under our protection and we'll make a canal-building treaty with *them* and then you may mark my words, boys, I shall make the dirt fly."

With jaundiced suspicion Pack regarded the costume worn by the President of the United States. It managed somehow to be both calculated and ingenuous. The outfit had seen hard service: slouch campaign hat, dark coat, soft negligee shirt with turndown collar, brown corduroy riding pants, soft leather leggins and stout stovepipe boots. It was the uniform of a hard-riding fighter—a man of the people—a working-man.

Yet Roosevelt had been born into a fortune, tutored for a life in the aristocracy, trained at Harvard in law and crew. By birth and heritage he was as much a working-man as Louis XIV. But he wore the rough clothes naturally—because he had earned them; even his enemies must concede that.

Someone else spoke; Roosevelt replied with his back turned, so Pack couldn't hear it; then the President strolled nearer and Pack heard him address Joe Ferris:

"And how's the hunting, old man?"

"Not much game left nowadays, sir. Everything's near extinct."

"I'm doing what I can about that in Washington, you know. We've got to protect these animals or future generations will never get a crack at them, will they now."

It was a topic that provoked Pack to drag his horse forward, prying a place amid half a dozen trudging strangers, to plunge in with a question: "What do you think of this new Teddy Bear they've put on the market?"

"An abomination," said the man who hated to be called Teddy.

"I'm not yet fool enough to believe what you boys say about me in the newspapers." Never slowing his quick pace he grinned and looked Pack straight in the eye: "I don't make a sport of shooting baby bears. It's your bloody cartoonists who're the ones who ought to be shot."

"Those cartoons haven't appeared in my newspaper, sir."

"But your editorials have."

Pack tried to reply to the President's broad grin in kind but he was no match for those teeth. And then he was squeezed back when the leader indicated, by climbing back aboard his horse, that it was time to resume the run.

Down along the riverbank Roosevelt galloped in a whirl of dust. On his heels drummed the gallant company of old friends. The President rode heavily, bristling, tipping pugnaciously forward in the saddle.

The final dash was a mad confused gallop, the horses strung out in a loose bunch, with Colonel Roosevelt a nose ahead of his old friend Huidekoper. The President rode into the clearing on the run, his horse heaving. Huidekoper, who had to be near sixty, riding like an Indian, slithered his horse to a pirouette and Roosevelt glowered at him. "You old rascal—tried to beat me!"

"I tried," Huidekoper agreed.

"Oh, boys, this is the life. Look at that stand of cottonwoods. By George it is still the loveliest spot in the Bad Lands." The President got off his horse and led it about. "This horse is breathing some—and then some."

The Elkhorn ranch house was gone, broken up for lumber, but there was still the great stand of trees to which he had referred, and beyond them on all sides the magnificent multi-colored slopes and buttes of the Bad Lands. Now Roosevelt whipped off his hat to drag a sleeve across his brow. In that dreadful choppy irritating voice he said, "'Thank God I have lived and toiled with men.' So spake my friend Kipling. By Godfrey, boys, I know every crease of this country. I've ridden over it, hunted in it, tramped it in all weather and every season. And it looks like home to me." He drew an immense breath into his barrel chest, slapped both palms against his breast in manly satisfaction, then poked a finger toward Huidekoper, then Eaton, then Johnny Goodall, then Joe Ferris.

"We'll set up our tents and you'll share my quarters, gentlemen, and we'll talk about old times."

And finally the poking finger turned toward Pack. When Pack looked up, the President's big square face was grinning right at him: that grin famous round the world—huge tombstone teeth, curry-brush mustache, Prussian-style close-cropped sandy hair and glittering eyeglasses—and suddenly Pack felt the full warmth of it.

"You too, Arthur," said the President. "I'll win your vote yet, by George, or die trying!"

With a hearty bellow of laughter the President slapped him on the shoulder and Pack felt a flush of heat suffuse his face all the way down into his shoulders.

Roosevelt moved on to the next crony. After a moment Pack swung away, awkward and uncertain, to stride to the edge of camp. His heart was pounding.

He felt weight beside him and turned to see Joe Ferris peering into the trees.

Pack felt the edge of the same fast-traveling thought that must have goaded Joe. "A nice spot for an ambush."

Joe nodded slowly. Then his expression changed and he began to shake his head. "No. Not Jerry Paddock. He's killed from ambush before, I guess, but this is a matter of pride. He'll come in straight up if he comes at all."

"And you are aiming to be ready for him."

"If it comes to that," Joe agreed with even-voiced gravity. "We lost one President to an assassin two years ago and I don't believe it would be seemly to have it happen again."

Joe left him then. Pack wandered the edge of the wood, annoyed with himself because even after all the intervening years he still didn't seem able to get close enough to clarify the fuzzy borders of his perception of Theodore Roosevelt. You listened to TR bragging and saw him for nothing but a blowhard—opinionated, arrogant, so full of himself he seemed ready to burst. And yet they all loved him, these men of wide experience and mature judgment.

There was no doubt in Pack's mind that in the days since Roosevelt had become famous by rough-riding his way up San Juan Hill and dispatching the fleet to the Philippines and swaggering his way into the White House at the unheard-of unseasoned age of forty-one, his past life had moved from the province of actuality to that of legend. Joe Ferris and these others were remembering the Roosevelt they wanted their hero to have been. They seemed conveniently to have forgotten the foolish ridiculous loudmouthed dude who had stepped off the train at that same spot exactly twenty years ago.

Pack sat down with his back to the bole of a tree and tried to remember how things really had been.

One

It had become the custom on the Little Missouri to greet trains by shooting into the air over the roofs of the railroad cars. The Cantonment had a reputation for deviltry and the boys felt a duty to live up to it. The Northern Pacific had learned to warn its passengers to cower beneath the sills because it was not extraordinary for the intoxicated frontiersmen to shoot through windows.

Some travelers, and even a few residents of the encampment, objected to this boisterous behavior on grounds that it was not only barbaric but downright dangerous. Personally Joe Ferris thought it was fair retribution in behalf of animals on the plains that had been maimed or slaughtered and left to rot by bullets fired by tourists from the bibulous comfort of their seats on the fast-moving trains. Sauce for the goose.

You had to admit, sometimes it did go a bit far. Last month "Bitter Creek" Redhead Finnegan, stimulated by an excess of bug juice, had emptied his revolver into the dining car. Two bullets had struck a breakfast tray carried by a waiter, scattering eggs and terrifying passengers.

Mostly, though, the ammunition passed harmlessly above the

railroad cars, eventually to plunge into what at the present rate must soon turn into a lucrative lead mine half a mile upstream.

Tonight the train was several hours late and the noisy welcoming ceremony awakened Joe Ferris from his temporary lodgings in the bare room above what used to be the sutler's store. He looked out the window and saw nothing. Darker than the inside of a cow out there. He heard an impatient chuffing of steam. Far ahead a trainman's disembodied signal lantern swayed and the train began to clank away. Nobody appeared.

Irritation turned Joe Ferris's mouth down. He wouldn't have come in today except for this train. He had received a letter from a man in New York named Theodore Roosevelt. Near as Joe could make out, it asked if he would take the undersigned out after game. The spelling was something awful. Joe had written a reply on the back of the dude's own letter: "If you cannot shoot any better than you can write, I do not think you will hit much game."

The response had come immediately, by telegram: "Consider yourself engaged."

Joe didn't want to take the dude out. He didn't want to go out at all. He didn't want to hunt. He hated the killing.

But a fellow had to eat. So here Joe waited, with the train pulling out, and he still hadn't seen anybody get off.

Must be near eleven o'clock. The front door of Jerry Paddock's bar flapped open, dropping a fan of lamplight across the alkali earth. The boys went inside; their silhouettes canted left, toward the foot of the stairs—time to go up to bed, now that the train had departed.

In the reflected glow Joe could make out shadows of the Cantonment's half-dozen drab structures. Then the door closed. Like a curtain descending on a play it effectively ended all discernible life: one moment bedlam and the next a Stygian silence.

May be the client had missed the train, or slept through his stop. It wouldn't be the first time for one of these dudes. There had been a pair two months ago that had drunk themselves into a stupor and slept half way across Montana. They'd sent a telegram from Billings and turned up three days later on the eastbound, woebegone from too many hairs of the dog.

Above the door lights began to glow behind the paper windows of Jerry Paddock's makeshift hotel dormitory where the boys were turning in.

Joe Ferris put a hand on the windowframe, ready to return to his blankets. Then he heard hammering across the parade ground. The door of the flyspecked saloon opened and a tiny stranger was outlined against the weak flame that guttered behind the smoky chimney of Jerry Paddock's lantern. Jerry wasn't a huge man by any means but he loomed ferociously over the newcomer.

So the little dude had managed to jump down off the wrong side of the train and now he'd carried his belongings across forty yards of sagebrush without anyone's knowing. *You'd make a fine Indian. For sure you are in the wrong line of work*, Joe told himself.

He could see the dude wore eyeglasses—an adornment said to be evidence of physical decay and defective moral character.

The newcomer went inside; the door closed, once again shutting off that light; there remained a few dirty illuminations from the papered windows of the second floor. Joe remained at his post a while, curious whether the half-pint dude would take a whiff of the unwashed men on the musty cots in Jerry's big common room and prefer, as Joe did, to sleep elsewhere—even outdoors if necessary. But the visitor did not reappear.

May be he not only suffered from poor eyesight but also lacked a sense of smell.

After a time Joe went back to bed and had trouble getting to sleep. Things didn't seem to be going well. He was making a living, unlike some, but never seemed to get ahead of the price of tomorrow's supper. It had been like that most of the time since he'd first come here seeking his fortune. The railroad brought immigrants to the West without charge; but try to return home and you found the ticket cost five cents a mile.

In the morning Joe Ferris went across to Paddock's first thing and found the newcomer already waiting by the horse trough. The initial impression was one of a high voice and a lot of teeth. Mr. Theodore Roosevelt had the look and manner of a brat from one of those academies to which wealthy folks sent their children to learn useless foolishnesses such as Latin, geometry and the overweening pronunciation of English through locked aristocratic jaws.

The dude was ready and eager, dragging a huge duffel bag,

carrying across his shoulder two cased rifles: a waif in a New York suit with a heavy revolver holstered squarely in front where it could do a man irreversible damage if it happened to go off by accident or if the buckboard seat should happen to lurch under him.

Behind the bravado of his sandy mustache he looked sickly, as if he had some wasting disease. He looked very young.

A few of the boys came outside and watched and snickered while Joe introduced himself to the stranger, confirmed to his dissatisfaction that the new arrival was actually his contract, winced at the screeching high pitch of the dude's voice and led the young man to the buckboard.

The boys paid close attention because there was naught else to hold their interest. Most of them had been hide hunters; now they were scratching to find work: they had come here to feed the construction men but the construction men wouldn't arrive in strength until next month. Nevertheless quite a few men on the drift had found their way to the Cantonment, may be because Jerry Paddock's pop-skull tonsil varnish was the cheapest whiskey on the plains. This morning you could tell most of the boys had been painting their noses with it.

Then this fellow Roosevelt piped, "I have come west to shoot buffalo while there are still buffalo left to shoot." He announced it loudly.

The boys laughed.

Evidently it was not the response the Easterner had desired. He glared at them.

Joe greeted the newcomer's boast with a dour grunt. He didn't tell the whole truth in reply; it might have cost him a badly needed commission. *You are about five months too late. They exterminated the last buffalo herd last spring.*

What he said was, "Bad Lands are a hunter's paradise. Plenty big game downriver just now, sir. Blacktail and whitetail, antelope, mountain sheep, beaver if you're so inclined, maybe a bear now and then, and I believe we'll find elk as well."

"Capital. And buffalo. Most important."

"We'll scare up plenty of game, sir."

This was going to be a glorious hunt, Joe thought. Glorious. He put his gloomy regard on the dude. This Mr. Roosevelt was a head shorter than most of the men in the pack. He could not weigh more than 120 pounds, Joe thought. The large blue-grey eyes seemed mournful and painfully sickly. They peered rapidly about from behind big gold-rimmed spectacles that kept slipping down his nose.

The boys had already sized up the new ground and found it wanting in just about every respect. One of them said, "Looks like his deck's shy a joker. Likely don't know near side from off side."

Roosevelt ignored the insults; perhaps he didn't understand them, or didn't realize he was the butt. He settled a disapproving glance on the buckboard. "What's this?"

Joe said, "Supplies for a fortnight."

The face twisted and clenched. He had a tic or something; he kept grimacing. "And how far might it be to the hunting ground?"

"This time of year, generally find your luck around the Killdeers. Fifty miles, give or take."

"I have not come a thousand miles to ride a wooden wagon seat, Mr. Ferris. Where's my horse?"

"I don't own any extra saddle horse, Mr. Roosevelt."

Wheezing, the dude turned to the onlookers. "Might any of you gentlemen have a spare horse?"

Jerry Paddock swept off his hat and bowed with a flourish. "E.G. Paddock at your service. I happen to have a little herd in my stable."

"Then I'll rent one from you. And of course saddle, bridle . . ."

"Well hold on," Jerry Paddock said. "We don't know you, do we." This morning Jerry's gaunt face looked exceptionally evil, like an illustration of a Mongol Tatar villain in a lurid dime novel.

"My name is Theodore Roosevelt," said the dude in his very strange Eastern accent.

"I hear you saying it."

"I'll be happy to pay in advance. Two weeks at, shall we say, seventy-five cents a day? Ten dollars and fifty cents, shall we make it?" He drew out his purse.

Jerry Paddock's eyes fell upon the purse as if it were a roast suckling pig and he hadn't eaten in a week. He said coquettishly, "We've had visitors ride away with our horses before. Anyways, how do I know you wouldn't mistreat my animal? Why, we had one here just last spring, rode my best horse to death and cooked it and ate the poor thing."

Jerry Paddock had what passed for a humorous glint in his eye. He was stringing the stranger; in a minute he'd be shooting holes in the dust around Mr. Roosevelt's polished boots. All in fun of course—but the dude's purse was likely to end up in Jerry's pocket before it was over.

With a reluctant sense of responsibility toward his client Joe tried to turn trouble aside: "Mr. Roosevelt, it's a long way to the Killdeers. You might be more comfortable on the wagon with me, sir."

"Nonsense." Roosevelt strutted toward the stable, talking sternly to Jerry Paddock: "Come along, my good fellow. If you won't rent me a horse I'm sure you'll sell me one. For cash."

That brought an end to the trouble then and there. Jerry brought out his sorriest mare—ugly wart of a bay, an old-timer named Nell—and Mr. Roosevelt cheerfully parted with half again what the horse and rig were worth, as if it didn't matter.

The boys trailed toward the saloon because the unexpected profit put Jerry in such a good mood he offered to stand them all a round of drinks.

The only man to refuse the offer was Roosevelt. "Thank you very much indeed, sir, but I do not partake of strong drink."

With hoots of derision the crowd tramped inside. In two shakes Joe was alone with the puny dude in the Cantonment corral.

Roosevelt overcame a coughing fit long enough to say, "Now then, old fellow, if you wouldn't mind showing me how to put the saddle on this animal . . ."

That was how the great hunt started. Its auspices were poor at best. It was with dismal foreboding that Joe made ready to put the wagon onto the trail.

Roosevelt was peering at the brick construction works across the river. "What's all that?"

"Abattoir," Joe said, "whatever that means."

"Slaughterhouse. It's French."

"Yes sir. So's the gentleman who's building it. The Marquis De Morès."

There was a glint, probably accidental, off Roosevelt's eyeglasses. "De Morès? Is he here?"

"Not now. Back East someplace. Big financial affairs. You know him?"

"We haven't met. I'm acquainted with his wife."

Joe considered the great heaps of fresh brick on the flats below the bluff. "The Marquis says he's going to build a whole town right there on the right bank. Abattoir and all. They say he's got ten thousand cattle coming north from Texas."

"A sizable enterprise." There was displeasure in the dude's piping voice. "The money comes from his father-in-law. The Marquis has no fortune of his own."

"I wouldn't know about such things."

Roosevelt seemed unwilling to let it drop. "I can't abide aristocrats. The stench of their blue blood despoils the clean air of America."

"Wouldn't know about that either, sir. I'm Canadian."

"And proud of it, are you?"

Joe felt the rise of suspicion. "I am."

Roosevelt smiled. "Good for you." His attention returned to the brick pile. "An abattoir? Credit the man at least with large aspirations."

Joe said, "All I know is, it takes plenty of game meat to feed his carpenters and masons, so these rough boys you see here will get plenty of work."

"What about you, then, Mr. Ferris?"

"I used to hunt meat. For the railroad. I don't any more."

"Why not?"

Joe wasn't ready to tell the exact truth. These weren't the circumstances. He said, "One time I was shooting buffalo the barrel of my rifle got so hot it near melted my hand. Decided to let some other fellow have a turn."

"How many buffalo did you kill?"

"That day? I don't know. May be four hundred."

"Great Scott! Those must have been glorious days!"

Heedless youth. Joe tasted the bile of recollection; but he knew better than to dispute the client. He kicked the brake off and the wagon rolled north.

Roosevelt came trotting cheerfully alongside on the old mare, unaware or uncaring of the fact that his Eastern-style posting up and down during the trot would be enough to get him laughed out of Dakota Territory if he didn't leave soon of his own free will.

Taking his time, Joe Ferris was ready to decide that he didn't like the little dude at all. Then Roosevelt unsaddled his own horse that night.

And when Joe began to unfold the canvas tent Roosevelt would have none of it: he bedded down on the earth, wrapped in the saddle blanket.

And in the morning the dude saddled up himself, not asking any questions, remembering precisely the instructions Joe had given him yesterday.

So then it was a relief to see that at least this dude meant to carry his own pack. Maybe he wasn't the worst after all.

"What do you think, Mr. Ferris—shall we cross paths with the buffalo tomorrow?"

"Never can tell, Mr. Roosevelt."

May be it would be best to reserve judgment a bit longer and see how the dude measured up on the trail.

Joe unhitched the wagon horse, clapped his old McClellan split-tree on it, endured the saddlesores and was moved to take pity on his guest. "Beg your pardon, sir, but they don't post on a Western saddle."

"That will suit me well enough," Roosevelt replied. But he kept a poor seat after that and never seemed to learn the trick of riding loose, sticking to the saddle, swaying with the natural movement of the horse. In general he bounced.

"Where are the buffalo, Mr. Ferris?"

"Whatever's to be found, I'll find for you, Mr. Roosevelt."

Ten days Joe guided his client around the familiar country of the Killdeer Mountain district. They saw no buffalo but nevertheless the expedition seemed to meet the satisfaction of the dude, who kept exclaiming with great enthusiasm over the abundance of game.

Most hunters would have thought it a bad hunt. The animals seemed to have scattered out of pure perversion. Joe Ferris rode more miles and raised more saddlesores than he ever had before. The insides of his knees were scraped raw. But Roosevelt loved it. They took pronghorn, mule deer, whitetail, an elk with a magnificent rack, a bighorn sheep.

Once in a while Joe tried to get a word in about his natural abilities with bookkeeping figures. He laid hints like rabbit snares, hoping the dude would step into them.

Roosevelt was more polite than most—his inquiries indicated he was listening to what Joe had to say; sometimes he even seemed interested in Joe's ideas about the great successes in Commerce that awaited a man who knew the country, knew the people, had vision and—most important—had capital to invest. "This country's going to need a good mercantile store and a solid bank. Why, a man like me for instance—all it would take to set me on my way would be a little seed investment. The man who staked me could just sit back and watch me do all the hard work, and bring in a handsome return, yes sir."

"I certainly admire your confidence and ambition, old fellow." Roosevelt beamed infuriatingly at him.

There was no progress. Day after day, conversation was all the encouragement Joe got out of his employer. And the conversation invariably returned to the same exchange:

"Buffalo today, Mr. Ferris?"

"We'll see, Mr. Roosevelt."

The dude coughed and wheezed and vomited with alarming frequency but he kept surprising Joe. He proved an accomplished skinner. He claimed to be an expert taxidermist and Joe had no reason to doubt his word. During the first ten days of the hunt they filled their bellies with game meat and Roosevelt burdened the wagon with a more than satisfactory load of trophy heads and pelts, along with a number of birds he shot—sharp-tailed grouse, Hungarian partridge, ring-necked pheasant—with the intention of mounting them and making drawings for an ornithology book he said he would write one day "in the tradition of the great John James Audubon, who in the interests of science and art killed more birds than any man in history."

That seemed an accomplishment of dubious worth. And anyhow if a man could not spell any better than Roosevelt, he didn't appear to have much future as a writer. But Joe curbed his tongue.

Again to his surprise the sick young dude proved to be an adept hunter. On the stalk he owned patience and endurance. He understood the importance of ranging downwind from the prey. And his incessant conversation came to a halt—it was the one circumstance under which he accepted the requirement of silence.

But as a shooter he was indifferent: his eyesight was imperfect even with the aid of glasses and his eager energy did not make up for a lack of simple dexterity. He used up a considerable arsenal of ammunition for each animal he actually felled.

At times the New Yorker had a hard time breathing. He would hunch forward over a painful cough and there would be a frightful chuffing and whistling as he tried to expel air from his chest; then he would drag in a breath—a sound like ripping cloth—and the desperate process would begin again. He couldn't get enough air in or out.

And there were times when he'd say, "Go on ahead, old fellow. I'll catch up." He'd dismount and go behind a bush. Sometimes it was the loose runs, as if he had worms; other times Joe tried to ignore it but couldn't help hearing him throw up.

The dude explained it once, as if the names of things mattered. "Cholera morbus and asthma. I've had them since I was a child. They come and go. Never mind."

It was the nearest thing to a complaint Joe heard from him.

At first Joe had taken him for a ridiculous little caricature, full of puffery and embroidery—all bombastic flourishes—but in fact he was turning out to be a cauldron of contradictions. In spite of the frailties his energies seemed to have no end. He would read an entire book each day in the saddle and another by campfire-light. Most of his huge duffel bag was filled with books. He was twenty-three years old—four years younger than Joe, but he made Joe feel old, what with his childlike enthusiasms and ignorances.

The dude was stupid and brilliant, oblivious and curious, foolish and sensible; he was a babe in the woods with the wisdom of a sage. Once offhandedly he remarked to Joe that he had graduated three years ago from Harvard University *magna cum laude* and Phi Beta Kappa and that before he grew too much older he had the ambition to contribute a few dozen volumes of his own writings to the learned libraries of the world.

Joe replied that it seemed to him there were already too many books in the world, for no man could possibly read them all.

"Perhaps not. But he can try," Roosevelt riposted with a horse-toothed grin.

"That what you do back in the States? Write books all the time?"

"Only sometimes. I'm the Minority Leader of the New York State Assembly."

Joe made no reply to that. He didn't believe a word of it. The dude was hardly old enough to vote, let alone get elected to high office.

According to habit Joe made a turn on foot around the camp. His shadow moved around him. He could see it—the moon was that bright; it reminded him that not too many months ago it wouldn't have been safe to go walking around straight up in moonlight sufficient to guide a Sioux arrow.

They spent one particularly long day in the saddle, part of it in a fruitless galloping pursuit of an elusive pair of whitetail across very rough ground. In the end they emerged on sweating horses at the head of a dry coulee and saw forty miles of sunflower prairie without a single beast stirring anywhere.

Heat pressed in on them. Joe pushed his lips in and out to keep himself from exclaiming aloud. This whole damned hunt must have been designed as a trial for him—or perhaps it was a message from the Almighty that he should follow his instincts and get out of this bloodstained business and find himself a respectable indoor trade.

"They must be up ahead somewhere," Roosevelt said.

"Yes sir. Be that as it may, we need water. I used up the last of my canteen at breakfast. Yours?"

"The same, I suppose." The dude shook his water bottle to make sure it was empty.

"Eight hours or more since then."

"I don't feel thirsty," Roosevelt said manfully.

"Yes sir. But these horses do." He looked at the foam on the animals' necks. "May be we'd best get off and walk, sir."

They led the animals along the escarpment from headland to headland, peering down the steep canyons into the Bad Lands for the greenery that would signal water at the surface.

Partly to distract Roosevelt from the increasing peril of their predicament and partly to advance his own schemes, Joe talked about his ideas: a drygoods mercantile store, perhaps a bank. He made it sound idle, but there was no doubt this silly little fellow was a very rich dude. So he talked on, more loquaciously than was his usual habit, allowing Roosevelt to see glimpses of his enthusiasm.

But Roosevelt remained unmoved. *Perhaps I am simply a bad drummer*, Joe thought.

He scanned the horizons with worry—embarrassed to realize he didn't know where they were. The last few days' wandering had taken them farther north than he had ever gone before. He didn't know whether they were in Montana or Canada. He did know he hadn't seen this particular God-forsaken stretch.

The wagon was a full day behind them, loaded with skins and heads; the meat was hanging from cottonwood trees and, knowing the proclivities of coyotes and wolves and bears and cats and Indians, Joe had his doubts whether there would be much left by the time they returned to claim it—if they emerged from this wretched adventure alive.

Just give me a desk and a chair someplace inside four walls and I'll never again put in jeopardy the life and good health of one of Your poor dumb creatures.

Roosevelt twisted an ankle over a loose rock but he limped on gamely, chattering with a high-pitched cheer that drove Joe nearly mad. "Do you know it reminds me a bit of the ancient desert lands of Egypt. My father took us there when I was a lad. I shot ever so many birds. My sister was furious—she couldn't stand the formaldehyde smell of the taxidermy chemicals." He giggled and lurched on, breath sawing. Then: "Across the desert we went on camels. . . . I half expect a valley of great pyramids just beyond the horizon there."

"Yes sir. Might be water down there. Let's have a look."

They descended toward a green clump that proved illusory; whatever waters had fed it were gone, dried by the approach of summer. But the coulee narrowed into a steep bend below. There might be pockets of water at the bottom. In forty minutes it would be dusk; it was no good continuing along the rim at this rate anyhow. So Joe led the exhausted horse downhill into the trap of the canyon. He leaned back and dug his bootheels into the clay, thought a silent prayer and did not bother to look around to see if the dude was following.

One quality a tired man shared with a lathered horse was that either could become the surprisingly quick victim of dehydration in country like this.

We could end up dry bones out here and no one the wiser.

The mournful knowledge put a taste like brass on Joe's tongue. He said nothing to Roosevelt; no good would be served by alarming the dude—there was no way to tell which way Roosevelt might jump. What if he folded up into a cowering ball and refused to go on? What if he had a fit?

The horses placed their feet with tired splayed abandon, stumbling down the clay slopes, trembling. Joe rolled a pebble around his mouth with his tongue to keep the saliva going. He pitied the big quivering creature whose reins he tugged.

The walls of the high gorge loomed, cutting out most of the sky. It was nearly dark. The horses seemed nervous; they kept tugging fitfully.

Roosevelt said, "Look there, old fellow. That seems promising."

He followed the line of Roosevelt's pointing finger and saw dimly a wide dish of stone in the shadows under the opposite cliff.

Probably nothing but a trick of the sun; but there was a chance it might indeed prove to be a sink—what the immigrant Texans called a *tanque*.

May be the dude's eyesight was improving.

"We'll have a look then."

They crossed the narrow canyon upon a rubble of shale rocks loosened by the past winter's storms; their passage set up a little avalanche that racketed down into darkness and hurled back ominous echoes.

As they entered the gloom of the cliff's shadow he heard Roosevelt exclaim, "Aha! I *thought* the horses smelled moisture."

It was muck: a gelatinous slime, the diminished leavings of a big pool that must have been deposited in this bowl of rock by the spring melt-off. The horses nuzzled it: lapped, snorted and drank.

Roosevelt without ado untied his neckerchief, scooped up a wad of muddy gumbo in it, twisted the cloth ends together and held the plump sack over his upturned hat. When he squeezed, brown water dripped from the cloth.

Joe gaped.

This damn dude had saved their lives.

It was downright mortifying.

They made a dry camp. Finally Joe was willing to ask, "Where'd you learn that trick with the bandanna?"

"From a Maine woodsman, a very fine friend of mine named Bill Sewall. Why? Did you think Dakota was the only wild country in all North America?"

The dude presented another hatful of strained mud to his horse, which drank gratefully. Then he tried to blow up the rubber sleeping pillow that he carried in his pack but he wheezed and hacked so badly that Joe was moved to take it away from him, inflate it himself and say, "You ought to see a doctor about those ailments."

The dude corked the pillow and suddenly burst into a barking merriment of laughter that quickly became a violent spell of coughing after which he struggled for breath and eventually spoke: "I've seen many a doctor, old fellow. The most eminent of 'em told me I hadn't long to live unless I elected a sedentary life. He said the strain of the asthma has weakened my heart, and any violent exercise may be immediately fatal. The fine fellow told me I oughtn't even walk up a flight of stairs without stopping several times on the way. Well I didn't think that sounded like much of a life. Not long after that I happened to be in Switzerland and I encountered a group of Englishmen who'd just come down from a two-day scaling of the Matterhorn, which as you probably know was never climbed at all until less than twenty years ago, and these Englishmen boasted so—as if no one else but an Englishman could ever make the top of that mountain—well sir I climbed it myself, just to show what an American could do, and I made it to the top of the Matterhorn in just three hours. And I am here alive to tell you the tale."

I may owe him my life but does he really expect me to believe these tall tales?

Roosevelt said, "Now do you suppose there may be a moral to this story, concerning doctors and their opinions?"

He broke into another fit of coughing. To Joe it sounded like death.

There was no wood for a fire and nothing by way of trees or even shrubs for tying the horses. It was a cold camp and, Joe thought, a miserable one. They'd had only a couple of dried biscuits to eat. The horses were hungry and didn't seem to like this place: they kept snorting restlessly.

After they rubbed the beasts down it was necessary to ground-hitch them for the night by laying saddles on the ground and tying a rawhide lariat from each saddle to each horse's bridle strap.

Roosevelt's horse kept pawing at the rock and looking nervously around and blowing through its nostrils. "There must be some wild predator about."

"Or two-legged animals," Joe said between yawns. "There are men around here, white and red alike, may be just as soon as not take our horses and our scalps as well."

It was mainly bravado to impress the dude; Joe felt immediately foolish but it was too late to retract and so he said, "Keep your eyes and ears peeled, now," and laid his head on his saddle for a pillow and was immediately asleep.

When it was jerked out from under him he came awake with a start. "What in the hell—?"

He heard hoofbeats clattering away down the canyon; he was clambering to his feet, still clearing his head of sleep when the boom of Roosevelt's rifle nearly made him jump out of his skin.

The muzzle-flame, so near his eyes, left him momentarily blind. "*What is it?*"

There was the metal racket of the dude's rifle—chambering a fresh cartridge, levering the breach shut—and then after a moment Roosevelt said in a calm enough voice, "Wolf, I think. I suspect I missed it. Great Scott, it certainly does seem to have frightened our horses."

This was, Joe determined as he tugged on his boots, most definitely the worst hunt he had ever endured.

"Come on then," the dude said cheerfully. "Isn't this bully? We'd best bring the poor steeds back."

"Or break our fool necks trying," Joe grumbled, and set out blindly down the canyon, feeling for footholds.

After an hour of tumbles and bruises they captured the beasts.

It was only just in time: thunder gave warning—rolling and crashing overhead with long ricochetting echoes.

"Come *on!*"

Roosevelt seemed to need no explaining. They led the horses swiftly up-canyon, collecting the bits and pieces of their camp, ascending from there at dawn. Then of course it began to rain. Another ten minutes and they'd have been caught in the flash flood that thundered down the canyon. They emerged at the rim with mud sucking at their boots; mounted the poor horses and rode for hours in the soaking downpour.

Along the escarpment it wasn't so bad but at the waning end of day when they began to descend the Bad Lands toward the place where they'd left the wagon they had to squelch and slither down hills on which the clay had turned to gumbo.

By the time they reached the little plateau and tied their horses to the wagon and ducked underneath the buckboard's bed they were so coated with the dreary slime they looked like fresh moist clay sculptures.

Joe wrapped himself in a sodden blanket and brooded at the abysmal torrent.

Roosevelt turned to him and grinned from ear to ear. "By Godfrey, but this is fun!"

In the morning the sun came up hot enough to dry the muddy clothes on their backs and Roosevelt's enthusiasm was larger, if possible, than ever. "Now what do you say, old fellow—buffalo today?"

"Well yes sir, I do believe today's the day."

In truth Joe had given up all expectation but he willed the buffalo to appear because he did not want any more of this absurdity.

He was even too tired to feel surprise when he saw two buffalo grazing along a grass slope.

He had to point them out several times before the dude spotted them. Roosevelt slipped his rifle from leather. Joe said, "Not yet, sir. Too far."

They moved forward. But all the same Roosevelt in his excitement fired too soon, from too far away.

Normally buffalo were too stupid to flee from the sound of gunfire—their bovine indifference to noise was one reason it had been so easy to exterminate them; that was one of the things that had altogether sickened Joe—but in this case a ricochet must have stung one or both of the lucky animals, for they were off in an instant at full gallop. Roosevelt fired his magazine empty but it was no good; and by the time the two horsemen found their way across the intervening canyons the hairy beasts had disappeared.

Joe concealed his relief. They tried tracking but lost the spoor in shale. Roosevelt was momentarily dejected but brightened quickly enough. "We'll go on until we find more."

"May not be any more to find," Joe said gloomily.

"Nonsense. Why, there are millions of them."

"Not any more."

"What's that you say?"

"Mr. Roosevelt, fact is the army and the railroads wiped the herds out." No good stringing the dude any farther; the truth might hurt him but without it they might be out here all winter long. Joe said, "They killed the last big herd last spring, sir."

"Why, that has the sound of utter nonsense!"

Joe was ready to take offense then. "It's my word."

Of course that was the precise moment when a good-sized buffalo bull browsed into sight not a hundred yards below in the tall grass of a butte-protected meadow.

"Aha!" Roosevelt cried in triumph. Quickly he dismounted and lifted his rifle.

"Have a care with the downslope," Joe said wearily. "And mind the wind off your starboard quarter."

The dude got down on one knee and sighted with care. Joe put his hands over his ears and squeezed his eyes tight shut. There followed the great crashing boom of the rifle shot and Roosevelt's exasperated "Drat!" and then another booming rifle shot and Roosevelt's delighted whoop.

Joe opened his eyes. He saw the buffalo stumble and go down. Roosevelt was clambering onto his saddle.

By the time Joe rode to the place the dude had already dismounted and was prodding the buffalo with the rifle muzzle to make sure the poor thing was dead.

Then the strangest thing happened. Roosevelt began to leap about, spinning violently in the air as if he had been possessed by infernal spirits. A violent grunting sound erupted spasmodically from his mouth. His arms and legs jerked; his feet barely seemed to touch the earth: it was as though he were being whipped hither and yon by some invisible giant puppeteer.

His lips peeled back. A high screech issued from between his teeth. And suddenly he whirled and stood with one foot planted on the carcass in the age-old gesturer of the conqueror. Eyes gleaming behind dusty lenses, he pulled out his purse and gestured his guide forward.

Hesitant, not knowing whether to expect another rictus St. Vitus' dance, Joe approached him.

"Jolly fine work, old man!" Roosevelt shook coins into Joe's palm.

Joe looked down. He spread the coins with a finger. Ten-dollar gold eagles and twenty-dollar double eagles. One hundred dollars' worth.

Well may be one buffalo more or less didn't matter that much after all.

Two

Ten months later it was quite a different and darker Theodore Roosevelt who returned to the Bad Lands.

Tuesday, June tenth, 1884: Joe Ferris knew his friend Pack's newspaper would mark it an outstanding day in the brief history of Medora town.

Roosevelt was not the first to alight. Before the train pulled forward to the depot platform, Madame la Marquise's private railroad car had to be detached and shunted onto the abattoir siding where, at some remove from the scene of the usual gunshots and profane antics, she could be spared unseemly excitement. Her attendants, concerned for her sensitivities, were determined that she and her two babies be spared exposure to the ruffians of the depot.

From her sumptuous railroad carriage the young Marquise—pert and delicate with masses of dark auburn-red hair—disembarked into the Dakota Bad Lands with two babies, twenty-one trunks and nine servants.

Nearly knocking Joe down when he trotted past, the Marquis De Morès rode his horse across the tracks with cool disregard for the snapping gunfire and hooting yells that greeted the rest of the train.

Much to Joe's disgust there was a cheer when De Morès stepped down to greet his wife. Evidently most of the town witnessed their impassioned embrace.

It was for sure a sizable crowd—Joe guessed it must have been the largest ever to have gathered in Medora town. Must have been at least five hundred, of whom perhaps two-thirds were employees of the De Morès ranch, the De Morès packing plant, the De Morès coal mine, the De Morès Hotel, the De Morès general store and the Northern Pacific Refrigerator Car Company (Marquis De Morès, Prop.).

The rest of the crowd was an assortment of the respectable and the verminous: hunters, trappers, guides, miscreants, cowboys, coal miners, whores, Indians, ranchmen and their wives, a few score townspeople. Not many were altogether sober, though it was not yet noon.

They'd gathered from everywhere. Bad Landers were taking the day off: many of them lived alone in the wilderness but they were not granite; the time came when they had to be with people or go crazy.

It might have been Christmas or the Fourth of July. De Morès had given his employees a holiday. He'd announced that his workers had earned it but the way Joe saw it he was aiming to impress the Marquise, his petite bride of three years—the lovely Medora after whom De Morès had named the town, either because he adored her or because he wanted to be on the good side of his filthy-rich father-in-law.

Impress her he undoubtedly did, with the most populous welcoming turnout in the history of Dakota.

Gangly tall Arthur Packard, "Pack" to his friends, caught up with Joe and accompanied him toward the tracks. Pack was youthful, big-eared and the editor-publisher of the town's only newspaper. Evidently he'd hurried around the corner of the half-built chapel in time to observe the Marquis dismounting to embrace his wife and kiss the two infant children who were held up to him by maidservants. "Really touches the heart, doesn't it!"

"Touches me someplace else," Joe said roughly. He was watching two dozen De Morès employees swarm around the private carriage, beginning to unload all the impedimenta. Along with the Marquise's twenty-odd trunks there were the servants' luggage, the elaborate Concord hunting coach—somebody had told Joe it was a custom-built replica of Napoleon's coach—an iron bathtub and a variety of massive furnishings and hunting equipment to augment the already impressive collection housed in the château on the bluff across the river. Relays of ox-drawn wagons would be going up and down the bluff for hours.

It was beyond show-off, Joe thought; it was downright indecent. But he held his tongue. No point stirring up Pack to argument. Pack was a De Morès man, heart and soul, and Joe had given up trying to reason with him.

By the time they reached the siding, the Marquis was riding up and down shouting instructions from under his white sombrero and pointing vigorously with his silver-headed bamboo walking stick.

The stick seemed a part of De Morès's personality. He carried it at all times and often held it out at arm's length. Stained dark and lacquered, it looked slender, even fragile—but Pack had told Joe how he had handled it on two or three occasions at De Morès's invitation; it was monstrously heavy, Pack assured him. De Morès had filled it with lead. It weighed ten or twelve pounds.

The Marquis claimed it was not a weapon. Its purpose, he said, was to exercise his duelling arm. It was said he'd killed several men in France in *affaires d'honneur*.

In fairness you had to admit a few things in his favor. De Morès was a handsome rapscallion, lean and sleek, so tall as to be commanding whether on foot or horseback; curly black-haired and golden-skinned with a supple beauty of physique that put Joe in mind of something feline. He seemed to have a good quick brain and no shortage of ambitious zeal. But Joe was not as impressed by the Frenchman as some of his friends were. There was a wickedness in the way the man used his power.

Today De Morès wore a loud yellow neck scarf and a blue yachting shirt laced with yellow silk cord; he wore black trousers and big-roweled California spurs on his polished black boots. Beneath half-lidded dark eyes his waxed-to-points mustache turned up rakishly at the ends.

With a casual savage sawing that made Joe wince, De Morès neck-reined the white horse deftly over the track embankment around the end of the private car and loomed above them, high against the bright azure Dakota sky.

"Joe." The greeting was without pleasure. Then the oily smile: "Arthur my friend. How good to see you."

The French accent was not pronounced; the Marquis was at ease with English and proud of his fluency.

Joe didn't mind having the Marquis's cold shoulder turned to him. The Marquis's friendship was not a thing he sought, or would have valued.

Men grunted and heaved, transferring cases to a wagon. There was no profanity. That meant Madame la Marquise was still about.

Pack said to De Morès, "Now, I'd like to speak with you and Madame, for the newspaper. My readers are avidly interested in what you both have to say."

"How flattering. I'm very busy today as you see."

Madame herself appeared in the open platform door. "Perhaps Arthur could dine with us later in the week, darling."

She smiled; and from the look of him, it was evident to Joe that Pack nearly fainted.

Joe kept his amusement to himself. He remembered the song that had leaped into Pack's lips the moment they'd first seen her, months ago:

Oh, my heart is gone and I'm forlorn,
A darling face has won me . . .

Joe suspected his friend had carried her image in his heart ever since.

She said in her gaily tuneful voice, "Joe, how good to see you. Arthur, dear, you look positively gaunt. We really must *feed* you."

"I'm fitter than I look, madame." Tongue-tied, Pack said no more.

Joe had to concede there was a fine beauty in the graceful carriage with which Madame moved, the composure with which she'd greeted him. There was a lively rhythm in her; it seemed impossible to be near her without picking up its tempo.

She returned his gaze with open candor; a demure smile saved it from impropriety. She was at ease anywhere and with anyone. She had a way of making a man feel like a goat. She treated all the young men of the town like truant children. It distressed Joe to feel she was laughing at him but he always suspected it.

Pack seemed to feel the same way but suffered the indignity gladly. May be he felt it was a small price to pay for the privilege of being near her.

De Morès, confident—unworried by the way his wife inspired the dreams of calf-eyed young men—turned in his saddle to watch the train lurch forward. The engine had come to a second halt in the center of the hundred-yard span of the river bridge. It meant the inconvenience of a double stop; the train would have to move a quarter mile and stop again to take on water at the old Little Missouri depot.

All this provoked Madame la Marquise's question: "Who on earth could be on that train?"

Joe said, "Assemblyman Roosevelt, ma'am."

"Teedie Roosevelt? Why on earth—"

"For the hunting, I imagine," her husband said. "I should like to meet him."

"So would I," said Pack. Then to Madame: "You know him, then?"

"Of course, poor thing. Fancy I didn't know he was on this train! Haven't you met him, Arthur?"

"Not yet," said Pack. "I'm looking forward to the pleasure."

For a moment she was clearly troubled. Then abruptly she gave De Morès her quick blazing smile.

Joe recalled vaguely from last year's hunt that Roosevelt had said something about being acquainted with De Morès's wife. It wasn't surprising, as they were about the same age and came from the same wealthy New York City Society. Seemed odd, though, that De Morès himself should be unacquainted with the rich dude. One naturally assumed they'd have known each other; such was the transcendent freemasonry of wealth.

Medora said to her husband, "I'm sure someone will introduce you to Teedie, dear." She smiled again at Joe and then at Pack, disarming him completely, as she always did. The way Joe saw it, Pack was more than just a little bit in love with the lady. So were most of the men in Billings County, if it came to that.

Joe indicated the vestibule of the train. "Here he comes now."

* * *

Quite some time later it was Mrs. Reuter, on one of her rare visits to town, who remarked to Joe on the irony of how Roosevelt had stepped down from the train lugging his own valises, while Madame De Morès had arrived in her private car with trunks, servants &c. The irony, Mrs. Reuter said, was in the fact that—from what she read—Roosevelt must have inherited considerably more personal wealth than De Morès.

"I mentioned it to Arthur Packard," she was to say to Joe, "but it was lost on him. I'm afraid he's a bit young yet for irony, isn't he."

With a grimace Theodore Roosevelt heaved his goods forward, coming down the step.

The sandy mustache was more weighty. Under it was that huge mouthful of tombstone teeth with which he rapidly chopped words into pieces.

"Here, here! Make way! Gentlemen, gentlemen, kindly be so good as to make way!"

The clipped talk in the thin strident voice was accompanied by those same facial squints and contortions of shoulders and elbows; had his arms been unencumbered with belongings he'd have been flailing like a drowning man.

Showing a certain deference the crowd made room. Roosevelt set down his valises. "Joe Ferris. Is Joe Ferris about? Joe?"

Joe made his reluctant way forward. He hadn't forgotten the adversities of last year's misadventure. "Right here, Mr. Roosevelt."

Roosevelt clapped him on the arm. "By Godfrey, it's good to see you again, Joe." He endeavored to grin. But it was strained. It came to Joe that he was acting out a performance. It didn't have the old enthusiasm inside.

The dude coughed. He was having trouble breathing but that wasn't it; that was his usual state. Joe sensed a melancholia in him: a new deep agony of pain.

Joe said, "Sir, some people here want to meet you . . . ."

Pack stepped forward. "Mr. Roosevelt—"

There was a moment's pinched displeasure on the dude's face;

then Roosevelt turned as Joe made the introduction: "Mr. Roosevelt—Arthur Packard. Publishes the newspaper here."

When Roosevelt heard the word "newspaper" a remnant of his politician's grin appeared; his hand wandered forward. Accompanying the emphatic but somehow unexcited "Dee-lighted to meet you" was his solid double-grip handshake—Joe had been the victim of it and knew it was quite firm, in contradiction to his apparent fragility.

"Dee-lighted." The eyes quickly lost their flash; they became somber again and it was as if Roosevelt hardly heard Pack's words: "Now, if I could have a few moments—your opinions about the Chicago convention, the political—"

"I think not," said Roosevelt, turning away. "I came out here for the climate. I've retired from politics."

"Sir, I'm sure my readers would like to know your view of the election ahead."

"I have no view," Roosevelt piped. "None whatever." He bent to gather his valises. "Joe, lead the way."

Joe was troubled. It seemed uncharacteristic for Roosevelt to refuse the opportunity of a platform from which to deliver his opinions.

Pack tried another flank. "Now, sir—if you've got just one moment, the Marquis De Morès asked especially to meet you."

It stopped Roosevelt. Again a momentary interest sparked in the wan eyes. "De Morès. Where is he, then?"

"Just over there." Pack gestured toward the private railroad car.

De Morès said, "Oh, I shall be the richest financier in the world." He smiled at Roosevelt when he spoke; but he meant what he said. The comment was in reply to Roosevelt's expressed admiration for the size and formidable solidity of the brand-new abattoir with its towering brick chimney.

"The Marquis will do it, too," Pack said. "Don't you find a mighty excitement in knowing we are here at the beginning, eyewitnesses to the birth of empire!"

Lord Almighty, Joe thought. *Spare us.*

Roosevelt was saying in a dull sort of voice, "Ambition's a fine attribute. I admire a man with determination and drive." While he spoke, his gaze drifted toward Madame. Joe saw Pack watching that exchange of glances as if he were trying to read something into it.

They had greeted each other with careful formality. Joe remembered Madame's earlier words: *Teedie . . . Poor thing.* Did everyone in New York refer to Roosevelt as "Teedie"? Or had it been a slip of the tongue, revealing something more than casual acquaintance?

Joe couldn't tell. In any event they behaved like virtual strangers under the perceptive eye of the Marquis.

De Morès said to Roosevelt, "You'll find good hunting to the north this time of year. The country's rough but the game should be plentiful. You may have the luck to find elk this month. Of course you'll be traveling with the proper comforts."

"I prefer to travel light," said Roosevelt, as if delivering a eulogy. "Hardships can be fine things." His glance may have remained on Madame's lovely face a moment or two too long. Once again Joe saw his friend Pack observe the exchange; Pack's face showed plainly that he was offended.

Roosevelt's piping high voice rattled suddenly, snapping words out in a rush, as if to cover a moment of embarrassment: "I'm sorry I couldn't have been at the christenings. I managed to miss them both, didn't I. Trapped in a crowded smoky room in dear old Albany. No rest for the wicked, they say. But my very best wishes went out to you, of course."

"Yes," she replied easily. "My father pointed out your card. 'That's from Teedie Roosevelt,' he said."

"I've left that childish name behind." He smiled—one of those facial punctuation marks that were his habit; all those great square *teeth*—and turned to De Morès. "I'm not sure, under the circumstances, whether to pronounce your title 'Markee' in the French fashion or 'Marquiss' as they say in England, and so I've decided," he concluded after drawing a wheezing breath, "that I'll just call you Mr. De Morès, because we have no marquises in the United States of America."

In the corner of his vision Joe saw Madame la Marquise avert her face to hide what may have been a quick smile—of amusement? Of memory?

Roosevelt offered his hand to De Morès. "That's settled then. I look forward to seeing you soon. And your delightful wife."

Demoted to an egalitarian Mister, the Frenchman accepted the proffered handshake only after a pause that was long enough to be insulting. Roosevelt didn't appear to notice. He shook hands briefly with Pack, bowed deeply—perhaps an inch too deeply?—to Madame la Marquise and summoned Joe with a jerk of his head.

Joe endeavored to help carry the luggage but Roosevelt refused to relinquish it. "Just show the way. I can carry for myself. Didn't come out here to be waited upon."

Joe pointed north and Roosevelt promptly tramped away.

Pack glared after him. "What an insufferable prig. What an utter disappointment."

You'll change that opinion when you get to know him, Joe thought.

Walking away to catch up with his client, Joe heard De Morès say with a bite in his tone, "Tell me, Arthur. Is he Jewish?"

"I don't think so. Dutch ancestry, I believe."

"I don't like him."

Joe caught up and led Roosevelt upstreet, ignoring the fit of coughing.

There was no paint on the town; the smell of new boards was in his nostrils—evidence that the wind was favorable, for otherwise they'd have smelled nothing but the abattoir's stink.

Roosevelt said, "I should feel sorry for Medora if I were you, old fellow. She's got herself a cavalier despot for a husband."

Joe was surprised by the remark. A year ago Roosevelt surely wouldn't have made it; he'd have been too filled with vigor—he'd have found *something* admiring to say about the couple.

Now there was a bitter note in the piping voice and an intolerance that hadn't been there before. Give him half an excuse, Joe thought gloomily, and the silly dude would get himself in serious trouble if he went around making those kinds of remarks about the imperial Frenchman. Joe felt he should warn Roosevelt that De Morès was too conceited to let an insult pass; and that he was well armed at all times. But he couldn't think of a way to do it that might not offend the little dude, so—just for the time being, he reckoned—it was all right to leave things alone.

Two months ago in the spring there had been rain—torrents. The river had run full, crashing down its banks. Two months from now by August it would dwindle to a fitful stream lurching through cut-clay channels not more than a foot deep. Just now it was half a river, stirrup-high, and they were able to splash their horses without trouble across the gravel ford a hundred yards downstream from the Northern Pacific bridge.

From there they struck south along the dirt track that passed for a wagon road. It took them across the rails and upriver beneath the bluff—Roosevelt's hatbrim lifted and turned as he focused his interest on the brand-new De Morès château up there—and around a bend through shade of cottonwoods that briefly interrupted the blast of afternoon sun.

Joe Ferris was thinking about the girl he had left behind in Newfoundland. In his memory he saw the laugh in her green eyes—as good as a kiss.

Must have been the sight of De Morès's big house that put him in mind of his girl. Didn't usually think about her in the daytime.

He heard Roosevelt: "It's said Mr. De Morès has killed two or three Jews in duels."

"Doesn't like Jews, does he?"

"I take him to be an unpleasant man all around," said Roosevelt. "Well despite all that, old fellow, it's good to be back. I feel as if I've come home. It's an enchanted country. D'you know Poe's tales and verses? These Bad Lands look just the way Poe sounds."

Joe scanned the scarred butte country. The ground was rent into fantastic shapes and splashed with barbaric colors. But after a while you hardly noticed.

He didn't know much about anybody called Poe. He'd done some reading in the books from school and from his mother's library bookcase and he had enjoyed some of them, especially the Sir Walter Scott ones, but none of it seemed to apply much to the country hereabouts, and he didn't know what Mr. Roosevelt meant but he wasn't curious enough to inquire further.

Deep in the horizon's haze he thought he saw antelope. He didn't remark it to Roosevelt; he did not hanker for several hours' hard riding followed by the acrid stink of shooting and the stench, even worse, of bleeding and skinning.

Safe enough not to point out the herd in the distance: Roosevelt, even with his storm windows, couldn't see well enough to discover it by himself.

Joe remembered that much from last time. Roosevelt still looked as frail as he'd looked last summer when he'd come for the hunting. *Consider yourself engaged.* That hunt had been a true misery. Please God let us not repeat it. Let this one be easy.

He listened absently to thudding hoof-falls and squeaks of saddle leather. As they rounded each bend there was a new shape to the horizon. Roosevelt said, "Don't the colors amaze you?"

"Guess so." They clattered across a rock-fall of loose shale colored like rainbows. Above, a few chalk-white lateral stripes had bled down over the darker strata, leaving stains like whitewash. This stretch wasn't much for green—nothing but a few stunted cedars on the hills.

"This air—" Roosevelt puffed his narrow chest to draw a wheezing breath, coughed, recovered "—fine clean sting to it, like the Alps. Like good tart cider. Look at the size of that sky. 'Wild Lands' I might better understand. But they're not bad. Who called them Bad Lands?"

"Everybody. Indians first."

"Which Indians?"

So he hadn't changed much; hadn't grown up any. He was still asking questions like a schoolboy. The dude seemed to want to stuff into his head every useless fact in the world.

Joe extended his hand palm-up in a gesture. "Indians. Lakota, Crow, Cheyenne, Arikara, Mandan, Gros Ventre. Whichever. You know. *Indians.*"

"They can't have all lived here."

Joe contained his vexation. "Indians don't live anywhere, Mr. Roosevelt. They drift on the plains. All the tribes camped and hunted here in the olden days. Sioux called the country *Mako Shika*, 'land bad.' Take a look at the old map in Arthur Packard's newspaper office—must be a hundred years old—you see where some French-Canada *voyageur* put down 'Bad lands to cross.'"

"*Mauvaises terres pour traverser.*" Roosevelt showed teeth, proud of his French. Then his face closed up again.

"They tell it twenty years ago old General Sully chased Sioux through here—he's the one supposedly called the place 'Hell with the fires put out.'" Joe considered the buttes. "He was partly wrong. Some fires still burning."

"I remember those. Wasn't there a coal vein burning near Huidekoper's?"

"Still on fire. Lignite. They burn for years."

"I make them 'Good Lands,'" Roosevelt insisted. "When you come from a life of crowded noisy little rooms filled with tobacco smoke—it's a stalwart country, Joe." His face twisted and squinted. "Why, when I was a boy my whole ambition was to take a horse and a rifle out on the prairie and ride day after day without encountering another human soul—far off from all mankind. That's freedom."

"Yes sir. For you I guess. I never did take to range-riding. I'll have four walls and a roof—I am of an indoor disposition. A little luck, I'll be the second banker in Medora."

"Who's the first?"

"Marquis De Morès."

Roosevelt made no reply; he gigged the horse and rode on. Not like him to be so uncommunicative and glum.

May be just a bad moment—he must be tired from the train journey. Better wait, drop more hints another time.

"We'll get outfitted at Eaton's ranch." Joe added hopefully, "Unless you'd rather go fishing?"

"I never fish," Roosevelt said. "Can't bear to sit still that long." He seemed on the brink of tears.

A three-strand wire fence crossed the trail. Someone had cut it and left the curled strands to dangle. When they rode through the gap Roosevelt said, "Is this Eaton's fence?"

"No sir. Marquis De Morès's."

"Doesn't the man know enough to put a gate where there's an obvious road?"

"May be they don't bother with gates back in France where he comes from."

Ahead three men hunkered in cottonwood shade, their horses tied to trees; one of the men trailed a fishing line in the river.

"Say, Mr. Roosevelt, be careful with these men now."

"Who are they?"

"'Bitter Creek' Redhead Finnegan and his friends."

"I don't believe I know them."

"Don't believe you'll want to," Joe said.

"By George, it appears I don't have a large choice in the matter."

Finnegan and Frank O'Donnell had stood up; O'Donnell had moved to his horse and now laid his hand on the buttstock of a scabbarded rifle. Finnegan had a revolver in his fist—not pointed at anyone, but the implied threat was obvious.

Joe drew rein facing them at the edge of the grove. Beside him he was relieved to see, out of the corner of his eye, that Roosevelt followed suit. The mood the dude was in, it didn't seem safe to trust his prudence; and if Roosevelt should suffer an attack of one of his unpredictable moments, God alone knew what effect it might have on the three trigger-happy hunters.

The third man remained below on the riverbank, squatting on his heels with the fishing pole in his hand; that was young Riley Luffsey. He had a rifle across his lap and looked at them over his shoulder with his customary cocky dare.

Joe said, "You can put up the firearms."

Pugnacious and surly, "Bitter Creek" Redhead Finnegan pointed the revolver vaguely at the dude. "What's this you got here, Joe?"

"Mr. Roosevelt from New York. Gentle down—we don't work for the Marquis. It *was* you boys cut the fence, I guess?"

"They strang it, we cut it," Frank O'Donnell snarled, as if it were an invitation to dispute.

Finnegan said, "That's a public road up and down the river. Man's got no right fencing it."

Joe said, "He claims to own all this land. Valentine Scrip."

Redhead Finnegan said, "He don't own nothing." As always he was in search of a fight. He had an evil reputation throughout the Bad Lands.

Joe pointed them out for Roosevelt's benefit. "Michael Finnegan—Frank O'Donnell. The lad down there with the pole is Riley Luffsey."

"Delighted to meet you," Roosevelt said without any evidence of delight. "And I agree with you that public roads ought to remain open." At least he had the sense not to dismount.

Finnegan surveyed Roosevelt, open condemnation in his glance. "Picked yourself a poor guide. If it's good hunting you care for, we'll take you to more game than a man can shoot with a Gatling."

"Sorry, gentlemen. No offense intended, but I have a contract with Joe Ferris."

"Your bad luck then. You'll go out two, three weeks and come in empty-handed. Count on it." Finnegan leered up at Joe.

Finnegan's curly red hair was thick and matted. He wore it shoulder-length like the late Wild Bill Hickok. His skin was as oily as Esquimeaux grease. Finnegan had a broad florid face and a taut stocky body that always seemed ready to spring like a trap: all his moves were sudden. His clothes were filthy.

More than one time Joe had heard Redhead Finnegan boast that he was from Bitter Creek, wherever that might be; and that the farther up Bitter Creek you went, the tougher and meaner the people got; and that he himself hailed from the fountain head of Bitter Creek.

Finnegan's sometime partner Frank O'Donnell was a big ruffian from Ireland whose cheeks bore the rough pits of smallpox. The stoic stillness of the Bad Lands had immobilized O'Donnell's features; he had built a wall around himself and inside it he must have dehydrated. Joe could not remember ever having seen him smile. Nor did O'Donnell talk much, except when drunk.

Story was, some of these Irish fugitives had slit the throats of their rich landlords and fled to the New World. Riley Luffsey was too young for that—only eighteen now, and he'd been in America long enough to lose his brogue—but the rumors might be true enough where O'Donnell was concerned.

Joe Ferris said, "We'll see you boys, then," and put his horse in motion. But Finnegan seemed unwilling to let the matter drop: he sidestepped in front of the horse, blocked Joe's way, locked his fist on the bridle strap. The horse jerked its head; Finnegan kept his grip. "Listen—every time we ride through here we hack down that fence, and every time we come back it's been put up again."

"Why talk on me about it?"

"Because you hang your hat around town and you have got the ear of Jerry Paddock and them," said the man from Bitter Creek. Joe's horse tried to bite him and he took his hand away without even glancing at it. "And now we hear Paddock and the Marquis are fixing to bring legal papers and that Valentine Scrip and jump claim on Frank's shack downriver."

"Any rascal jumps me," O'Donnell said, "jumps right into his grave."

From the edge of the river Riley Luffsey shouted, "I'm the best and fastest shot in Dakota with long gun or short. They want to try something, I'm ready to stand with Frank."

"And so am I. And others too. You tell that to Jerry Paddock, Joe," said Finnegan.

"Tell him yourself. He's no friend of mine."

Finnegan glared at Roosevelt. "What about you, little man? Whose side you on?"

"My own. I've no quarrels here."

"Keep it that way," Finnegan adjured.

Joe said, "Be that as it may, Red, I'll give you good advice. Take it or not as you please. You stir it up with Jerry Paddock and the Marquis, I'll venture folks may walk wide around you so they don't have to look too close at the destruction." Then Joe smiled. "I hear the Marquis loads his ammunition with exploding bullets."

Riding away at a brisk trot with spine braced against a half-expected bullet, Joe glanced at Roosevelt beside him and wondered at his silence.

He'd worried himself near sick back there that the boisterous New Yorker might be moved to utter a harangue about right and wrong, law and principle, good and evil. A year ago it would have been impossible to shut him up. Finnegan probably would have shot him out of the saddle for a loudmouthed fool.

But this time there had been next to no moralizings. Roosevelt hadn't said much of anything beyond his approval of their fence-cutting and his cool statement of neutrality. That was a surprise worth remarking. The man surely did seem distracted. Either that or his whole personality had been squashed—and you'd have thought it would have taken a granite avalanche to do that.

They trotted around a loop in the river. There was lowland meadow here, grass standing three feet high. Joe looked back, and caught Roosevelt doing the same.

Finnegan and his partners were out of sight. Joe's shoulders loosened.

Roosevelt merely said, "I take it those three are not ranchmen."

"They hunt, do some trapping. Guide visitors when they can."

"Rough riders, are they? I admire any man who lives on the rough side of things—so long as he keeps his conscience intact."

"More than rough, those three. And I have not seen much

conscience on them. You don't mind my advice, might keep your distance from them. It is said Redhead and his friends don't mind spending money from a stranger's purse."

Roosevelt made no answer. They forded the river's several channels and rode into a grove of ash. Chilly in here.

Joe thought the subject had died but after an interval Roosevelt revived it: "From what you say, Finnegan seems cut from the same cloth as the notorious Jerry Paddock. I'm surprised they're enemies."

"I guess they're so alike they just *had* to hate each other," said Joe Ferris.

"Seems to be plenty of acrimony on this frontier," Roosevelt murmured.

"A man with good sense stays above it."

"A man with sound moral underpinnings will seek out the right and wrong, and choose his side according to the right."

That was easy for a man to say when he was merely a visitor and didn't have to live here. Joe waited for Roosevelt's further comment but it was not forthcoming. The dude relapsed into gloom.

Long shadows sprawled in the coulees; warmth was draining out of the afternoon. The horses carried them south at a lazy gait. Half asleep in the saddle Joe recalled Roosevelt's earlier trip west.

He remembered how the dude had said, "Joe—my little war dance when I got my buffalo. I wouldn't like the little pink wife to hear of it. My Alice teases me sometimes about my wild barbarian ways. I don't mind, really—she's too lovely and lovable a girl, you can't mind anything she does—but I prefer not to give her unnecessary ammunition, don't you know. You'll keep it to yourself, then?" And Roosevelt had all but winked at him, man-to-man.

Now he marked the difference in the man. Roosevelt had been as frail then as now; but his enthusiasm had been unquenchable last fall. Joe remembered most of all Roosevelt's absurd grin—and wondered what had become of it. This Roosevelt, wrapped in gloom, was a different and darker man.

Three

A.C. Huidekoper took one of his pleasures from listening not simply to people's words but to the music and rhythms in their speech. Just now—above the voices of several men and women in the hot smoky room—Howard Eaton's penetrating tenor was a prominent melody:

"The Indians will have to learn to herd—or they'll starve."

Huidekoper let the talk roll around him while he watched the crowd. Most of the others in Eaton's big low-ceilinged front room were talking of hunting and of the arrival in town of the beautiful young Madame De Morès, with regard to whom Mrs. Eaton and Huidekoper's wife and three other women kept their voices to a twitter of murmurs, their conversation circumspect because there was a De Morès man in the room.

Huidekoper stroked his muttonchop whiskers and smiled when spoken to; he made himself appear at ease because he didn't care to reveal the expectant abeyance with which he watched the door for the appearance of the Cyclone Assemblyman from New York.

They made for a sizable crowd—more than a dozen ranchers tonight, four or five wives, several Easterners wearing the trappings of wealth. It was not unusual; Howard Eaton, who loved beer and loud argument, had made his Custer Trail Ranch as much a beacon for visitors as were its lamplit windows for the insects that swarmed against the glass.

The voices were young; it was a country for youth. It occurred to Huidekoper that at thirty-seven he might be the oldest person in the room. Most of them, even the owners of the big herds, were still in their twenties.

All the young energy, abetted by the generosity of Howard Eaton's bar, made for a boisterous din. But now a lapse in discourse rippled the length of the long room, muting the racket. Alerted, Huidekoper looked over his shoulder and saw that—in spite of his vigilance—they had managed to take him by surprise after all.

Joe Ferris, compact but wide-shouldered, showed himself in the doorway. In alarm Huidekoper at first thought Joe was alone—he was so short it was difficult to believe anyone might be concealed beyond him. But then Joe stepped inside and behind him in the doorway, diminutive and pale in the waning afternoon light, appeared his dude—New York State Assembly Minority Leader Theodore Roosevelt.

Make that *former* Minority Leader, Huidekoper reminded himself. *And if he stings badly enough from the licking he took, he may just be in a mood to be our savior.*

Roosevelt's quick piping voice made a new disharmony. He was greeting Eaton and Gregor Lang and others he already knew from the time of his previous Western trip; he was being introduced to the ones he didn't know; amid the murmurs and polite rumblings his magpie bursts were as discordant as an out-of-tune fiddle.

As Huidekoper moved toward the drinks table with studied nonchalance—waiting his moment—he heard Joe Ferris tease Johnny Goodall:

"We came on Redhead Finnegan on the road. Pulling down one of your fences."

"Then we'll just have to string it up again," Johnny said with his usual equanimity.

Joe Ferris, unsmiling, was having his dour fun with De Morès's man: "Redhead said a few unfriendly words about the Marquis."

"I don't expect the Marquis is fixin' to lose a heap of sleep over that," said Johnny Goodall. From this distance Huidekoper couldn't tell if he was amused or irritated; Johnny's Texas twang seldom gave away his feelings.

"Being none of my concern," Joe Ferris told him, "but you might give a mind to Redhead and his mates. They're armed and they take their pleasures in making trouble. Trouble for the Marquis—trouble for you one day."

"They do and I reckon they will end in a shallow grave," Johnny Goodall replied without heat. He glanced at Huidekoper and gave him the benediction of his brief polite nod. Johnny Goodall stood a head taller than most others in the room. He had a big man's slow way about him. He was smiling courteously and he had a good-humored manner; but Huidekoper had caught the brief pale dancing flash of danger in his eyes.

Coming to the beer keg Johnny moved with the slow wary caution of a dog amid an unfriendly pack. For—despite the fact that he was generally liked and respected—Johnny Goodall was range foreman for the Marquis De Morès, and his presence put tension in the house. Men spoke guardedly so long as he was present.

Theodore Roosevelt had penetrated deeper into the room and Huidekoper thought, *It is better to get this over with.* He poured his cheer straight and turned toward the young New Yorker. "Sorry to hear about your ladies. A terrible misfortune." He drank his tot and felt the burn when it went down.

Roosevelt, turning to speak to someone else, stopped in mid-swing and blinked. Then he continued to pivot away, purporting not to have heard Huidekoper's solicitous remark: he gave Huidekoper his back.

It was a blunt rebuff; Huidekoper thought, *Why, I am a fool.* He should have intuited that the young man might prefer not to discuss his personal tragedies.

So it would be necessary to come to him from another side; for it was important to get the New Yorker's ear tonight, while he still had the fresh clean viewpoint of an outsider—before the damn fool dreamers could blind Roosevelt to the alarming truth.

Joe Ferris leaned over the table and had his look at the beer keg and the bottles. He seemed a bit lost; he nodded a greeting to Huidekoper and said, "Feel like I'm getting narrow at the equator. Anything to eat around here?"

"Bacon and beans in the kitchen."

"I might have known," Joe Ferris said. "Always a pot on the stove at Custer Trail."

"If you can hold your horses, I'm sure Mrs. Eaton will be serving up supper in just a bit."

"Then may be just one drink first." Joe poured, tasted and considered.

Huidekoper offered, "Genuine forty-rod coffin varnish."

"Two weeks old if it's a day," Joe Ferris agreed.

Huidekoper said, "Around here that's *aged* whiskey, my friend."

"No dispute it'd make powerful snake poison." Joe Ferris did not smile. He rarely smiled. His demeanor appeared to derive from a fundamental recognition that life was neither frivolous nor amusing, but mainly a serious business.

Joe touched Huidekoper's arm with a forefinger. "What was that you said to him about his ladies?"

"Didn't you—no, I suppose you didn't. They kept it mainly out of the newspapers, didn't they. I had it in a long letter from one of my relations in New York."

Joe Ferris watched him with a wry sort of patience. Huidekoper knew his own reputation for roundabout longwindedness. It didn't trouble him. There was time enough for everything; in any discourse many things must be considered—especially here: it was a sudden country, where men often blurted and acted too swiftly.

Taking his own course, Huidekoper said, "He's had dreadful political defeats. You know about those."

Joe gave him a very quick nod and a very small smile, meant to show that he knew what Huidekoper was talking about; but it was clear Joe knew nothing of the kind. Huidekoper scolded him: "Joe—what do you know?"

"I don't pay a lot of mind to your American politics."

"Then allow me to be the instrument of your edification. You *must* know, of course, that your friend acquired a certain fame as the youngest Minority Leader in the history of the New York Assembly . . ."

"Well he told me he was Minority something. I thought he was running a sandy on me."

"Nothing of the kind. Why, that young idealist was so brash he out-politicked Tammany Hall—just about single-handedly passed a Civil Service Reform Act." Huidekoper dropped his voice to a confidential drone. "But now you know he's fallen as fast as he climbed. Did you follow the Republican Convention this year?"

"I had a few other things to do."

"Well Theodore Roosevelt there was thought to be an important figure. But I can tell you that his hand-picked candidate for the presidential nomination—that Vermont Senator whose name even now I cannot recall: a politician not only incorruptibly honest but also soporifically dull—was not merely defeated but squashed on the final convention ballot. And by that time, so much scandal—none of it attached to Roosevelt, so far as I know—had been exposed in the press that quite a few of the most influential Republicans bolted the party. In fact all that remains is a skeleton crew. It was a debacle. Are you sure you don't—"

"I'm fresh and green, A.C. You may as well finish my instruction. Make it faster before I fall down from the starvation!"

"It's unforgivable that you don't apprise yourself of these events. You may be a foreigner but you're on American soil now."

"We're not in the States, A.C."

"All the same. Why, some are opining the Republican Party has no future in American politics. And many more, I hear, are opining that Theodore Roosevelt has none."

"Well, then," Joe said uncertainly.

"Yes indeed. The question is—do we see the contentious young New Yorker coming west to lick his political wounds—or, as some of our Eastern cousins have been speculating, to build a new constituency?"

"You aiming to vote for him?"

"He's not running for office, is he." Huidekoper moved closer to his companion and dropped his voice another pitch. "A few years ago, you see, his father died."

"Mr. Roosevelt's father?"

"Yes. In his forties. And the young fellow was just eighteen. They were very close. I understand he took his father's passing very hard. But he still had a brother and his sisters and surely you've heard of the mother, very bright woman, a Southerner—one of the Bullochs of Savannah. Heroic ancestors in abundance . . . Anyhow that boy there went back to Harvard after his father passed on—completed his studies and met a young lady up there and married her—Alice Hathaway Lee by name. Hopelessly enchanting girl, I have heard. And by the by a close relation to the Cabots and Saltonstalls."

"Patrician stuff," said Joe Ferris.

It took Huidekoper a bit by surprise. "Just so," he said.

"One of those arranged marriages?"

"The contrary. He was expected to marry one of the Carow girls of New York, I can't remember which one, but he left his sweetheart behind and went off to Boston and met the Lee girl and fell hopelessly out of control over her. Even out in the wilds of Pennsylvania we heard tales about it—sonnets and songs, romance of the season, so on. An authentic love match."

"Come to think of it he said something to me about his wife."

"Last year that would have been."

"How'd you know that?"

Huidekoper could see Roosevelt by the window, conversing with Howard Eaton. Roosevelt's voice sputtered out its notes as if from a half-obstructed trumpet—a shrill strained determined squeak, the words struggling to get out and tumbling over one another in bursts.

Huidekoper returned his attention to his companion when Joe Ferris said in a dry way, "I am trying to picture him in love."

"For God's sake don't tease the poor man. It's been a fearful tragedy."

"What has?"

"Valentine's Day. It was Valentine's Day, just a few months ago. I had a good lengthy letter from my—"

"Come *on*, A.C."

Huidekoper sighed. He loathed being rushed. It was important to lay the proper groundwork for a revelation. But he gave in to the young Canadian's impatience. "Early in the morning, or so I understand, his mother died of salmonella typhoid fever . . ."

"Oh. Sad thing."

". . . and later the same day—the very same Valentine's Day, in the very same house in Manhattan—poor Alice Lee—Bright's Disease—nephritis of the kidney; there's speculation she may have had it for months, but being with child masked the symptoms. In sum, you see, the young bride whom he loved with all his heart, having just given birth to a baby girl, died as well, on the same day as his mother, and in the same house."

Joe Ferris blinked. "God in Heaven."

"There was a double funeral. And just a day or two later your young client was back in his seat in the Albany legislature. I had a letter speculating that he tried to lose himself in a flood of hard work—he refused to accept any sympathy, he declined to show any interest in his new baby daughter, and some of his closest colleagues seriously suspected he was losing his reason. And then, you see, his political career was dashed as well, and now he's decided to come west and here he is before you."

Joe Ferris cleared his throat with noisy effort and dragged a palm across his face. "God in Heaven," he said again. "No wonder he's low."

He seemed near tears—a surprising thing, for Joe had a phlegmatic countenance and was no more given to displays of open emotion than was any other Bad Lander.

Seeking to distract his companion from his gloom, Huidekoper looked around the room and took notice of one trifle. When people went to the outhouse they took pains to conceal their destination. What gave away Gregor Lang's intent was his carrying a copy of the *Police Gazette* outdoors into the night. Even that was too blatant for Deacon W. P. Osterhaut, who turned and glared until the door closed softly behind Lang. Huidekoper directed a half-stifled smile toward Joe Ferris and said out of the side of his mouth, "Seems the Deacon forever quests after causes for outrage."

Joe Ferris said gravely, "From the look on his face may be he never got the stink of that polecat out of his nose."

Huidekoper changed the subject carefully: "Are you taking Roosevelt out again? I thought you'd given up guiding hunters."

"I thought I had too. Be that as it may, he wrote to me by name."

Huidekoper saw his glance slide toward Roosevelt, who still was engrossed in conversation with their host.

Huidekoper, who thought himself a judge of character, estimated that Joe Ferris was feeling shamed because he had been cultivating Roosevelt in the hope of prompting a grubstake that could move him indoors. Everybody knew about Joe's zeal to put four walls around him. Joe hated the killing: he was sentimental about animals.

Couldn't blame the man for that. The music of the animals was, in the main, sweeter than that of men.

Huidekoper kept his voice neutral. "He have anything to say on the ride out here?"

"About what?"

"Your run-up against Redhead Finnegan?"

"He didn't have much to say at all," Joe Ferris replied. "Which I understand now."

Huidekoper tried to sound casual. "He didn't happen to offer any sentiments on the subject of the Marquis de Morès?"

Joe Ferris squinted at him. "I don't think he likes the Marquis much."

"I can't begin to tell you how happy I am to hear that."

"Not my concern, is it." But Joe gave him the beginning of a smile.

Huidekoper knew how Joe had stood up against that faction on more than one occasion—against Jerry Paddock especially; even in the old Cantonment days Joe Ferris never had had any use for Paddock; and when Paddock had joined forces with the Marquis, Joe became one of the few who did not cowtow to either of them.

Huidekoper liked Joe Ferris. Was it time to take him into his confidence?

Not for the moment; not just yet.

Somewhere in the room there barked the complaint of a hard bitter voice, a voice that would cut glass: Deacon Osterhaut's. It was not unusually loud; but Huidekoper with his especial sensitivity to sounds was cursed with an inability to disregard the unpleasant ones.

Roosevelt came forward. Joe Ferris lifted his glass inquiringly. The New Yorker declined the offer with a vast display of teeth.

"At Harvard, old fellow," Roosevelt chattered, "they initiated me into the Porcellian on the occasion of my twentieth birthday, and I was persuaded to celebrate the event with the ingestion of a voluminous excess of wine. The next day I learned the full dread meaning of that horrendous term 'hangover.' It was enough to persuade me never to drink again."

"I've learned the same lesson myself," Huidekoper observed. "Several hundred times."

Roosevelt laughed—appreciatively; politely; but it was a sham. Last year's gusto was missing.

Little wonder, Huidekoper thought, considering what the poor fellow had been through. Still—it was important to get in past the grief and impress upon him the urgency of the situation.

He tried to move closer but Roosevelt eeled away through the swirling crowd. It was clear Roosevelt was deliberately evading him. "Hallo there, old fellow—delighted to see you!" Huidekoper couldn't see who it was. Wadsworth perhaps, or Truscott or Gregor Lang if he'd returned from the privy—one of the handful who'd been here last fall. *Damn*, Huidekoper thought. *So stupid to talk to him of his loss. It must be the last thing he wants reminding of.*

Preceded by the sound of his wheezing cough, Roosevelt came back into view to shout past several people at Howard Eaton: "I see no diminution in the remarkable hospitality of your ranch. Has this room ever been empty?"

"I recall a day or two in the dead of winter," allowed Howard Eaton, with a wide smile beneath his heavy drooping mustache.

Eaton was a pioneer: he had settled in the Bad Lands in 1881—three years ago. Now Eaton was superintendent of the Custer Trail Cattle Company and the Badger Cattle Company, with the tacit financial backing of one A.C. Huidekoper, who at the moment was asking himself, *Do I need Howard's help to bring Roosevelt into this?* He hoped not; it would require persuading not only Roosevelt but Howard Eaton as well, for Howard was not yet in agreement with Huidekoper about the extent of the impending danger.

Abruptly Johnny Goodall appeared at Huidekoper's shoulder. The Texan said, "Little dude sounds like a foreigner. English?"

"No," said Huidekoper, "that's New York Silk Stocking."

They watched Roosevelt accept a glass of lemonade from Mrs. Eaton, who said, "Is this another short visit or is there truth in the rumors that you intend to stay out here?"

"I bought a share in a herd last fall," Roosevelt said.

It was something Huidekoper already knew—something, indeed, he was counting on.

Roosevelt was talking to Mrs. Eaton—measuring his words,

Huidekoper thought, in a way that was unlike the Roosevelt he'd met last year: "We've had a good increase. I may make ranching my regular business. Haven't made up my mind yet, don't you know. I am out here because I cannot get up any enthusiasm for the Republican candidate, and punching cattle is one good way to avoid campaigning, but . . ." and his voice dropped so that Huidekoper scarcely heard it, "in truth, dear lady, I haven't much to go back to. I may stay—I like this country."

Huidekoper was reminded just then of an afternoon several years ago in the coal hills of Pennsylvania: youths on wagons bounding furiously across the bright green meadow in a Mardi Gras buckboard race. Huidekoper had been in the crowd, shouting with the rest of them, urging his friend on. There had been great laughter and exultation and then a sudden pall when one of the wagons had flipped at full gallop and slammed its driver hard against the ground. What Huidekoper recalled now was the way the laughter had been cut in two as if by the blade of a falling axe; and the way none of them had quite been the same ever after, once they learned the seventeen-year-old driver had been crushed to death in the accident before their eyes.

Roosevelt was like that now—not merely subdued but a different young man altogether from the exuberant chatterer of last summer.

He's got to be handled with caution, Huidekoper thought, *or he'll bolt like a fawn*.

Johnny Goodall was gazing over the others' heads at Roosevelt with a hard challenge in his stare; then he turned his back and said in a mild drawl to Huidekoper, "Appears to me this beef bonanza belongs to dudes who invest from back East and never get to know the business from the back of a cow horse. I expect they stand to lose their millions."

"That particular dude may take you by surprise," said Huidekoper.

"We'll see—we'll see." Johnny, after all, was in a short temper tonight.

Huidekoper said, "A year ago you'd have numbered me among those dudes investing from back East." Out here everyone was an immigrant. Those who had been here more than six months counted themselves natives.

Johnny Goodall said, "You're different, Mr. Huidekoper. You're a horseman."

It took Huidekoper by surprise: it was a considerable compliment to an Easterner from a Texan.

"Hell," Johnny Goodall said obscurely, "nothing's like it was." And moved away.

Mystified, Huidekoper watched him go. At the door Johnny Goodall stopped and looked at every face. Then he made a deliberate pivot and strode out.

As if a hangman had departed, the noise of voices in the room climbed quickly; Huidekoper heard barks of nervous laughter and loud talk that was too hearty.

It meant things really were reaching an impossible pitch.

It wasn't Johnny Goodall, really. It was what Johnny represented. The damnable Frenchman.

We've got to bring Roosevelt into this.

Having located his prey he waited his opportunity with the patience of a stalker; it did not arrive until after supper—near sunset when half the guests had departed; finally he seized his chance when he saw Roosevelt slip out the side door. Huidekoper followed shortly thereafter and lurked discreetly by a corner of the horse barn. Westward the clouds appeared to reflect some violent conflagration taking place just beneath the horizon. When he heard the crunch of Roosevelt's approaching boots from the direction of the outhouse he turned the corner, hands in pockets, head thrown back—a casual stroller out for a breath of fresh air. "A fine evening."

"Very pleasant," Roosevelt agreed.

Huidekoper said, "I wonder if I might have a word. A matter of cattle business," he added quickly.

It slowed the New Yorker's pace and, in the end, brought him to a halt. His shoulders dropped a fraction in relief; there was gratitude, of a sort, in his face when he turned, for Huidekoper had not reopened the wound by attempting to apologize for his earlier gaffe.

"I'm at your disposal," Roosevelt said with reluctant courtesy.

It pleased Huidekoper to approach it delicately, obliquely. "My ancestors came from Amsterdam. I suppose that gives you and me something in common. My family owns estates in Pennsylvania and New York."

"Yes, I know that, Mr. Huidekoper."

"You've an investment of some substance—eighty horses, isn't it, and something like four hundred fifty head of cattle under the Maltese Cross brand?"

Roosevelt eyed him with quick darting probes. "That's so. What the locals insist upon calling the Maltee Cross."

"They reason if it's only a single cross it oughtn't to have a plural name." Huidekoper ventured a smile.

Roosevelt said, "You've been making inquiries about my investments?"

"Only to the extent that I've made it my business to identify all the stock owners in the district, and their relative holdings. Not prying, I assure you. We're facing what, not to put too fine a point on it, one might elect to describe as difficulties. We'd be obliged to have your assistance."

Roosevelt watched him, blinking rapidly, waiting to hear what he had to say. A year ago, Huidekoper thought, he would have jumped right into the opening with both feet. But now—Roosevelt's attention hardly seemed to have been stirred at all.

Huidekoper said, "Within reason this is good country for grazing. But it may be a mistake to listen to fools who go around boasting that if it was good enough for millions of buffalo then it must be equally well suited for beef cattle."

"Is that so." It was polite; not really interested. Roosevelt's eyes wandered.

Huidekoper said, "The buffalo had vast prairies to roam—tens of millions of acres. They kept moving, don't you see. The grass replenished itself behind them. You don't have the same qualities with a sedentary herd of beef cattle."

"If you're trying to discourage me—"

"Not at all. We welcome your participation; in fact I for one am eager to have you among us, because I think you bring with you a sorely needed sense of justice along with a practical understanding of how things work. We desperately need your kind of leadership. But I think it's important you be acquainted with the realities here. Please hear me out. It's a matter of the utmost urgency.

He could see that Roosevelt wanted to turn his back; he wanted to be left alone. Huidekoper saw the desire plainly in Roosevelt's twitching face—and prayed the politician's fatal curiosity in him would hold him in his tracks.

Roosevelt watched him—and finally said, "Go on, then."

"Thank you." Huidekoper made a vague gesture with his hand, suggesting they walk; Roosevelt acknowledged it with the barest nod and they began to stroll up the slope, the better to view the sunset.

Huidekoper said, "Stock-raising country needs three things. Good nutritious grasses, clean drinking water and natural shelter against the weather. We've got all three in abundance in the Bad Lands."

They passed the corner of the corral fence and continued up the pasture. Huidekoper peeled one eye for droppings, out of concern for his freshly cleaned boots. "We graze our stock on open range—the public lands. Here in Billings County we've got three million acres of free range within our round-up district—surely an ample supply of land, one might think. In labor and goods it costs a sensible ranchman about a dollar a year to raise each head of cattle, so a four-year-old steer ready for market and raised from a calf should cost around four dollars. It can be sold in today's market for twenty dollars. From these kinds of facts a large and growing number of investors have calculated their potential profits. Yourself among them, perhaps."

Roosevelt rapidly squinted his large blue eyes. His facial contortions were quick and strenuous. "If you're seeking capital investment—"

"I'm not, Mr. Roosevelt. Please hear me out. The matter is one of considerable menace."

"Menace?"

"There are those—enthusiastic ones—who refuse to believe this country has limitations. They keep pouring in with their cattle. They don't see how easily the Bad Lands can be overgrazed. For myself I've concluded that horses are best able to adapt themselves to the prevailing natural conditions—but that's by the way. Have you ever heard of Valentine Scrip?"

"I heard the term this afternoon for the first time. I don't command its meaning."

"Ten years ago," Huidekoper commenced, with a familiar sense of enjoyment in exposition, "the Supreme Court upheld a Spanish land grant claim by one Thomas Valentine, who said he was the rightful owner of a good part of the state of California under the terms of an old grant that survived the changes from Spanish to Mexican to American government."

"I don't recall the case."

"You'd have been thirteen or fourteen. In any event—hundreds of people were settled on the lands that Thomas Valentine claimed, and rather than displace them the Supreme Court ordered the general land office to compensate Valentine by giving him an equivalent number of acres of unappropriated public lands."

"A fair settlement, if his claims were valid."

"Quite. But he wasn't given title to any specific ground. The land office issued scrip to Valentine, rather like blank deeds to unspecified sections of land, and he promptly turned around and sold it in dozens of transactions. He made a huge profit."

"Enterprising fellow."

"I dare say." Huidekoper couldn't help smiling a bit, anticipating his companion's reaction; he had prepared the ground thoroughly, he thought, and now was the time to sink the spade:

"Five of the allotments of Valentine Scrip were bought by Baron Nicholas Von Hoffman of New York City, whom you know. His son-in-law is the Marquis de Morès."

"Yes . . ."

"De Morès had already bought fourteen sections along the right-of-way from the Northern Pacific Railroad—for his cattle pens and feeding lots and the plat where he built the town of Medora. That's fair enough. But then he acquired the Valentine Scrip from his father-in-law. And here is the curious fact. The Valentine Scrip in De Morès's possession entitles him to file claim to just two hundred and twenty acres—but he's been stringing fences for *miles* up and down the river."

"I saw one of them today," Roosevelt said, with what appeared to be a spark of regard.

Huidekoper said, "He's claiming thousands of acres of bottom land as his private range—and waving pieces of scrip in the faces of any men who object."

Roosevelt scowled. "Is he claiming the land where my Maltese Cross stock are grazed?"

"At Chimney Butte? No." Huidekoper let the silence hang long enough for maximum effectiveness: "Not yet."

He watched Roosevelt react to that; then he said, "He's been limiting his eviction attempts to the little hardscrabble fellows. For the moment. But he'll swallow every inch of ground in these Bad Lands if he's not stopped. I'm convinced of it."

"Do the other ranchmen agree with you?"

"Not many. They don't see what I see. They believe De Morès is a gentleman, and they believe gentlemen don't steal from other gentlemen. They're flattered to be invited to dine with him. They push one another aside to gain favor with him. Half the grown-up men in the county would give a month's income for the privilege of an invitation to join the Marquis on one of his luxurious hunting expeditions. Some of the best men in the district—men I'd have thought wiser—have been investing hard cash in his pipe-dream schemes." Huidekoper allowed a quick small smile to break across his face. "One is encouraged to recall George Washington's dictum—'Beware of foreign entanglements.'"

"De Morès's operations are prosperous, from what I've read."

"He's got the ear of the press," Huidekoper said dryly. "Some of us don't believe everything we read. The newspaper publisher here, Arthur Packard, very pleasant young man but I'm afraid the Marquis seems to have thrown something of a spell over him."

Roosevelt folded his arms, unfolded them and shifted his stance; Huidkoper observed with alarm that clearly, after all, he'd prefer to be somewhere else. "Look here. If the man is claiming land falsely, as you say he is, then surely you should take up the matter with the government authorities."

"We'd like to do just that, you see, but there's a difficulty."

"Why?"

"When you leave the United States and come out into the wilderness you soon come to an understanding that there may be changes in the rules. Take for example Billings County. It's a fiction—it exists solely on paper. There are no commissioners. No county government. For administrative purposes we're attached to Stark County and there's a Justice of the Peace at Dickinson—forty miles east; you came through it on the train—but the nearest sheriff is at Mandan, one hundred and fifty miles away. We're on our own out here."

"Then why not organize Billings County with your own government and sheriff?"

"And call it what? De Morès County? That's how it would resolve. De Morès employs—I don't know, perhaps two-thirds of the men in the county who are of voting age and might be inclined to come out of their hiding holes long enough to cast a ballot. And anyway—" Huidekoper endeavored not to appear too sly "—the stock-growers have expressed a certain resistance to the notion. If the county were organized they might have to pay taxes."

"By federal law they have to pay taxes anyway, to the nearest county seat."

Huidekoper said, "Yes, that's the law. But consider, if you will, the picture of a tax collector based right here in Medora as opposed to one based one hundred and fifty miles away in Mandan, who hasn't a hope in Hades of keeping track of the movements of cattle out here on the Little Missouri. If I may be boldly candid, the last time the assessor appeared—last fall—word preceded his arrival by several weeks, and at the time of the assessments most of the herds somehow managed to have wandered over into Montana until the assessor's departure. . . ."

They had achieved the rump of the low hill behind Eaton's ranch house; they strolled in the lee of a looming face of rock. The sky was fading through pinks and lavenders. Roosevelt stopped, turned a slow circle on his heels and faced Huidekoper. The force of Roosevelt's eyes, magnified by the dusty glass of his spectacles, was enough to discomfit Huidekoper.

Roosevelt said, "You can't have your cake and eat it. You must either accept the rule of law or choose to get along without it and suffer the consequences."

"Perhaps. A few of us feel there may be a third alternative. There's been some talk of forming—within the proposed Stockmen's Association—a committee of safety."

Roosevelt blinked rapidly. "Vigilantes? To what purpose? The lynching of the Marquis De Morès?"

"Hardly that." Feeling the rise of Roosevelt's anger, Huidekoper sought to deflect it. He thrust a finger toward an inscription scratched in the rock above them. "Hard to read in the twilight, but they carved their names just eight years ago. W.C. Williams,

Company H . . . F. Healy, Company M. Two soldiers in Custer's command."

Roosevelt peered up at the carvings. "In actual fact Williams and Healy were not with Custer's column at the Little Big Horn. They're still alive."

"Where on earth did you learn that?"

"Eaton showed me this rock last year. It made me curious, and I sent a letter of inquiry to Washington."

"That's precisely the sort of initiative we need here, to get us organized. No one listens to me—I'm just the windbag from Pennsylvania. You've earned fame and respect. They'll listen to you."

"I didn't come out here for politics," Roosevelt said; he flung his anguished face toward the sky and confided, "I've reached the ebb of my life, old fellow."

"Perhaps you need a challenge then."

A faint wind ran in from the direction of the gentle deepening twilight. The swift darkness dropped sharply, like the deliberate extinction of a lamp. The moon was up, just barely; its light laid a pewter band along the crest.

Roosevelt said: "A challenge? No. I need solitude. Privacy. I'll make a life somewhere in these hills—on my own, by myself. I'm sorry, Huidekoper, but I want no part of your damned vigilantes."

Four

Arthur Packard set out to meet the train; today was Tuesday. Every Tuesday he pushed a wheelbarrow full of freshly printed newspapers down the two blocks to the platform for delivery to Mingusville and the other towns along the railway line to the west beyond the nearby Montana border.

Today seemed unexceptional. Of course he didn't expect a Lunatic to bolt from the train.

Pack, with an itch somewhere under the cobwebby dark beard that he cultivated in an effort to make the world recognize that he was mature and responsible, teetered along the rough ground, balancing the precarious tower of newspapers and resolving, not for the first time, to hire a boy to act as printer's devil and general chore-handler for *The Bad Lands Cow Boy* so as to absolve the owner-publisher from the indignity of picking up the four hundred newspapers that fell off the wheelbarrow at least once during each week's perilous trek. If the papers didn't topple of their own accord there had been until recently a contingent of ne'er-do-wells from Big Mouth Bob's Bug Juice Dispensary to tip the load "accidentally" and inspire brays of yelping laughter from the saloon porch.

It didn't matter that Pack, enraged, had boxed two of the ruffians to their knees within the month of April. Too drunk to feel the punishment, they and their friends had only continued laughing.

Then one of them—the kid, Riley Luffsey—had come forward in a brief show of cocky conscience. He was a lout, no more than eighteen, who strutted everywhere with an insolent swagger and tried to appear dangerous. Pack had heard him announce more than once his life's ambition to become a *pistolero* as celebrated as the late Wild Bill Hickok; yet on that singular occasion, moved by some stray impulse from a better world, Luffsey had found the decency to help Pack gather up the spilled newspapers and wipe off the worst of the clay dust and help him heap them in the wheelbarrow.

But the kid had been assailed with such a thunder of hazing and hoo-rawing that he'd seen better than to come to Pack's aid a second time.

Later the same Riley Luffsey had come to the side door of the *Cow Boy*. Pack remembered the kid's hushed confession—"I can read and write!"—as if it were a secret of felonious shamefulness.

When Pack had offered the job of printer's devil Luffsey had reared back on his dignity—"I'm a hunter, sir, not anybody's hired hand!"—but he'd looked over his shoulder as he said it, and Pack got the feeling the bravado was mostly for the benefit of any of the ruffians who might be eavesdropping. Pack had tried to invite the boy in for a look at the printing press—there was something you couldn't help liking about the kid, despite all his boasting—but Luffsey declined, hurrying away skittishly to rejoin his friends.

Like the rest of Redhead Finnegan's unsavory crowd Luffsey usually could be found hanging about Bob Roberts's saloon, sometimes weeks at a time, awaiting the arrival of trains carrying dudes who might be induced to hire guides and wranglers for big-game expeditions into the Bad Lands.

Luffsey might be tractable but his companions were incorrigible. Pack sometimes thought of buying a revolver but realized what an invitation to disaster that could be. At the same time certain notions of order and decency, inculcated in him since infancy, had to be defended.

Therefore last month he had taken to carrying a type iron in the wheelbarrow.

It was a metal side-stick that he used for locking type forms in the press—three feet long and heavy. Pack, having been a baseball batsman of some repute at Michigan, knew how to swing it.

That Tuesday a month ago "Bitter Creek" Redhead Finnegan and his assortment of ruffians had circled round in their customary baiting taunt and Pack, setting down the wheelbarrow with unhurried care and picking up the type iron, had knocked the nearest of them to the ground with one blow.

Since then no one had molested the wheelbarrow.

Today therefore he had no gantlet to run. All the boys were down at the Northern Pacific line, preparing the ritual hoo-rawing of the train. Pack had the street nearly to himself; there was only a desultory traffic of pedestrians and horsemen, and there were the two young men on the porch of Nelson's drygoods store, catty-corner across the wide intersection from the shack that housed the *Cow Boy*. Pack set the wheelbarrow down in front of Nelson's steps, stood up, jammed both fists in the small of his spine and arched himself backwards.

Swede Nelson, pink and plump, shifted the weight of the shotgun on his shoulder. He was preoccupied—staring down the street toward the cafe; when Pack looked that way he saw the girl Katie by the cafe door. She came out every morning to watch the train. She would stand motionless until the train disappeared to the west. For several months now she had watched it with dreamy despair.

Pack said to Joe Ferris, "Now, I thought you were on the trail with Theodore Roosevelt."

Joe only grunted.

Pack said, "Where's Roosevelt then?"

"Hunting, I expect."

"Without you?"

"I am tired of trundling tenderfeet," Joe Ferris said.

"Good money in it, though," said Swede Nelson, his gaze intent upon the girl down the street.

"Be that as it may," said Joe, "it's my life's aim to work indoors."

The girl who stood at the cafe watching for the train was sixteen or seventeen and had a quick bold eye and a restless body. When Katie and her mother had come to work in the cafe it had been easy to see she was ripe to be plucked by the first sharp-dressed man who might step off the train for a day and give her a second glance on an evening when her mother was looking the other way. She wasn't a whore but she was known to have stepped out with quite a few men who were not reputed to be gentlemen.

Lately somehow the bashful storekeeper Swede Nelson had worked up the boldness to approach her. During the past few weeks Pack had seen them arm-in-arm several times. He wondered if it was serious between them—or for just one of them.

Now Katie looked up this way and Pack saw the way she smiled at Swede before she stepped off the wooden sidewalk and strode, hips swinging healthily, toward the Northern Pacific platform.

Pack heard the whistling exhalation of Swede's pent breath.

When he caught Swede's shy grin, half pride and half guilt, Pack said, "Why don't you go along there with her?"

Swede made no answer, other than a vague shifting of the shotgun on his shoulder.

Joe Ferris selected a soda cracker from the open barrel. He said, "Swede's afraid if he leaves the store alone the boys will clean it out again."

"In broad daylight?"

Swede made a face. "Night or day don't matter. Can't afford another loss."

Joe Ferris bit off half the soda cracker with his neat teeth. "I keep telling him he's got too much inventory of goods that nobody wants much—stocks that don't turn over fast enough. What's the news today, Pack?"

Pack unfolded the top copy. "Chinese Gordon's still under siege in Khartoum." He glanced through his inside-page headlines, reading upside-down. "Major league baseball elects to allow overhand pitching as well as underhand—batsman to call his choice."

"Well now—that could be fun. We going to inaugurate that rule Sunday?"

"I'll put it to a vote." Pack glimpsed one brief item before he folded the newspaper. "In New York City they've opened a swank new apartment block they call the Dakota. Because it's so far north in the wilderness. Isn't that a howl?"

"Someday I want to see New York," said little Joe Ferris. "May be I'll open a bank there."

Still plugging along on a previous train of thought, Swede

Nelson said calmly, "If you keep a shop you must keep everything folks may want. Otherwise they buy at the competition."

"They won't go to the competition long as you keep under De Morès's prices," Joe Ferris argued. "Which is not hard to do, the way Jerry Paddock keeps doubling the price of things over at the Markee's general store. You've put a crease in that, which is why he wants you out of business. *He* minds the competition. Jerry Paddock does. He'll do you harm. He's got no compunctions. Bullet or knife, and likely in the dark. And he's got the Markee's protection. Swede, I keep telling you, you're stretched too far."

"A man's got to take risks if he's to get ahead," said Swede.

Joe Ferris swung his face from side to side; he tossed a bland glance at Pack. "There's prudent risks and there's foolish risks."

Swede put his owl-wise gaze on Pack. "Listen to the mercantile master." He pointed a thumb at their friend Joe Ferris. "Joe gets his experience in high finance from cutting trees. And from laying track like a Chinee."

"And wrangling stock and guiding damn fool dude hunters," Joe Ferris said. "Be that as it may, you got yourself at risk with the commission house in St. Paul. You've bought too much goods on credit, and friend Paddock knows that. I hear he's been buying up your IOU notes from the commission house."

Swede's mind was nearly transparent. Pack watched him while he decided to pretend he wasn't alarmed. Swede let a ragged moment go by before he permitted himself to ask quietly, "Where'd you hear that?"

"He had a little conversation elixir in the hotel bar and he was bragging. I heard him."

"It's not true," Swede decided. "Jerry Paddock wants to scare me. He knows you'd tell me what you heard."

"I don't think he knew I was there," said Joe Ferris. "But you're right he's a liar." He looked at Pack. Joe Ferris was short and easygoing and very thick everywhere except in the brain. He had the muscles of a man twice his size. He wore a plaid shirt and coarse butternut trousers; he was a rough young man from the woods of Canada but somewhere he had learned an agreeable grace. His droopy mustache overhung a mouth curled into a quick and sometimes dour sense of humor. "What do you think, Pack? I wonder how much you could win on a bet that Jerry Paddock wouldn't know the truth from one of his own black lies?"

"Now, nobody's proved a thing against him," Pack said. "The Marquis seems to trust him."

"And that's good enough for Pack," Joe said to Swede Nelson. "Pack's a true believer. Why, the way he's convinced of the Markee's infallibility, you'd think the Markee was the pope of Dakota Territory."

"I do think he's a great man," Pack conceded. He lifted the wheelbarrow's handles and resumed his journey toward the train.

Behind him Joe Ferris said, "Be that as it may, your great man's bringing in ten thousand head of sheep. What do you think of that?"

Pack called back over his shoulder: "You hear that nonsense from Jerry Paddock too?" And went on his way.

Pack knew he needed to have a serious talk with Joe Ferris. For a man who was ambitious to get ahead in the world Joe had an altogether too jaundiced view. Cynicism had no place on this frontier. It ought to be a man's mission to alert the world to the benefits that derived, as Pack had written jubilantly in *The Bad Lands Cow Boy*, "from ingesting the electrifying purification of the fresh pure ozone of the Bad Lands."

Everything that happened in Medora stirred Pack's proprietary feelings. Sometimes it was as if he (and not the Marquis) owned the town.

In actual fact the Marquis De Morès owned just about everything in sight. But then, Pack told his friends, the Marquis had a couple years' jump on him. After all, the Marquis was twenty-five years old; Pack was merely twenty-two, and not yet a year out of the University of Michigan.

At any age the Marquis was a singular figure. Pack thought him a Great Man. He had said as much more than once in his newspaper—and not simply, as cynics would have it, because De Morès was *The Bad Lands Cow Boy*'s biggest advertiser. Anyone with half a brain could see the Marquis was a Visionary. It wouldn't be long before the world would be mentioning him in the same breath with Astor, Carnegie and Morgan. The dashing Marquis De Morès was bringing reality to the Dream: he was putting meat and flesh on the bones of the nation's imperative Manifest Destiny.

For a Frenchman he was the next best thing to Lafayette: an American Hero.

Medora town's streets had been plotted and surveyed on a tidy grid strictly by the compass, due north-south and due east-west, with haughty disregard for the fact that the town's basic intersection—that of the railroad bridge with the river—ran on the diagonal, with the river flowing northeast while the Northern Pacific track sliced across the butte canyons to the northwest.

The interesting result of this clash between nature's reality and ambition's rigidity was that every single street in Medora led to the railroad.

From wherever you stood in town you could see—at a forty-five degree angle—the high abutment that supported the steel tracks.

The town sat on river flats on the east bank of the Little Missouri sheltered by scarred looming bluffs of clay and stone and lignite coal. The buildings, of brick and of lumber, had been constructed of materials imported by rail. Already more than a dozen blocks on the plat had been built nearly to capacity, and this was remarkable because the town had been founded as recently as the spring of the previous year.

Before that there had been the tiny community on the far side of the river—the scrofulous camp called Little Missouri: an outgrowth of the army's Bad Lands Cantonment, inhabited by those who had remained behind after the Indian-fighting troopers and railroad-building roughnecks had departed.

Little Missouri—one big shabby hotel-saloon and a seedy litter of shacks and tents—had been presided over by the sinister Jerry Paddock, onetime sutler and permanent man of mystery.

The Marquis De Morès, planning a site for the headquarters of his proposed meat-packing empire, had disdained the Cantonment and built his private railroad siding on the east side of the river. Here he parked his sumptuous private railroad car the *Montana* and used it for a residence while he directed and paid for the construction of the packing plant, the mansion on the overlooking bluff, and the town.

Not quite seven years after George Custer had camped here en route to his Centennial Summer appointment with catastrophe the young Marquis De Morès—who only a year earlier had been clerking in a New York bank—had cracked a bottle of French champagne over a tent-peg on April Fool's Day, 1883, and christened the place Medora after his bride, who happened to be the daughter of the owner of the bank that had employed him.

The metamorphosis from ambitious dream to brick-and-wood reality had taken place with amazing speed. De Morès, Pack saw, was a man who understood his own dreams. Within months the town had been built and populated . . . herds and herdsmen had arrived from as far away as Texas . . . Jerry Paddock, taken into the Marquis's confidence and onto his payroll, had cooperated eagerly in the demise of what was left of the Cantonment and had moved his enterprises, along with those of his few neighbors and colleagues, into the brand-new settlement on the right bank . . . and the De Morès abattoir's butchers had begun slaughtering beef by the ton and shipping it east by rail aboard the Marquis's refrigerated freight cars.

From no building in town was it more than three blocks to the railroad, or more than four blocks to the slaughterhouse.

These proximities might have been convenient for the residents were it not for the noise and smell and ash. Still, the few ill-tempered skeptics had been encouraged to leave town or to think less about their discomfort and more about the advantages of modern progress.

Today fortunately the abattoir was downwind of town and the breeze was robust enough to keep the flies off the streets, which were empty of inhabitants in any event; and so Pack's journey with his wheelbarrow to the railroad platform was uneventful and pleasant enough until the Lunatic grenaded into his life.

The usual racketing fusillade of enthusiastic gunfire greeted the train as it entered town. The sulphurous acridity of black powder smoke stung Pack's nostrils and eyes as he heaved the wheelbarrow up the ramp.

The onset of De Morès-style civilization had done nothing to curb the custom of greeting trains with .44-caliber barrages. Passengers were wise to duck low. Just last month the Marquis De

Morès's father-in-law, the irascible New York banker Nicholas Von Hoffman, had stepped off the train wearing a derby hat—a certain invitation to target practice. Several shots had been fired. The hat had been shot off the banker's head by party or parties unknown in the crowd.

When found an hour later the derby hat was a shredded ruin.

The banker was humiliated, the Marquis indignant.

De Morès had posted a two-hundred-dollar reward for the identification of the marksman.

Nothing had come of that. Generally it was assumed "Bitter Creek" Redhead Finnegan or one of his friends had ventilated the derby hat but no one had sought the reward; it was taken for granted that the two hundred dollars would have to be collected by the heirs of any such claimant, for Finnegan was malevolent—as untamed as a mountain lion.

The Marquis had been furious. For a while he had taken to bursting unannounced into saloons, perhaps in the hope of catching someone in the act of boasting about the celebrated victory over the derby hat.

In turn, Finnegan and his friends had doubled their armament and made clear how they intended to defend themselves if any libelous accusations were laid against them by that son of a bitch of a Markee.

Tempers only eased after Pack, as the representative of the community, assured the Marquis that the derby hat never would have been assaulted if the culprits had known the man under the hat was related to him. A brand-new derby hat was presented with the compliments of the citizenry, and the Marquis—perhaps because his father-in-law had returned to the East—allowed himself to be mollified.

Today to Pack's relief Finnegan was nowhere in evidence. He hadn't been in town for several days; possibly he was on a hunting or stock-stealing trek. The sun shone bright, the breeze was good, the day was festive and the town was blessed by the absence not only of Finnegan but also of young Riley Luffsey and one or two others among Finnegan's wild Irish friends.

So the shooting today was desultory and did no harm; it only contributed a fewscore balls to the lead mine upstream.

* * *

Mrs. Reuter—muscular ranch woman—was helping an injured passenger down from the train. For a moment Pack thought with alarm that one of the roisterers must have aimed too low. Mrs. Reuter was pressing a cloth to a bloody streak at the side of the passenger's neck—a bullet blaze by the look of it. The man kept jerking his head away from the cloth and stout Mrs. Reuter said brusquely, "Stop making such a fuss. I never heard anyone go on so about a little gunshot wound."

Struggling, the conductor with the aid of two passengers manhandled a huge youth down the steps from the vestibule of a passenger car. The conductor said, "Who's in authority here?"

Someone pointed to Pack.

"I guess I am," Pack admitted, inasmuch as he was the Medoran who possessed the key to the jail.

The conductor's captive heaved and lunged in frantic determination to get free of the grasp of the three big men around him. The conductor held the back of his collar; each straining passenger gripped one of the demented prisoner's arms.

A curious crowd gathered. "Now, what's all this?" Pack said.

"Damn to hell Lunatic," said the passenger with the neck wound. He took the cloth away from Mrs. Reuter and examined its bloodstains accusingly.

The Lunatic—a child six feet tall, two hundred pounds or more, shaggy, filthy, dressed in rags—made inarticulate sounds: he howled like a wolf in a trap. Yet his eyes appeared to know a profound secret: Pack thought he looked as if he had seen the inside of his dreams. . . . He lurched about, carrying three men with him, wearing the furious scowl of a child denied a toy.

The conductor said, "He took this gentleman's revolver. Seemed to think it was a toy. Shot up my train."

"Not to mention my neck," said the passenger irritably.

Pack said, "Any other casualties?"

"No," said the conductor. "By God's grace and through no fault of the Lunatic here."

"How'd he get on the train?"

"Don't know."

"Where'd he get aboard?"

"Don't know."

"No one's claimed him?"

"No. Hell—would you?"

"Can he talk?"

"Not that I know of. Just howling and growling."

Someone in the crowd said petulantly, "I don't know why he should be our responsibility."

"I can't have him on my train, that's all I know."

Pack turned to the injured passenger. "Now, you'll have to go back and see the sheriff in Mandan if you want to press charges—"

"Not if I have to stay in this Dakota place." The passenger swatted Mrs. Reuter's ministrations away, turned and climbed back aboard the train. His parting words were, "I wash my hands of the matter."

Mrs. Reuter yelled up at the train, "You are welcome!" and strode away toward town.

Pack said to the conductor, "Now, look here, I don't know if we legally can—"

That was when the Lunatic flung his head down and bit the hand of the passenger who held his right arm.

The passenger yelped and leaped back, loosing his hold.

The Lunatic, one arm freed, flailed with mighty strength—broke loose and butted his way through the surprised crowd and ran with an oafish thudding stride toward town. His cry sang as if from a coyote drunk on the moon.

The bitten passenger cried, "What if he's got hydrophobia?"

If there was a reply Pack did not hear it. He was running full speed, giving chase. Behind him the crowd came thundering.

Ahead the Lunatic disappeared among the buildings of Medora.

Assuredly the Lunatic would not continue to elude capture for very long. And indeed it was only a few moments before he was sighted lumbering up over the railroad embankment, heading for the river flats to the south. The crowd, baying like Huidekoper's pack of wolfhounds, gave happy chase. The race had become a game.

Pack, winded, let the others take up the baton. He stopped, hands on knees, chest heaving, trying to get breath.

From a distance he had a glimpse of the Marquis De Morès riding his horse across the tracks. For a brief instant he was reminded of the promised dinner interview. Next week perhaps? That assuredly would sell newspapers. (Masthead: "The *Cow Boy* is not published for fun, but for $2 per year. Arthur T. Packard, Prop.")

Shortly thereafter the Lunatic ran back into town, arms and legs pounding with energetic desperation. He seemed to have the stamina of a locomotive. The pursuers lagged quite far behind; some had dropped out altogether.

Expressing keen displeasure under his breath Pack took up the chase once again.

Joe Ferris and Swede Nelson had not deserted their posts on the porch of Swede's store. As Pack loped by he heard Joe Ferris's call: "He's around behind the store."

"Help me turn him," Pack gasped, and skittered around the corner. In the edge of his vision he had a glimpse of Joe Ferris vaulting the porch rail and dashing around the far side of the building.

They caught the Lunatic between them. Joe Ferris threatened him with a lofted baseball bat. The Lunatic threw himself flat on his back behind the store and commenced to suck great gasps into his cavernous chest.

"Don't get too close," Pack said. "He bites."

They stood warily above the Lunatic. A few others came in sight and stopped. There was a hush of uncertainty; then a sound—something Pack didn't hear, but it made Joe Ferris wheel with an abruptness that betrayed his trigger-poised nerves.

Jerry Paddock strutted into sight. His eyes flicked around, quick as a terrier's, surveying them and the prone Lunatic with shrewd and aggressive contempt.

Jerry Paddock didn't say a word but his malignant presence was enough to erase whatever amusement had graced the moment. Pack watched him resentfully.

Paddock, who had cloaked himself in a kind of seedy elegance since he'd met the Marquis, was wearing a black vested suit, its image spoiled by the grime around his celluloid collar and the unkempt shaggy droop of his dark goatee and stringy mandarin mustache, which accentuated the hatchet sharpness of his features.

Jerry Paddock tended to keep his own counsel. Everybody knew him but he probably had no friends; no one seemed to like him. He had no particular coterie or faction. Yet still he dominated the community—largely by means of fear.

Pack had no idea how much truth, if any, there was in the rumors that Jerry Paddock was the direct cause of at least five of the stones and crosses on Graveyard Butte. He did know that he had never heard Paddock make any effort to deny the rumors, and he suspected that Paddock himself probably was responsible for having started some of them.

Jerry Paddock enjoyed alarming people. It pleased him to have a reputation as a villain. When he stroked his beard the gesture had a sinister deliberation; did he rehearse it before a mirror?

Joe Ferris looked down at the panting Lunatic. He said to Pack, "You got him. What you want to do with him?"

"Well—"

Jerry Paddock said in his sandpaper voice, "Shoot him or hang him. Put him in the bone orchard."

Pack ignored the villain's suggestion. He looked around at the men, seeking a majority sentiment, but found mainly bewilderment in their faces.

Swede Nelson glared at Jerry Paddock and said, "You've got no call to lynch him. He ain't done a crime."

Glancing into the Lunatic's eyes Pack again caught an elusive glimpse of some secret intelligence. It was curiosity as much as anything that made him say to Joe Ferris, "Let's lock him in the Bastille."

"Then what'll we do with the drunks?"

"Chain them in the open. The weather's mild enough."

Jerry Paddock removed a snap-lid watch from his vest pocket, opened it and held it out to the limit of its chain, squinting at it. "Who's going to look after him, then?"

"Not you, Jerry," said Pack, "that's for certain."

"Bet your bottom," Jerry Paddock agreed. "You caught him. He's yours. Do what you want. But you're a fool if you don't put him out of his misery." He closed the watch, dropped it into its pocket and swung away with an abrupt snap of his skeletal shoulders.

When the villain was gone Joe Ferris put his bleak glance on Pack. Joe said, "He may be right. You might do the boy a favor by hanging him."

"Now, I don't imagine anybody wants to hang anybody."

"I know. I wouldn't either." Joe grinned. "Got yourself a tiger by the tail, Pack."

"At least help me get him to the jail."

The Bastille was a windowless shack of railroad-tie logs, eight feet by ten feet, built by the army for some now-forgotten purpose and employed lately to contain citizens who ventured so far from sobriety that they became unable to distinguish between inanimate revolver targets and human ones. The Bastille had been christened by Pack the first time he had incarcerated Redhead Finnegan in it and watched with satisfaction while Luffsey and three others gave up after a half hour's vain attempts to breach it.

The crowd watched them lock up the Lunatic. Swede said, "I could get it something to eat, I guess. What do you think it eats?"

"Human ears and rusty nails, I imagine," said Pack. He gave the padlock key to Swede. "Don't let him jump you."

"What are we going to *do* with it, Pack?"

"Hell," Pack said, "I wouldn't know. Let's think about it another time."

And so, for a time, the Lunatic became a resident of Medora town.

Sunday. Madame la Marquise had come by, riding sidesaddle, and had spent three minutes as a spectator to the baseball game. That had been twenty minutes ago but Pack's cheeks were still hot.

Pack windmilled his arm, flicked a twist at the last instant and hurled the stitched leather underarm. The pitch was a distracted simulation of the curve ball for which he'd been infamous on the University of Michigan team; it was no good. Joe Ferris swung his bat and there was the crack of ball against wood and when the projectile hurtled above Pack's head he lost it in the sun and missed his catch.

There was a boastful display of partisan allegiances: seventeen players and threescore picnicking Sunday-afternoon spectators yelled derision or encouragement.

Pack felt redoubled heat in his cheeks. What a fool to let the mere sight of the lady Medora transform him into a tanglefooted child.

The centerfielder pursued the bouncing leather with enthusiasm. Pack turned steadily on his heel to watch while Joe Ferris reached third base, cast a quick eye at the fielder and made his dash for home. His short legs pumped like locomotive pistons.

Near the left-field boundary at the stockyard fence a fight commenced among spectators—some of the De Morès butchers and stock wranglers. They'd been drinking beer all afternoon and there'd been a great deal of noise from that quarter and the outbreak of a fight did not take Pack by surprise.

Boots pounding clay, Joe Ferris made it home ahead of the fielder's inadequate throw. Bob Roberts the saloonkeeper, Umpire by common consent, called in his loud precise basso, "Runner is safe!"

Joe Ferris beamed. Pack tried to put on a sportsmanlike smile. His Cow Boys were losing to Joe's Bad Landers 14–31 and it was the seventh inning—an utter disgrace: he rued the day he'd introduced the baseball craze to Medora town.

The game had gone awry in the moment of Madame's appearance. Shaded under her huge white sugar-loaf sombrero she'd sat smiling at the players. On the high perch of her sidesaddle, with boots demurely concealed by the rich folds of her long skirt, she had contrived magically to appear both stately and as tiny as a doll. Her delicate aristocratic dignity had imposed a hush on these rough men. They'd removed their hats in respect and smiled like angels.

That had been two innings ago. It was as if the scent of her delicate perfume lingered in Pack's nostrils.

The leather rolled to his feet and he scooped it up. At the fence the fight petered out. There must have been one or two good blows; one man was bleeding at the nose; but it was all right because the combatants were helping each other to their feet and their friends were laughing.

Pack swiveled with ill grace to face the next batter. Altogether it had not been an auspicious day, ever since he'd looked in the mirror and realized that the attempt to sprout a full beard was becoming a humiliation.

He scowled at the batter and began to wind up but that was when Swede Nelson ran hollering onto the field, waving his plump arms in frantic despair.

"God help me, boys, they've gone and cleaned me out!"

Pack looked around the store and pronounced, "Now, you've been ransacked for certain."

Desolate devastated perdition. Debris on the shelves. Broken scraps of furnishings and glass, a menace underfoot—evidence of the thieves' haste.

They must have spilled liniment—or emptied it deliberately: the floor was stained and the smell sickening.

Swede's face had gone bright pink. "And they emptied the stockroom in back."

Joe Ferris planted his fists akimbo. "Last night?"

"No, I slept here armed all night. Had to be this morning while I was at circuit tent service."

Joe Ferris sneezed. "I don't suppose Jerry Paddock was in church."

Swede said, "I didn't see him."

"Now Jerry Paddock can double his prices till you get restocked. Prob'ly take weeks."

Swede said in a gentle sad voice, "I'd have bested him in a fair competition."

"There's a few too many in this country who wouldn't know fair play from buffalo chips." Joe Ferris swung angrily about. "Damn you, Pack, don't you ever carry a gun?"

"I'm no good with them . . . . What's this? I'm not chief of police here. Why air your lungs at me?"

"Well it gives me a bellyache," Joe grumbled.

It was enough of an apology.

Pack suddenly realized he still had the baseball in his hand. It seemed mortifyingly foolish.

The girl from the cafe appeared in the door. Swede faced her helplessly. "I've lost it all, Katie."

She stared, eyes big as dollars. Pack thought: *She'll turn her back on him now, faster than you can say Jack Robinson.*

He saw the girl take Swede's hand in both of her own as if it were a lovely flower. "It's all right," she said. "We'll start again."

Swede brooded at her and finally brought himself to say to Joe Ferris, "I can't pay you back the hundred dollars."

"You'll pay it sometime," said Joe.

"I guess not. I just can't stay on. No longer."

Joe and Swede were not meeting each other's eyes. Pack felt the discomfort coming off both men. The girl Katie said to Swede, "You're going to have to decide."

"Well I know that."

"Decide, then."

"All right. I've decided."

"What? What did you decide?"

"I've decided," he said, "that I don't know what to decide."

"Then I'll tell you what you're going to do." She leaned close to whisper to him. Pack watched them in mild disbelief.

"I've lost it all, Katie. How can I marry you when I've lost my reputation?"

"I don't mind," said Katie. "I lost mine quite a while ago."

Her smile was so sweet it tore Pack's heart.

And Swede said to Joe Ferris, "All right then. Is this building worth a hundred dollars to you?"

And so it came to pass that Swede Nelson signed over his store to Joe Ferris, in cancellation of a hundred-dollar debt and in an effort to keep the store out of the hands of Jerry Paddock and his ilk; and the very next afternoon, Monday, Swede and Katie departed in Swede's old freight wagon, inasmuch as they lacked train fare and had no particular destination in mind anyhow.

Outside the newspaper office Pack and Joe Ferris stood watching the freight wagon rattle out of town.

Katie's mother, slat-sided wilted woman who seldom ever spoke, stood on the cafe stoop shading her eyes with her hand. Katie looked back once and waved. The mother put her eyes down and wiped her hands on her apron. Perhaps she was wondering if Swede really meant to catch up with the circuit parson in Montana. Pack reminded himself to reassure her at supper about that. Swede was a man of his word.

The wagon went by the meat-packing factory—sprawl of peaked tinroof buildings skewered by the towering brick smokestack, toward which Joe Ferris made a face. "Smell always puts me in mind of Indians burning prisoners at the stake."

"You ever see an Indian burn a prisoner at the stake?"

"Why, no. But this is just what it would smell like. I just know that."

"Price of progress," said Pack. He watched the wagon ford the river and make its way along the bend on the far bank where squatted the splintered grey drooping remains of what used to be the town of Little Missouri—"Little Misery" to those who had known it.

He saw Jerry Paddock standing in the shadows two blocks away. From this distance Pack could not tell if he was smiling.

Alerted by Pack's expression, Joe Ferris turned his head that way. At sight of the villain he said in an ominous voice, "One day . . ."

"Now, what if he wasn't the one?"

Joe snorted. "What if the sky's not blue?" He stared furiously at the dark sinister figure. "Back before you came here, I remember old what's-his-name from Arkansas. Jerry Paddock owed him three hundred dollars, I believe it was. The man got shod into a funeral procession—kicked to death by a horse, or so Jerry Paddock told it. It sounded pretty peculiar if you happened to know anything about the ways of horses."

It was true, Pack thought, that to Jerry Paddock morality meant no more than grammar. But he said, "Don't take up for Swede with your eyes shut, Joe. You find the stolen goods or a witness who saw the deed and we can go to Mandan and call in Sheriff Harmon. But without evidence—"

"Sometimes you just exasperate the hell out of me."

"Is that so."

After a moment Pack's good-natured poultice of patience drew the outrage out of Joe Ferris; he said crossly, "You should've been a preacher."

"I know too little about men and nothing at all about the Almighty."

"You do pretend to know more about right and wrong than a fire-escape sin buster."

"My prayer book's *The Bad Lands Cow Boy*, and my rod and my staff they comfort thee."

Following the Northern Pacific's right-of-way to the west, the wagon disappeared past the knee of Graveyard Butte.

When it was gone the mother went back into the cafe without any expression at all on her face.

Joe Ferris said, "D'you imagine we'll hear from them sometime?"

"Possibly. If the Indians and road agents and blizzards don't get them."

Joe said, "True enough. Well then. We fixing to finish that baseball game next Sunday or you boys willing to forfeit?"

"What was the score?"

"Thirty-one to fourteen. Seventh inning."

"I'll put it to a vote." Standing at the front door of the newspaper office, regarding the building diagonally opposite, Pack said, "Got yourself a store."

"Some board lumber is all. No stock of merchandise and no money to buy it."

"One thing at a time. At least it's four walls and a roof. That's what you wanted."

"I can sleep there anyhow. If Jerry Paddock doesn't mistake that for competition."

Joe took a hitch in the gunbelt around his waist. Pack glanced at it, for it was unusual to see Joe wearing a weapon in town. The revolver in the holster was big—a Remington from the look of it; probably a .44—and the loops in Joe's prairie belt held thirty or forty cartridges. It made Pack uneasy.

Joe saw the direction of his friend's glance; he looked sharply at Pack.

Choosing to change the subject Pack cocked an eye toward the angle of the sun. It was time to feed and water the guest in the Bastille.

As they set forth he said, "I had Katie fixed in my mind as six months away from a painted shanty queen. I knew for certain she'd put her back to Swede—and look what happened. How old does a man have to get before he has the wisdom to understand the first damn thing about a woman?"

"Old enough to grow wrinkles on his horns, may be. All the same, wish I had *my* young lady here." There was a moment while Joe considered things. He frowned over his shoulder toward the vacant store.

"Why do we let Jerry Paddock have his way? Even a baseball game has got to have rules."

They waved their way with violent hand-flappings through a plague of flies. Pack said, "Always rules, and always those inclined to flout them."

"That's why you elect an Umpire . . . Now *that's* what this town needs! An Umpire."

The abattoir smell was terrible today. Pack turned his face out of the wind. "Now, I may have a word with the Marquis."

"About Jerry Paddock?"

"Just so," Pack said. "The Marquis may be too trusting." He added, "Now, I believe it's a typical weakness in geniuses."

They found hunters at the Bastille—Redhead Finnegan and Frank O'Donnell and young Riley Luffsey and four of their drinking companions.

The louts were amusing themselves by throwing stones and empty bottles at the door of the windowless prison cabin.

The rattling racket was loud enough out here; Pack could imagine what it must do to a man's ears inside the echoing strongbox; he did not wonder at the bellowing screams of bewildered fury that roared pathetically from within. The door shook—not so much from the rataplan of stones and bottles as from the pounding of the prisoner's enraged fists.

"Now boys," Pack said, "I expect that's enough."

The ruffians swung to peer at him. Riley Luffsey put his brash grin on Pack. "That critter needs his exercise, don't he? We're just helping him out."

Joe Ferris said, "What's the matter—you boys run out of fences to cut?"

Full of good nature, Riley Luffsey laughed. "Sure. Come on, Joe, give the critter his exercise."

Pack felt the ill will in "Bitter Creek" Redhead Finnegan's scowl. With very little provocation this could become something with which he would prefer not to tangle. Uncertain, searching for a fair resolution, he said, "Might not hurt to give him an airing."

"That's right," said Luffsey eagerly. "Open the door and let it run some."

Redhead Finnegan's eyes were crowded with a bright blue tension. After some visible thought he said, "The kid will bring him back," and nearly smiled at Luffsey. "Won't you, kid."

Joe Ferris said dryly, "And if he doesn't?"

"Can't nothing get away from me," Riley Luffsey boasted.

Redhead Finnegan's skin was as sticky as overboiled rice. He said, "We'll chip in two bits for the kid if he catches him. If the

Lunatic gets away from the kid, we'll whale hell out of the kid." He leered at the youth.

Luffsey was full of the devil today; he let his bravado get the better of him. "For two bits I'll run all day and all night. Turn him loose, then—let's go."

Frank O'Donnell's rusty voice scraped at the youth. "How much head start you aim to give him?"

"I'll give him fifty foot. Hell, make it a hundred foot."

An unpleasant expression stretched Frank O'Donnell's rough pitted cheeks. Perhaps it was intended as a smile. He said to Finnegan, "Half a dollar on the Lunatic—and if the kid don't catch him I'll help knock his ears down."

"Even bet," Finnegan said. "One to one."

Pack said, "Now hold on . . ."

Riley Luffsey thrust his face eagerly toward Pack. "Come on, Mr. Packard. Turn it loose. I won't let it get away. I can run faster than anything in Dakota. I'm aching to heat my axles. I can run faster than the wind." To Finnegan he said, "You ought to give him ten-to-one odds."

"One to one," Finnegan replied. "I never seen you run a distance." He glared around him. "Any disputation?"

Three of the ruffians dug coins from their pockets.

Joe Ferris said mildly to Pack, "Give us a chance to swamp the place out."

Pack considered it. After a moment he warned Finnegan: "Mind he's brought back here without harm."

Joe Ferris said to the kid, "Chase it through the river while you're about it—give it a bath. Getting so you can smell it a hundred yards downwind."

Riley Luffsey pressed something into Redhead Finnegan's hand. "I'm betting on myself."

Pack realized they were staring at him. For a moment he couldn't fathom why. Then Joe Ferris said, "The key."

He approached the building and hesitated with the key poised at the big padlock. Joe was right, the odor was ripe, even through the thick door.

He turned the key and silently lifted the padlock off its hasp and stepped back out of the way and pulled the door open.

The Lunatic loomed, arms half-raised defensively before him. Plainly he was bewildered, face screwed up in a painful squint against the sudden brightness.

The stink was God-awful. Pack wanted to back away but he felt pinioned and could not move.

The Lunatic's eyes came open and swung slowly to bear upon Pack's face and once again there seemed to be something profound in that strange huge round smooth childlike face.

Pack said softly, "Can you talk? Can you talk to me?"

The Lunatic cocked his head to one side with the quizzicality of a dog listening to an unfamiliar sound.

For a moment their glances interlocked; then there was the *thwack* of a thrown stone against the Lunatic's tattered trouser leg.

The Lunatic bolted along the embankment; the chase was on.

The ruffians got him well started, following in full cry and pelting him with stones until the Lunatic went past the end of town, fleeing at a dead run.

After a bit the crowd stopped. Pack and Joe watched from the door of the Bastille. Young Riley Luffsey waited, playing fair, giving the Lunatic his lead, and when Luffsey began to run Frank O'Donnell tripped him with an outflung foot.

Pack observed that it was typical of the fair play observed by that crowd: O'Donnell was simply protecting his bet, and it did not occur to any of the others to chastise him. The ruffians laughed aloud as Luffsey fell hard—his palms and knees must have taken a bad skinning—but he was up in an instant and giving chase without even a glance at O'Donnell, who by the agonized contortion of his face evidently was trying to smile again; and then, with Finnegan, O'Donnell led the little mob away in a lumbering effort to keep the two runners in sight. Luffsey soon distanced them all.

Pack remained where he was. Joe Ferris said, "What if it gets away?"

"Then Riley Luffsey will take a beating he won't soon forget. And I'll have to borrow your horse and track down the Lunatic."

"What for? Let it go," Joe Ferris said. "It's a wild animal anyhow—leave it free."

"Free to starve? Free to be eaten by bears and wolves?"

"For that critter it'd be better than being locked up in a cage."

* * *

Soon the ruffians adjourned to one of their watering holes for refreshment; but ten minutes later they returned *en masse*, their ranks swollen with curiosity seekers. The mob lurched past the jail up onto the embankment and Pack heard someone shout, "There they are, by damn. Coming back this way—see them there?"

"Looks like Riley's closing in."

"No, that's only the angle you're looking."

Pack watched them until it was clear no mayhem was forthcoming just at the moment. Joe Ferris said, "I'll get it something to eat," and went away for a bit. Smelling the slaughterhouse, listening to Finnegan and his crowd, Pack had his look around at the bluffs. Their dominant hue was a faded buckskin. If you put your weight on the dry soil it tended to crumble; everything crunched underfoot—sagebrush, grass, clay, twigs, rocks. But on the gentler slopes there was greenery for livestock to feed on; that was the secret wealth of these Bad Lands.

A beer keg passed from hand to hand through the mob of toughs. Joe Ferris returned with a covered dish. He set it aside and Pack helped him swamp out the filthy jail with soapy water. They swept it onto the clay, where it was absorbed instantaneously and left a chalky white rime. Pack said, "We'll find a way to help you stock the store."

"There is an investor I can put the touch on."

"If you're thinking of the Marquis de Morès . . ."

"The Markee'd give me nothing except the hard end of that heavy stick. Your French friend knows what I think of him . . ."

"You're wrong about him. Why are you so stubborn on that subject?"

"I know a four-flusher when I see one," Joe said. He walked away toward the embankment, plodding as resolutely as a man stamping out spiders. Pack caught up with him at the tracks. They stood off to one side a piece from Finnegan and the half-drunk toughs who were braying toward Luffsey as he chased the Lunatic into the river a quarter mile upstream, just below the château on the bluff.

Joe wasn't looking at those two. His attention was directed back the other way—north, downriver. He said, "Speak of Beelzebub!"

It made Pack look that way. He saw a jouncing diminutive horseman emerge from the shadow of a cloud. He was startled.

"Roosevelt? You think you'll get a penny out of him? I thought you'd had a falling out."

"What? What gave you that notion?"

Pack said, "You took him out hunting. Now, two days later you came back alone."

"He changed his mind, that's all. Decided to ride by himself. I judged he wasn't hunting game; he was hunting solitude. May be he wanted to look the loneliness square in the face. I know he had some things he wanted to forget."

"Lost his wife and his mother," Pack said. "I know all that. Is that what makes him so disagreeable, or was he born like that?"

"He's got his own way about him," Joe said. "What makes you think he's disagreeable?"

"Thinks a lot of himself, doesn't he. Great hunter. Fortunate he didn't find himself looking a bear square in the face."

Joe hitched up his cartridge belt with the flats of his wrists. "I guess he didn't, as you see. Know Blacktail Creek?"

"Heard of it."

"Downstream on the east bank, thirty miles north of here, may be more. Anyhow a fair day's ride. There's a good ford. I've taken hunters in there a few times—good big stand of cottonwoods and some bottomland pasture, and the river's wide and gentle about the bend, so you find game often as not. One of the boys told me Mr. Roosevelt staked it out last week. Say he's planning to build a house there. He's calling it Elkhorn Ranch because he found a couple racks of shedded elk antlers interlocked on the ground. Stocking it with a herd of Eastern shorthorns and he's already wired two of his hired men from back East to drive 'em out here. Fellow has got money, Pack. And I can show him a good opportunity to invest a little bit of it."

Joe watched the horseman's ungainly approach. "Well," he said dubiously, "good luck to you."

Riley Luffsey brought the Lunatic across the embankment, half dragging the poor creature. Luffsey did his best to pretend he wasn't winded. The crowd trailed them toward the Bastille. Downriver the approaching Roosevelt must have noticed the activity, for he changed course and advanced.

Pack saw him coming but was drawn by something more vital; after a moment he forgot about the horseman altogether as he kept close watch on the Lunatic in case those eyes, with their profound secret, should rise to meet his own; but the Lunatic stood with his head down, chest heaving, and never gave him a glance. Pack felt obscurely betrayed.

Pack felt the familiar pressing urgency—an insistence to know more. He needed to get beneath the surfaces of things and find out what was hidden in their crevices and shadows and dreams, for only in such inaccessible and guarded places could one hope to find the important secrets.

"I ran him till he dropped," Luffsey boasted, puffing. "You all see when I butted him into the river there? Gave him a right fine bath. He 'most bit my nose off but look at him now—not an ounce of fight left in him."

Frank O'Donnell growled, "Kid, you ought to be playing with a string of spools, all I can say."

The Lunatic stood in bleary silence while Joe Ferris tried to entice him into the shack with an uncovered bowl of cold rice and beans. Breathing very fast, the Lunatic watched it but seemed too tired to follow Joe.

Riley Luffsey said to Finnegan, "I'm a mind collect on my bet."

Pack heard growls of agreement from some of the hunters. They all were ready to gather their winnings.

Finnegan scowled at them. He wasn't the sort to take a loss with good grace. His red hair hung long, tangled thick along his shoulders. He glared at Luffsey and angry muscles stood out along his jaw like the strands of a tight hard rope.

Young Luffsey appeared to be unmindful of the displeasure of the man from Bitter Creek. The youth whooped at the sky. He grinned lavishly at Pack. "I'll be famous now, won't I?" Playful, he stretched a foot out behind the Lunatic and pushed, so that the Lunatic fell backwards like a tree that had been axed. In an instant young Luffsey was upon the felled giant, boisterously pummeling him, shouting exuberant nonsense. The great oaf rolled onto his side, cringed, curled into a protective ball, wrapped his hands over his head against the bewildering blows and whimpered.

Joe Ferris ripped the revolver from his holster and pointed it in Luffsey's direction and shouted, "*Let it go!*"

Luffsey rocked back and stared up at Joe.

Pack was astonished.

A growl of dangerous anger rolled through the crowd.

Joe Ferris glared at them all.

The Lunatic crawled around fearfully like a half-squashed insect, knees drawn up, hands over his head.

Joe waved the revolver in a sweep that brought the entire mob within its intimacy. "What a pack of big brave men we got here! You coyotes take your pleasures from watching this poor dumb critter chew gravel?"

Luffsey was getting to his feet. He seemed unable to decide whether to make his face surly or cocky. He took a pace toward Joe Ferris.

Joe cocked the Remington: a loud scraping ratchet of warning.

Pack said, "Now, wait now—"

Fearful and intent, he nearly jumped a foot when Theodore Roosevelt came beside him and stopped his horse at the edge of the crowd. "What's all this?"

Joe Ferris had all his attention on the ruffians. His revolver stirred back and forth, keeping them at bay. "Pack, get the critter's feet under it and put it back in the box where it'll be safe from these drunks."

Before Pack could move, Roosevelt's piping voice cut forward overhead: "Is this the strange fellow I've heard of?" He dismounted and walked unhurriedly to the Lunatic. "What is it, my friend? Have you something to say? Have no fear."

Roosevelt's own fearlessness astounded Pack; but then he thought it likely it wasn't courage at all, but merely ignorance.

Anger put a chalk-white strain on Frank O'Donnell's mouth. He had a revolver in his belt. His hand strayed near it but Joe Ferris said, "Frank—don't do that."

Roosevelt helped the Lunatic to his feet. "Nothing to say, have you?" The New Yorker peered through his dusty eyeglasses at the assembled hunters, and at Pack, and finally at Joe Ferris with the revolver in his hand. Roosevelt said, "This poor fellow deserves care, not ridicule. He certainly doesn't belong *here*." He pointed an angry digit at the Bastille.

Joe said, "Belongs out in the woods to be its own free natural self—or else someplace where somebody can look after it. Poor critter should not be a toy for the amusement pack."

"Perfectly right, Joe old fellow. He should be taken away for observation and treatment. There's an asylum at the territorial capital, I believe."

Redhead Finnegan's hard eyes raked the dude from head to foot. "He belong to you, does he?"

Roosevelt said, "In the sense that one has a responsibility to those who are not fortunate enough to be able to care for themselves. Yes, he belongs to me. He's my responsibility, and yours, and yours, and yours."

"You have got a leaky mouth, mister."

Privately Pack agreed with Finnegan. This dude was displaying very bad manners, meddling and preaching; it was unseemly behavior, at the very least, for a greenhorn foreigner.

Frank O'Donnell said, "He's nothing but a half-pint lunger. Ain't got enough wind to blow out a match."

Roosevelt said, "It appears to me, Joe old fellow, that your friends might benefit from a word or two about such subjects as kindness and decency and moral probity."

Finnegan said in a low growl, "Storm Windows, I'll make wolf meat out of you—and your friend Ferris too."

Joe Ferris pointed the revolver at Finnegan. "Not this afternoon, Red."

"Just where in the hell did you screw up enough foolishness to point a gun in my face?"

"You know this isn't worth a fight, Red."

Finnegan thought about it.

The Lunatic puffed and blinked. He had most of his attention on Roosevelt; evidently his curiosity was drawn by the irritating screech and the unfamiliar vowels of the dude's talk. Pack found himself glaring at Roosevelt with a resentment that surprised him. There was something odiously vexatious about him. It was enough to put anyone out of countenance.

Joe Ferris's revolver stirred. "You boys don't really give a damn about the critter one way or the other, and I don't believe you want to do injury to a gentleman like Mr. Roosevelt. Red, why not just take the boys back to the saloon and buy a round of drinks. You owe it to them, for those bets you lost."

Evidently it was the right thing to say, for the tone of the crowd's growl changed. Someone yelled, "Red's buying!"

There was a loud and, Pack thought, somewhat ominous cheer.

Finnegan, sensing the shift in interests, backed down.

"Just one round. On my chalk."

Joe Ferris essayed a bit of a smile; for some reason Riley Luffsey laughed aloud and that broke the malice.

Finnegan, still irascible, pointed a menacing finger at Joe and then turned it to aim at Roosevelt, but had nothing to say; he walked away and the hunters walked with him.

Riley Luffsey had one more look at the Lunatic, laughed again and bounced swaggering away, calling out ahead: "Wait on, wait on. Don't forget my winnings. I'm faster than a slough pig—I tell you boys I am the speediest man in Dakota! I could've outrun a bullet from Wild Bill himself!"

The Lunatic groveled and groaned. Joe Ferris put the revolver away and studied his own hand with surprise. Theodore Roosevelt skinned his teeth; his tusks gleamed. "Masterful. By Jove, you're a capital fellow, Joe."

"Just trying to keep the peace." Joe cleared his throat manfully. "Now if I had the fare, I would be willing to deliver this poor critter to Bismarck, sure enough."

Pack noted that the sun had peeled skin from Roosevelt's face; he looked mottled as if he'd been too close to a bad fire. Roosevelt said, "I'm seldom mistaken in my judgements of men, and I knew from the outset that our Joe Ferris here was of a finer stamp."

Pack felt a sarcastic anger that felt unfamiliar: he said to Joe Ferris, "Now, you are sure enough the hero of Medora. Why it's *you* who's the Umpire you were talking about." He said to Roosevelt, "In generations to come they'll be erecting statues of Joe Ferris all over the nation—people will salute them as they go by."

"I don't know why you're picking on me, Pack. All I want is a fair shake for everybody and a chance to stock the shelves in my new store and give the competition a run for its money."

Joe's sly glance edged toward Roosevelt. He said to Pack in a sincere voice, "I wish you had the capital to back me, Pack. We'd show the world. Just a few thousand's all it would take to get me started."

Pack made a face. He looked at the dude to see if Joe's unsubtle hints were taking effect.

The terms he'd seen attached to Theodore Roosevelt by the press were words that seemed to describe a whirlwind rather than a man:

histrionic, *harsh*, *heroic*, *ebullient*, *upright*, *downright*, *forthright*, *bumptious*, *smug*, *impatient*, *loud*, *opinionated*, *spoiled*, *garrulous*, *gallant*, *blunt*, *clear-thinking*, *stubborn*, *impulsive*, *swashbuckling*, *inexhaustible*, *vehement*, *snobbish*, *dyspeptic*. . . .

The slight and slender young man who stood before him now did not have the shoulders to support all those words.

The New York dude climbed onto his horse and settled his feet carefully in the stirrups, adjusted the reins and finally looked up to study the two of them through his gold-rimmed spectacles. His regard settled on Joe Ferris and he delivered himself of a theatrical sigh. "If only to bring an end to your unceasing broad hints," he said, "five thousand and not a penny more—and I shall expect you to look after my money with a zeal equal to that which you've just displayed in looking after this poor insane chap."

Without waiting a reply, Roosevelt neck-reined away, lifting the horse to an immediate canter.

With a straight face Joe Ferris said to Pack, "I told you he'd invest."

Pack pouted at him in suspicion. "I wish I could believe you were genuine all the way through. Now, how much bravery did you invent for the dude's benefit?"

Joe Ferris smiled. "Be that as it may."

Five

The prairie put Wil Dow in mind of the Maine sea: it seemed to consist of nothing but horizon. He chased a steer into the herd, eased back on his saddlesores, watched the dusty backs of the cattle and was content to make slow passage through the thick rippling grass that grew chest-high to the horse.

His quick eye caught it far off when a frightened pronghorn doe bolted; the signal patches of her rump flashed white with alarm and Wil Dow heard the grunt of her peculiar utterance, half bay and half snort. Then he saw her pursuers—a pair of hungry coyotes. The doe soon distanced them and was gone.

This was truly a grand adventure.

He saw Uncle Bill Sewall emerge from the fog of dust. Uncle Bill was caked with clay. They had been on the trail from the rail yards at Dickinson two days—just long enough so that the sight of his uncle on a Texas-rigged horse no longer startled Wil Dow.

"Heat could make a rattlesnake pant," Uncle Bill Sewall complained. He tugged a burr from his bright red beard.

"In the shade there's most always a breeze."

"The grand trouble is, no shade to get in." Uncle Bill squeezed his eyes shut. He had lived all his life in the deep woods of Maine and seemed to have trouble adjusting to the glare of the open land. "It's a dirty country, Wil, and very dirty people mostly."

"Why it seems healthy to me, Uncle Bill. Where's Mr. Roosevelt?"

"Out front. Good thing he found us last night. I don't see a profusion of landmarks for navigation around here."

"He's in dreadful low spirits."

"He went down into a blackness that few can ever know. But I believe he'll turn out all right. All his life they've told him he was too little for this, too weak for that, too sick to do a thing. You can see how much that wisdom has slowed him down."

Wil Dow and his uncle had guided young Roosevelt on a good many hunting expeditions through the wild woods of Maine and during the very first of them, when Wil had been just a boy and Roosevelt had been even younger, Uncle Bill had warned Wil Dow, "The doctor said Theodore ain't strong but he's all grit and he'd as soon kill himself before he'd even say he's tired." The upshot had been that neither of them had been able to keep up with the sickly New Yorker.

Now he'd wired them in Island Falls and had guaranteed them a share of anything they made in the cattle business, and if they lost money Roosevelt said he'd absorb the losses and pay their wages. Yesterday at the railroad corrals, shaking hands with their employer, Sewall had said, "It is a pretty one-sided proposition. But if you think you can stand it, I think we can."

Sewall had told Wil Dow he suspected that perhaps Roosevelt had invited the two to join him because they reminded him of his Alice Lee. She'd been a New England girl.

An eerie howling moaned about the camp. Wil Dow wheeled to keen the darkness.

Roosevelt stopped wheezing long enough to say, "Wolves—the evening concert. The first time you hear it, it can frighten you out of your wits. Never mind, Wil. Contrary to legend they are most harmless beasts, except to livestock."

Wil lied, "I'm not afraid, Mr. Roosevelt."

The New Yorker regarded him with squinting blinking thoughtfulness. "It's all right to be afraid. I used to be afraid of everything. *Everything*. But by acting as if I was not afraid, I gradually took control of it. You'll see. Look here, Wil—fear makes your perceptions keener—adds to your energy and helps you perform beyond your usual capacity." Roosevelt's voice piped high. "Being afraid can be a friend. But it depends, don't you know, on whether you're in control of it—or it's in control of you. Don't say you can't be frightened. Of course you can be frightened. Anyone can. The trick's to stay in control after you do get frightened."

Wil had learned to accept Roosevelt's ways but he thought he never would understand why it seemed so natural for Roosevelt to lecture a man that way. Wil was a few years older than Roosevelt and he'd spent nearly ten years guiding city hunters through the woods and tapping maples and building boats and delivering coal but still he thought of himself as a youth; here Roosevelt was as undersized as a half-grown teen-age boy, frail and sick and much given to unseemly boasting and unsolicited advising—but men seldom laughed to his face; they paid attention when he spoke. It sure was a mystery.

Uncharacteristically Roosevelt fell silent. The wolf chorus carried on. Wil Dow endeavored to smile; but pretend as he would, the howling put a chill in him.

Roosevelt said, "Of course there is nothing to fear when there is nothing to live for."

"Got your baby child to live for," Sewall replied in a gentle voice.

"My sister can take care of little Alice better than I can. She'll be just as well off without me."

Uncle Bill Sewall poked up the campfire and pounded the dottle from his pipe into his palm, reversed the bowl and refilled it from his pouch. He wiped the underside of his tobacco-stained mustache and when Roosevelt went into a coughing fit, by common habit Wil and his uncle ignored it.

When the wheezing subsided, Uncle Bill said, "I guess you won't always feel that way. Black care rarely sits behind a rider whose pace is fast enough."

Roosevelt's face lifted an inch. "I've heard that before. Who said that?"

"You did."

Roosevelt took his saddle close by the fire and propped himself against it. For a while he stared at a blank page in his notebook. Then he began to write. When he was finished he took his blanket a few yards from the fire and sat wrapped like an Indian with his back to the flames, looking at the stars. He had left the notebook behind, within Sewall's reach. Without turning his head he said, "You may want to read that."

With a raised-eyebrow glance of surprise at Wil, Uncle Bill reached for the notebook. He squinted to read it in the firelight; he considered it for a while and then closed his eyes, sat breathing deep and slow, and finally passed the notebook to Wil Dow.

> Alice Hathaway Lee. Born at Chestnut Hill, July 29th 1861. I saw her first on October 18th 1878; I wooed her for over a year before I won her; we were betrothed on January 25th 1880, and it was announced on Feb. 16th; on Oct. 27th of the same year we were married; we spent three years of happiness greater and more unalloyed than I have ever known fall to the lot of others; on Feb. 12th 1884 her baby was born, and on Feb. 14th she died in my arms; my mother had died in the same house, on the same day, but a few hours previously. On Feb. 16th they were buried together in Greenwood.
>
> For joy or sorrow, my life has now been lived out.

Wil Dow closed the notebook and put it back where Roosevelt had left it. The little New Yorker still sat with his back to them, coughing violently. It sounded saw-tooth painful.

He met Uncle Bill's glance and nodded his head to indicate he understood Roosevelt's purpose. It was clear enough: Roosevelt never wished to hear or speak of his departed wife and mother again.

On the following hot afternoon they moved the herd across more of the high plain. When a sod-roof cabin came in sight Roosevelt trotted back to join the two Maine woodsmen. "Take the herd for ten minutes, Bill. I want to do business at this house." He pulled awkwardly away, dragging high at the reins. "Come along, Wil, if you care to meet one of the famous locals."

Wil rode at Roosevelt's stirrup toward the unpretentious soddy. A short heavy woman stood in the door holding a rifle. When she saw the two men guide their mounts carefully around the perimeter of her tidy vegetable garden she illustrated her approval by setting the rifle away inside the door.

Roosevelt said, “Are you Mrs. Reuter?”

“I am. Mostly they call me ‘Old Lady Reuter’ which I take to be a compliment on the maturity of my character, as I’m hardly forty years of age.”

Wil Dow was not accustomed to hearing ladies admit their ages aloud.

“My name is Theodore Roosevelt.”

“Heard of you.”

“This is Wil Dow, in my employ.”

The woman made a gesture. “Come in. You mustn’t mind the untidiness of my house.” She had a deep hoarse voice. She wore a proper bonnet and a heavy bodice and a wraparound overskirt but no bustle.

In the dark it was a moment before Wil Dow could make out detail—a good cherrywood table, a foot-powered loom, several lithographs on the walls, a small pump organ: the place was homelike and he was surprised.

Roosevelt said, “Why it’s a splendid house, Mrs. Reuter. Splendid.”

The woman made a bit of a curtsy. “You’re very gallant. Won’t you sit down? I have some tin airtights of peaches and apricots.”

“Many thanks, madame, but as you see we’re driving a thousand steers into the Bad Lands. I’m afraid we can stay only a few moments. They’ve told me you make the finest deerhide clothing in Dakota.”

“Whoever could have told you such a thing? My, what exaggeration.” A coquettish smile was startling on the woman’s broad sun-browned face; Wil Dow laughed aloud. She made a face at him. If she was gruff she was also full of fun.

Roosevelt said, “I want to have a suit of fringed buckskin.”

“Then you’ll have one.” She found a coiled measuring tape and began to span the scale of his bones with matter-of-fact swiftness.

Roosevelt said, “A handsome suit that I can show off to my friends back East. Perhaps a bit of Indian design work. I shall bring my own hides to you next week. They’re hanging now—”

“I use only my own,” the woman said. “I kill them, I cure them,

I sew them. Then I know what I am doing, and you know what you are getting."

Roosevelt held his tongue. His retreat surprised Wil Dow; it reminded him what low spirits his employer was in. After a moment Roosevelt said to the woman, "You must eat a great deal of venison—or waste it."

"What I can't eat I give to the Indians, who haven't got sufficient ammunition of their own. It's a sin to waste good meat."

"My sentiments," Roosevelt agreed. "If you kill an animal you've a responsibility not to waste any part of it. When we're hungry we kill but I despise a man who'll kill a beast for a trophy or a single taste of its flesh."

Mrs. Reuter looked him in the eye with mischievous challenge. "What I heard was that Theodore Roosevelt was in the habit of mounting stuffed animal heads on his walls. What I heard was, Theodore Roosevelt likes to kill for sport."

"And animal rugs on my floors—blankets for the divans—horns for hatracks—leather for my furniture and game meat in my belly and cured jerky in my pack. I'm a student of naturalism and I am experienced in taxidermy, and when I kill an animal I use every portion of it. Anything less would be an offense to Nature."

Wil Dow examined a patterned Indian blanket that hung from the low ceiling, dividing the cabin into two rooms. He'd heard Mr. Roosevelt's discourses on naturalism before; there were things that interested him more. He said to the woman, "Any wild Indians around here?"

"Not so wild any more," Mrs. Reuter said with regret in her voice. To Roosevelt she said: "They say you're Dutch."

It took Wil Dow a moment to catch up with her abrupt change of topic.

Roosevelt said, "From Holland by ancestry, long ago. I am an American."

"My husband's name is Johann. They call him Dutch."

"Dutch Reuter. We met last year when I was here hunting."

"He's a good man sometimes, my husband, but being Dutch—"

"In fact I think he's Prussian, isn't he? Or Bavarian?"

"Isn't it all the same? Being Dutch he's not just stubborn. He's impossibly, irrationally, inexorably obstinate. I'm used to dealing with your sort, Mr. Roosevelt." She beamed at him.

Roosevelt flashed his teeth. "I'll try to remember my manners."

The woman wrote numbers on a scrap of paper. "You shall have your suit in two weeks, if it please you to call back then."

Wil Dow followed him out into the blinding sun. As they climbed aboard their steeds Roosevelt touched his hatbrim to the lady in the door. They rode out toward the great dust cloud.

"I understand she kills rattlesnakes with a hoe," Roosevelt said. "Did you hear her on the subject of the Dutch! And they say *I'm* opinionated!"

Wil saw a swarm of little creatures scampering about. There was a high-pitched warning bark. Abruptly a hundred dusty dark rodents scurried into their holes, instantly out of sight.

"Gophers?"

Roosevelt said, "Prairie dog town. Wise to give it berth—your horse could crack a leg."

They went around it and in a while rejoined Bill Sewall and the shorthorns; Roosevelt galloped out ahead to lead the trek.

For a while it was easy work, just now and then riding out to head a stray back into the flow. But toward four o'clock Wil Dow became aware that the herd was bunching up.

"Come on," Uncle Bill Sewall said, and set about kicking his steed energetically about the flanks. The horse responded sluggishly. Wil watched with fond amusement. He gigged his horse easily to a canter, caught up and rode abreast the old Mennonite.

The cattle had got themselves into some kind of log jam. They crowded into one another's rumps, mooing and milling.

When the two horsemen reached the front of the herd they found Roosevelt squinting down past the lip of a steep drop. Wil Dow heard his uncle's sharp intake of breath.

"*Terra damnata*."

Below he saw a marvelous vast litter of broken country all heaved and buckled, striped with lateral ribbons of vivid colors. Junipers on the hills were fat and conical and dark.

"The Bad Lands," said Roosevelt. "Some of those piles of rock look like fallen ancient temples I've seen in Egypt and Greece. What do you think, then, Bill? Capital country, isn't it!"

"This river of yours somewhere in all that?"

"It is indeed."

Wil Dow grinned. "Then let's go."

Sewall gave him a look. Within the red beard his lips were pinched together in stern disapproval.

Through the afternoon the pilgrims from Down East taunted and bullied Roosevelt's herd of one thousand shorthorns toward the river. Wil Dow's horse was surefooted and he enjoyed the work but it had an unspeakable effect on his sore knees and thighs and rump.

Toward the bottom they threaded clusters of box-elders and junipers and scrub-oaks. The cattle had taken the scent of water and were moving westward with resolute purpose; it was no longer necessary to prod them. The riders reined up onto the side-slope of the wide gully to let the beasts pass; then they followed at a leisurely pace, squinting against the risen dust.

There were clumps of deciduous trees on these sheltered slopes; their roots must have access to some sort of artesian water. Beneath outcroppings they skirted cannonball boulders two or three feet in diameter—perfect spheres that must have weighed tons. The air had a fragrance of juniper. Wil Dow inhaled deep and felt a thrill of pleasure.

There were groves of tall cottonwoods on the riverbanks. Bill Sewall watched the cattle churn mud as they drank their fill; he said, "That river's the meanest apology for a frog-pond I ever saw. It's a queer country. I reckon cattle will starve on it."

"Looks green enough to me," Wil Dow observed.

"Sooner or later—I expect sooner—there'll be a winter storm or a summer drought, and there'll be no more cattle here."

"I don't agree, Uncle Bill. I believe what Mr. Roosevelt said, a venture of grand promise." He enjoyed ragging his uncle. Anyhow the old pessimist needed it to keep him from going sour.

The greyish leaves of the cottonwoods rustled in the breeze and there was a music of doves and magpies. The western sky was a slash of flame.

Roosevelt had a coughing fit. It provoked Uncle Bill into reviving his complaints. "I shall never like this country for a home. I have no ambition to become a cowboy. I expect the best a man can do is regard his time in Dakota as a sentence to be served out."

Roosevelt scoffed. "Nonsense. I think it's perfectly bully." He pointed across the backs of the cattle at the lush land across the river bend. This country along the river was green with vegetation and its soil was darkened by rich silt. Trees were clumped thick in the lowlands. Roosevelt said, "We shall build my Elkhorn Ranch here. We have eighty horses coming in from A.C. Huidekoper's stock, so our first task is to build corrals. Then I want you to build me a ranch house."

God in Heaven, Wil Dow thought happily. I am in the Wild West.

There would be eight rooms, seven feet high, and a sheltered piazza along the outside of the east wall. They would build the house of cottonwood logs and they would shingle the roof with pine and Roosevelt insisted that the inside walls be finished with pine boards planed on one side. Then they had to put up outbuildings: two stables with a wagon shed between them, a cattle barn, a lean-to for blacksmith work, a chicken house. And all the while they had to look after a thousand cattle. No denying there was a great deal of work to do.

But Wil Dow didn't mind. The country was beautiful just then: at its best, Mr. Roosevelt reckoned. There were acres of blooming wild roses; there were wild morning glories, June berries, plums and pomegranates, and fields of brown-eyed yellow daisies.

Wil Dow teased his uncle: "I didn't come out here to be a carpenter. I want to learn cowboying."

Uncle Bill said, "I've had enough cowboying in the last three days to last my lifetime. I sure don't know what you see in it."

Wil laughed at the old boy. "You need more Romance in your soul."

"I didn't know Romance smelled so bad," Sewall said.

They went out in the morning to continue cutting timber for Mr. Roosevelt's new house. Near an ugly Medusa of a tree he had paced out the corners thirty by sixty, back in the shade of the cottonwoods and up a commanding slope where spring floods wouldn't take it. A handsome spot under an enormous sky.

Mr. Roosevelt picked up his axe. "What was our tally yesterday?"

Bill Sewall considered the stack of logs. "I cut down fifty, and young Wil about forty, and I believe you, sir, beavered down about twelve."

Wil Dow tried to keep his face straight. He pictured stumps he'd seen that beavers had gnawed down.

Mr. Roosevelt didn't seem to mind. All he said was, "I shall have to do better today."

Wheezing heavily, Roosevelt hauled his axe away. Wil Dow set out to follow.

Uncle Bill Sewall fell in step, striding easily, a long-boned man with shaggy hair that was darker than his flaming beard. He was tall enough to appear thin but in fact he had a logger's musculature. He was strong of back and strong of heart, as Mr. Roosevelt liked to put it; Wil was too familiar with Roosevelt's stout opinion of how his uncle was a fearless wayfaring warrior, full of backwoodsman's self-reliance and muscular resource, who stood for laconic courage and everything else that was to be found in true heroes. Wil Dow knew his Mennonite uncle better than that; and indeed Uncle Bill himself did not enjoy the fuss—he counted himself a man of plain common sense and he did not disagree when Wil Dow suggested Mr. Roosevelt might be able to see the simple truth better if his head weren't so filled with book-learning.

"Of which you could use a bit yourself," was all Uncle Bill said.

To that, Wil Dow's constant answer was, "I got my learning out behind the barn, thank you sir." He could read and write and do sums. That was enough.

Wil prepared a noon meal. While they ate, Roosevelt was reading Keats and listening—head cocked—to the hooting of mourning doves. He knew the song of every variety of bird, and had the annoying habit of identifying them for Bill Sewall's edification. Wil Dow listened to him with eager interest—"Sharp-tailed grouse . . . Hungarian partridge"—but Uncle Bill gave Roosevelt no more than a bilious glance each time.

It was different from the way it used to be. Back East the New Yorker had dedicated himself to these interests with avid pleasure, like an eager child. Now he was pursuing them in a transparent effort to keep his mind occupied. He snatched at anything that might prevent him from thinking about the things he didn't want to think about.

It was natural enough, Wil thought. He understood that a little patience was required of all of them.

Two horsemen appeared, threading their way through the herd. Sewall watched them approach. "Our first visitors."

Roosevelt squinted through his eyeglasses. When the horsemen were near enough for him to make them out he said, "The tall one is Johnny Goodall. Range manager for the Marquis De Morès. The other one's called Jerry Paddock. Saloonkeeper, mainly."

Wil watched the two men ride up from the riverbank. There was a squeaking of saddle leather when they reined in and shifted their seats. Johnny Goodall said, "How do," and laid both hands on his saddlehorn. "Handsome herd of cattle."

"I expect them to prosper here," said Roosevelt.

The one called Paddock looked like an undertaker, Wil Dow thought. He had a drooping Oriental sort of mustache and evil black eyes. Paddock said, in a voice that would cut glass, "Who are these?"

"William Sewall and Wilmot Dow. My friends from Maine—self-reliant outdoorsmen whom I admire for their grit and pluck and abilities. They're here to build and manage my ranch."

"Ain't your ranch."

Roosevelt pushed his glasses up on his nose. "What's that you say?"

"You're squatting on my property," said Paddock.

"Nonsense. This is open range."

"Used to be, before I put up my cabin across the river there."

Wil Dow said, "There's nothing over there but a few rotted old logs."

"Well I keep meaning to rebuild it." Paddock's sudden grin was shocking—a yellow display of crooked teeth.

Goodall said mildly, "Mind if I get down?" He dismounted and had a careful look at the stakes that marked the outline of the house that was to be. Then he studied Wil Dow and Bill Sewall in turn, and finally Roosevelt.

Wil studied him right back, with equal boldness.

This Johnny Goodall was tall and weathered; his wide shoulders were a bit stooped as if he were always ready to go through doorways that were too low for him. Despite the leathery texture of his skin and the unhurried confidence of his manner, he appeared to be young—perhaps in his middle twenties; no older. He kept his eyes on Roosevelt a long time, as if measuring him.

Wil Dow picked up his axe and swung it idly by the handle.

When Jerry Paddock's hooded eyes whipped toward him, Wil gave the horseman a slow wide smile.

A rifle stood muzzle-up, propped against the log where they had been eating; it was kept at hand in case game animals should put in an appearance. Uncle Bill Sewall picked it up without any pretense at stealth; he laid the rifle across his forearm. It wasn't quite aimed at Paddock.

Paddock said, "Easy now. This don't call for guns."

Roosevelt said to Paddock, "Anyone could have left those ruins."

"I'm just explaining to you, Mr. Roosevelt, you are squatting on my claim."

"There's no record of ownership in the land office. I've looked. If you've built any other improvements show them to me."

"No need to show a thing. My word stands, in this Territory."

Behind the glasses Roosevelt's large blue eyes were angry. "This is *open range*." He turned to Johnny Goodall. "Your friend's trying to run a bluff on me. Does it work on other settlers?"

"I couldn't say," Goodall replied. "Never seen him try it before."

"Are you part of it?"

"No. And he's not exactly my friend." Johnny Goodall's voice was mild, unhurried, a pleasant Texas twang. He kept sizing Roosevelt up as if he couldn't decide what to make of the little dude.

"Then what are you doing here together?"

"Me, sir, I am taking a look over the land and picking up a few strays. Jerry came along and asked to ride down here with me. Might as well say I'm here out of curiosity."

"Which led to the demise of the proverbial cat," Bill Sewall reminded him.

"What part of Maine you from?"

"Island Falls."

"Never heard of it. But then you probably never heard of the patch of chaparral I'm from, either."

Roosevelt said to Johnny Goodall, "If you're picking up strays, where are they? I see no cattle with you."

"Penned upriver a mile or so. Don't take after me, Mr. Roosevelt. I'm not a liar like certain folks."

Paddock stiffened with indignation but it was wasted; Goodall was not looking at him.

A mistral stirred; leaves shivered in the glade. Roosevelt said to Bill Sewall, "I believe Mr. Goodall is curious to see if we can prove ourselves to his satisfaction. I believe he came along to find out if we Easterners have any sand." He swung abruptly to look up at Paddock, who had not descended from his horse. "I might care to take you seriously," Roosevelt said, "but to do so would be to affront your intelligence."

"What in hell's that supposed to mean?"

"You must take me for an awful fool." Reflections glittered from Roosevelt's eyeglasses. "You're a vulgar brute. Take your blackguardly declarations away with you."

Paddock glanced at Wil Dow's axe and Bill Sewall's rifle, and showed his yellow smile again. "It don't matter a whole lot to me personally, I guess. But I aim to be selling my claims to the Marquis De Morès. So I expect you'll hear from the Marquis."

Roosevelt said, "You may tell Mister De Morès that I am at his disposal any time."

Johnny Goodall seemed interested in the way Roosevelt said that. But he didn't say anything. He merely got back on his horse. "Expect I'll see you gents." He wheeled his mount effortlessly and trotted away. Wil Dow thought, *Someday I want to be able to ride like that*.

Paddock remained where he was, gazing darkly at the ranchman until Roosevelt said, "Is there something else?"

"Not just yet." Paddock jerked his horse away and plunged toward the river, scattering cattle as he pounded away.

Bill Sewall said, "I suppose that there's a sample of your famous Western hospitality." He put the rifle down and poked a warning finger toward Roosevelt. "The Texan kept that loon-crazy Paddock in rein. That may not be the case another time."

Wil Dow held the axe near its head, balancing its weight in his grip; he bounced it lightly in the circle of his fist and thought this was not exactly the sort of adventuresome challenge to which he had been looking forward in the Wild West.

Roosevelt said after a moment, "I suppose I'll have to see about this."

Six

Monday morning Pack opened the front door wide; the heat was so powerful that despite flies and stench, ventilation was preferable to suffocation. He rolled up his sleeves and set about composing the front page of tomorrow's edition of *The Bad Lands Cow Boy.*

Alerted by something he felt rather than heard, he turned to see Riley Luffsey standing in the doorway. Luffsey's stance was aggressive—fists against flanks, head thrust forward. Low on his right hip hung a revolver in an old army holster from which the overflap had been cut off so as to make for quick access to the handle. It wasn't the sort of holster you could wear on horseback, Pack observed; the revolver would bounce out.

"Morning, Riley. Change your mind about working for me?"

"No."

"Something I can do for you, then?"

"Well I was wondering." Some of the bellicosity went out of Luffsey's attitude. "Dutch Reuter says you know a lot about Custer and Hickok and them all." He watched with interest as Pack set a bar of type.

"Now, all I know is what I used to read in the newspapers when

I was a boy. My father put out a newspaper, you know. Still does. When Custer and Hickok died I was about fifteen. Now, I remember the reports. I guess everybody does who was old enough at the time. What did you want to know?"

"Dutch says he actually saw Wild Bill Hickok once, down in Kansas. He says you saw Hickok too. That true, Mr. Packard?"

"Wild Bill? Yes, I saw him once. My dad took me to see him on the stage in Chicago when he was traveling in that show with Buffalo Bill and Ned Buntline. I was eleven or twelve. I was mighty impressed."

"What's he look like?"

"He looked tall, I guess, but then all grown men look pretty tall when you're a kid looking up at them from a theater seat. He had hair down to his shoulders—"

"Golden hair, like a lion?"

"No, it was brown as I recall, and he had a mustache, and he was dressed up in a buckskin outfit that my dad said he never wore except in that make-believe play. Why do you want to know all this, Riley?"

"Well I'm just kind of curious, is all. What kind of holster he carry his gun in?"

Pack gave him a suspicious look. "Now, what did Dutch Reuter tell you about that?"

"Said he carried his guns in cut-down army holsters."

"Like that one you're wearing there?"

"Yes sir, like this one."

"Now, I happen to know Hickok didn't like holsters. Never used them."

"Where in hell'd he carry his gun, then?"

"Hickok had two guns, in the first place."

"Dutch didn't mention that."

"What did Dutch tell you, exactly?"

"I don't know. Just things. I guess Wild Bill must have been the best gunfighter ever, wasn't he?"

"And look at the good it did him," Pack said.

"He lost his eyesight. That wasn't his fault. Up until he started to go blind there wasn't anybody could beat Will Bill with any kind of handgun."

"Now, that may be true," Pack conceded; give the devil his due.

"You said he wore two guns. What kind?"

"I think they were the old style forty-four army Colts with no top-strap—Theuer cartridge conversions, I believe. I could be wrong about that but that's what I remember. I do know he was partial to wearing a wide sash around his waist. He was a big eater and he was vain about his looks and he liked to hobble in his pot-belly with a sash. He generally wore the Colts inside the sash, with the handles sticking out over."

"That ain't what Dutch said."

"Dutch has a flexible way of telling the truth sometimes."

"I don't see how you could draw a gun very quick if it was all knotted up inside a big sash."

"I never heard of Hickok having to draw his gun very quick. When he sat down to play cards, I understand he'd keep one revolver in his lap under the table, just in case. He generally walked around with at least one gun already in his hand if he felt there might be any need of it. Now, that got him in trouble—I guess you heard."

"What kind of trouble?"

"Hickok was a man with a unique talent for marksmanship—he could hit anything, at any distance, without even seeming to aim—but he drank too much whiskey and when he was drunk he got belligerent and trigger-happy, not unlike some of your friends hereabouts, and there was one time, I think in Abilene, when he was chief of police there, and he was walking around drunk one night and he heard somebody come up behind him and he already had that gun in his hand so he just turned around and shot the man behind him, and it turned out to be his own town constable."

"Oh, now, Mr. Packard, I do believe you're runnin' a sandy on me."

"No, it's the truth. It was in all the dispatches. Hickok was fired after that little mishap. Now, he couldn't get a job enforcing the law anywhere after that, so he went on the stage with Cody for a little while but my dad told me he just couldn't stand play-acting, and his eyesight was starting to go bad on him so he just drifted around, drunk mostly, until somebody shot him in the back. He was thirty-something years old. It's not a very glorious life if you were thinking of following in his footsteps. If I were you I'd read more newspapers and not so many dime novels."

Riley Luffsey said, "I don't take partial to having my leg pulled, Mr. Packard."

Pack was too busy setting type to argue the point. And next time he looked up, the kid was gone.

Luffsey had strange dreams, sure enough; but he was a likeable youngster and Pack hoped he'd outgrow some of his turbulence. Keep nudging him along gently and it might yet be possible to make a printer's devil out of him.

That afternoon Pack received a visit from Joe Ferris, who put his head in the door of the *Bad Lands Cow Boy* shack and said, "News."

"What?"

"Come on and see."

Pack closed the newspaper door and joined Joe Ferris on the boardwalk. They had to wait out a traffic of half a dozen horsemen—Pack recognized two or three of them as hands who worked around the De Morès corrals; he wondered momentarily why they were heading east, for the Marquis had no nearby enterprises in that direction.

In the drovers' dusty wake Pack and Joe stepped down into clay powder that half-buried their boots.

Jerry Paddock's place was the first saloon they came to. Against Pack's nostrils a thick current of whiskey and beer and tobacco smoke rolled out through the half-open door. He didn't need to see the inside of Paddock's saloon with its low ceiling and small paper-covered windows; even in the daytime the place had an aura of dim dusk—the better to cloak Jerry's habits of behavior?

Pack reached for the door but Joe's hand stayed him. "Not here," Joe said. "I'll walk a little farther and spend my money in Bob Roberts's place if it's all the same to you."

"All right," said Pack. They walked on. "How's trade?"

"Picking up." Joe had stocked the store with provisions ordered on the strength of his loan from Theodore Roosevelt and Pack had seen a fair stream of customers in and out of the place in the past week. He had also made note of the Remington revolver Joe wore at all times, handle-forward on his hip, and the bellicose challenge with which Joe stared back at those of Jerry Paddock's crowd who made it a point to drop in each day to inspect his progress.

Pack said, "Who's minding the place?"

"I rigged traps," Joe Ferris said. "Anybody tries to bust in, we'll hear it."

"Hear what? Pots and pans?"

"More likely screams," Joe said. "They're bear traps."

"Now, isn't that a little ferocious?"

"I'm not Swede Nelson," Joe replied. "They're not going to break me."

At the corner, smiling in a shapeless burlap dress and a pathetic sunbonnet, stood Jerry Paddock's professed wife, a painted woman known around town as Little Casino. In dubious distinction she probably was the most famous or infamous madam in western Dakota. At this moment she was bending the ear of young Riley Luffsey, who giggled at everything she said. She looked up as the two men walked by, said, "Hello boys," and winked at Pack.

Pack granted the stiff nod the occasion required. Joe Ferris muttered a greeting as they went by.

Pack had spent a silly hour once with Little Casino and she had treated him like a dirty little boy. Apparently that was what most of her customers liked. Pack hadn't enjoyed it at all; he preferred a softly languorous vulgarity that allowed room for dreams of Romance.

A wagon was parked in the alley beside the De Morès store; a small boy slept full length on its seat. Children, Pack thought—a sure sign of growing civilization.

But he felt irritable. Booster's passion seemed to have deserted him on this ragged afternoon. Instead of an incipient metropolis the town for all its raw newness seemed but a shabby camp: ramshackle and makeshift. It probably had less to do with architecture than with the clinging dirt, the glutinous smell, the ubiquitous insects and the barren landscape that, by overhanging the place, dwarfed it. But on this particular day he found himself wondering if Progress was, after all, worth the price.

"What news is coming to town?"

"You'll see."

"What's the mystery?"

"Seeing's believing. Best for you to witness it with a fresh clean open mind. I wouldn't want to go coloring your editorial opinions."

"Now, Joe, you're an exasperation."

"I know I am." Joe seemed pleased with himself.

They walked on, bootheels kicking up little whorls of powder dust. Masking his nose with a curved palm against the abattoir stink, Pack recalled the six or seven De Morès horsemen who'd ridden out east just now. Something odd about them nagged at him and it struck him now that all of them had been carrying rifles and wearing holstered revolvers. He glanced at Joe Ferris's belted sidearm and wondered what things were coming to.

Riley Luffsey came hurrying up behind them. "Mr. Packard? I hope that's not a wool shirt you're wearing."

"Why?"

Joe Ferris made a face at Luffsey and pushed Pack forward into Bob Roberts's Bug Juice Dispensary. There was much more of a crowd than one should expect at this hour on a Monday afternoon; and come to think of it, why was Joe Ferris closing the doors of his store in the middle of the afternoon?

A man nearly backed into him; Pack put his hand gently against the man's shoulder and eased past him. He heard someone say, "Strong? Naw. I wouldn't say this snake juice was strong. But you give a shot of it to a fifteen-pound puppy and he'll pull a freight train."

Dan McKenzie, the blacksmith, was swapping tall stories with a friend. "Why that's nothing. Just last fall I seen a petrified bird sitting on a petrified tree singing a petrified song."

Some of them were onetime buffalo hunters fretting their lives away in unemployed bitterness. But why wasn't McKenzie at work?

Pack sensed expectancy in the air. He said to Joe Ferris, "What is it?"

"May be we'll find out soon enough."

By the barroom piano a group of men sang in rough voices the popular song "What Was Your Name in the States?"

At the long plank bar Redhead Finnegan—surly, unkempt, quarrelsome, thickly muscled, chin like a curbstone; the man from Bitter Creek, Pack thought dryly—was holding court amid his louts and sycophants. Pack bent an ear in that direction. Sure enough, Finnegan and O'Donnell and Luffsey were vying to see who could utter the gamiest threats against the Marquis, whereupon Dutch Reuter—as inebriated as the others, and trying to eat with one hand while smoking a Single Twist with the other— stopped feeding his Teutonic appetite momentarily and lurched away from the free-lunch tray proclaiming, "I in the war of Franco-Prussia fought, and I always to go after any Frenchman am ready!"

Finnegan yelled, "The fences cut the game trails. And they cut off all us ranchers from the river. And the God-damn French cattle kingdom driving out the game. And I ain't going to have it no more. I'm tired of riding sixty miles to find game and I'm tired of cuttin' wire."

"You want to know what I think?" asked young Riley Luffsey. No one encouraged him but he went on anyway: "I think he's no French nobleman at all. I think it's a lie—just a way to avoid having to hobnob with common folks."

Frank O'Donnell said, "I don't care if he's the king of England and France both—he comes on my outfit I'll shoot that son of a bitch of a Markee like a dog on sight."

Pack drew breath to retort but Joe Ferris pulled him aside. "You want a Donnybrook? Keep it quiet now," he adjured. "They're right, Pack. You need to learn to listen to them. The hand of De Morès is upon everything in this place and they're sick of it."

"Now, don't scream at me, Joe."

"I thought we were friends. Why have a friend if you can't scream at him? I'm trying to save you a beating—or worse."

"The Marquis has every right to fence his own land."

"Sure, I know. The Markee can do no wrong. To hear you tell it, the sun shines out of his hind end. But don't tell it that way in here—these boys will make wolf meat out of you."

Dutch Reuter came weaving away from the bar, drunk and mildly angry. "They not ready yet to fight are. What good they are?" He pushed toward the door.

Joe Ferris said, "Where you going, Dutch?"

"Clearing out. Someplace where a man the air can breathe."

"Don't you like it around here any more?"

"Like, not like—no matter, Joe, I got no job. Maybe Dickinson I try, maybe Black Hills."

"Wait then. I know a man who may give you a job. I'll have a word with him." Joe moved away, his arms across Dutch's shoulders. Pack recalled that Joe had ridden with Dutch back in the buffalo-hunting days. If you had ever been a friend of Joe's you could always count on his help.

Behind the bar Bob Roberts examined both sides of a paper-money note before he shoved it in his pocket and counted out a handful of coins in change. A filthy hunter elbowed his way to the bar, leaned across and spoke rapidly in Roberts's ear. Roberts looked startled. Then he threw his head back. His big round voice boomed out into the room. "They're coming!"

At first Pack had no clue to the saloonkeeper's meaning; but in the abrupt silence that followed, he heard a faint drumming thunder.

The crowd listened with a religious intensity of silence. The rataplan grew slowly louder.

Bob Roberts broke the spell:

"By the Lord God, it's true then!"

There was a continuing stillness of some duration, punctuated by a growing racket of hoofs and followed by a surprisingly quiet statement from Redhead Finnegan:

"The blackhearted devil."

There was a surge toward the doors. Pack caught Joe Ferris's eye. They waited out the crush and afterward followed the crowd outside.

By then three point riders had entered the head of the street and Pack finally understood when he saw the dust-caked woollies behind them—a sea of bobbing sheep, funneled into a tight-woven carpet by the buildings on either side, unrolling forward at the insistence of yipping dogs and whooping riders.

The breeze, having shifted around to the east, brought with it a new odor—the stink of sheep oil. It set Frank O'Donnell to sneezing. Pack found it less obtrusive than the abattoir's smell but it had an astonishing effect on the faces of the men around him. Above the rataplan of hoofs and the baying of sheep and the yapping of dogs and the whooping of drovers there were quite a few sneezes and Pack heard a great deal of angry comment—all of it profane.

The sheep bobbed like corks. Their faces, Pack thought, were truly innocent. They crowded against one another in a suffocating jam—a single flow of tangled dust-caked wool. Curly capital on the hoof. Pack felt a swell of pride as if they were his own. *Progress!*

One block short of Roberts's saloon the point riders turned the herd left, heading them toward the embankment. A single horseman posted himself at the near side of the intersection to prevent strays from wandering this way. He didn't seem to have any difficulty; the sheep trotted around the bend as obediently as children in a follow-the-leader game. They looked like four-legged flour barrels.

The Bad Landers were aghast.

Joe Ferris said, "How many? Five, seven thousand goddamn sheep? Didn't have to drive the stupid critters right through town. Take two inches of topsoil off the streets."

Finnegan said, "Rubbing our faces in it. Son of a French whore."

A hundred yards away Jerry Paddock stood in the doorway of the De Morès office building. Dressed all in black, he watched the sheep's progress. His face was not legible beneath the lowered hatbrim; the droop of his Oriental mustache gave him a sardonic look in the misty dust.

Young Luffsey, half full of whiskey, stepped past Pack and lifted his revolver toward the flowing sheep. Before the youth could steady his aim Pack grasped his arm and pushed it down.

Pack said mildly, "Might hit one of the riders."

"I's just gonna shoot a couple muttons."

"Destroy the Marquis's property in front of fifty witnesses and you'll have the sheriff on you."

"Hell, Mr. Packard, Sheriff Harmon's a hundred and fifty miles away and he doesn't even know where this town is. He couldn't find Medora on a bet."

"All he's got to do is step on the train and step off the train, Riley."

Luffsey turned and looked uncertainly at Redhead Finnegan, as if for instructions.

Finnegan had other things on his mind. He was brooding in the direction of the De Morès offices. Jerry Paddock seemed to feel the strike of Finnegan's stare; with a toss of his head the villain retired into the doorway.

Finnegan said, "I heard it but I didn't believe it—I didn't believe even the Markee could be that stupid. Ain't no end to what the damn fool crazy Frenchman don't know about sheep. Nibble the grass right down to the quick, don't they. So close to the ground they kill the roots, ruin the pasture for game and cattle and they leave you nothing but dust and clay that'll wash away next rain."

Frank O'Donnell, who was quite drunk, sneezed violently and aimed his .45 at the horseman on the corner, who steadied his mount and lifted his free hand to indicate his peacefulness. O'Donnell yelled, "Take a message to De Morès—the word's out he's to be shot on sight like a dog!"

O'Donnell was only tossing raw meat at a distance—bait. His eyes watered. He seemed too drunk to know what he was doing, but Finnegan turned on him in contempt: "Hell, Frank, you want to transmit messages, why'n't you just send the Markee a telegraph wire—give him twenty-four hours to get out of Dakota?"

Indignation made O'Donnell rear back until he nearly lost his balance. He lost his grip on the revolver; it flew away through the air and struck someone who cried out in annoyance.

O'Donnell sneezed again as he lurched toward Redhead Finnegan. "You think I won't do it? I'll send him a note, I swear I will!"

"Go ahead, Frank. Write the Markee a letter. I bet it just scares the chaps right off him." Finnegan sniggered. "Hell, you fool, either kill the man or don't kill him—don't mess with sending *messages*."

O'Donnell swayed, gathered himself with a determined scowl and said, "Riley? Where in hell's Riley Luffsey?"

"Right here, Frank."

"You write the message for me. You can write, can't you?"

There was a general round of derisive laughter. O'Donnell sat down unintentionally on the edge of the board sidewalk and pitched over on his side and the crowd made way around him in a general movement back into Bob's Bug Juice Emporium.

Luffsey hung back, revolver still in his fist, and Pack watched closely until finally the youth put the weapon away in its cut-off holster and made a face and slammed into the saloon.

O'Donnell lay snoring on the edge of the walk. Pack thought about picking him up but a rebellious *To hell with him* welled up, and he put his back to the unconscious drunk and went inside with Joe Ferris.

He could see that Joe was in a dangerous fuming silent rage. Joe tramped around behind the bar and poured himself a full mug of beer from the keg and drank the whole thing down without pausing for breath. He closed his eyes. "There's your news story, Pack. Write it up with the usual enthusiasm."

Joe drew another beer and came away from the backbar. He breathed heavily in and out; he looked resentfully at Pack and said, "Jerry Paddock convinced the Marquis there's money in it. Got something like twenty men signed solemn contracts to herd sheep for the Marquis. These're just the first batch, you know. Fifteen thousand of those Merinos coming in, boys, like it or not."

The thundering racket was diminishing out there. Riley Luffsey's eyes bulged. "Fifteen *thousand?*"

Joe Ferris belched and interjected, "Jerry Paddock is lower than a snake's vest button. What he did to poor Swede— "

There was a burst of sudden laughter from Redhead Finnegan. "Merinos, hell—they won't stand one winter up here. What you bet these boys eat all the mutton their bellies can hold and then go complaining to the Markee about the terrible losses to coyotes and wolves and snow?"

Pack said, "Now, you have my sympathies, gents, but it's no good standing in the path of improvement. Now, I know you hunters resent the Marquis. But with his capital he's doing more to stimulate the development of the Territory than all the hunters and squatters put together. You won't turn the calendar back. There is a world of cities out there hungry for beef and mutton and wool, and now that the Marquis has shown the way, the industry will boom with or without him. You may as well quit your threats."

Redhead Finnegan said, "You're in the wrong bar room, Pack."

Pack knew what they thought of him. He knew he invariably presented an innocent expression of eager curiosity. But there were things you couldn't let a ruffian get away with. Pack met the stare of the Man from Bitter Creek. He expected Finnegan's faithless glance to break away but Finnegan never blinked; he only said, "You'd be dead by now except I don't pick fights with a man who ain't got the grit to go armed."

"I'm armed with my wits, Red, which is more than I need in this company."

"Go peddle the Markee's fish-wrap—whyn't you just print the damn rag in French? I'm telling you again—you're in the wrong bar room, you vile dirty whangdoodle low-down Frenchman's toady," Finnegan roared; and Pack felt the prod of Joe Ferris's hand.

Bob Roberts sought to break the moment with a bellow: "Time to fill the empty ones!"

Pack felt himself gripped from behind. By reflex he resisted but then he recognized Joe Ferris. Propelled urgently out of the place by his friend, Pack gave Joe a resentful look and broke away and surged earnestly toward *The Bad Lands Cow Boy*, his bearded head preceding his body; he lunged ahead with such force that he felt capable of exploding straight through any object that might block his path.

On his way through the office he snatched down his burlap apron and green visor and paper cuffs stained with ink. In the press room he scribbled the paragraphs quickly. Anger stiffened his hand:

> It has been our endeavor to build up a paper that would be of substantial benefit to Dakota and Dakotans; and we had hoped our undertaking might meet with the approval of all who feel an interest in the development of the Territory and who believe that fair and impartial advertising of its resources will hasten the march of progress.
>
> Low, vulgar abuse has never found a place in these columns, and it never shall, and though we shall ever wage war upon corruption and wrongdoers, and attempt all in our power to sustain principles of right and justice, we do not believe that personal vituperation will in any way tend to root out the corrupt nor advance the cause of truth and purity.

He paced urgently around the table, reading it back, squinting in the smoky kerosene lamplight.

It needed no correcting. He went on to the composing desk and began to sort through the week's collection of Western Union wire stories and clippings from the most recent of the national magazines and newspapers that cluttered the room in unruly havoc.

Then he went through his charts, made a note to remove two advertisers because of their nonpayment of third-notice billings, canceled five subscriptions that were three months overdue, and gathered the three new advertisements that were to make their debut appearances in this week's issue: Anderson's Restaurant

("Refreshes the Inner Man!"), Dan McKenzie ("Blacksmith and Horse-shoeing"); and Michael Knott ("Keeps All Kinds of Wines, Liquors and Whiskies").

Through it all, fury was a hot spiral through his innards. He rehearsed and refined what he was going to write. When he was able to steady his pulse, his pencil flew:

> America's divine predestination is being achieved in Billings County. The Marquis De Morès, that brave soldier in the army of Manifest Destiny, once again emblazons history with his deeds of Vision and Progress.
>
> The Marquis De Morès is already famed for bringing modernity to the beef industry. His score of highly trained butchers dress cattle in a spanking new abattoir on the range beside the railroad, thus eliminating the cost of shipping live animals to the East. One might have thought it should have been obvious to any fool that three fifths of the weight of a live steer is inedible, and therefore the man who ships live cattle pays more than twice as much for transportation as he need do, but evidently this brilliant stroke has never occurred to Mr Armour, Mr Swift or any other of the Eastern packers.
>
> Blocks of ice, chopped and harvested from northern rivers throughout the winter, are stored in insulated relay ice-houses every 200 miles between Medora and New York. M De Morès's Northern Pacific Refigerator Car Company has built cold-storage facilities in Helena, Billings, Miles City, Medora, Bismarck, Fargo, Brainerd, Duluth, Minneapolis, St. Paul and Chicago.
>
> He has half the transport cost and none of the middleman cost of the meat-packers of the Chicago Trust, and we predict with confidence that this means nothing less than a Revolution in the meat industry.
>
> The NPRCC has recently increased its capital stock from $200,000 to $1 million. When the range is fully stocked and the abattoir operating at full capacity, it is anticipated the Medora industry will provide the fattening, slaughtering and marketing of at least 40,000 beeves yearly, thus dashing the strangle-hold of the Eastern

monopolies. We anticipate the De Morès triumph will create a considerable drop in prices for the consumer and, in turn, encourage a sharp increase in the demand for beef.

And now upon this auspicious date the *Cow Boy* is pleased to report the arrival of the first domestic sheep in Medora town, thanks to the foresight and genius of the community's leading citizen.

In sum and in short, the Marquis De Morès has become a stirring symbol of the ethos of Prosperity and Progress on the Frontier.

He read it back with satisfaction. That would most certainly take the wind right out of the sails of Finnegan and the ignorant ruffians.

It remained to put *The Bad Lands Cowboy* to bed. He set his type with the speed of long practice: son and apprentice of a newspaper man. Pack—publisher, reporter, editor, make-up man, press man, printer's devil—made up the forms and slapped them on the bed of the Washington hand press and jammed the type-bars in place and thrust the first sheet of wet-down paper on the tympan points and unhooked the swinging frisket and brought it down to protect the margins of the paper and distributed ink on the composition roller and slid the bed under the platen and slid it back again, his deadline determined by the schedule of the morning train. Eyes on the clock, oblivious to the familiar rumble of the press, he heaved the lever fore and back, freeing sheets of sticky printpaper, straightening the new stack for back-side printing, needing six arms and possessing but two.

When he looked up he saw Riley Luffsey's face pressed to the window. Pack reared back in alarm. But the kid only smiled, in an odd shy way. Pack beckoned, inviting him in. Luffsey came hesitantly to the door and nearly stepped inside. But then he looked behind him, saw something that changed his mind, and hurried away with swagger restored.

Pack was returning from the train with empty wheelbarrow and type iron when he saw two horsemen converging toward the abattoir. Recognizing them, Pack dropped the iron into the wheelbarrow, left them at the edge of the street and hurried toward the abattoir. For the two riders were De Morès and Theodore Roosevelt.

The smell grew worse as Pack ran toward the smashing racket of boilers, vats, crashing mechanical pumps.

Amid the metal-roofed factory buildings the two riders approached each other like challengers in a joust. They stopped; neither dismounted; the horses, made uneasy by the noise and stink, pranced around each other in a short-fused minuet. Through it all the Marquis sat his horse like a centaur—a noble figure in sombrero, wild yellow shirt and flaming red neckerchief. His golden skin seemed to glow. When he greeted the diminutive New Yorker, De Morès slapped the heavy lead-filled bamboo stick against the palm of his hand.

Roosevelt wore butternut trousers and a flannel shirt under his brown Eastern-cut jacket. He wore a wide-brimmed hat that didn't quite seem to fit. Covered from head to foot with the dust of Bad Lands travel, he kept grabbing leather as the horse jumped about. While he fought to control the beast he was speaking swiftly, jaws chopping, head jutting emphatically.

De Morès, easily keeping his seat as the spirited stallion skittered around, replied with equal vigor. Clearly it was a confrontation of some kind. Pack ran full out.

He approached in time to hear the Marquis say,"I'll have the secretary look into the papers. I don't foresee any difficulty. As to Paddock, when I came here I understood very quickly that to control the town I must control the worst of its denizens. You will leave him to me—that's a good chap. Now if you'll forgive me I must be about my business. We must always keep moving. Otherwise time will cheat us of our good years—you agree?"

De Morès acknowledged Pack's presence with a casual wave and urged the horse away. The Marquis always wanted to go faster; it was one of his few failings—he had no patience.

Pack looked up at Roosevelt, who was watching the Marquis—watching, perhaps, the quality of De Morès's horsemanship.

Pack said tentatively, "Mr. Roosevelt?"

"Good day to you, Mr. Packard."

"Conducting business with the Marquis?"

"I do admire his plumage."

"Is there anything my readers should benefit from knowing?"

"Thousands of things, I've no doubt," Roosevelt replied. His teeth made a brief but large appearance.

Panting from his run, Pack gathered breath for another try but his attention was drawn by Madame la Marquise. She came up from the ford in a surrey driven by a coachman in livery. Roosevelt rode out from between the factory sheds to meet her. Pack ran along behind him.

As Madame approached, Pack tried not to stare at her large brown eyes and masses of lovely red hair. She was so beautiful she made his eyes ache.

The coachman drew rein and braced his foot against the brake handle. There was a screech of chock against rim. The sudden high noise frightened Roosevelt's horse; it reared, nearly spilling the rider.

When Roosevelt regained control Madame said, "I'm so sorry. I didn't mean to—"

Roosevelt said, "I disapprove of self-reproach. Please don't apologize."

She seemed about to speak again but then her glance touched on Pack; she changed her mind. "Hello, Arthur," she said gaily. "It's a wonderful column about Antoine. He felt very complimented."

"Thank you. Merely writing the truth as I see it."

She said to Roosevelt, "Have you seen the paper?" And suddenly it was in her hand. She held it out of the surrey at arm's length and Roosevelt awkwardly spurred his horse forward, leaned out of the saddle and nearly toppled as he took a fingertip grip on the newspaper. After all that he dropped it. Pack stepped forward to pick it up and handed it up to him. In that moment, when perhaps they thought he wasn't looking, Pack thought he saw a spark of something more than ordinary friendliness in the way Medora's eyes met Roosevelt's.

"Thank you," said Roosevelt. "And now if you'll excuse me I must be on my way." He touched the folded newspaper to his hatbrim, gave Pack a glance and a nod, and rode off into town. Something about his carriage—something in the posture of his back—conveyed a quiet melancholy.

The afternoon was filled with explosive noise and destructive danger. It was mostly O'Donnell and Finnegan—drunk and shooting up the town. Using the Marquis's importation of sheep as an excuse they had a rip-roarin' time. There was a great promiscuity of gunfire that made Pack wonder, not for the first time, how these boys could afford such profligate expenditures on ammunition. The De Morès Hotel was shot full of holes. Blaspheming vigorously, the boys shot up all the stovepipes they could see.

During the fusillade Pack stayed indoors like any prudent citizen but it nearly didn't save him; as he was studying the reflection of his face and thinking about shaving, a bullet parted his whiskers and smashed his mirror.

By evening the celebrants were sleeping it off somewhere, probably in the scabrous dormitory above Paddock's dingy saloon. With the danger abated and the pressures of his weekly deadline in abeyance, Pack emerged from his toilet in stiff collar and cravat with his hair all wet down and his bottle-green frock coat dusted clean and his evening boots polished to a patent-leather gleam.

The sun was low above Graveyard Butte when Pack strolled across the railroad bridge—it was that or use the horse-and-wagon ford downstream, and a man dressed for dinner at the château could hardly select that alternative, regardless how hot his feet might be.

He was intercepted at the end of the bridge by a man on horseback. At first Pack could not make out the man's face against the sunset—but he recognized A.C. Huidekoper's Pennsylvania voice. "Beautiful evening."

"It is indeed."

Huidekoper dismounted with the easy grace of a born horseman. He was dressed with odd formality, as if for courting, in a lingerie shirt and a boiled collar. He removed his hat in a sort of punctuation to indicate an emphasis upon the importance he attached to this meeting. He was slight but not delicate, a compact man with a small round bald head and bright alert birdlike eyes.

"I've been lying in wait for you." Huidekoper pronounced his words with care. Pack envied the Pennsylvanian his ear for mimicry; depending on the occasion he was capable of speaking innumerable appropriate varieties of English from cowboy to proper to stuffy.

"Now, that's ominous." Pack smiled with his mouth.

"You've been summoned to an audience with De Morès. Possibly as you grow a bit older you'll learn to pick your dinner companions with more care," Huidekoper said, "but as it happens, I'm pleased you're going up there tonight. I've a message for him."

"Why not give it to him yourself?"

"Hell will freeze over before I get an invitation to visit that house. I've made no secret of my feelings against him. But I'm not the sort of fool who's eager for carnage—any civilized man has a duty to head off catastrophe if he can. Will you try to make clear to De Morès that he's courting a violent debacle?"

Pack didn't want to hear more. He had suffered his share of the garrulous horse-rancher's fulminations. He liked Huidekoper well enough: the man was good-hearted and well-intentioned. But everyone knew Huidekoper's eccentric prejudices against Progress and Industrial Growth, and Pack was in no frame of mind to be buttonholed this evening for an endless harangue.

Pack made as if to continue on his way. With a departing flap of a hand he walked down off the NPRR embankment and approached the bend in the wagon-road that led up toward the De Morès residence.

Huidekoper, leading the horse, hurried along beside him.

"Tell him we ranchers are not going to tolerate it any more—his fences and his Valentine Scrip frauds, and the irresponsible arrogance with which the man disregards the rights and feelings of his neighbors. The sheep are the last straw. There'll be an explosion of tempers, mark me."

"Will there? Most of the people around here owe their prosperity to the Marquis."

"There's a growing population that does not. Why are you so determined to see only one side of the issue?"

"It's the side that counts." Pack lengthened his stride. As soon as he could reach the vegetable garden at the foot of the driveway he'd be able to leave his companion behind, for Huidekoper had spoken the truth about one thing: he was not welcome on the Marquis's land.

Huidekoper, half a head shorter, had to hasten awkwardly to keep up, tugging all the while on the reins of the saddle horse.

"You've got his ear. He respects you. For Heaven's sake warn him off. Tell him to pull back before it's too late."

"Why? Because a few saloon ruffians have been shaking the leaves?"

"There's talk of shooting. There's talk of assassinating De Morès."

"Now, there's always talk. I don't believe the Marquis sets much store by it."

"These are not university boys, Pack. They're a rough crowd."

"The Marquis is no shrinking violet, you know. He's killed several men."

"He claims to have done. But these toughs don't abide by the rules of formal duelling. More like a shotgun from a dark alley. Is that what you want? Bloodshed upon bloodshed? Unrestricted range warfare?"

"It won't come to that. They're only a few hotheads with nothing better to do than hang around bar rooms and boast to one another about what bad men they are. Why, I had a run-in with a roomful of them just yesterday. They had every chance to rend me limb from limb but nothing came of it except a drunken idea to send a threatening letter to the Marquis. Ease your mind. They're not gorgons and hydras and chimeras dire."

"What's that? Shakespeare?"

"Milton."

They reached the garden fence at the foot of the drive. Huidekoper stopped, as Pack had hoped he would. He climbed into the saddle and removed his hat and wiped a sleeve across the round ball of his hairless scalp. "It's not just the hunters and wild ones your friend up there has antagonized. The sober element as well. He makes enemies too easily. It's a habit that could cost him his life. Please understand what I'm saying, and why I'm saying it."

Now, you're an old woman, Pack thought. He walked on.

Huidekoper called after him: "At least tell him to keep away from the windows!"

Château De Morès overlooked the town, the railroad and its bridge, the river, the abattoir and the horizontally streaked colors of the heaving Bad Lands. On the lowlands along the river bend beneath the bluff were coach garage, stable and a house for the coachmen—and beyond them a pattern of corrals and vegetable gardens from which Pack commenced the strenuous climb to the wide terrace on which stood the residence of the Monte Cristo of the Bad Lands.

There were deer horns over the door. The house was large—twenty-six rooms looming two stories high at the edge of the bluff on the eastern promontory of Graveyard Butte. Everyone in the Territory knew it had an indoor bathroom—the first in Dakota. The walls were clapboard wood painted French grey with slate grey trim; the roof and shutters were deep red. The front porch faced the southern sun and was outfitted with easy chairs overseen by racks of antelope and elk horns—trophies of the De Morès's hunts.

It was the Bad Landers who had named it "the château"; in fact it was an ordinary frame lodge, though a large one, and its owners preferred to call it "the summer house" because once their operations were fully organized they intended to spend their winters in the East.

Pack as usual was punctual; the Marquis and Marquise as usual were not. A maid admitted Pack to the front room and the butler came through quickly, dismissed the maid and led Pack to the front corner parlor. There he was left to himself for several minutes to consider the staring enormous buffalo head and the square Kurtzmann piano from which Madame la Marquise's impassioned renditions of Verdi and Bach and Liszt sometimes could be heard in the town across the river when the wind was right.

Pack stared enraptured at the celebrated portrait of Madame Medora. It was an excellent likeness, beautifully rendered by the celebrated Charles Jalabert; it captured Madame's delicate beauty and impish good humor and the richness of her masses of auburn-red hair.

He knew these things about her achievements: she spoke seven languages fluently; she painted well; she played the pianoforte with accomplished technique and great feeling; she created divine needlepoint; she was an accomplished horsewoman and huntress. There were some, Huidekoper among them, who said she could outride and outshoot her own husband. In a *Cow Boy* column two weeks ago Pack had christened her the Diana of Dakota.

Pack found it significant that the hunting trophies—the envy of every sporting gentleman and lady in the Territory—were juxtaposed matter-of-factly with shelves of books and magazines published in more than half a dozen languages, all of which both the Marquis and his wife could read effortlessly. There were books on cattle and banking and finance and history and the French monarchy—as well as volumes of Longfellow, Hugo, Emerson, Goethe. The family De Morès, making no concessions to wilderness, had brought every refinement of Civilization to the Territory. Therein, Pack was sure, resided the hope of the Future.

Fitfully distracted by Huidekoper's alarums, Pack wandered through the dining room, laid with its settings of Minton china; the complete set contained five hundred pieces. Fine table linens, delicate crystal glassware and expensive silver caught his eye. Like all rooms in civilized homes the chamber was wallpapered. The dominant color was deep red, to go with Madame's hair.

His interest lay mainly in the windows just now. There was still daylight; he peered out one pane and then another, judging angles of fire. . . .

He prowled past several hard-working servants in kitchen and scullery to the long trophy room where most guests tended to congregate during gatherings here. The maid who'd admitted him was on her knees polishing the floor. Except for the rugs, which were from the Orient, most of the furnishings and draperies were French. Here and there, sometimes with startling rudeness, a Wild West artifact boomed: a red Mackinac blanket over a chair, a racked elk head above the doorway and of course that magnificent grizzly bearskin and the huge knife beside it. Pack recalled his previous visit when the Marquis had pointed out the knife, eyes glittering with pride, and gripped Pack's arm until Pack thought gangrene would set in. The Marquis's voice had trembled with feeling: *I adore the thrilling excitement of the chase and the hunt. It's no longer enough to shoot game. The spirit craves more. With glistening steel I met this grizzly bear. I wrestled the great beast with nothing but my knife.*

Every time Pack saw the knife his awe was renewed.

To keep the establishment functioning there was a considerable population of servants. Pack had catalogued them for the newspaper's ardent readers: butler, French cook, wine steward, Madame's private maids, seamstress, six Italian chambermaids, dining room maids, laundress, scullery maids, maids for the children, stable boy, four German gardeners, a guide, four handlers to care for the horses and carriages and hunting dogs, a doctor for the Marquise and her two infant children. Pack had interviewed several of them to provide incidental stories here and there in the *Cow Boy.*

He moved along the north side of the room, having his look out the windows. The lawn was wide; no cover within easy range of the house. Only a fool would try the half-blind luck of long-range shooting, whether by night or by daylight when he faced nothing but reflections off the surfaces of the windows.

No, it was nonsense. Huidekoper was getting exercised over nothing. Pack put it from his mind.

Lady Medora entered, skirts brushing the floor; behind her came a train of womanservants who took the two children into the kitchen. Madame la Marquise watched the little ones fondly through the open kitchen door as she pointed Pack toward a seat.

"Antoine apologizes for his rudeness. I hope you haven't been too bored." She smelled delectably of washed linen and sachet. "You look very handsome, Arthur."

Pack knew if he spoke he'd only stammer. He smiled, shook his head, kissed Medora's lovely hand.

She said, "Dakota is a better place to rear children than New York, don't you think?" In the kitchen he saw the high chair—Medora's own; her parents had saved it twenty years and given it to her for her firstborn. The children—daughter Athenais and son Louis—of course ate in the kitchen with the servants; they would not be allowed to eat in the dining room with their elders until they were judged fit to behave properly. That would be a while yet—they'd have to be somewhere between the ages of twelve and sixteen.

Madame's skirts rustled. "I'm pleased they're completing the church so quickly."

"It seems to be going very nicely," Pack agreed. That was the brick Roman Catholic chapel she was erecting in town as a thank-you offering after the births of her two children. It was to be the only church building of any denomination in Billings County.

She smiled with infinite sweetness and said, "The inhabitants of these Bad Lands do seem to feel less in need of theological instruction than of the spiritual consolation provided by Forty-Mile Red-Eye. But we mustn't let such things stand in the way of bringing the influence of civilization to the West. I'm employing a schoolteacher from the East, did we tell you?" She looked up past him and beamed. "Ah—Antoine."

De Morès entered—tall, dashing, slender, erect, wafting cologne, wearing a blue shirt with yellow silk lacings. Pack stood and bowed. It was a practice De Morès preferred to the American habit of handshaking.

Pack said, "Your fine lady certainly adds more than a touch of charm to the Bad Lands."

"She adds magic to whatever she touches," De Morès said. He was watching the way Pack glanced at Madame; he seemed not resentful but, rather, pleased. His dark flashing eyes missed nothing.

When Madame excused herself from the room, Pack said to the Marquis, "Some of the ranchers seem to have misgivings about your personal safety. They feel you and your family may be in danger from the wilder crowd. I don't know how seriously you ought to take these vague threats but I feel obliged to pass them on to you."

"I'll take them under advisement." The Marquis smiled. "Thank you for not mentioning these trivialities in my wife's presence."

"I shouldn't have mentioned them at all, save for concern toward Madame and the children."

"We are grateful for your steadfast gallantry."

Over sherry De Morès slouched on the davenport and spoke to Pack of his ambitions. He touched the barbed ends of his longhorn mustache, the points of which had been waxed and twisted to glorious perfection.

"We're chartered to do business in every state and Territory from the Atlantic to the Pacific. I shall keep building. Tanneries. Soap factories, glue factories, shoe factories. I shall expand the mining of lignite coal not only for use in the abattoir but also, I anticipate, for sale to the railroad and the inhabitants of the region. I'll raise cabbages—fertilize them with offal from the abattoir and deliver to the East in my refrigerator cars. The city of Medora will become the livestock center of North America. Ultimately it will be the capital of the state of Dakota." He smiled for emphasis. "In the past half-century America's population has quadrupled to fifty million. Someone has to feed them—*I* shall feed them!"

"How many sheep did you bring in?"

"That was the first of some fifteen thousand Merinos this season. Ultimately I shall maintain a herd sufficient to allow the slaughter and shipment of ten thousand lambs and muttons each year."

"There's been grumbling about the sheep. The Bad Landers don't like them."

"The bumpkins don't like anything new till they've have time to grow accustomed to it. They'll learn to enjoy the taste of lamb—even if I have to force it down them."

That was another mark of his strength: De Morès would rebuild the whole world, if need be, to fit his own visions.

Madame reappeared. "Shall we dine?"

De Morès graciously allowed his guest to take Madame's elbow. Pack's heart raced as he escorted Medora to the dining room.

Dinner was venison, flavored by the touch of the French chef and garnished with a vegetable variety from the cultivated half-acre along the river that was tended by the estate's four German gardeners.

"Our friend Roosevelt seems to have decided to raise cattle on a little ranch north of here," De Morès said, as much to his wife as to the visitor. "I really don't understand it. He has money, hasn't he?"

"His family has," she said. "He's not the eldest son."

"Ah, but the older brother—what is his name?"

"Elliot."

"A drunken wastrel, no? Off sailing the oceans or visiting maharajahs in India. I don't imagine the family should have entrusted the fortune on that one."

"I don't know much about the family fortune," she said. "Their father died several years ago."

"I gather he was wealthy."

"I think so."

"Jewish?"

"No, Antoine, not Jewish."

"I don't believe it." De Morès's brilliant eyes wheeled and challenged Pack to deny him. "You only need to *look* at him, *n'est-ce pas*? The weak little boy, the eyes squinting with suspicion behind spectacles—and the sly deviousness. Does he come right out to challenge me in open competition? No. He slips a small herd of cattle in, very quietly, hoping I won't notice. He pretends he wants only a few acres of open range and a little log ranch house. Roosevelt—a nester? A small rancher? What do they call it, Arthur? A two-bit sodbuster. Ridiculous. He's at least as rich as I am. There is more than meets the eye. He's plotting. Something devilishly clever—I can feel it."

Madame la Marquise said, "I don't think that's true, Antoine. He's not a sneak. Even his enemies in politics complain of his bluntness, his forthrightness—not his deviousness."

"I don't know what he wants," De Morès insisted, "and I don't trust him." Then with the sort of bewildering change that was typical of him he turned to Pack. "Arthur, have you been to Deadwood?"

"No."

"It's still quite a boom town."

"That's what I hear." There had been more gold discoveries in the Black Hills since the Custer days; Deadwood was more than merely the site of the murder of Wild Bill Hickok.

"If you examine the map," De Morès said, "you will note that the closest point on the railroad to Deadwood is the point where you are now sitting."

Pack was surprised. "What about the Central Pacific?"

"Twice as far. From here to Deadwood is only two hundred miles. There's a great deal of freight and passenger traffic in and out of the gold camps. It only needs a convenient connection with the railroad terminus here, and we'll become the gateway to those rich mines. Now I should like your advice, Arthur. I have an idea to start up a stagecoach line from here to Deadwood. What do you think?"

Pack, pleased to be made privy to such important confidential information, felt his cheeks redden with pride.

"Now, it's such an obvious idea," Pack said. "I wonder no one thought of it before."

"Every great idea is simple," said De Morès, "and every great idea appears obvious after it has been discovered. I am a man who takes only an instant to comprehend things that other men may puzzle over for years. That's why I shall be more than merely another J.P. Morgan or Andrew Carnegie or John Jacob Astor. I shall be the richest financier in the world." When he lifted his cup to drink he deftly pushed the points of his mustache out of the way with two fingers of his left hand.

Pack believed him. "Now, what will you do with all the millions you'll make here?"

"Do you know why I left the French army? I am, as you know, a graduate of St. Cyr and took my officer's training in the Saumur cavalry school. I was commissioned and I served. But I took leave of all that—because it is an army without the sense to feel shame. It is a disgrace. Its commanders have not sought revenge on Germany, they have not sought to restore the French throne—they are milksops."

Unable to sit still, De Morès swiveled his chair and pulled open a drawer. Out of it, to Pack's surprise, came a gunbelt and a holstered revolver. The dining room sideboard seemed an odd choice for an armory; but then that was part of the Marquis's genius—always doing the unexpected.

De Morès lifted the blue steel weapon out of leather. In the way he regarded the revolver when he spoke, he reminded Pack of a man taking an oath. "Upon the death of my father I shall become Duc de Vallombrosa. I am an Orleans—a royalist with the God-given aspirations of my royal bloodlines." His eyes lifted. They drilled into Pack's core. "With those millions I shall buy the French army. I'll gain control of the high command and recapture the throne of France."

"Now, may I publish that?"

"By all means. I make no secret of it." De Morès opened the revolver and looked at its loads like a soothsayer studying entrails.

Madame said gently, "Shall we serve cognac?"

De Morès snapped the thumb-gate shut. When he spun the cylinder it clicked like a rattlesnake. He enjoyed mechanisms and melodramatic gestures; it was part of his childlike charm. He said, "Cognac by all means. And one of your tunes on the pianoforte—to remind the press what an oasis we are in the wilderness."

"The press needs no reminding," Pack said; "but it is delighted by the prospect." He took one side of Madame's chair; the Marquis took the other; together they pulled it back. Madame in bustle and floor-length gown rose to her feet like a flower gracefully rising to meet the sun. As she led them into the front room Pack had to quell the impulse to see if he could span her waist with his two hands. The willowy grace of her spine was enough to make him dizzy.

There was an abrupt confusion of shattering glass and violent movement. De Morès slammed into Pack and as he tumbled toward the floor Pack heard the slam of a gunshot. It took his mind a moment to catch up. De Morès flew past him, struck Madame and knocked her to the floor. There was the loud echo of another gunshot: a rifle, somewhere outdoors. Pack realized—as he broke the fall with the flat of his hand and rolled to one side—that the two bullets had smashed the window and struck something on the interior wall.

My God.

All in the same fractured instant De Morès braced himself athwart Madame, shielding her with his body, and whipped up the revolver, which by odd Providence was still in his grasp. Pack saw him flick back the hammer and aim at the already broken window.

The angle of fire was upward; it would hit nothing but the night sky—Pack did not understand.

Another rifle bullet crashed through, breaking up more glass in the same pane, and De Morès fired swiftly—skyward, through the shattered window.

Immediately the room went pitch dark.

Then Pack understood. Concussion from the gunshot had knocked out all the lamps and candles in the room. Pack marveled: it had been very quick thinking.

He heard angry voices yelling in the night. They sounded drunk. There was a fusillade of rifle fire. Bullets whacked into the house; Pack heard them strike—*felt* their vibrations—and then at the window De Morès's revolver roared several times in the darkness: shooting, Pack supposed, at the telltale muzzle flames of those cowardly rifles in the darkness outside.

There was silence. Pack's heart raced. He heard soft voices:

De Morès: "Where are you going?"

Madame: "To get rifles."

De Morès: "Stay down."

Pack said, "I'll get them. On the porch?"

"Never mind. They've retreated."

"How do you know?"

De Morès made no answer. Everything went still. Pack held his breath. Then he heard a sudden clatter of hoofbeats—several horses running away.

De Morès: *"Sauve qui peut! . . . Ma chérie—ça va?"*

"Nothing injured but my bustle. Antoine? Are you all right?"

"Of course."

Suddenly the front door was open: a faint rectangle defined by starlight. De Morès stood outlined in it. He was making a target of himself, Pack thought—hoping to draw fire; but the cowards had fled. He saw De Morès stoop to pick up something. It rustled—a piece of paper, tied around a small rock on the porch. De Morès waited long enough for anyone to draw a bead on him, then came inside, shut the door and shoved the paper in a pocket. He fumbled about; after a moment he struck a match and held it to a lamp.

Madame said, "Such drunken lawlessness can no longer be tolerated. We must send for the sheriff." Pack helped her to her feet. She groped a bit and sat down quickly and a bit weakly on the piano bench. In the weak light she looked pale but resolute. A woman of remarkable courage, Pack thought. He endeavored to smile reassuringly but it was difficult; his pulse continued to pound, nearly deafening him.

"Sheriff Harmon is at Mandan," De Morès muttered. "One hundred and thirty miles away."

Pack shoved his hands in his pockets. He didn't want either of them to see how badly he was trembling. "Madame's right. Send for him. You can't have this riffraff laying siege to your house."

"Hardly a siege," De Morès said. "Who were they, Arthur? Roosevelt?"

Madame said sharply, "Antoine!"

Pack said, "I don't know Roosevelt, really. I couldn't say, sir."

Madame said, "It wasn't. Teedie Roosevelt? Don't be ridiculous."

The Marquis soothed his wife, stroking her hair. As if to mollify her he said, "Very well, Arthur. Who was it, then? Finnegan and his fools?"

"Now, if I had to guess—that would be my first thought. Maybe you'll find something by daylight. They must have left tracks."

"Tracks all look the same in Bad Lands clay. But we'll see what we'll see. Very well—I shall send for the sheriff, if only out of propriety." De Morès was reloading the revolver. "Where the devil are the servants?"

Madame said, "They're not soldiers, Antoine. You'll probably find them in the wine cellar—and please don't berate them."

Pack said, "Did they put a note on the porch? May I see it?"

De Morès pulled it from his pocket and handed it to Pack without a word.

Git out Or Git killt.

Pack said, "Vile cretins."

De Morès's voice was low, well modulated, controlled; he was furious. "I shall post armed guards, with orders to kill. God help the soul of any craven poltroon who places my wife in danger, for he shall find no mercy from any hand here on Earth."

Seven

Wil Dow climbed onto a fresh pony. It tried to buck him off and he ran it down into the river to cool it out.

Five minutes later on the bottomland bank he lit out in pursuit of a skittish heifer.

He rode at full gallop and his eyes fell upon a deep sinkhole immediately before him; there was nothing to do except slam both palms down onto the saddlehorn and swing himself up as high as he could on his arms. He was still kicking free of the stirrups when the horse plunged both forefeet into the chasm.

The horse went down and Wil was in flight then, an amazing sensation for a moment before he hit the clay running and couldn't keep up with his feet and toppled over, breaking the fall on one shoulder.

When he hit ground it felt as if he'd rattled the brains inside his skull.

He got up quickly, testing his joints with a reckless need to find out if any bones were broken, and was nearly caused to jump out of his boots by the earsplitting crash of a gunshot.

He wheeled to stare behind him.

Standing over the dead horse, Dutch Reuter was punching an

empty cartridge case out of his revolver. "Very fast you jump—save your balls. A cool head you have got. But next time you will try not ride a hundred-dollar horse into a leg-breaker hole, yah?"

"Sweet Jesus, you scared me half to death. You have to do that to the poor horse?"

Dutch loaded a new round into the chamber. "Both legs broke."

"How'd you know?"

"Heard them snap. Seen it." Dutch buttoned the revolver into its holster.

"Well Jesus, you scared me."

"Yah, yah. Go on, go to work. The horse dispose."

Wil Dow glanced across the river. He could see through the narrow wagon-gap they had thrashed through the dense mat of thorny brush.

Up on the knoll, visible amid the cottonwoods, Roosevelt was watching them. He had been taking pictures of the site of the Elkhorn Ranch. He must have seen Dutch shoot the horse but evidently he decided it was all right because Wil Dow saw him return underneath the hood of his tripod-supported glass-plate camera. Shaded by the stately trees it stood on the site of what soon would be the verandah, which the boss insisted upon calling the piazza—a term that seemed peculiar to his class of New Yorker; the boss pronounced the word to rhyme with a minstrel-show darky's "Yassuh."

Dutch Reuter gathered the reins in easy synchronization with his swift rise to the saddle. He loped off toward the horse corrals. Wil Dow stripped the tack off his dead horse and was trying to decide what to do with the carcass when Uncle Bill Sewall emerged on horseback from the trees, driving a little gather of beeves. "You shoot that horse?"

Wil Dow had to explain what had happened.

Sewall grunted. "Killed it and left it. What's he think you are—his servant? These Westerners have got no manners at all. That Dutchman offends me. People here go ragged and as dirty as they can be. Can you point out to me one social advantage of the Bad Lands? Half the time I don't even know when Sunday comes." Uncle Bill wasted no opportunity to express his opinion of Dakota, which was a jaundiced one at the best of times. He allowed no one to go ignorant of the fact that he saw no future in this God-forsaken country.

"Dutch is all right." Wil Dow was eager to learn cowboying and he was learning it from Dutch, whom Mr. Roosevelt had hired on the recommendation of the storekeeper and had brought back from town to break horses and assist in the building of the ranch.

There was a puckered two-inch scar below Dutch's left temple—souvenir of perhaps a fight or a tumble from a horse, or a woman. He had unkempt hair and a greying beard wilder and thicker than Uncle Bill Sewall's, and bloodshot little eyes that looked weak but seemed to miss nothing. He was a lumpy sack of a man with no grace whatever except in the confident economy with which he did his work.

Sewall complained continually about Dutch—they'd even had to teach the barbarian to use the outhouse. Not that he didn't know how, but he preferred open-air squatting; he said nobody should have to put up with the stink inside an outhouse—and he didn't seem to care who might be around to see him relieve his bowels on the open ground.

For all that, Dutch was a first-class plainsman and Wil Dow found him an excellent teacher.

In the afternoon a young horseman came along the river with a worried smile. Dutch watched him approach and said out of the side of his mouth, "Riley Luffsey. You heard of him?"

"No."

"He is good boy."

Inasmuch as that was more of a compliment than Wil Dow had heard Dutch utter about anybody, he watched the newcomer with interest.

It was customary to invite a visitor into camp; this was done, and Roosevelt came down from the knoll. "We have met." He said it in a neutral way, leaving Luffsey the choice between friendship and bellicosity.

"Upriver," Luffsey acknowledged. "We was cutting the Markee's fence. I cut two more today." He watched to see how Roosevelt would take that.

Roosevelt said, "You're the chap who gave that Lunatic a race. The fastest runner in Dakota, they were saying."

It seemed to please Luffsey. "There's not even an Indian can outrun me, sir."

After an exchange of pleasantries about the weather, the condition of the trail from Medora and two sightings of game, Luffsey turned to Dutch Reuter. "I don't know if you heard—some boys with rifles punched some holes in the château the other night."

There followed Roosevelt's interested "Great Scott!"

"Shot the house up?" Dutch seemed delighted.

Roosevelt said, "Anyone hurt?"

"Naw. Only the Markee's pride. And his wife busted her bustle." Luffsey snickered.

Roosevelt said, "I'm not sure I find that amusing."

Dutch said in a careful voice, "Who did it? They know?"

"Johnny Goodall hired some Indian and they found some tracks but they got lost in the river. Could've been anybody. Nobody knows a thing." Wil Dow saw the private-seeming glance that the visitor traded with Dutch. There was an undercurrent here that he had trouble tracing.

Luffsey said, "The Markee's posted guards all around the place now. Forted up like you wouldn't believe. Says he's just protecting his wife and babies—but they got enough guns for a middlin' war."

Shrewd old Uncle Bill Sewall said, "You rode thirty miles down here to tell us about that?"

Luffsey showed his palms in a gesture of candor. "They are saying Jerry Paddock told the Markee that old Dutch here was one of the shooters." He said to Dutch, "Paddock's had it in for you. He told the Markee how you were in the Prussian army—how you fought in the Franco-Prussian War against France."

Dutch Reuter was indignant. "Me? Me? Hell, I never in any army been. Never in no war fought. Me? Hell."

Luffsey was astonished. "Dutch, I was in Bob Roberts's place—I *heard* you boast about your soldiering."

Dutch blandly said, "Such a thing I not possibly could have said. Because it is not true."

Luffsey said, "You were drunk."

Dutch said, "Ah, well then," and blessed them with a big beaming smile.

Uncle Bill Sewall uttered a disgusted sigh.

Young Riley Luffsey said to Dutch, "I thought you'd want to

know. They think you had a hand in it and they could be waiting next time you go into town. And by the way—any man hires you ought to know it's asking for trouble with the Markee."

That last was addressed to Dutch Reuter but it was meant for Roosevelt. Wil Dow watched his employer with close interest.

Roosevelt studied Luffsey's callow face. There was a certain gloom in his face when he said, "I'm not worried about whether or not I may place myself in Mr. De Morès's bad graces. Several days ago I had a word with him about a matter of possible contention and I believe I have made my neutrality clear to him and headed off any possible differences between us. There's plenty of room for everyone in this vast country."

Dutch Reuter said, "About that you not can be sure. If you wish me to be on my way—"

"Nonsense. You have a job here as long as you want it. I won't be intimidated by rumors."

Riley Luffsey flashed a quick nervous smile. "Well it's nice to see you gents." He got on his horse and rode back the way he had come, leaving Wil Dow a bit mystified and a bit uneasy.

An hour later Roosevelt came down into the meadow where the three men were putting the last corral rails into their posts. The boss was leading a pack animal on which sizable bundles depended. His own saddle was double-scabbarded—rifle and shotgun. He rode a big blaze-faced sorrel gelding he'd bought from A.C. Huidekoper; the horse was called Manitou and seemed to have taken a liking to Roosevelt—it had learned to follow the boss around and nibble at his elbow until the boss gave up the crust of bread he kept ready.

"We need meat for the camp," he said. "I leave you men to continue construction."

Wil Dow said, "If you need help—"

"Thank you. I don't care for company." Roosevelt rode away.

The log house went up quickly. Indoors it had the shine and scent of new lumber. By the time the boss returned from his solitary hunt there was a roof for his head and he expressed satisfaction.

There always seemed to be sick cattle to be nurtured and bogged cattle to be freed. Wil Dow took his lessons from Dutch Reuter and there was time enough in each day for playfulness as well: he learned to spin his riata loop and ride backwards and wrestle calves.

When the water was at all high, they found it was not possible to ford the river. Roosevelt had ordered a Mackinaw boat. It was shipped in by rail from St. Paul. They had rented a wagon from Jerry Paddock to haul the boat out to the ranch. The flat-bowed scow was no more than a skiff but it was big enough to take three or four men across the river and stout enough to withstand the severe currents.

The boss had been in the Bad Lands a couple months by now and had spent much of the time out on his own, living off the land. He seemed to be gathering strength bit by bit; he seemed to Wil Dow a little less dispirited as the weeks went by. But he still preferred his own company and he remained subdued by comparison with his old self.

Finally one day the three of them—Roosevelt and Dow and Sewall—left Dutch behind to tend the ranch while they rode up on the escarpment to bring down outlying strays and to stop by Mrs. Reuter's place so that Roosevelt could collect his new buckskin suit.

They found the woman in the vegetable garden sitting on a stool with a churn secured between her knees. It contained cream from the cow; she swung the handle sturdily, conserving strength for the long patient work of making the butter and then kneading and bricking it.

Three Indians on tangle-maned ponies were rushing away from the shack.

"Sioux," Mrs. Reuter said. "They were hungry so I fed them. They get an average of one good meal a week. But they heard you coming."

"Why," Roosevelt said, "what are they afraid of?"

"Axelby tried to steal their horses. They caught him and got their horses back."

Bill Sewall said, "Who's Axelby?"

"Neighbor of yours. Twelve, fifteen miles upriver. And I guess you could say he was a horse thief."

Wil Dow perked up. "They scalp him?"

"No," Mrs. Reuter said, "they just disarmed him and turned him loose. Now they're making a run for the tribe before anyone can come after them. I think they were afraid you might be Axelby with a posse. There's a big party of them camped six or seven miles north of here. I think they've been hunting in the Killdeers."

Roosevelt said to Sewall, "Stealing horses seems to be an Indian game. One steals another's horse, the other steals it back."

Mrs. Reuter said, "It used to be more serious than that but we have got them scared half to death. It's not fair at all. I told them I didn't see why they should have let that man go. What makes it right for Axelby to steal an Indian's horse if it's a crime to steal a white man's? I told them if they ever see Axelby again, they ought to take *his* horse—and if he objects, kill him. I'd never tell on them!" She set the churn aside and stood up. She looked heavy, as if she felt full with the weight of herself. "Come inside, then."

When Dutch Reuter had heard their destination he had told Wil this much: he used to live in the soddy with that woman but she had sassed him and he had set out to beat her and she had damn near broke his face with a stove-lid lifter and called in a couple of passing Indians to haul him away.

Since then Dutch had left her peacefully in full possession of the house. He advised Wil to give that woman wide berth.

Now Wil Dow heard Mrs. Reuter's version. She had ejected her husband, she said, after "such profanity as I never expect to hear again."

She hadn't intended to settle for the first man who asked. She had wanted to wait for a man who would talk to her, who would listen to her, who would pull back her chair for her. But times were hard. Dutch had got half drunk and proposed marriage—and she'd had no other offers. "I am a plain woman. But I have made a good life for myself here. It is a good place." The abrupt smile, cozy and jolly, illuminated her face.

Roosevelt came out of the back room dressed in his new suit. Wil Dow's eyes opened wide with admiration. He couldn't recall ever having seen such soft golden buckskin. The fringed yoke and the cut of it made Roosevelt look taller and more powerful—handsomer all round.

Uncle Bill Sewall said without enthusiasm, "You'll be the most beautiful cowboy in the corral."

Mrs. Reuter enjoyed provocation. While Roosevelt was admiring his suit she poked his arm. "I want to know why a woman can't vote in this free country. You are a politician. I want you to look me in the eye and tell me why I can't vote."

Roosevelt seemed pleased to be asked: he seemed both amused and serious. "Well I'm no longer in politics, you know. But I still have opinions. I feel it is exactly as much a right of women as of men to vote. I believe in suffrage for women, because I think they are fit for it. But the important point—man or woman—is to treat suffrage as a duty. A vote is like a rifle. The mere possession of it will no more benefit men and women not sufficiently developed to use it than the possession of rifles will turn untrained Egyptian fellaheen into soldiers. You see I believe, for women as well as for men, more in the duty of doing well and wisely with the ballot than in the naked right to cast the ballot."

"If we women had the vote we wouldn't be so ready to send young men off to war."

Roosevelt said, "As to that, madame, war is not necessarily a bad thing. It can be beneficial when it encourages people to forget their selfish concerns and lend themselves to great national effort."

"My father was killed in the war," she replied. "I hope your outfit suits you."

Roosevelt studied himself in the mirror she'd handed him. "It's a splendid suit. Splendid." Whether or not he realized he'd been chastised, he said no more to Mrs. Reuter about the benefits of war.

It was too late to ride home; they camped for the night not far from Mrs. Reuter's.

"How do you spell Audubon? One *o* or two?"

Sewall said, "Two *u*'s, one *o*."

"I'm a dreadful speller."

Roosevelt could read things at amazingly high speed while simultaneously carrying on a running conversation. He seemed to see and hear everything—at least he had strong opinions about everything. Wil Dow saw him find endless magic in the books against which he squinted every evening in the inadequate light of lantern or campfire. He had an especial passion for natural science books and made notes as he read them.

Roosevelt considered the page on which he was writing. He seemed agitated with a hint of his old enthusiasm. "D'you know,

Bill, narrow ideas cannot survive on these prairies. This is a wholesome place to dream in."

Sewall only grunted; but Wil Dow was pleased to see even so small a sign of recovery in Roosevelt.

Suddenly, for no particular reason, it struck him that Roosevelt had no sidewhiskers this season; he thought back and decided Roosevelt must have shaved them off in 1883.

The pencil scratched across the tablet. Roosevelt was writing a book about ranching. It was a serious endeavor; he had already written a book that had been published—a history of the naval battles of the War of 1812—and now it seemed his literary ambitions were revived. Maybe that was another good sign.

After a while he set the notebook aside and took out his letter-writing paper. He had received several letters along with the last batch of possibles that Dutch had picked up at Joe Ferris's store. Most of them, Wil gathered, were from his sister Bamie. Now Roosevelt opened one of the letters, consulted it briefly and began to set down his response. A soft smile hovered around his mouth.

That night he didn't seem to wheeze as much as usual.

In the morning Roosevelt impishly decided they must sate their curiosity with a visit to the Indian camp that Mrs. Reuter had told them about. Wil Dow nearly danced with eagerness.

As they broke camp, Dutch Reuter appeared from the coulees and joined them without comment; it was as if he had been spying on them from afar in order to join them as soon as they were clear of his formidable *frau*.

Dutch rolled a quirly from his makin's. He offered it to Roosevelt, who said, "I have a gentleman's distaste for tobacco." Dutch, not offended in the least, kindled his snoose and puffed away with content. They rode along together and presently Sewall saw something out yonder on the plain. "What's that? Big rock?"

Wil Dow searched the distance and found it—a white spire, perhaps a pyramid.

Dutch studied it a while before he replied. "Tepee, I think."

It was evident by the way he squinted at the horizon that Roosevelt couldn't see what they were talking about. He yanked off his glasses and polished them.

They rode forward for a good half hour before Dutch said quietly to Wil Dow, "How you find her?"

"Your wife?"

"Yah, yah."

Wil Dow was uncertain how to reply. Finally he said, "Fine stout woman."

"For me she don't pine," Dutch said. "That's good."

Wil Dow grinned. "You miss her, do you?"

Dutch licked his fingers before he pinched out the lit end of the cigarette stub between thumb and finger. He dropped the remains into his tobacco pouch and did not look at Wil Dow at all.

In the end the white pyramid turned out to be an Indian tent, shut up against the world. Dutch clapped his hands in lieu of knocking. There was no reply. He let his call sing out in English and in French. After having observed those amenities he lifted the flap and looked inside.

The smell hit them immediately. Dutch said, "*Mein Gott.*"

An Indian man lay curled up on his side on a blanket. Roosevelt said, "Is he dead?"

Old Bill Sewall said, "Dead and ripe. A 'good Indian'—isn't that what they say? The only good Indian?"

Roosevelt dismounted and crouched for a better look. "I say. He doesn't seem very old."

Wil Dow said, "I expect he took sick and the rest of them left him here."

Uncle Bill Sewall said, "They just left a sick man behind to die?"

Roosevelt said, "I understand that's their way."

Uncle Bill backed away, making a face against the smell. "Barbaric."

Wil Dow said, "I don't know. It makes sense, you think about it."

Roosevelt was holding his nose, still hunkered to peer inside. "What tribe is he?"

"Teton Sioux," Dutch said. "East from they usual range." He scanned the horizons. "If there be trouble, better not you take cover. Before you know, crawl up on you they do. Better stay in open—they coming, you see them—with your rifle you must make a show. You good rifle shot, you scare them. Most of them very poor shots unless inside bow-and-arrow range they get."

* * *

Dutch yipped and whooped as they approached the encampment. It was considered good manners, he explained, to announce yourself as loudly as possible. It showed you had nothing to hide.

There were quite a few lodges on the high ground. They threw long shadows in the evening sunlight. Indians were converging on foot and horseback from the day's hunt, some of them dragging the game they'd killed.

Their outfits varied. Dutch identified them as Sioux and Mandans and Gros Ventres. "Friendly ones," he said.

"I remind you Sitting Bull surrendered only three years ago," Uncle Bill Sewall growled.

Dutch Reuter said, "No war today. Is etiquette to do a bit of trading." He winked at Wil Dow, which made Wil feel better: it restored the confidence that had been draining out of him as they drew closer to the crowd of Indians who were emerging before them. Dutch knew what he was talking about. He was a genuine specimen of a frontiersman. He had been mail carrier and scout and free trader and hunter ever since he had come to America. He said he had been shot with bullets seven times and with arrows five times, and once had his head split open with a tomahawk. Of course he had also said he'd been in the Prussian army. But he'd been drunk on that occasion. From what Wil had seen, Dutch had plenty of scars to prove his injuries.

A group of women came forward, took their horses by the bridles and led them quite a way through the encampment. The women wore beaded deerskin dresses. The inhabitants of the camp regarded the visitors with an interest intense enough to set Wil Dow's nerves on edge but still he had the presence of mind to note the elaborate variety of color and styles amid the Indians' costumery and the intricate designs painted on the slopes of the leather tepees. The colors were as rich as fine paintings in the dying sunlight.

There was a great deal of chattering among the Indians; it dispelled at once Wil Dow's previous understanding of them as laconic savages who grunted at intervals. These people were as animated and talkative as ladies at a Sunday social.

Naturally it was Roosevelt who commanded the most attention. The Indians regarded him with admiring astonishment. Some of them squinted and shaded their eyes, pretending to be blinded by his regalia. By their reaction they incited Wil Dow to have another look at his employer's outfit, which included not only Mrs. Reuter's fringed buckskin suit, which he was breaking in, but also a wealthy New Yorker's idea of wilderness wear: alligator boots, silver spurs, leather chaps, huge beaver sombrero, engraved Colt revolver in an elaborately tooled holster on a carved belt with an enormous silver buckle upon which was sculpted the head of a snarling bear, and silver-decorated hunting knife from Tiffany in New York.

Then there was his horse Manitou—as handsome a beast as could have set foot in these people's midst. Wil Dow was not pleased by the fascination with which the Indians examined the big gelding.

Undismayed, Roosevelt dismounted and went about energetically examining everything with the belligerent scowling interest of a new dog sniffing his way around a pack's home ground.

Wil Dow followed Dutch's lead: he dismounted with the rifle in his hand and kept it there.

With cartridges and gold pieces they purchased moccasins, war plumes and cured buckskins from a happy old pirate called Sitting Owl. Roosevelt kept going back to a red blanket with five parallel black stripes. "How much does he want for it?"

"Buffalo blanket?" Dutch spoke rapidly to Sitting Owl and the old Indian talked back to him. Dutch's English might be atrocious but it appeared he could speak Gros Ventre as well as any Indian; Sitting Owl seemed to have no trouble conversing with him. There was a great deal of headshaking and shouting.

"He says worth twenty gold dollars. More like four or five, you ask me."

"What about that robe?"

The Gros Ventre buffalo robe was beautiful, Wil thought. It was painted with quills and flowers. Sitting Owl said he had been offered twenty-five dollars but Dutch argued amiably with him until he gave it up for eight, being hard up—"I am a deadbroke Indian"—and the blanket for five. They bought war plumes and a mountain lion skin.

To settle a matter in his mind Roosevelt asked Sitting Owl which white men had discovered the Bad Lands first—French? Spanish? English?

After several Indians broke into raucous laughter, Dutch translated the Indian's reply: "'Then it's true—You think nothing can exist before by a white man it be discovered.'"

Then Dutch said, "Horses you want to buy? A bargain here." You could buy Indian ponies for forty to eighty dollars; that was good business if you were capable of training the animals because anywhere in cattle country a more-or-less tamed saddle horse could go for ninety-five to a hundred and twenty-five dollars.

But Roosevelt said, "We've more than enough horses to keep tame as it is."

Then there was the matter of scalps. Sitting Owl brought them out, appended to a pole; they were dried and shrunk down to a few inches across. Among the dark ones it was hard not to take note of a single scalp of pale sandy hair. It was about the hue of Roosevelt's. Dutch said, "Five dollar. Don't buy. Cheaper take one yourself, if you want one."

Roosevelt said, "I don't think I want one that badly, thank you."

Uncle Bill Sewall's long red whiskers captured the interest of Sitting Owl, who clearly was a leader of fashion among the Indian dandies; he wore beaded finery and his hands were bejeweled with brass trade rings. He looked at Sewall's whiskers, felt of them, then began to braid them. Sewall dourly let him work while Wil Dow urgently watched Dutch Reuter to find out whether he should be alarmed. Dutch didn't seem concerned. The Indians were laughing, taking it in what Wil Dow hoped was good nature. After Sitting Owl got Uncle Bill's whiskers braided he reached for a very large knife and that was when Sewall grabbed him by the top of the head quick and lofted his free hand threateningly.

Sitting Owl shrank back; the other Indians laughed—but the crowd was pressing in closer and Wil Dow tasted fear.

Dutch said in a calm way, "Wil, the deadfall yonder—you see?"

He glanced nervously toward a fallen tree beyond the camp. "I see it. Why?"

"Shoot roots off."

"You better do that yourself, Dutch."

"You the best shot."

"My hands are shaking something awful."

"You shoot, you steady all right."

He looked at Roosevelt and saw the big grin with which the boss regarded the Indians and remembered what Roosevelt had said to him about being afraid.

Dutch was talking fast to Sitting Owl, who drew himself up and with immense dignity accepted the loan of Dutch's rifle, aimed it imperiously at the distant fallen tree and blazed away so furiously that Wil's ears rang.

Afterward the old Indian had to step aside to peer past the great cloud of black powder smoke.

As far as Wil Dow could see, the tree remained intact. He lifted his own rifle, smiled confidently at the crowd, tried to will his hands to hold still, and squeezed off a shot. It knocked the tip off a root of the deadfall. An admiring mutter ran through the crowd. He moved a pace and fired again. When this shot also chipped wood from the target, the Indians went altogether silent.

Roosevelt said, "Excellent shooting, old fellow. First class."

Wil Dow knocked another branch off with another bullet. His heart felt hollow. But Dutch said, "Enough, that is," and that seemed to be the end of it: the crowd eased back and everyone was all smiles.

Dutch reclaimed his rifle from Sitting Owl. He said to Wil Dow, "Yah, yah, first class, yah. No red fellow fixin' with us to mess now. Good boy."

Wil smiled, pleased by Dutch's praise. Sitting Owl smiled right back at him, showing a mouth full of cracked teeth and blackened gums.

Dutch talked briefly with the old boy while he reloaded the magazine. Sitting Owl grinned his ugly grin and led them into his lodge.

An old woman tended a fire inside the tepee. She bowed her way back toward the entrance flap, which evidently was the place of lowest honor, while Sitting Owl moved all the way to the back of the lodge where he sat down beside a tripod from which dangled what looked like a canvas poke. Dutch pointed to it and said, "Sacred medicine bundle. Best not touch that." Sitting Owl pounded his fist on the robe that formed the floor of the lodge and Dutch sat down, indicating they all should follow suit. Sitting Owl spoke. Dutch said, "We to take supper are invited."

Roosevelt said, "But they have very little food."

"Just so."

"Ask if we may share out our food with them—if it's not a breach of etiquette."

Dutch hesitated. Roosevelt said, "Go ahead, ask him. Be very polite. Tell him I don't know their ways—tell him we mean no offense."

Dutch spoke more slowly than before. He spread his hands and smiled through his beard, and when the Indian replied, Dutch eased back with relief. "Used to be insult. But not these days."

"We are poor Indian," Sitting Owl said. "Hungry Indian."

And so they ate tough fried meat from a pan and afterward they were invited to observe the council. The long pipe of peace was smoked. Sewall passed; Wil Dow eagerly took a whiff and was instantly dizzy. The Sioux sang their songs, accompanied by drums, and the visitors watched them dance. Roosevelt's eyes were merry behind the dusty glasses; he grinned with pleasure; and Wil Dow thought, *Now I'm a frontiersman for certain!*

Eight

The beard seemed overnight to have thickened, darkened, become respectable. It pleased Pack.

Riley Luffsey stood hipshot against a hitching rail. A folded newspaper jutted from his back pocket. He smiled hesitantly. Pack nodded a greeting to him and strode catty-corner across the intersection into Joe Ferris's store and found the proprietor in an apron waiting on a customer. When the transaction was completed Joe said to Pack, "One more good month and I'll turn a profit."

"Good for you."

"Swede could have succeeded if he'd stood his ground."

"Now, Swede never had your gumption," Pack told him.

"He never had Theodore Roosevelt's financial backing."

"The Marquis isn't happy about that."

"Isn't he," said Joe Ferris without inflection.

"He feels it's an affront for Roosevelt to support the competition."

"Plenty of room in this town for two mercantiles—we keep each other honest. Or we try to. Hard to do sometimes, with Paddock chalking up cutthroat low prices for the goods he stole from Swede."

"I've said it before, Joe. Prove that, or be more careful of the accusations you toss around."

Joe Ferris only made a face. "Train's coming."

"How do you know?"

"Feel it in the floor."

Pack was about to dispute him when he heard the wail of the engine's steam whistle. Joe grinned wickedly at him.

Pack said, "The soles of your feet are more observant than mine."

"I hear Sheriff Harmon's on the train."

"You hear that in the soles of your feet too?"

"It was on the telegraph."

"I saw the wire. I still don't believe he'll turn up. He's been consistently bashful about investigating any crimes against the Marquis. I wouldn't expect him to lose a lot of sleep just because the man's family was nearly killed and his house all shot up." Pack felt thorough disgust. "Isn't it scandalous to treat our leading citizen this way? Who does this pipsqueak sheriff think he is?"

"May be he thinks he's his own man, and not some Frenchman's lackey." Joe untied his apron. "Your beard looks like a bird's nest. Whyn't you shave the thing off? Come on—let's go see the fun."

They found the Marquis De Morès riding back and forth before the station in leather leggings and a yellow flannel shirt with a bright red scarf about his neck. He carried in his hand a French breech loader and in his belt a Bowie knife and two long .45 Colt revolvers. The high-strung horse sidestepped away and the Marquis, by not speaking to Pack, indicated his haughty disapproval of Pack's choice of companion.

Quite a few citizens were hanging about. Everyone had heard about the telegram. Even blacksmith Dan McKenzie was on the platform pretending to study a timetable. Bob Roberts scratched his sidewhiskers and gave Pack a friendly nod. A block away Jerry Paddock—dark, sallow, dissipated—watched from a safe distance.

As the train made its noisy way into town Pack was astonished to see three men ride boldly forward on horseback. They came across the tracks not far ahead of the engine and wheeled in line abreast to face the Marquis.

They were the three who reputedly had shot up the château: Redhead Finnegan, Frank O'Donnell and Riley Luffsey.

"Got the *cojones* of a brass spittoon," muttered Joe Ferris.

The three horsemen carried rifles across their saddlebows and ostensibly they were cold sober.

The Marquis watched them approach. His chest swelled.

Something stirred in the far corner of Pack's vision. Finnegan caught it too, for he turned his head as he steadied the horse, and the moment was so still that even at this distance Pack heard him say lazily, "Stay put, Jerry."

At the door of his store, Paddock stopped dead. His shoulders lifted. He turned slowly to show his face.

"Just stay put," Finnegan said again.

A portly man in a brown suit descended the train's steps and pulled back the lapel of his coat to display the badge on his vest, as if inviting anyone who had business with the law to step forward. He stood blinking like a slow-witted owl until the Marquis De Morès reined his horse thither. "Sheriff G.W. Harmon?"

"I'm his brother. Henry Harmon, Deputy Sheriff. Who're you? The famous Markee?"

"I see. Not only does the High Sheriff regard our business in Medora as being of such low interest as to spend more than sixty days in responding to a request for assistance, but he can't even bother to come in person."

"He's right busy. Anyways we didn't think it was a matter of almighty urgency to come down here. Nobody was hurt, was they?"

"My house was fired upon by men with rifles. Cowards firing from the night."

The Marquis was looking straight at Finnegan when he spoke. Finnegan, fifty feet distant, displayed no reaction that Pack could see.

The Marquis said, "It was only through good luck and quick action that my wife and my children and Mr. Packard here and my own life were spared."

"Not to mention a houseful of servants," said Joe Ferris acerbically.

The Marquis paid him no attention. His righteous anger was directed elsewhere for the moment. He said to Deputy Harmon, "I've sought to charge these men with attempted murder. But you don't regard that as a 'matter of almighty urgency.'"

"I sure do like them bright colors you're wearin'. Anybody identify the shooter or shooters?"

"I know who they are. Those three men right there. Finnegan, Luffsey, O'Donnell." The Marquis pronounced their names as if he were reading from a list at a memorial ceremony for war dead.

The deputy regarded the three accused men as if he had not noticed them before. His eyebrows arched high under his hatbrim as he made a show of studying the three. It was clear—comically obvious—that he would have quit right then and got back on the train if it wouldn't have looked bad.

They sat their horses like figures on a frieze. Finnegan did not stir at all. O'Donnell made no motion except to cock his rifle with as much noise as he could make. Luffsey showed a slight nervous grin. When Pack caught his eye the kid gave a nervous apologetic little shrug of his shoulders.

Up-street, Jerry Paddock looked on with hooded eyes and, no doubt, a gun under his undertaker's coat.

Joe Ferris took an involuntary step back and bumped into Pack.

Pack felt half strangled by quivering tension. He prepared to drop flat.

The deputy's voice broke in, unnaturally mild. "Anybody see these men do the purported crime?"

The Marquis said, "They've been heard boasting of it in the saloons."

"Heard by who? You?"

"I don't habituate saloons."

"They sign confessions?"

"Don't be a complete ass."

Deputy Harmon made a show of examining the three hunters and their rifles and their stony faces.

Finally the law man said, "If nobody seen them do it, and they ain't volunteered no formal confession, they ain't a whole lot the law can do here."

The Marquis's horse skittered back and forth. He controlled his temper with what Pack felt was admirable restraint. "Let me just ask you this, since even under these ridiculous circumstances it is still my intent to abide by local custom and law. What course of action do you recommend I take?"

"Why, shoot," Harmon said.

"Yes?"

"Shoot. Shoot, man. Somebody shoots at you, shoot back."

"And that is how you advise me?"

Deputy Harmon grinned. "Sure is."

Finnegan grinned back at him.

Suddenly Pack understood that Deputy Harmon and Redhead Finnegan were friends.

The Marquis said, "Suppose *I* advise *you* to arrest the men."

"And if they kill me," Henry Harmon said, "what do you advise me to do then?"

Riley Luffsey snickered. The Marquis's head snapped toward him and for a moment Pack was certain the shooting was about to commence but the Marquis only drew a deep breath and said with equanimity to the craven deputy, "If they kill you, then I and my men will consider ourselves deputized and will prevent the murderers' escaping. You may be assured of that."

Harmon pretended to consider that.

Pack heard a low fluttering sound. It barely reached his ears. A moment went by before he realized it was a chuckle of amusement from the throat of Jerry Paddock.

Deputy Harmon exchanged knowing glances again with Finnegan. Then he turned without hurry and stepped back aboard the train just as it pulled away from the platform.

The three ruffians gave the Marquis plenty of time to act, should he be so foolish. Redhead Finnegan's hatbrim lifted and turned as he looked past the Marquis. "Come on, then, Jerry. You want to start a ball?"

As isolated as if he were quarantined, Paddock spread his open hands wide, like a dark preacher to his flock. He was grinning wickedly.

The three riders presented their backs to the Marquis and rode away at an insolently slow gait. Luffsey rode tall and straight. Pack felt, not for the first time, that there was a good deal to be admired in that youngster and it was a shame he had elected to take up with such low companions.

The Marquis glared at their backs with high indignation. "Vile cowardly vermin!"

They heard it. Pack saw Luffsey's back stiffen: Luffsey looked at

Finnegan, then O'Donnell. But neither of them responded. They continued to ride slowly away.

Joe Ferris showed Pack a troubled brooding scowl.

De Morès then decided—sensibly, Pack thought—to ignore the entire matter. It was the magnanimous act of a truly civilized gentleman. Pack tried to explain this to Joe Ferris but Joe only jeered. Anyway the Marquis was entertaining visitors—Russian royalty. Surrounded by servants and hounds he took them away on a hunting expedition out toward the Yellowstone.

For once his wife did not accompany the Marquis. One of the children had a touch of fever and she remained to minister to the baby. Within a few days the child had recovered, and Madame la Marquise was seen more often riding along the bluffs and through the town. Pack's heart leaped whenever he saw her.

On a hot Saturday late in August he rented a horse and was saddling in the livery corral when he saw two riders enter town: the lady Medora and, of all people, Theodore Roosevelt. They were riding together stirrup to stirrup. Pack's jaw dropped.

"I've been showing Mr. Roosevelt our landscape," she said unabashedly to Pack.

"And I've been admiring Mrs. De Morès's paintings," Roosevelt said.

Pack said stiffly, "I'm on my way to Eaton's. There's a hunt today."

"I know," said Roosevelt. "I've been invited. I'm afraid we shall be late."

Medora gave Roosevelt the bounty of her smile. "Very nice to have seen you again."

"The pleasure's entirely mine, madame." Roosevelt touched his hatbrim.

Pack, besotted with suspicions, now saw it right before him. Why, they were hiding it right out in the open. He marveled at their boldness.

Of course now that they were in town tact imposed an absolute modesty on whatever it was that they had between them. Pack could not bring himself to give it a name; but it took no great leap of imagination to envision the deep flood of feeling that must be concealed behind the polite smiles with which they regarded each other on this public occasion.

He felt befuddled. No matter how contrary women might be, he had difficulty believing what the events implied. It was beyond credence that there could be anything truly unseemly in the lady Medora's disposition toward Roosevelt. Not only was her husband handsome, gallant and titled—while Roosevelt was unprepossessing at best—but it had been clear from the first moment of her arrival in the Bad Lands that she worshipped the Marquis with an adoring and unquestioning passion.

Still, it was possible that, as she was from New York, she might have acquired an inappropriate sense of Theodore Roosevelt's importance and power. Women, Pack had observed, sometimes had such propensities. And if that was the case, was it possible that Roosevelt could have been so caddish as to have played upon those strings?

Leaving no answers in her wake, Madame la Marquise rode away. Dan McKenzie came out of the livery and said sarcastically to Pack, "D'you think she can cook?"

Pack scowled at the ill-mannered oaf. Roosevelt did more than that. He dismounted behind McKenzie and gripped his shoulder. When the blacksmith turned, Roosevelt said, "Apologize for your tone, sir."

McKenzie only grinned. Perhaps it wasn't for Roosevelt to know that McKenzie's preferred answer to everything was the hammer or the fist—two objects that were nearly interchangeable in McKenzie's lexicon—but Roosevelt was about to learn it; and Pack took a certain sly satisfaction in being witness to the dude's lesson.

McKenzie said, "What'd you say?"

"Apologize."

McKenzie, still grinning, hauled a roundhouse left up from hip level. What happened then was odd. It appeared to Pack that Roosevelt, flinching from the blow, must have tripped over his own bootheel; in any event McKenzie's powerful swing sailed over the dude's head and before McKenzie could recover his balance, Roosevelt hit him at the hinge of the jaw.

It happened so fast Pack wasn't sure what he had seen, but McKenzie—twice the dude's size—was down and then Roosevelt was helping the man up. "Go to the trough and wash yourself.

When you're in the presence of a lady, henceforth conduct yourself like a gentleman—or suffer the consequences."

McKenzie's eyes narrowed. Roosevelt said, "I studied boxing with the master prizefighter John Long."

"Aagh," McKenzie said, disbelieving it. "One lucky punch—I wasn't looking."

"If you'd care for a match I shall accommodate you at any suitable time and place. Here and now will do, if you like."

Madame was two blocks distant, riding away; she had noticed none of it. Pack felt vaguely gratified: at least Roosevelt's brazen act of fraudulent chivalry hadn't impressed her.

McKenzie looked down upon Roosevelt. "Hell, I ain't going to pick on a man your size."

"As you wish. The choice is yours."

McKenzie shook his head in a display of exasperated disgust, glanced at Pack and walked back into the stable.

Roosevelt got back on his horse. "If we're both bound for the Custer Trail, I should be pleased to have your company."

Pack could think of no suitable grounds for refusal. He rode along southward with the four-eyed dude. To cover his confusion he said, "Now, the Republicans seem in serious disarray. What do you think?"

"Don't ask me about politics. I'm out of that. I've far more interest in the coming round-up than in politics—the round-up's far more respectable."

Theodore Roosevelt, political apostate. Pack wondered if the ridiculous man realized how pompous he appeared, all decked out in his pretense to have cornered the market on moral absolutes.

But then, to be perfectly honest, was that any worse than going along from day to day like a mere witness, devoid of the passionate commitments of involvement? Pack daily threw himself with increasing resentment against the bars of his cage of inaction. He saw everything; he participated in nothing. It seemed life had not begun for him yet. He was nothing but a spectator. *Nothing serious will ever happen to me*, he complained to himself.

Howard Eaton's front yard was decorated with chunks of petrified logs, cold to the touch.

Wolves had been taking down livestock. Some of the ranchers

had organized a Dakota version of an ancient tradition: a rugged frontier interpretation of a fox hunt, with grey wolves as the prey. In place of red coats the hunters wore whatever seemed practical. A.C. Huidekoper kept a pack of wolfhounds he'd imported all the way from Imperial Russia, and on these high social occasions they were set loose to lead the spirited horsemen at breakneck pace across the Bad Lands.

This time the crowd was swelled by a dozen visiting Eastern sportsmen. Most of them seemed bemused; but the local hunters were in foul spirits because some practical joker had found out where Huidekoper planned to start his wolf hunt, and had dragged the skin of a fresh-killed wolf from that spot directly back to Eaton's well. The hounds had led the crowd directly home to the well, where Pack and Roosevelt arrived to find the hunters dismounted and crowded around. A few bloody claws had been found at the rim and a man had to be lowered into the well. Now he climbed out and shook his head; he'd found nothing amiss at the bottom.

A wrangler came out of the barn with a shamefaced countenance. "There's a wolf hide in the loft. All tore up and dusty. Better not bring it down here while those dogs around."

Huidekoper—a squire out of Fielding—assisted his handlers in pulling the dogs away from the well; he said, "This has Jerry Paddock's stamp on it."

Pack said, "Now, I doubt that. Jerry has no sense of humor."

"The man who did this has no sense of humor," Huidekoper retorted, and stamped into the Custer Trail ranch house, undoubtedly to proceed directly to the bar.

Pack watched with satisfaction and amusement when two of the boys asked Roosevelt if he'd like to help out with the acorn harvesting. The dude fell for it, fool that he was. Huidekoper came out of the house with a drink. He and Pack trailed along at a discreet distance when the boys took Roosevelt to the pigpen and handed him a long stout pole. "Now you pole the hogs with this . . ."

"What the devil has this got to do with harvesting acorns?"

"Well sir, everybody knows pigs just love acorn shells. Now you just take that pole and stick it up the pig's hind end and hold him up so he can reach the acorns . . ."

Roosevelt blinked rapidly, then after a long interval burst into a hearty peal of laughter that struck Pack as being embarrassingly false. "By George, you fellows nearly had me there!"

Huidekoper took Pack away. "Haven't we had enough cruel joking? Arthur, you might show more tolerance to the Easterner. We all were Easterners once. He's only, what, twenty-four years old?"

Pack said, "Around here that's a full-seasoned age for a man."

"Is that so," Huidekoper said dryly. "And how old are *you*, my friend?"

They moved toward the house. Pack glimpsed Roosevelt beyond the side of the barn—bent over, coughing ferociously, evidently retching. Feeling a snarling contempt, Pack followed Huidekoper inside.

These northern summer days were long but finally shadows invaded the tortured folds of the land. Pack made his way through the gathering in Eaton's front room, helping to light the lamps. Through one window he saw a three-quarter moon floating low on the horizon.

The door came open and Deacon W.P. Osterhaut insinuated himself. No one had invited him but he always seemed to know when gatherings were to take place; he seldom failed to impose his undesired presence. He was a short man with a plump stomach, a fat shrewish wife and a marked Southern accent, having served in the Rebel army during the war. Pack heard him talking to a rancher named Pierce Bolan. Osterhaut said, "I hear little Roosevelt there had a run-in with savages and saved the lives of his men by putting on a shooting exhibition that impressed the barbarians. He must be a crack shot."

Pack said, "Who told you that yarn, Deacon? It wasn't Roosevelt. It was one of his hired hands. Wilmot Dow." He'd written up the story for next week's paper. He'd heard it first from the Maine woodsman Sewall and this afternoon, riding out here, he had asked Roosevelt to confirm it.

Pack poured himself a cup of beer from the keg—the Eatons always had an endless supply—and heard Huidekoper buttonhole Roosevelt nearby. "Theodore, I want your advice." Evidently both Huidekoper and Howard Eaton were permitted to call Roosevelt by his first name. It was a club Pack felt no urgent wish to join.

Mrs. Eaton was at the door welcoming another newcomer. "You've come just in time. Supper's on the table."

Howard Eaton came curling past Pack with his customary big smile. Eaton clapped Huidekoper on the shoulder and said to Roosevelt, "It's too long a ride back to your place. Of course you'll stay here the night."

"My thanks for your kindness, but you seem to have a full house of visiting sportsmen."

"Nonsense. We enjoy company—more than anything."

"Thank you again, but I've arranged to stay in town."

"In the De Morès Hotel?"

"In Joe Ferris's spare room above the store." Roosevelt smiled with a display of teeth that reminded Pack not favorably of a gopher. "I haven't the nerve to join the horde of your friends who've availed themselves of the Eaton hospitality until they're in danger of losing their self-respect."

"You make a witticism of it," Howard Eaton replied, "but we've got too many friends who refuse our hospitality for just that reason."

Roosevelt said, "Then why don't you make 'dude-ranching' a business?"

"Charge money?"

"Don't be horrified, old fellow. Your friends will jump at the chance to enjoy your hospitality without feeling they're taking unfair advantage."

"Well I don't think—"

Roosevelt said, "Guides and hunters charge for their services. Hotelkeepers charge. No one faults them for it. Without the fair exchanges of honest commerce, few of us would survive."

Quick interest brightened Eaton's face. "Food for thought," he said. "You may have something. Yes, by George, you may have something there, Theodore. We'll discuss it among ourselves."

Huidekoper ran a hand across his bald pate. "I feel a need to air a few topics myself—such as the troubles caused by the Marquis's fences and sheep. We live in an isolated village. What affects one affects all. I believe the time has arrived for consideration of the formation of a committee of vigilance."

Pack tipped the point of his shoulder against the wall and listened without overwhelming interest. Whenever Huidekoper began talking, the promise was one of lengthy and prudent and rarely fascinating discourse.

Perhaps knowing Huidekoper well enough by now, Roosevelt nipped it quickly. "We don't need vigilantes. We need a stockmen's association, so that difficulties and disputes may be settled by a civilized vote among ranchmen, rather than by the present every-man-for-himself chaos."

Pack saw nothing wrong with the sentiment but he found himself resenting the cocksuredness with which Roosevelt presented it and the rude speed with which he had interrupted Huidekoper, and the ill-mannered haste with which he now changed the subject: "I come to another matter now. Perhaps it's already been discussed amongst some of you. We ranchmen must organize a round-up for the fall."

"No question of that," Huidekoper said. Wasn't he irritated? Didn't he *mind* being pushed aside by the little upstart from New York?

Huidekoper went on, "The question is, who's to lead it? We need an experienced round-up boss."

"Then I'll propose one," Roosevelt said. "Johnny Goodall."

Pack bounced away from the wall, astonished.

The others were equally amazed. Howard Eaton said, "I thought you were something less than a staunch supporter of the Marquis and his men."

"It's nothing to do with Mr. De Morès. We need the most able man for the job. Beyond question, Goodall is that man. Does anyone doubt his ability—or his integrity?"

Eaton said, "What a singular man you are, Theodore."

Huidekoper said, "I respect Johnny. But as to his loyalty—his employer has an unhealthy taste for empire. And for other people's property."

Pack felt obliged to speak out. "Now, the Marquis has title to his acreage."

"No one disputes that," Huidekoper snapped. "The question is, *which* acreage? The Marquis's land seems to keep moving about to suit the convenience of his ambitions." He turned back to the others. "The De Morès expedition's departure for the Yellowstone has left his many enterprises to run themselves. And it seems some of them are running themselves into the ground—"

Pack said, "The Marquis's businesses are so well set up as to need little supervision."

"With Jerry Paddock providing the supervision," Huidekoper retorted, "I suggest things look unpromising to say the least. But the point I was about to make is that Johnny Goodall has his hands full in De Morès's absence, and I doubt—"

Very angry now, Pack said, "The Marquis will be back before the beginning of round-up. Now, if you're looking for an excuse to blackball Johnny, you can't use that one."

Howard Eaton said in a mild voice, "Don't be such a hothead, Arthur. Try not to judge people too quickly."

Pack turned away, feeling red in his cheeks, and went back to the bar to replenish his beer. Deacon Osterhaut was there, a smear of cigar ash greying the lapel of his worn black suit; the Deacon was telling someone that same inaccurate story about how Roosevelt bluffed a war party of Indians with his fancy shooting. Pack didn't bother to correct the Deacon again; all too obviously it would do no good. Osterhaut was the sort of person who preferred rumor to truth.

Pack carried his beer back the way he had come; he felt an irascible need to get back into the fray. He pushed his way through the boisterous crowd and found the same group clustered around Roosevelt. Pierce Bolan, who ran a small outfit downriver, had joined them. Huidekoper was complaining: "Before De Morès came—"

"Before De Morès came," Pack said in a voice strong enough to override Huidekoper's, "there were wild Indians and coal fires, and badmen and thieves in the old Little Misery Cantonment. I am not much of a believer in the good old days."

"At least we had opportunity to run our little outfits without fear of this mob of human vultures who've flocked to peck at us now." Huidekoper wouldn't give up an inch. "Dive-keepers and tinhorn card mechanics and diseased shanty queens. You can smell the brimstone from twenty miles downwind."

"That's the Markee's slaughterhouse you're smelling," Pierce Bolan interjected. Everyone laughed a little—everyone but Pack.

Roosevelt said, "Shall we return to the idea of forming a stock-growers' association?"

Pack said, "To exclude whom?"

They all looked at him.

He took a step backward. Then he narrowed his eyes and stroked his beard. He managed a wise smile. "I don't see a need to create an association if there's nobody to be kept out of it."

Huidekoper said, "No one's suggested any exclusions."

"Isn't that the whole reason to form an association—to keep somebody out? Who is it? The Marquis De Morès?"

Howard Eaton said, "Now you know we live in a country that's almighty attractive to the criminal element. Just try and find a man who's hiding in the buckbrush out there in the ravines, with the Montana line just west and, if he needs it, the Canada line only a few hours' ride north."

By then Huidekoper and Bolan were looking toward the door with new interest. Pack turned to find out what had alerted them.

It was Johnny Goodall, entering late. He paused inquisitively, trying to get the hang of the conversation.

Eaton called, "Johnny. Glad you could make it. Come over here."

When Goodall came forward, Eaton said, "Mr. Roosevelt here has put your name forward as round-up boss."

"That's mighty kind." Johnny Goodall had fine manners. His voice was soft with a careful courtesy in it. But the look he gave Roosevelt was one of puzzlement. Johnny was no fool. He knew Roosevelt stood against the Marquis.

Howard Eaton said, "What do you say to it, then?"

At a time like this a man had to test his enemies, not his friends. Johnny turned to Huidekoper. "What do *you* say to it, sir?"

"It's been put before us that you're the most experienced and able man for the position. Can you think of any reason why you might not be able to fill the job with good conscience and complete impartiality?" There was dubious challenge in Huidekoper's gaze.

Johnny Goodall said, "I can do the job—if every man agrees to let me do it."

"I admire your confidence," Huidekoper said—too dryly, Pack thought.

Howard Eaton said, "While we're at it let me propose as chairman of the Little Missouri Stockmen's Association a gentleman among us who has a political record well known—Theodore Roosevelt. We'll meet to draw up rules and resolutions. What do you say?"

Johnny Goodall, looking straight at Roosevelt, said, "I say there ain't time now for that much jawing and writing. I say we wait till after the round-up, and then we can see what we need and who's fit to say so."

Pack watched Roosevelt meet the Texan's gaze.

Roosevelt said, "That certainly seems fair to me."

Now, it was doubtful, Pack thought, that Roosevelt would ever become chairman of anything in Dakota; by the time round-up was over, the little dude would be the laughingstock of the West.

Nine

Round-up camp was enormous; it looked to Wil Dow like a town. There must have been two thousand horses, two hundred men, a dozen chuck wagons each pulled by four drays and driven by a testy teamster-chef whose job seemed to incorporate the imperative of a ferocious temper.

By agreement the Roosevelt outfit was attached to the Huidekoper wagon, as were two other small ranchers—Deacon W.P. Osterhaut and Pierce Bolan.

It was clear from the outset that Theodore Roosevelt had his enemies. Men walked out of their way to avoid him. When Wil saw it happen he gave them his best snarl but no one paid much attention.

Horseflies were numerous and ripe smells were pungent—horses, leather, dung, not to mention the dreadful stink of steaming vats of coffee that had been defined for Wil Dow by Dutch Reuter: "You drop horseshoe in. If horseshoe don't float, strong enough it ain't."

Horsetails swished and unshod hoofs pounded earth as the animals fought an endless war with the flies. There were creakings of saddle leather and tinnient chimings of spurs. Horses grunted, whickered, whinnied, urinated and dropped patties with soft thumpings.

Johnny Goodall stood on the open tailgate of a Conestoga. He sounded a bit as if his mind were somewhere else; he'd probably delivered the same sermon five times today. His voice carried across the crowd:

"Listen up. This round-up will work its way one hundred miles down the river from here to the Killdeer Mountains. I expect the wagons to move eight miles a day, zigzag. Each man's responsibility to keep up. Expecting a seven-week round-up to cover ten thousand square miles. Rough estimate calls for forty thousand head of cattle. Tame the kinks out of your horses today because we start tomorrow before sunup. Breakfast at three in the morning. Good luck, boys."

It was still dark when the bellowing cook roused Wil Dow from his blankets. By firelight he tugged on boots, buckled chaps and gunbelt, lodged his hat hard down over his ears and was ready for whatever the day might mete out.

Following Dutch's example Wil rolled his blankets, tied the roll with whipcord and turned it in at the chuck wagon so that the cook could carry it on to the next night's campsite. Otherwise, Dutch reminded him, it would be left behind and he'd have to sleep cold on open ground for the remainder of the round-up.

At the fire they helped themselves to a stark breakfast and a hot metal cup of coffee that lived up to Dutch's description: it had the consistency of molasses and the impact of a horse's hoofs against the ribs.

Most of the hands ate squatting on their toes; Wil preferred to stand—there'd be enough sitting during the day on horseback.

Pierce Bolan was having the devil's own time trying to saddle up. In a rage he cursed the horse at length. At the end of it Deacon Osterhaut—late arriving for breakfast—said loudly, "You'll answer to the good Lord one day for that cussing, Pierce."

Pierce Bolan swung aboard the horse and it bucked like the wrath of God. Bolan gasped, "Answering for it right now, Deacon."

Watching the bronco buster, Mr. Roosevelt applauded. "A fine ride—a fine rider. I admire dogged staying power."

Wil Dow heard someone's Arkansas twang—no effort to lower the voice: "Who's the little squirt to be admirin' anything in a cow camp?" But it wasn't possible to identify the speaker; it hadn't been said to Roosevelt's face. He might be a figure of ridicule but he was an owner.

Osterhaut poured a cup of coffee. "For what we are about to receive may the Lord make us truly thankful." When he put the cup to his mouth Wil saw his eyes grow round. The Deacon spat it out, spraying coffee across the ground. He made a dreadful face. "Sweet dear Jesus!"

The cook leered at him with nasty satisfaction.

Osterhaut said, "I shouldn't laugh if I were you. If the coffee hasn't improved by tomorrow, I personally will see that you're fired and that you never work on this range again."

The cook sneered. "Take your Christian charity to some other wagon if you don't like the taste of this one."

Pierce Bolan had the horse under control now. He said, "Watch out now, cookie, or Deacon Osterhaut personally will see that you're lynched." He said it in an uncannily accurate imitation of Osterhaut's thick Southern accent. A ripple of easy laughter ran around the campfire. Osterhaut threw his cup at the cook's feet, but the vessel landed at an angle and splashed what was left of the coffee across Osterhaut's own boots. Amid louder laughter the Deacon stalked away.

In the first soft grey of dawn the night wranglers drove the day's *remuda* of cow-ponies into the rope corral. It was expected that each rider would wear out several horses during the day; but only the mounts for the first shift were brought in at dawn.

Uncle Bill Sewall was unhappy because most of the Elkhorn's eighty horses—many of them well trained by Dutch Reuter—had been contributed to the round-up's pool of livestock; it was the custom for each man to draw straws for the horses he would use each day. It meant you never knew whether you were drawing an untrained animal.

Each man, upon learning the identities of the beasts in his string, would curse for an extended interval; that was the ritual. Wil could see by Mr. Roosevelt's face that the boss disapproved as strongly as the Deacon did of such excessive profanity, but Roosevelt held his tongue. He seemed more than usually distracted this morning. Wil thought perhaps it was a matter of insufficient sleep—several times in the night he'd heard the boss coughing and retching—but Uncle

Bill Sewall said, "He has got nobody now and he still thinks that's his tragedy. Never mind—hard work cheers a man, and I expect he'll find a woman before long. There's your horse, Wil."

The best ropers in the outfit were the only men trusted to go into the corral. Wil said, "I'd just as soon rope out my own horse."

But Dutch pulled him back. "You let rope fall wrong, just once, and maybe stampede you got."

"You taught me to rope as well as any."

"Not these horse. You wait, Wil. 'Patient, ever patient, and joy shall be thy share.'"

"Where'd you learn that?"

"The good wife," Dutch said in a grunt. "Your horse—that one. I tell the roper."

When the roper brought the horse out—a bay, fifteen hands, with an amiable eye—Wil expended a good deal of effort jamming the bit between its clenched teeth and slipping the bridle over its tossing head. Then it was a matter of coaxing the animal with gentle words and caresses to hold still long enough to adjust a saddle-blanket across its spine, settle the heavy kak on its midsection and have it cinched up before the horse could get rid of it.

Half the ponies in the cavvy seemed to have learned the trick of puffing themselves up with air so that when you tightened the cinch they could exhale and leave so much slack that when you tried to mount up, your weight in the stirrup would slide the saddle right off until you were hanging upside down.

Wil had to agree with his uncle on one thing: the equine species was characterized by its malicious sense of humor.

The trick was to plant a boot in the beast's ribs and poke hard while tightening the cinch.

A small audience of cowboys, interested to see how the Down-East boatman would do, watched while Wil untied the reins, gathered them at the withers, hopped on his right foot while he tried to jab his left boot into the stirrup, and went dancing around on one toe while the horse pirouetted.

Finally he swung up onto the animal. Then it was a contest of wills. The bay went to bucking. Wil had to endure the shouts and laughs of cowboys who had mounted their older and tamer steeds without incident.

The horse was not terribly serious about its rebellion but it sunfished enough to make Wil grab the saddlehorn to keep from flying off. This act of cowardice was enough to make the audience jeer. "Don't go to leather, Wil. Ride him honest!"

Hot-faced, Wil let go and lifted his right arm in the air to show he meant to play the game by the rules. It was fortunate the horse had a mild temper, for it eased down almost immediately.

Uncle Bill Sewall and Roosevelt rode forward to join him. By the luck of the draw they seemed to have tractable mounts this morning. Several riders moved away pointedly when Roosevelt approached.

Uncle Bill was unimpressed with his mount. "One's no better than another. I'm no lover of horses," he said. "They're vicious stupid beasts, and dangerous. They'd as soon kick you as bite you. They'd break their own backs if they could fall on a man and crush him. And as for stupidity—what other animal on the face of the earth would let a man ride it to death?"

At the moment Wil was not inclined to dispute the point. Dutch Reuter, Pierce Bolan, Deacon Osterhaut and four of Huidekoper's hands joined them. Roosevelt, clad in horsehide chaparajos, buckskin shirt, silk neckerchief and enormous sombrero, pointed east toward the many-colored stripes of the malpais. "That's our district for the morning. The job is to collect every head of cattle. Come along, fellows."

It was a twelve-mile ride to the edge of the Bad Lands. Nobody talked much. It was clear to Wil Dow that the Huidekoper cowboys were under strict instructions not to be rude to Mr. Roosevelt, but from the clandestine glances they exchanged he could see what was in their minds.

At the crest they looked out across the plain.

"Nothing but dust and heat and mosquitoes," said Bill Sewall.

His sour tone made Pierce Bolan laugh.

"Not to mention blisters and bad food," said Deacon Osterhaut; but no one laughed this time. Uncle Bill's complaints were amusing; Osterhaut's were not. Evidently he never heard the offensiveness of his own disagreeably whining voice.

As for Uncle Bill Sewall—all he wanted, he kept insisting, was to return to his home back East in the States. But it had not escaped anyone's attention that he had made no effort to accomplish that goal. His threats were funny because they were empty.

The buffalo grass was yellow. Patches of it had been grazed to the ground by Merino sheep. The few cattle that had wandered up this far were easy to spot and easy to collect; they'd been fattening on what was left of the plateau's little blue-stem grasses. Two of the Huidekoper men rode out to gather them while Pierce Bolan said, "Rest of us may as well split up by twos. Each take a coulee and follow it down. Any cattle you find, push 'em ahead of you."

Wil Dow said, "What about sheep?"

Dutch Reuter said immediately, "Shoot them."

Pierce Bolan was entertained. "That's the right idea. Anybody care for a mutton dinner?"

It brought a scowl from Osterhaut and a flash of sun from Mr. Roosevelt's sunglasses. "Let's have it clear. If we come across sheep we'll leave them alone."

Bolan said nothing to that. He adjusted the reins in his grip. "We'll join up at the creek five miles down. All right?"

"It's a practical plan," Roosevelt commented. "Who'll ride with me?"

There was a moment's awkward silence. Then Sewall said, "I will."

Pierce Bolan pointed quickly to Wil Dow. "You come with me." It was pre-emptive—Bolan didn't want to end up paired with Osterhaut. Neither did anyone else and it might have been quite awkward but Dutch Reuter generously offered to accompany the Deacon.

Wil Dow ran along the rim of the escarpment with Pierce Bolan. A mile south of their starting place they dropped down into the notch of a coulee where there were cow pies that appeared to be reasonably fresh.

Over the western horizon appeared the slanted grey shadow-streaks of falling rain: an isolated squall moving away north. Otherwise the sky was bright and deep. The glare of sun on the malpais beat against Wil's eyes. Red clay caps on the occasional formation were evidence of lignite fires that had fused the clay.

They worked their way down, switchbacking when the pitch turned steep; they skirted sharp cuts and gullies, picked up a few scattered cattle and made their way into the treacherous windings of the eroded bottoms.

The earth was dense with heat down here. They picked up

another dozen head in a black tangled mass of trees, waved their hats and whooped and drove the little herd on.

Pierce Bolan said, "Been west before?"

"No. My first summer," Wil said. "You been here long?"

"Few years. Came north to build the railroad. Ten spikes the rail, four hundred rails the mile—thirsty work. Built up a stake, bought a little seed herd, got myself a cabin on Wannigan Creek. It'll work out now. I had hard luck in Texas the last two times I tried. Lost one herd to Comanches and the other outfit to drought. But I can feel it's going to be different here. Thinking about sending east for a mail-order bride next year. You got a girl?"

"I have."

"Now you're a lucky man. Fixin' to bring her out here?"

"Expect I will marry her and bring her out here if this turns out to be permanent."

"Why shouldn't it?"

"My uncle thinks the cattle business will go bust soon as there's a hard winter or a drought."

"Your uncle don't know much, then. The Little Missouri ain't never dried up, and there's plenty shelter in the Bad Lands no matter how hard the winter. Finest place on earth to be in the cattle business." Pierce Bolan was young and heavy-chested. He had freckles and yellow hair that hung long enough to be bleached lighter at the tips where the sun had reached it, and wrinkles of easy laughter around his eyes. A likeable man.

Bolan said, "Tell me about little Four Eyes, then. What's he think he's doin' out here?"

"Why, same as you, Pierce. Running a cattle outfit."

"I seen him coughing and throwing up half the night. I hear he's rich. If he's so sick why ain't he back East in some big mansion lying on a davenport and being waited on by sixteen nurses?"

"You'd have to ask him."

Wil took dinner off the chuck wagon at ten in the morning and was back on his horse by ten-fifteen. Drovers kept coming in for the next two hours with cattle.

The second half of the day consisted of identifying and sorting cattle—separating them by age, gender and ownership—and of wrestling and marking and castrating the unbranded calves and yearlings. Cutting such beasts out of the herd was no easy task. "Tell you something about these critters of the bovine species," said Pierce Bolan. "Cattle are like buffalo. Gregarious. Hard to separate them, for branding or anything else."

Round-up to Wil Dow was a wondrous kaleidoscope of impressions. First it was a matter of prodding each animal out to the rim of the herd and then chasing it away. The calves had an especial talent for veering back into the herd; it wasn't unusual for three or four horsemen to be thundering about with a great deal of commotion and sinuous galloping convolutions—all in pursuit of one hapless half-grown calf that wanted nothing more than to rejoin its bawling mother.

"Look at old Four Eyes go!"

It was Pierce Bolan's shout; it snapped Wil Dow's head around. He saw Mr. Roosevelt dashing across the edge of the herd at a dead run in pursuit of a comically recalcitrant calf. A cowboy—one of Huidekoper's men—loped toward them to intercept the calf; Roosevelt skidded his horse to one side, the calf bolted past the Huidekoper hand, and Roosevelt shouted at the man:

"Hasten forward quickly there!"

There was a sudden silence, as if pails of cold water had been thrown over every man in earshot.

The cow hand spun his lass rope expertly, dropped its billowing noose over the calf's neck and pulled it tight.

Someone giggled.

The calf ran out to the limit of the riata, came up against taut rope and flipped over on its back.

The giggle provoked someone else's bark of laughter.

Chastised, the calf lurched to its feet and came obediently along on its rope-leash behind the cow hand, who rode away with his head slowly turning while he kept his dumfounded stare on Roosevelt.

Half a dozen men were laughing now—at Mr. Roosevelt.

Pierce Bolan came riding past Wil Dow. He said, "Hasten forward quickly there," and erupted in an outburst of laughter so ferocious it nearly unhorsed him.

There was a standing-wave pattern of chaos as cowboys ran from one bunch to the next, passing the word. A half hour later, far away at the most distant edge of the herd Wil Dow saw a tiny horseman throw his arms in the air; he could nearly hear the man's explosion of laughter.

Roosevelt took it all in good spirit, smiling a bit sheepishly, joining halfheartedly in the laughter until one cow puncher came out of the herd prodding a maverick heifer. "This one's up for grabs." He spied Roosevelt riding by. "Hey Teddy. Hasten forward quickly there!"

Roosevelt wheeled his horse. There was no smile. "I expect to be called Mr. Roosevelt."

The cow puncher was ready to retort but something—perhaps the set of Roosevelt's shoulders or the glint behind the glasses—changed his mind. Wil saw him swallow. "Yes sir."

With relentless inevitability the truant calves were driven to join the rest of the cut, and once the cut had itself become a herd the job was easier, for the animals quit trying to escape.

Wil Dow heard Uncle Bill Sewall say to Pierce Bolan, "When he was little they called him 'Teedy' and his late wife took to calling him that. She called him 'Teedy' until she died. Since then he hasn't allowed it. Doesn't want anybody calling him that name—reminds him of Alice Lee, I expect. He hates the nickname now. You want to start a fight with him, just call him 'Teddy.'"

"Hell, why would I want to start a fight with a sick little dude like that?"

Fires were kindled and irons brought out, unbranded beasts of all ages were lassoed with leather riatas and dragged forward one at a time, and from the branded and cauterized calves came a pitiful blatting.

Toward evening came the tallying and gathering. Yet another new herd was formed: these were the cattle destined for market—each beef identified by brand and written down as a slash-mark on its owner's page in the wagon-boss's tally book. This herd, Pierce Bolan told him, would grow daily and would need constant fresh graze.

The rest of the cattle were turned loose and chased back into the country that had already been swept, so that they wouldn't be rounded up a second time.

It was near dark when the riders found their way to the Huidekoper wagon. They exercised their teeth on stringy fresh-killed beef.

Bill Sewall said, "I'm awful tired."

"Don't be peevish, Uncle Bill."

Johnny Goodall came by, making his rounds. He was riding a buckskin mare with three white stockings. He observed the determination with which Roosevelt's jaws worked on a mouthful. "Afraid this isn't exactly your Delmonico restaurant."

"It tastes jolly good to me."

"I swear I don't know what you're doing here."

"Looking after my interests, old fellow."

"Go on home, Mr. Roosevelt. There's men here who can do that a lot better than you can."

"I shan't know that until I've tried. And I shan't learn much if I *don't* try."

"You're too rich for round-up camp, Mr. Roosevelt. Don't you see that?"

"Will it satisfy you if I explain that I scorn the slothful ease of the mollycoddled?"

"Well then," said Johnny, "you'll just suit yourself, I guess. You just keep on hastening forward quickly there." A rare smile crossed his face before he rode away.

Everyone knew that Roosevelt had to prove himself to Johnny Goodall. The challenge Johnny had set him—regarding the stockmen's association and who should be chosen to lead it—was common knowledge on the round-up, and Wil Dow knew that everyone was waiting to see if sickly little "Silk-Stocking Roosenfelder" could possibly survive the next two months' gruelling labor and show the Texan that he was wrong.

It didn't begin well for Mr. Roosevelt. Not only did he have to endure it with good nature every time a cow hand ragged him with a hearty "Hasten forward quickly there"—some of them even managed pretty well to mimic his odd Eastern dialect—but then on the third day, after his first assignment on night-herding duty, he came riding into camp in early sunlight, blinking perplexedly behind his glasses. "By Jove, I seem to have been lost. I was trying to find the night herd and it was so pitch-dark I must have got started in the wrong direction."

A hand—one of Johnny Goodall's men—squinted wearily at the dude. "I had to stand double guard because of you, Mr. Roosevelt. Believe I must've lullabied a thousand cows with one chorus apiece of 'Bury Me Not on the Lone Prairie.' You going to do something about that?"

"I'll stand your next night guard. It's the only fair thing."

"You bet you will," the hand agreed.

After that the boys were even more cool to him. Before, they had teased him; now they avoided him. Wil kept hearing their criticisms—uttered behind Roosevelt's back:

"Greenhorn got himself lost inside half a mile of camp. I hear at home he needs a map and a lantern to find the outhouse."

"Appears to me like he's got more teeth than a man needs."

"How can you trust a man don't drink or smoke or swear?"

"He won't last out the first two weeks. The booger'll get sick or for certain he'll get himself a gallopin' case of cold feet in hot country."

There were days when Roosevelt rode in, trail-worn and wilted, only to have to saddle a fresh horse and go straight out to night-herding, where twice Wil Dow ventured out with his uncle to keep an eye on the boss and they found him, thinking he was alone, giving way to violent attacks of asthma and cholera morbus. There were days when his hands bled, raw from the rope, and he kept pulling his glasses off to wipe his face because of the scalding sweat that stung his eyes. And still the boys ridiculed him, and Johnny Goodall did nothing to curb it.

They learned quickly enough that the buckskins they'd bought from the Indians were the only things worth wearing in the brush, for the thorn bushes could wear out a pair of good stout duck pants in two days.

Wil hated it when he drew the middle shift of night-riding; it interrupted his rest and got him so keyed up he couldn't get back to sleep.

"Quiet one, at least," said Pierce Bolan one night as their paths intersected. "The ones you want to look out for's the loud nights—lighting, thunder. Ain't nothing on earth half as deadly as a night stampede. Lost both my brothers in a stampede—night before we crossed the Red River."

They all were young men, with one or two exceptions like Dutch Reuter; nobody knew just how old Dutch was—possibly in his forties or fifties. Bill Sewall was thirty-nine years old and the hands called him The Old Man. Sewall was sometimes in a frame of mind to declaim poetry in a very loud voice with his Down-East accent. It caused a good deal of ribbing and laughing. Uncle Bill didn't seem to mind. He was sure of himself, to the annoyance of the Westerners; he was never too bashful to tell them how wrong they all were. He said to Johnny Goodall, "The stock business is still new here and I can't find anybody as has made anything in it. They all expect to—but I think they have all lost money. Even your Markee."

As for Dutch Reuter, Wil had developed a keen respect and liking for his cowboy mentor. Dutch had earned that rare encomium from Roosevelt "a capital fellow." Roosevelt seemed much taken by the fact that Dutch, who could not read or write, could retain in his memory long complicated lists of instructions. Uncle Bill Sewall, with characteristic dour wit, described Dutch's English as "unspeakable" and in truth the accent sometimes made him nearly impossible to understand; but they'd learned on the ranch that you could recite a lengthy order to him and he would ride away in the morning with his pack animals and return next day to the Elkhorn after sixty miles' round-trip ride with packsaddles filled with precisely every item on the list, even though he may have had to visit every establishment in town to fulfill them all.

But Dutch was by no means admired by everyone. Once he had been a hunting-guide partner of the surly Frank O'Donnell; Dutch was taken to be a friend, or at least an ally, of O'Donnell and his friends—Redhead Finnegan and Riley Luffsey and the other wild ruffians who had made clear their opposition to the Marquis de Morès.

The matter surfaced one noon when a large number of rifle shots was heard in the distance. It was a great fusillade but it only lasted a minute or two. A while later Dutch Reuter and Bill Sewall came separately into camp driving small pick-up herds of strays. The two men were riding parallel on converging courses but they had not been working together. Dutch turned his cattle in, unsaddled and went to the chuck wagon for dinner; he had nothing to report. Sewall said to Johnny Goodall, who happened to be eating here today, "I don't know if it means anything but I saw Redhead Finnegan and his friends hanging around the edges of the round-up."

"When?"

"Two hours ago."

Johnny glanced at Dutch. "You see them too?"

Dutch looked at him, looked at Sewall, then returned his attention to his meal. He made no answer of any kind.

Sewall said, "And there was a pretty big flock of sheep. Buzzards picking at more than two dozen of them. They'd been rifle-shot."

"By Finnegan?"

"I wouldn't know that for certain. I heard shooting but I didn't see it done, and when I saw Finnegan and the others they were a mile or more away from the sheep."

Dutch continued to eat. Johnny Goodall walked to Dutch's saddle and touched the stock of the scabbarded rifle. He looked at Dutch, as if for permission. Dutch watched him without a word or a sign. Johnny said, "Mind if I look at it?"

Dutch only stared at him. After a while Johnny slid the rifle out of leather, watching Dutch every moment, and jacked it open. He put his thumb in the breech and peered down the muzzle, sniffed at the weapon, snapped it shut and returned it to the scabbard. "Fresh cleaned."

Pierce Bolan said, "It does get dusty on the trail, Johnny. I clean my rifle at least a couple times a week."

"While you're on horseback?" Johnny Goodall saddled a fresh horse. When he rose to the saddle he said, "Dutch—you got anything to say to me?"

"About what?"

"Sheep."

"Don't like 'em."

"Redhead Finnegan."

"I mind my own business, yah?"

"Destroying another man's livestock—that's a serious thing, Dutch."

"You see me destroy?"

"You're on thin ice, you old bastard."

Johnny rode out in the direction Uncle Bill pointed him.

That evening Wil heard it said around camp that Johnny had engaged in some very plain talk with Finnegan, threatening to lynch the whole crowd if any cattle were stolen or any more sheep massacred; but no one knew very much for sure and Johnny said nothing about it. Nevertheless Wil kept hearing louder and more frequent expressions of concern among the ranchmen about the profusion of rustlers in the Bad Lands, and the need to do something about them.

The round-up worked its way downriver to the outskirts of Medora town. Quite a few citizens came out to observe the activities. Among them was the lady Medora, Madame la Marquise—sidesaddle on a pretty mare, her delicate face shaded beneath a Mexican sugarloaf hat that was wider than her shoulders. Mr. Roosevelt walked through the crowd to greet her.

Johnny Goodall turned his head alertly to watch them. The ligaments of his neck stood out tight against the weather-bronzed flesh.

Wil Dow wasn't close enough to hear the words Roosevelt exchanged with the lady; he did see Roosevelt's flashing smile.

Just then Wil happened to notice Johnny Goodall with a wicked sort of grin stride to the wagon, hold brief colloquy with one of the De Morès top hands, and run across the camp like a man with bright mischief on his mind. Johnny, in his round-topped flat-brimmed hat, went prowling into the remuda as if heedless of the danger of being kicked or stomped or crushed by any of the wild-eyed horses, and came out a minute later leading a skittish vicious-looking beast. He and the top hand wrapped a blindfold around the horse's head and fought hard to get it saddled.

Wil watched with increasing suspicion until Johnny led the monster to Mr. Roosevelt and handed him the reins. Johnny lifted his voice so that everyone could hear him. "Here you go, Mr. Roosevelt. A plumb gentle horse."

Wil jumped off the fence and hurried forward while Roosevelt met the round-up manager's gaze. Johnny put on a guileless smile. Roosevelt did not smile back. Wil stopped then, because it was clear they both knew what this was about: yet another in the exhausting sequence of tests the Texan had contrived for the dude—and this one in front of Madame Medora, which could not help but increase Mr. Roosevelt's humiliation, whether he should decline the challenge or accept it and be made a fool by the savage horse.

There was nothing Wil could do about it. He backed away slowly with a scowl.

Johnny Goodall said, "You just ease yourself—the horse will do the same. You trust him, he'll trust you. You give respect, he'll return it."

Cowboys gathered. Wil Dow found Pierce Bolan beside him. "Watch this," Bolan confided. "Johnny will tell you any horse that's been roped is a broke horse. But that's a bucker if I ever seen one."

Roosevelt spoke another half-dozen quiet words to the lady and then turned to accept the bucking horse.

Wil Dow stated agape at Madame Medora. It was the first time he'd seen her close up. Her riding habit was black. She wore hobnail boots with soft leather leggins; of course it was not done for a woman to show the least bit of ankle. Lady Medora's skirts would have dragged the ground if she had been standing upon it. Even so, Wil Dow knew that if a gentleman should give her a hand up into the sidesaddle, he was required by custom to look away, lest he catch a glimpse of limb.

He'd heard it said that Madame la Marquise was considered quite risqué because—rumor had it—she now and then sunned herself in a full-length outfit that had half-sleeves and actually revealed her forearms.

Two men boosted Roosevelt into the saddle. They stepped back, grinning.

The horse exploded under the boss and Wil Dow winced; he could feel the hard shocks that must have run up Roosevelt's bones.

The horse leaped high in the air, all four hoofs far from the ground, spine bowed—and came down with a crash that swung the rider far over. The horse pivoted; the rider was clutching at things but there was sky visible beneath the crotch of his trousers and it was just a matter of instants now. His hat and glasses were gone into the dust. Wil Dow saw the revolver bounce out of Roosevelt's holster. There were shouts from the men: "Go to him, cowboy!"

"Stay by! Stay by!"

There was a great deal of laughter: nobody expected Roosevelt to stay on board. But he was making a good fight of it. Wil worried: Roosevelt had more than his share of stubbornness and it seemed all too clear that this horse was going to be ridden—or Roosevelt was going to get hurt.

Oddly, it was Johnny Goodall who ran out and rescued the eyeglasses.

The horse reared, kicked, came down hard two legs at a time—that second shock nearly twisted the rider in half. It brought a cry from Madame la Marquise. The horse planted its front feet and kicked its hind hoofs high in the air. Roosevelt would have come off if the horse hadn't slammed forward under him, as if catching him. Then it ran forward, stopped dead in its tracks and dropped its head between its splayed front legs. It arched its back and swirled, gone mad.

Somehow the rider was still up. But then the horse went straight up in the air as if it had been hit from underneath by a cannonball. When it came down it rolled sideways and the rider pitched off—and a good thing too, Wil thought, because it might have crushed him otherwise.

The cowboys cheered, their humor being as cruel as it was rough, but when the horse clambered to its feet Roosevelt was right there, reins gathered, both fists gripping the horn.

He hauled himself back into the saddle as the horse sunfished end-for-end. He hadn't secured his seat; his feet were half out of the stirrups; and the horse was swapping ends fast enough to make a wooden cigar-store Indian dizzy. It was no wonder Roosevelt flew off.

The lady Medora gasped; the cowboys cheered the horse; Johnny Goodall squinted with a calm smile, trying to see through Roosevelt's eyeglasses; Pierce Bolan said to no one in particular, "That horse is pure outlaw." And Roosevelt got back on the horse.

The outlaw's teeth snapped together; it uttered a loud malevolent grunt; it surged and lashed; and at last—just when it seemed inevitable the rider must soar away yet again to wheel shoulder-first against the dusty earth—the horse gave up and ran.

Tamed for the moment, it galloped full out while the rider resettled his seat and his composure.

Madame Medora clapped her hands energetically. Sewall and Dow followed suit. Dutch Reuter and several of the punchers joined in the applause. But several others did not; and Johnny Goodall only watched, not moving, until Roosevelt turned the running horse and brought it back toward the fire, dropping it to a canter and a trot and finally a walk. Then Johnny Goodall stepped forward and handed the rescued pair of glasses up to Roosevelt.

Wil Dow saw that Roosevelt's ferocious grin was aimed at the lady. "What a rattling good time."

Madame Medora smiled back demurely under her hatbrim.

Roosevelt looked down. "I rode him for you, Mr. Goodall. All the way from the tip of his ear to the end of his tail."

Johnny Goodall made a deliberate pivot and strode away.

Pierce Bolan said dryly to Roosevelt, "Next time Johnny tells you he's got a plumb gentle horse for you, you want to look out."

Roosevelt's blue eyes flashed behind the dusty lenses. "Nonsense. It's all good fun. I think it's perfectly bully!"

The lady returned to her château; the round-up went on into the evening, at which point there was a great turmoil of men trying to find teetotalers willing to take their places on night-guard. Roosevelt and Uncle Bill immediately volunteered, as they did not drink. A considerable amount of pressure was brought to bear upon Deacon Osterhaut, who finally agreed to stand a watch but not without berating the boys about the Wages of Sin. "It is not God's will that *any* of you patronize the fleshpots of this evil Gomorrah."

Wil Dow thought of going into town to See The Elephant with the rest of the boys. It was tempting. But he decided to save his money and his health. He enjoyed a drink now and then but it would give him a dread headache and that was something he did not care to endure on the back of a bucking horse. He took Pierce Bolan's place on night duty and earned the rancher's undying gratitude.

By the next morning it was Wil who was grateful. For the others there followed two days of painful sobering up as the round-up moved its memorable hangover downriver. Uncle Bill and Deacon Osterhaut regarded the suffering cowboys with smug satisfaction. The boys joked with Uncle Bill while they returned Osterhaut's surliness in kind. Some men simply had a sweeter flavor than others, Wil observed.

Mr. Roosevelt wisely held his own counsel. One afternoon he was out with his glass-plate camera making pictures of the round-up. Johnny Goodall came by. "I'm giving out assignment orders. Mr. Roosevelt, you'll ride circle twice tomorrow, the outer swing. Next day find the wagon and take your turn cutting out and branding, and you'll have a turn on night-herd guard."

"Fair enough," Roosevelt replied. Perhaps he didn't realize he'd just been ordered to ride more than a hundred miles without rest and to perform nearly forty hours' work in the next forty-eight. Wil Dow was on the point of speaking a protest but Uncle Bill shushed him.

Then Johnny Goodall did a strange thing. He said to Roosevelt, "A word of advice. Pick out the gentlest horse you can find, picket it near the wagon every night, and use it for night duty. Hard enough to have to get out of the blankets in the middle of the night—you don't want to have to fight a mean horse to get it saddled. Besides, sometimes you have to move sudden at night."

Johnny moved away without leaving time for a response. Roosevelt called after him: "Thank you. You're a capital gentleman."

If he heard, Johnny made no sign of it.

Wil Dow said to his uncle, "Looks like Johnny's relenting."

"I doubt it. He's not sorry for anything he said or did. He's just being practical. Wants to keep things calm and head off any mutinies."

"You think he's that calculating?"

Wil Dow knew he invariably presented an innocent expression of eager curiosity. He went after Johnny Goodall, found him dismounted, and asked him straight out, "Why do you work for a man like De Morès?"

"For one hundred dollars a month," Johnny replied.

Reason enough, perhaps. It was three times the wage of a top hand.

Johnny walked away with the slightly bowlegged ungainly rolling gait of a horseman, the rowels of his big Mexican spurs chinking with each hard confident stride: he planted each boot hard enough to jab a distinct heel-print into the tough clay. He never seemed to hurry. All his movements were measured and laconic. Yet he managed to be everywhere at once; nothing escaped his keen attention.

Wil's kaleidoscope kept spinning as the end of the long round-up approached. The days cooled; leaves turned; bushes and shrubs made a rich variety of color.

They were near the Killdeers. Headquarters camp had been

pitched in the vast curve of the Little Missouri where it emerged from the Bad Lands onto the virgin prairie. Wil Dow and Dutch Reuter were pushing a batch of cows into the herd. Roosevelt swung by them, neck-reining one-handed. "You want to keep a careful eye on that steer over there—the one with the tip broken off the left horn. Bed him down and watch him, for he'll keep getting up again and he'll lead the others to mischief if you let him."

He went to turn his mount again—and the horse slipped and fell hard, pinning him.

Wil leaped down and tugged the horse. Dutch was with him; they worked together until the beast scrambled off the boss. Wil had his own horse by the reins and used it as a shield to fend off milling cattle. Dutch was trying to help Roosevelt to his feet but when he pulled at Roosevelt's hand the boss cried out with pain.

Dutch let go. Roosevelt stood up slowly by himself and tried to lift his arm. It wouldn't move.

"Well," he said offhandedly, "probably just a strain."

Dutch took him by forearm and elbow and began gently to manipulate the limb. "That hurt?"

"Like the devil."

"Something broken in the shoulder, I think. Dr. Stickney you go see."

The clenched fist of Roosevelt's uninjured hand revealed his pain; but he said, "No doctors."

Wil said to Dutch, "Boss has a low opinion of doctors. They've told him a lot of lies."

"I've broken plenty of bones in my time," Roosevelt said, as if he were some sort of old man rather than a youth of twenty-four. "No doubt I'll break plenty more before I'm finished. It's nothing."

Dutch said, "All right. Then you wait." He borrowed Wil's horse to go after his own. After a lively chase he caught his mount and brought it back, dismounted and dipped into a saddlebag, poured a few drops from a small bottle into a metal cup half full of water and offered the stain to Mr. Roosevelt.

Roosevelt regarded it suspiciously. "What's this?"

"Laudanum. You'll ride better."

"Very well." Roosevelt swallowed the mixture and made a face.

He carried his arm in a sling thereafter but he did not stop working. Once Wil Dow saw him rassling a calf one-handed.

Johnny Goodall saw this. He rode off without saying anything. Covered with clay from head to foot, Roosevelt dragged the protesting calf to the fire and waited the branding iron.

It was agreed, grudgingly in some quarters, that the dude New Yorker, who was five-foot-eight and weighed no more than one hundred and twenty-five pounds, had acquitted himself some better than anybody expected. He was an indifferent roper—his eye was poor—and an inferior horseman; he talked like a priggish schoolmistress and he would never make a fair cow puncher, let alone a top hand. Nevertheless he had carried his share; he had kept up. He had a tenacity that amazed the Westerners. As Pierce Bolan put it, "He ain't a pretty rider but he's got grit."

He was given the nearest thing to an official stamp of approval when Johnny Goodall came to him in camp, looked at the sling on Roosevelt's arm and said, "If you still want to be chairman of the stockmen's association, you have got my vote."

Roosevelt and his men drove their cattle onto the De Morès siding. Wil Dow helped Uncle Bill; they began to chute the beeves into a holding corral.

Flanked by Johnny Goodall and half a dozen horsemen, the Marquis came along on a big black stallion and Wil surveyed him with keen interest. Here then was the fabled Monte Cristo of the Bad Lands. No denying he was picturesque in the extreme in his fringed hunting coat. Under the great white hat De Morès wore bright-colored clothes punctuated with two Colts, each on its own cartridge belt, and a scabbarded hunting knife of enormous size. He carried a large stick in one hand and there was, Dow noticed, a rifle of what looked like very large caliber on the saddle within his reach. The Marquis was a one-man arsenal.

Roosevelt was on foot outside the corral, examining his cattle. He still carried his arm in the sling; evidently it was quite painful but he didn't allow that to show if he thought anyone was looking. When he saw the Marquis he came pounding forward with his choppy aggressive stride.

They exchanged good-afternoons. The Marquis said, "It's unfortunate you couldn't have brought them in yesterday."

"Why is that?"

"The price has dropped."

Roosevelt said, "We agreed on a price yesterday, did we not?"

"That is true. Seventy cents less than the Chicago price. This morning there has been a drop in the price of beef on the Chicago market. I can show you the telegram if you like."

Roosevelt said, "If the Chicago price had gone *up* I still should have made delivery at the agreed terms. A bargain is a bargain."

"Just so. Seventy cents less than the Chicago price."

"Seventy cents less than the price as quoted when we made the bargain."

De Morès's reply was a dissenting grunt. "No. I do not control the Chicago market."

"But you control your own actions, Mr. De Morès. I insist you keep your word."

Wil Dow saw the rising roughness in the Marquis's face. "I have offered to do just that." The brim of his white sombrero cast a sharp line of shadow across his face. "I am not trying to Jew you down."

"I find that expression offensive, Mr. De Morès."

"Do you." The Marquis's eyes flashed, as if he had scored some sort of point. "I find some things offensive too. One of them is the fact that you've chosen to employ a man who's been firing his rifle into my house and my sheep."

"What man is that?"

"You know perfectly well. Dutch Reuter."

"I know nothing of the kind. Have you evidence?"

"If I had, your man would be hanging from a tree."

Roosevelt looked up at the horsemen who flanked De Morès. His gaze settled for a moment on Johnny Goodall, who looked on in flinty silence. Finally Roosevelt faced the Marquis. "Mr. De Morès, I ask you one last time to keep your word. If you will not do that, then henceforth I will not do business with you."

"I am fully prepared to keep my word. Seventy cents less than the Chicago price."

Roosevelt turned to Bill Sewall. "We will drive the animals back out of the yards."

The breath caught in Wil Dow's throat. His eyes flashed from face to face. He shifted his hand nearer his revolver and turned to face Johnny Goodall squarely, leaving the Marquis to Mr. Roosevelt. If it was to come to shooting, he wanted his target clearly identified.

Menace hung in the stinking air like a blade poised to drop.

Then Johnny lifted both hands onto the saddlehorn in a quiet but clear gesture of peace.

De Morès said to Roosevelt in an arrogantly amused way, "What do you intend doing, then? These are the only shipping pens in town."

"I shall drive them to the next town and ship them from there."

"All the way to Dickinson? You'll drop thousands of pounds off them."

"You leave me no choice."

The Marquis glared at him. "I'm sorry you can't see the proper side of this." He turned his horse and rode off.

Johnny Goodall said to his men, "All right, boys, give Mr. Roosevelt a hand getting these cattle out."

"Thank you," said Roosevelt.

"That's all right," Johnny drawled.

And so Wil and Uncle Bill Sewall drove the beeves three days to Dickinson and put them on a train, fifty-five yearlings to a boxcar, and shipped them to the Chicago stockyards. Mr. Roosevelt was pleased because the price had gone back up and he got a dollar more per head even after payment of shipping charges than the Marquis would have paid him.

But the incident left little doubt that they were going to have to sleep light from now on.

Before it was over, Wil Dow thought, there was going to be hell to pay.

The anticipation of it made him feel alarmed and pleased, all at once. He couldn't fathom that; but he rode through the ensuing weeks in a state of excitement that made his senses keener than they ever had been.

Ten

The Indian Summer heat was oppressive. Pack found it difficult to breathe inside the shack. He could hear rats scurrying in the roof. When he'd finished dressing in his evening suit it was impossible to stand the stifling closeness any longer; he went outside and tried to fill his chest but the air was rancid with slaughterhouse stink. That was but a small price to pay, however—all you had to do was take a look at the train of refrigerator cars, each painted with the Marquis's NPRC legend, making its slow way out of town, hauling dressed Bad Lands beef to the Eastern markets.

It was an evening that might prove interesting. Despite the dreadful heat Pack looked forward to tonight's formal dinner with the Marquis and Marquise and their honored guests.

He saw Dan McKenzie emerge from the smithy, remove his apron and toss it back inside, wipe sweat from his face and trudge toward the Senate Billiard and Pool Hall, licking his lips in anticipation of beer.

Riley Luffsey, who had returned three days ago from guiding a moderately successful game hunt for a party of Belgians, was jawing on the porch of Joe Ferris's store with Little Casino. Luffsey was slapping a rolled newspaper into his open palm, punctuating his ribald talk. He had just turned nineteen and, judging by the monumental scale of his celebration the other night, inevitably still must be suffering from the hangover; the insolent swagger of his manner was in no way muted, however. He flashed a proud grin at Pack and went right on talking to Little Casino. Pack couldn't hear their words but he saw Luffsey speak with dry cocky impudence and he heard the madam's bawdy whiskey-baritone laugh.

They were an odd pair, the curiously touching—almost endearing—youngster and the hardened whore. Little Casino had a soft spot for Luffsey; everybody in town knew it, including her husband, but then Jerry Paddock never seemed to care whom she sported with, or how she felt about them. Jerry's main interest in his wife seemed to be how much money she brought home.

Speak of the Devil: down the street Jerry Paddock stepped out of the De Morès store. For once he was without his funeral coat; he was in shirtsleeves and seemed a bit wilted. He glanced down toward the competing emporium, saw his wife engaged in intimate laughter with the young hunter, and wheeled abruptly back inside, sudden danger and menace implicit in his every twitch.

Pack wondered at that. Something new here?

Jerry Paddock, for all his surly conspiratorial mannerisms, was a contradiction. His dominant characteristic was an air of personal isolation; it kept him at a rigid distance from everyone. Pack saw him every day but had yet to comprehend him.

After a moment's thought, however, Pack realized why there probably would be an earsplitting row later tonight in the Paddock household. It had nothing to do with any normal feelings of masculine jealousy; if Jerry resented his wife's friendliness with Riley Luffsey it would be solely because the villain did not care to have his wife consorting with the Irish crowd of anti–De Morès hunters. He probably had forbidden it—and she seemed to miss few opportunities to defy his proscriptions.

A De Morès mechanic was driving one of Cyrus McCormick's one-hundred-twenty-dollar wheat-reaping harvester machines through town, lashing the air above the horses' ears and yelling hoarsely. Redhead Finnegan, the man from Bitter Creek, so filthy he was surrounded by his own personal cloud of flies, came out of Ferris's store followed by Frank O'Donnell, who kept rubbing his pitted cheeks and batting the flies away. Finnegan said something that took all the laughter out of Little Casino's face, and took Riley Luffsey in tow and plodded through the heat toward Bob Roberts's saloon.

Poor Luffsey, Pack thought. Given half a chance the kid might do just fine. But his chosen campanions had filled him up with dreams of ruffianly glory; Luffsey wanted nothing so much as to be another Wild Bill Hickok. It did no good to try and point out to him the squalor in which Hickok had ended his sorry days.

The sun had disappeared beyond the bluffs; the sky was grey and thick. Pack idled down the street to the cafe and was about to go inside when he saw Theodore Roosevelt ride into town with two of his hired hands. Roosevelt carried his arm in a leather sling. He was all dressed up in an elaborate buckskin suit. Sight of him stopped Pack in his tracks. Had the man ridden thirty-odd miles into town on this particular evening by sheer coincidence? Why was he wearing his Wild West best?

Roosevelt stepped down off his handsome horse and went inside Joe's store. The hired men, Sewall and Dow, came on to the cafe, towing two pack horses laden with carcasses. Curious, Pack followed them inside. They had shot more deer than they could eat; they had the excess on the pack animals outside and Pack watched the old Mennonite transact business with the slat-sided proprietress. "Five cents a pound," she said.

Sewall—his beard jutting as ferociously as a Viking's—said, "Six," and the woman stared back fearlessly. They settled on five and a half.

Pack said, "Now, Mr. Roosevelt appears to be dressed for a wedding."

Wil Dow said, "He got an invite card to dine at the château."

Sewall said, "And if you are aiming to ask why Mr. Roosevelt tolerates the French son of a bitch, don't ask me."

Wil Dow said, "Mr. Roosevelt says you have to recognize that people from different parts of the world have different ways of doing things."

Sewall growled, "He said he'd never do business with the Markee again."

Wil Dow said, "Well, Uncle Bill, this isn't a business matter."

Pack said with some astonishment, "I take it then that he's posted an acceptance of the invitation?"

Sewall said, "He is suffering great pain from that broken shoulder bone and has been taking laudanum and I'm afraid it's diminished his judgment."

If he ever had any, Pack thought, *which I doubt very much*.

But the promise of confrontation between Roosevelt and De Morès, after what he'd heard about their *contretemps* at the railroad corrals, put an excitement into him that drove him immediately back outside.

He saw Roosevelt and Joe Ferris in front of the store in the same patch of shade that had been occupied a few minutes earlier by Luffsey and the whore. Roosevelt, despite his leather sling and buckskin outfit, did not seem to mind the stifling heat. Half-drunk on laudanum, no doubt. Joe Ferris was gesturing and talking probably trying to impress the dude with the zeal with which he had been guarding Roosevelt's investment. Someone had tried to break into the store the other night and Joe had fired several shots, one of which had hit the wall of Pack's office, and he'd had words with Joe about that. But afterward they had shared a meal and laughed about it.

Pack walked to the store. He arrived in time to hear Roosevelt say to Joe Ferris, "Your friend Dutch has been doing fine work with us. I'm grateful for the recommendation. . . . Now this horse Manitou is a magnificent creature of great endurance. Take good care of him. I shall see you later if you're still awake, and I shall appreciate it if you don't shoot me for a prowler."

Joe said, "I may just make that mistake if you keep letting that mustache grow. It's starting to droop as bad as Jerry Paddock's."

"They're saying you have a score to settle with Mr. Paddock."

"He stole every scrap from this store. Drove Swede Nelson out of town. Keeps trying to rob me blind."

Pack interjected, "Now, you've never proved a word of that, Joe."

"Hell, everybody in town knows it. Let him sue me for slander—may be the truth will come out then!"

Roosevelt looked Pack up and down. "A fine coat you're wearing. May I take it you're bound for Mr. De Morès's house?"

"I was about to ask you the same question," Pack said reluctantly.

* * *

There hadn't been any appreciable rain since last spring. The river was shallow beneath the railroad bridge. Pack accompanied Roosevelt along the ties and up the hill. "I heard about your disputation with the Marquis. I'm surprised you'd accept an invitation to dine at the château."

Roosevelt said, "It's better all around if a cordial relation be maintained, as befitting two civilized gentlemen."

Perhaps, Pack thought. But there might be another side to it—perhaps Roosevelt did not wish to be cut off from contact with Mme. Medora . . .

In a way he nearly felt compassion for the silly dude, for Pack knew something of such things. When he'd been at the University of Michigan he had fallen disastrously in love with an ethereal girl whose pale delicacy and enormous shy brown eyes had entranced him. Unwilling to risk her diamond-engraved engagement to a world-traveling timber-and-railroad heir, she had dallied harmlessly with the helplessly smitten Pack; in the entire collegiate year he had obtained not so much as a kiss on the cheek, and in the end she had gone off gaily to marry the wretched heritor without so much as a word of regret.

After an exchange of a few more desultory politenesses with Roosevelt, he found himself at the château. Several guests were already there, outdoors on the verandah trying to pick up what little breeze came across the butte. There were half a dozen wealthy Easterners and seven Europeans, including two of the Belgians from Luffsey's hunt and a titled couple from Denmark. Madame la Marquise wore a henna-colored gown that set off her red hair. Eaton was there, and the famous Montana cattle king Granville Stuart, and a barrel-bodied rancher named Pierre Wibaux, proprietor and manager of the W-Bar Ranch on Beaver Creek. Wibaux was from France and, although he was not from the Marquis's social class, the Marquis generously extended frequent invitations to him because he was a fellow countryman.

From the outset things went badly. The French flag waved on its staff before the château and Roosevelt made an issue of the impropriety of this. The Marquis evidently had decided to humor the New Yorker, regardless of provocations. Perhaps it had to do with Roosevelt's injury. A servant was summoned and in short order the American flag was hoisted, with the French flag beneath it; then Roosevelt pointed out that the sun had gone down and therefore it was not proper to fly *any* flag.

Pack thought he wouldn't blame the Marquis if he threw the insufferable dude off the premises and told him never to return.

But of course the Marquis was too civilized for that. Roosevelt went inside with the others and soon was the animated center of a cluster that included Eaton, Wibaux and several others. Passing by, Pack overheard Roosevelt say to Howard Eaton jocularly, "By Godfrey, sometimes I think the Devil put women on this earth to make fools out of men."

Madame la Marquise was not in earshot but all the same Pack gave Roosevelt an outraged look. Roosevelt didn't seem to notice. Pack moved on, his back stiff in disapproval. Suddenly the Marquis was by his side, taking his elbow, steering him to the trophy porch at the rear of the house. "Arthur, I'd like you to put a few articles in the paper. I'm going ahead with the Deadwood stagecoach line. We're acquiring four Concord coaches from Gilmer and Salisbury. It's been recommended we maintain at least one hundred and fifty stage horses. What do you think?"

Pack was flattered. "I'd like to know more."

"It is two hundred and fifteen miles to Deadwood and we are building a station every ten to fifteen miles, the precise interval depending on terrain. We've finished five. Soon there will be thirteen stations along the route."

"You're putting them up now? That's quick work."

"A coach will leave three days a week and will make its midday dinner stop on the south fork of the Cannonball. That coach will continue south while its driver doubles back on the afternoon stage coming into Medora. In that manner each driver will need to memorize only the details of his own section of the route. He will use four fresh teams a day, and he will cover about a hundred miles round-trip. The coach, having left Medora in the morning, will arrive in Deadwood on the evening of the following day."

"A thirty-six-hour trip?"

"Just so. Passenger fare will be ten cents a mile."

"And freight?"

"Express charges ten cents a pound. A coach can carry a ton of cargo—"

Pierre Wibaux, coming through to examine the trophies, interrupted: "In that country? Muddy roads and steep hills?"

"I'm assured it can be done, Pierre. Twenty-five hundred pounds, in fact, and four passengers as well."

"Whose estimate is that? Jerry Paddock's?"

Annoyed, Pack turned on Wibaux. "Now, Jerry Paddock knows horses and wagons."

"He's probably stolen enough of both," Wibaux agreed.

Madame Medora swept forward; some intuition had brought her. Her beauty immediately erased the growing tension. "Come along, Antoine, it's time to feed our guests."

Dinner was a splendid affair, served on costly Minton china. It began with Mumm's champagne from the wine icebox. The table sat eight. The servants brought forth plovers' eggs and truffles from Park & Tilford, Apollinaris water, finely sauced pheasant and a St. Julien Château LaGrange from Bordeaux that the Marquis tasted and pronounced splendid.

At table Pack found himself studying the Marquis and Roosevelt. It might have been said by someone who did not know them that the two men had quite a bit in common. They were the same age. They were wealthy; they were avid hunters; they were born aristocrats; they loved the Bad Lands; they were, or purported to be, fearless men of adventure; they were exceptionally well educated; they had interests in financial matters and political affairs.

But in spite of those things they were at opposite poles, really. De Morès had grand ambition and energy; he had impeccable manners and personal habits, which set him far apart from the childish New York dude with his desultory small-rancher desires and his rapid priggish voice. Roosevelt's personality and mannerisms made Pack cringe.

Madame la Marquise said to Roosevelt, "Does your arm hurt terribly?"

"Not a bit of it. I feel capital. Capital. Especially in such charming presence as yours, dear lady."

Pack felt a sense of personal shame every time he caught Roosevelt exchanging secret smiles across the table with the lady Medora. At least he thought they were secret smiles. It wasn't possible to be sure. The suspicion had occurred to him that the entire matter existed solely in his own mind and that he might be misinterpreting innocent gestures. As a journalist he tried to be fair and objective but the effort was maddening; how did you draw the line between impartiality and indecision?

Lady Medora smiled at him. He felt shattered into pieces.

After dinner there was coffee. De Morès—by birth heir to one of the Orléans dukedoms and a "white lily of France"—sat in his favorite deerhide chair. When he lifted his cup to drink, he deftly pushed the points of his mustache out of the way with two fingers of his left hand. He wore a pinch-waisted grey suit and a starched white shirt. He said, "The buffalo will be extinct in a few years, they say. That suits me well enough." He chortled. "It will make my trophies worth all the more." He described how the thrill of the hunt no longer satisfied his cravings for excitement and therefore he had faced that grizzly bear there with glittering steel—he bade everyone examine the knife.

Medora, upon her husband's request, played Beethoven on the piano. She caressed the keys so beautifully, Pack thought—such warm passion. But the interval put him in mind of guns blazing in the night. . . .

Roosevelt listened with polite restlessness and afterward Pack overheard him confiding in Howard Eaton, "I fear the only music my ear comprehends is the song of wild birds." Pack glared at him.

When cognac had been distributed the Marquis led the gentlemen onto the trophy porch. Continuing a discourse to his foreign guests he gesticulated toward a framed photograph of the abattoir and declared, "The object of the undertaking is to provide on the range facilities for fattening, slaughtering and marketing forty thousand beeves yearly, thus doing away with the risks and losses arising from live-animal shipment, transport shrinkage, middlemen and of course Jewish monopolies. You see," he went on without a break, baffling Pack as he so often did with his abrupt change of direction, "I can trace my nobility back to the King of Aragon five hundred years ago—and now I shall become the richest financier in the world. It is only fitting. We of the aristocracy are uniquely suited to rule the world, don't you agree?"

His remarks had not been addressed to Roosevelt but it was Roosevelt who replied. "I've no patience, Mr. De Morès, with attempts to fall back into the tyrannies of old ways. History ought to mean progress—and I believe democracy to be the most noble principle we have to offer the world. I hold that men like you and me are not entitled, simply because of family or wealth, to an ounce of privilege. In fact I think we ought to be held to an exceptional accountability. A good deal has been given to us, and therefore people have a right to expect a good deal of us."

Howard Eaton was looking on, visibly impressed, perhaps not so much by Roosevelt's egalitarian sentiments as by the stout courage with which he had uttered them in the face of the daunting Marquis.

Obviously feeling he had scored a point, Roosevelt said with boyish smugness, "Hem, hem!"

The Marquis said, "I should not expect the son of a merchant to agree with me," and turned his back haughtily to speak with one of the Belgians.

Pierre Wibaux took Roosevelt's elbow and said mildly, "You ought not call him 'Mr. De Morès.'"

"It's jolly well the American way. We have no titles here."

What a prime silly fool, Pack thought. What an ass.

"No, no," said Wibaux. He was a little drunk and slurred his words, but his English was excellent. "I mean 'De Morès' is not his name, it's his title. His name is Vallombrosa. He is either Mr. Vallombrosa or the Marquis De Morès. You see?"

The Marquis was swinging about. "Wibaux, what business have you with this man?"

"What?"

"I heard you'd bought six horses from him for an absurdly high price."

"You're mistaken. I've bought nothing from him."

"Now you call me a liar! I won't be called a liar in my own house!"

The Marquis was more than a little drunk; Pack only just realized it. The Marquis pulled two sabers from their scabbards and tossed one belligerently to Wibaux. "Defend yourself!"

The rancher caught it by the hilt in mid-air—a matter of reflex rather than decision.

"*Alors?*"

"*En garde!*" The Marquis was on him in an instant, blade flashing. Wibaux fell back, defending himself vigorously, slashing back and forth, not quite fencing but somehow keeping the Marquis at bay by the sheer energy of his flailing defense.

It was serious swordplay. These weren't foils; they were cavalry sabers, heavy enough to decapitate. Pack felt a chugging sensation in his innards. A sudden sweat cracked through his skin. "Wait a minute. Gentlemen! Gentlemen!"

Roosevelt had already thrust past him. "Stop it, De Morès. Stop this—right now!"

The Marquis ignored him. He lunged; Wibaux parried desperately; there was the crash of blade upon blade, the sickening hiss of sliding steel. Wibaux had his back to the wall now.

The European visitors watched the combat with jaded impartiality. Theodore Roosevelt was dodging elbows, trying to reach out and grasp the Marquis.

Pack watched Roosevelt and felt scorn. The damn fool was likely to get his arm chopped off at this rate.

That was when Madame Medora swept into the room. Somehow her delicate voice penetrated everything. "Antoine!"

The Marquis stepped back. He lowered the saber. An easy smile spread beneath his mustache. "*Ça va.*" He endeavored to laugh. "Just having a bit of sport, aren't we, Wibaux. Amusing our visitors with a bit of Wild West adventure, eh?"

Wibaux had nothing to say; he was breathing heavily—the blood had rushed into his face and he tried to put on a smile for the others but it wavered. He tossed the saber to the floor and walked unsteadily from the room.

Roosevelt watched the Marquis with a fixed narrowed gaze.

Pack began to relax. He smiled. It was nothing, really. Two hot-blooded gents got a bit drunk and showed their tempers; nobody hurt.

It brought the evening to an abrupt and ragged close.

A sense of propriety led Pack reluctantly to seek out Roosevelt, to walk back to town with him, but he found that the dude had already departed.

In a sense he felt relief. But there was also a degree of frustration. In challenging the Marquis, Roosevelt had thrown raw meat on the floor. Pack knew De Morès would not let it lie there to grow maggoty. There was a clear conflict between the two men—their attitudes, ambitions, even their very personalities were clearly marked for collision, and Pack wanted to see it concluded. He wanted to see the boisterous little New Yorker's comeuppance; more, he wanted this potentially hazardous obstacle removed from the Marquis's course of destiny.

In the morning Pack returned to the château to ask the proprietor further questions about the stagecoach line for his article in the *Cow Boy*. He found the Marquis on the verandah awaiting the arrival of his saddle horse. Pack began to speak but he'd hardly got four words out when, triggered by his instant reflexes, the Marquis wheeled.

Pack hadn't heard a thing, but when he looked that way he saw a horseman coming uphill from the river bottoms.

It was Jerry Paddock. He arrived with a rifle in his scabbard. He was dressed in his threadbare formal clothes but he hadn't quite groomed himself accordingly: Pack observed that as usual he hadn't stood quite close enough to his razor. The early sun sliced in under the hatbrim and glittered off the slitted surfaces of Paddock's hooded eyes. He scowled; his eyebrows crawled together like black caterpillars. "Frank O'Donnell and Dutch Reuter and Riley Luffsey been seen on their way into town armed to the teeth. They been bragging about how this time they going to burn the château down. You got to teach them a lesson, and there is only one kind they understand. The kind with gunpowder behind it."

Pack said, "Now, they're just baiting you. It's the custom to hoo-raw foreigners."

"They shot up my house. They endangered the life of my wife. You were here, Arthur."

Misgivings made him say, "I didn't see their faces. Neither did you."

"I know who they are, Arthur, and so do you. The sheriff and his brother—that craven deputy!—have elected to remain away from here and take no part in the matter. Very well. I've given the law every chance. I'm not a greenhorn any longer. If these men want a fight I shall be pleased to give them one."

Several of the Marquis's men arrived—the news had spread; perhaps Jerry Paddock had dropped a word at the stable on his way up here. The Marquis told them to remain where they were, and Pack saw the disappointment in their faces. He watched the

Marquis smoothly mount his handsome but mettlesome cream-colored stallion. On a Navajo blanket the Mexican saddle was ornamented with silver horn, cantle and taps.

The Marquis said, "I shall deal with the hunters—we'll see how they appreciate the French code of law."

Pack noticed Jerry Paddock riding away at a casual angle into the brush. Behind him he heard one of the hands say, "What's old Jerry armed with? I didn't get a look at it."

"Springfield trapdoor."

"Army carbine?"

"Rifle, not carbine."

"Long range, then. Big cartridge."

"It's chambered down to .38-56. And only one shot."

"One's all you need, if you know where to put it."

The events that followed were confusing. All anyone knew at first was that there was the racket of shooting—a lot of it.

LUFFSEY KILLED

> . . . The *Cow Boy* has learned that The Marquis De Morès saw Luffsey, O'Donnell and Reuter riding toward him at full speed with guns drawn. De Morès raised his hand as a gesture for them to stop, but this gesture was returned with gunfire.
>
> De Morès opened fire and the riders' horses were soon down, the hunters using them for cover as they fired at De Morès. During the ensuing gun battle, which took minutes, Luffsey was killed by a bullet through the neck; O'Donnell was wounded, his thigh shattered, and Reuter was slightly wounded. All three horses were killed. The stock of O'Donnell's rifle was smashed, so badly so that it could not be used.
>
> O'Donnell and Reuter seeing Luffsey dead tried to make a run for it. In the face of this rout, the Marquis must be credited with great restraint. In this part of the West more men are shot where their suspenders come together than any other spot on their anatomies, but De Morès held fire.

In Bob Roberts's place that night there were varying degrees of maudlin drunkenness. The morose hunters rehearsed obituaries and vowed retaliation.

Pack confessed, "Now, I miss him a bit, you know. He had a bad streak, no doubt of it, but there was good in the lad. Given a better chance he might have made his mark on the world."

It was the extent to which he was willing to display his sense of loss in this company. In truth he felt a deep sorrow—perhaps in part for what the youth might have become. If the wildness could have been tamed in time Luffsey might have come to something; he'd had intelligence and enthusiasm and you just couldn't help liking him. Pack had tried to enlist the lad as a protégé and the regret ran deep that he had failed.

He heard Joe Ferris say, "Only one way Frank O'Donnell's rifle could have been busted up that bad. One of the Marquis's exploding bullets."

Pack said, "What of it? Luffsey must've got off several shots before he died, for his rifle was empty and there were three empty cartridge cases in his revolver and two loaded ones. The Marquis was defending himself, it's plain to see."

Dan McKenzie remarked, "The bullet that killed Luffsey went straight through. Nobody found the slug."

Bob Roberts said, "Could it have been a .38-56?"

"Who knows."

Joe said to Pack, "So maybe the Marquis wasn't out there by himself all alone face-to-face with three murderous miscreants. What do you say to that?"

"There's no evidence of anything of the kind. Even Reuter and O'Donnell don't claim to have seen more than one man, although they say the Marquis opened fire first. Naturally they'd claim that. Otherwise they're finished."

"Your big brave Marquis went out there all alone to face three seasoned hunters armed to the teeth. You really believe that hog swill, Pack?"

"Now, I saw him ride out by himself. It is the truth." And so it was.

Amid gossips in town the killing of Luffsey was laid, without evidence Pack could credit, on the doorstep of Jerry Paddock, because he was disliked generally and was said to be a killer and probably was the best shot of any of the men the Marquis employed. Never mind that nobody could place Paddock at the scene of the event. It was assumed he had lain up in the brush and done the long-range shooting from across the river.

The Marquis himself was not generally believed to have fired the lethal shot, because the bullet that had killed Luffsey had not been of the exploding kind. The reasoning was specious, of course. The boys were far too quick to assume the Marquis carried only exploding bullets.

Pack found a certain savage satisfaction in being able to report in the *Cow Boy*, to what he hoped would be the chagrin of the loudmouths and cynics and especially his misguided friend Joe Ferris, that the Marquis had manfully agreed to submit to arrest any time by Sheriff Harmon, and meanwhile was endeavoring honestly and earnestly to calm things down by guaranteeing to remain available within the jurisdiction at any time for hearings and/or trial in custody of the territorial courts.

Nevertheless, to Pack's profound disgust, by the time the story of the gun battle on the Little Missouri had made the rounds it had grown into a full-scale massacre.

And not two days after the gunfight, Joe Ferris remarked softly, "You notice who hooked up his private car to the train this morning and headed out east? None other than the great Innocent—your friend De Morès. So much for his promise to stay put in the jurisdiction."

"Roosevelt's gone east too," Pack sputtered.

"What the hell's that got to do with it?"

"I don't know," Pack admitted. It had been something to say, to fill the empty moment that seemed to require a response. He felt foolish. He said, "You may call the Marquis quite a few things but hardly a coward. He will be back."

In that, as it turned out, he was quite right.

At the boneyard on the butte Luffsey was planted with his boots on. Huidekoper, the Langs, Joe Ferris and others were in attendance—most of the mourners being people who had had little or no use for him during his lifetime, but this was a show of force and a choosing-up of sides; thus the incongruous adjacence of Ferris and Finnegan, and the notable absence of the Marquis and all his men.

Pack noted disapprovingly that Joe Ferris wore his Remington revolver blatantly on his hip—a rudeness, God knew, at a funeral; but there it was.

Did Joe expect Jerry Paddock to blaze away from ambush at the funeral party?

As the new white wood cross went up there was a great deal of muttering, much of it old-sod accented. "Why, darlin' Riley Luffsey had so soft a heart, he could hardly kill a fly."

Frank O'Donnell was not there; he was confined to his bed by his bullet wound. But Dutch Reuter had the gall to put in an appearance, and was surrounded with immediate loyalty by Redhead Finnegan and a crowd that seemed to include every Irishman in the district. Finnegan kept running his hand down his face—pretending to wipe away his crocodile tears, Pack thought savagely. They are such brazen hypocrites in their bleeding sentimentality.

Tempers ran very high. Dutch Reuter was not bashful in honking out his story. He had just happened to encounter O'Donnell and Luffsey on the trail, and accompanied them on their quiet ride toward town. They were peaceful folks. They nobody no harm meant.

If this were indeed the case, Pack thought angrily, how was it that the Marquis was able to show such a large number of bullet holes through his clothing and a soft lead bullet smashed against the buttstrap of his revolver?

Deacon Osterhaut, reading over the corpse, said self-righteously, "Perhaps it is true young Luffsey may have been headed for certain eventual arrest. Yet we cannot know anything but his Innocence in the eyes of the Almighty. In any event he now is in the Highest Custody."

As the Deacon intoned the prayer, Pack saw Little Casino try to hide a tear in her eye. He felt moisture in his own eyes; and it occurred to him that there was hope for us all in the knowledge that even so low a creature as Luffsey had friends and loved ones to cry for him.

Sotto voce, Joe Ferris said in Pack's ear, "You know damn well it was Jerry Paddock killed the kid from ambush."

"Nonsense. Paddock wasn't even there."

Joe's suspicions obviously had to be chalked up to his foolish prejudice against the Marquis and his virulent dislike of Jerry Paddock.

I don't like the villain any better than you do, Pack thought, *but that's no proof he murdered Luffsey.*

It must continue to be Pack's mission to set his misinformed friend on the path of Right and Truth.

Eleven

Joe Ferris climbed up on the seat and ran the wagon out of town, happy to get away from slaughter smell and treacherous tempers—these latter still running high after several weeks of a strange suspension during which none of the principals had been on the scene. The Marquis and Marquise were away, allegedly on business, for nearly a month. Redhead Finnegan hadn't shown his face in town during that time. Frank O'Donnell was recovering slowly from his wound after a bout with blood poisoning; he drank profusely but kept to himself. Dutch Reuter had stayed away from town. A.C. Huidekoper seemed to have been spending all his free time traveling from ranch to ranch trying to organize the owners and managers against De Morès, with no success Joe could see. Even Roosevelt had been away in the East for three weeks, taking care of family business matters.

But now he was back. And so was the Marquis.

It seemed inevitable there was going to be a dust-up between those two gents. Somehow you could feel it coming.

The trail north to the Elkhorn crossed and recrossed the Little Missouri River more than twenty times. At intervals Joe went bouncing in the ruts past holding pens where hired hands were gathering cattle for the ravenous De Morès abattoir. He passed the turnoffs to Wibaux's ranch and Pierce Bolan's. As he came onto the Elkhorn the colors of the Bad Lands changed subtly—the horizontal stripes seemed to become more pale and there was more greenery on the slopes. The trees in the bottoms were lush, even this late in the year. Easy to understand why Roosevelt had chosen this location.

Joe tied the team in front of the log ranch house. Dutch Reuter evidently had watched his approach; now he set aside a rifle, came up from the barn and lifted a dipperful of water from the basin by the door. Dusty and shaggy, Dutch gulped a refreshing drink and then poured cold water over his head so that it ran down his face. It dripped from his beard. He wiped at it clumsily. "That French bastard still going me to shoot?"

"I expect he knows better, Dutch. He wouldn't try it a second time. Most likely you're safe, specially long as you're under Mr. Roosevelt's protection."

"Don't need nobody's protection." Dutch took out his tobacco, rolled up a paper-collar stiff and ignited it. Then he said, "Before, he Mr. Roosevelt did not like. Hate, now."

Sometimes it was hard to decide what Dutch meant; his fractured English made for poor understanding. Joe said, "You mean the Markee hates Mr. Roosevelt—more than he did before?"

"Just so. And worse if I stay. He Mr. Roosevelt try to kill, maybe."

"I don't think even the Markee's that big of a fool."

"I hear cowboys talk about Roosenfelder the Jew bastard. This from the Markee they got. He Jews don't like."

"I met a couple Jew folks," Joe said. "I buy from them all the time, stocking the store. They ain't nearly as crazy as some. They don't shake, they don't refuse to ride the railroad, they don't mind if you take a drink or a smoke. Practical folks. What's the Markee got against them?"

"Don't know. Ask him. Hey, Joe—Mr. Roosevelt, he Jewish?"

"Not that I know of."

"Sure be funny if he was not." Then Dutch said, "Maybe I favor for boss make—kill Markee and go away." He suddenly grinned, as if to take the edge off it; but Joe wasn't entirely sure he was joking.

At one side of the barn Wil Dow was milking a cow, squeezing loud jets one-two, one-two into an echoing tin pail. This probably was the only childless ranch in the territory where they took milk. Mr. Roosevelt's fondness for drinking the stuff was one of his suspect foreign traits. Like his eyeglasses and his accent, it set him apart and made him the object of saloon jokes that were more insulting than fond.

Joe said to Dutch, "I expect the Markee isn't happy about Mr. Roosevelt keeping you on. But let Mr. Roosevelt worry about that, Dutch." He helped himself to water and tried to keep his tone casual. "What really did happen out there?"

"Heap of shooting."

"I know that." Exasperation nudged Joe's patience. "Who did it?"

"Didn't see 'em."

"How many, then?"

"Don't know."

"Tell me this. There's talk you boys were riding on the château to set fire to it. That a fact?"

"Hell no."

"Well then. Was De Morès the only one?"

"Paddock—on the rise of the hill, us he saw. He horse turns, back out of sight rides—back to the Marquis, I guess. That mile we go. Over hill we go, and everyplace guns was. Three, four, five, don't know. Too busy we was, from horses jumping."

"Hidden guns? You never saw who was shooting?"

"Yah. Never saw." Dutch stepped to the edge of the piazza to drop ash on the ground. The breeze carried it away. "What happen, you want to know? I you tell, Joe—too scared, we was. Too scared to remember. Too scared to see."

"I guess I can understand that. Who started the shooting, then?"

"Don't know. Wasn't us."

"Was it De Morès?"

"No. Was from the bushes."

"Ambush. Jerry Paddock. That bastard Markee."

Roosevelt came riding in past the house. Joe turned toward him in indignation. "You hear that, Mr. Roosevelt?"

"Hear what?"

"Dutch and his friends were ambushed. They were fired on from the bushes. I always knew the Markee was a shifty son of a bitch, but this—"

Roosevelt thrust a rigid index finger toward Dutch. "Have you changed your mind? Do you want to file a complaint and press charges against Mr. De Morès?"

"No. No law stuff."

Roosevelt returned to his gaze to Joe. "There you have it. It would appear there's little to be done."

"We could organize a party and hang him for murder."

"Not without due process of law, by thunder! Not while there are men of civilized decency left alive!" Roosevelt dismounted. As he led the horse toward the barn he called back over his shoulder, "Are you ready to head west in the morning?"

"Sure enough," Joe replied without enthusiasm.

Roosevelt had tolled him into this two days ago when he'd returned on the train from back East. The New Yorker wanted to go out on a hunting expedition before the onset of winter. He wanted Joe Ferris with him. Joe didn't care to go hunting but it seemed a prudent time to be away from town for a while; anyhow he needed money to keep the store alive; so he had agreed, after McKenzie and Pack had offered to take turns looking after the store in his absence.

Roosevelt had been in a good mood in spite of the fact that he had the *other* arm in a sling. Seemed he'd no sooner arrived on Long Island than he'd gone out on a hunt, following the hounds, and his horse had pitched him into a stream, breaking some bone or other in his arm. It really wasn't safe to allow the poor dude near any sort of horse.

But Roosevelt had been cheerful when he'd stepped off the train and he couldn't wait to set out into the wilderness.

Joe couldn't help wondering what had perked him up so. He knew of few things that could have such an effect. Strong drink and pretty women, mainly. Joe knew this much: Roosevelt didn't drink.

Did he have a woman back East?

If he did, he wasn't talking about her.

In the morning Dutch Reuter came along. Dutch drove the wagon; he was to be mainly the cook. Bill Sewall was invited to accompany the hunters but the old Mennonite stayed behind to help young Dow look after the ranch—he said he preferred that to traveling the endless boring prairie.

It was easy to see by the way he moved that Roosevelt was

favoring the injured arm. Nevertheless he was carrying his entire armory. "I want a grizzly bear above all. And a mature buffalo—a great bison bull."

Joe made a face.

They came across the cabin at midmorning, that first day out. Joe remembered the place all too well. From the outset that shack had been fated ill.

Mr. Roosevelt said, "I've passed this place a score of times and always wondered about it. It seems sound enough. Why doesn't someone live in it?"

"It happens you're asking the right man that question, sir. I can tell you the whole sorry story of this miserable excuse for a house."

Joe went on to tell it:

Two years ago in the railroad-building days, someplace nearly two hundred miles away south in the Short Pine Hills, some poor fool had thought to make his fortune cutting logs for ties. The fool aimed to float the ties north down the Little Missouri and sell them to the NPRR.

He was a fool because he should have asked. Anybody could have told him not to trust that river.

A storm had swelled the Little Missouri; the fool had lost control of his ties—the binding ropes snapped, his rafts splintered into giant toothpicks, and after wild rides the logs had been tossed helter-skelter onto riverbanks from here to Louisiana.

No one knew how fate had disposed of the fool. May be he'd been swept along in the flood; may be he'd given up in good cheer and gone farther west.

One accumulation of ties got trapped in a whirlpool eddy at a sharp bend 25 miles north of Medora town. When the flood subsided it left the stack of logs high and drying.

That was two years ago; Joe remembered it because he had camped here with Dutch and a hunting party, waiting out the storm. As they'd broken camp, Dutch had made a note of the location of the lumber pile. Then a couple of months later when the wood was mostly dried Joe had helped him set the ties on end like stockade fencing and they'd packed the chinks with mud and laced a sod roof across it and hung a horseshoe points-up over the doorway. They had nailed paper over the window openings and

Dutch had talked vaguely about settling his wife here but then Deacon and Mrs. Osterhaut had offered fifty dollars for the place, which was far more than its worth, and without a second thought Dutch accepted the money.

Dutch would have kept it all, too. Joe remembered having words with him in Big Mouth Bob's Bug Juice Dispensary. It had required three drinks' worth of reasoning, after which Dutch had parted with a double eagle and a half eagle. They'd shaken hands and bought more drinks and forgiven each other. At the drunken end of the evening they'd lurched outside into the darkness and been rolled by a hard-breathing villain who had escaped in the dark with their gold pieces.

Joe always suspected Jerry Paddock had done the deed but he couldn't honestly swear he'd recognized the man by sight or by scent, dark as it was and drunk as he was.

So no profit had come, after all, from the cabin of ties. It had started hard-luck and stayed that way.

Joe had gone back to work hunting. Dutch had disappeared into the wilderness according to his habit.

Now, riding beside Roosevelt, Joe looked back at the wagon to make sure Dutch was not in earshot; then he reined closer to Roosevelt and confided, "You know, sometimes Dutch ain't the most reliable of men."

Joe liked him anyhow. He'd put up with Dutch for a whole season during which they had provided the NPRR construction crews and dining-car passengers with fresh-killed venison for five cents a pound.

When it got to be too much killing for Joe he quit. But nothing seemed to get Dutch down. He was what flap-eared Arthur Packard called a free soul.

There was for example the time when Joe and Dutch rode across the tracks complaining of the heat and noticed an eastbound passenger train approaching in the distance—and the next thing Joe knew, Dutch was flagging down the train.

It labored to a juddering halt with great effort. When the engineer shouted down at Dutch, inquiring what the emergency was, Dutch only waved with great cheer, climbed aboard the dining car and helped himself to a pitcher of ice-water.

Joe watched from his saddle while, in the face of the train crew's outrage, Dutch leaped off the train, still clutching the silver pitcher of ice-water. He drank deep and then proffered it up to his companion but Joe didn't have the nerve and only shook his head. Dutch had another swallow and then tossed the pitcher up into the hands of the surprised conductor. He said in his German accent, "The alkali water in the river I don't like. Thank you," and made a cheerful bow of thanks before he gathered the reins and mounted.

Joe remembered how he'd cringed as they rode away followed by shouted threats upon the safety of their persons.

He remembered it all as they approached the cabin he and Dutch had built. Its luck hadn't changed. It stood abandoned, weeds crowding the doorway, windows gaping vacantly. Joe said, "I'm not sure if it's still Osterhaut's."

"What happened, then?"

"Ever put your nose in the door?" Joe replied.

Dutch watched with amusement. Roosevelt reined toward the cabin. The sorrel tried to shy away. Controlling it with difficulty the Easterner bent low to peer inside. "I don't see anything."

Dutch said, "Go closer."

The horse balked. Roosevelt sank his heels. "Great Scott!" He lashed the rein-ends across its flanks; it only shied back.

"It doesn't like something—"

There was a gust of wind. The sorrel all but pitched its rider; just the same, Joe saw it when the stink hit Roosevelt's nostrils: his face contorted violently. The nervous horse backed up.

Now at last Roosevelt understood the animal's behavior. He allowed it to trot back to the trail.

Joe said, "May be ten years before the smell clears out, if it ever does. They tell it, the nice kitty was under the bed when the Deacon and Mrs. Osterhaut came home with the hired hand. The hired man favored waiting for the nice kitty to leave. Mrs. Osterhaut put her chin in the air and said this and that. You met them—you recall their dispositions? Hired man tried to talk reason but Mrs. Osterhaut made a fuss and the Deacon wasn't ready to listen to a hired man, so he went in after the skunk with a pitchfork, with the result that you can smell."

By now Dutch had caught up with the wagon and began laughing. "Polecat Hollow, this place his new name."

Roosevelt wrinkled his nose. "And where are the Osterhauts living?"

"Trying to farm beef cattle over on the Little Cannonball. As you can tell from the round-up tally they aren't making much of a go of it. He makes a dollar here and a dollar there for doing confirmations and such—I guess it's enough to keep body and soul apart." He chuckled then. "That skunk didn't improve their mood any. Deacon's still complaining about everything in sight."

"It baffles me," Roosevelt said, "that such fellows fail to realize how their complaints make people dislike them. Everyone despises a whiner."

There was one thing, Joe conceded in the privacy of his thoughts, that you could say for Roosevelt: he never whined.

In fact that was one of the exasperating things about him.

Under a racket of rattling rustling cottonwood leaves they departed the river bottoms and climbed west toward the high prairie, dragging the wagon up sharp-pitched slopes until they reached an eminence from which they could see clear across the colorful Bad Lands behind them.

Not far ahead of them a wolf stood alone on a promontory. With gentlemanly generosity Roosevelt said, "Your shot, Dutch."

Dutch Reuter found his rifle under the seat and slid it from the scabbard but he did not lift it. He cocked the hammer, uncocked it and put the weapon away. The wolf ran down off the skyline and disappeared. Roosevelt said, "Why didn't you shoot?"

"I am no good shot."

"You made your living shooting buffalo."

"Buffalo was big target, close by, not move." Dutch waved toward the promontory. "Three, four hundred meters must be."

"Then you need more practice. Most of us are not born experts. If we choose resolutely to apply ourselves, we can by sheer industry make ourselves fair rifle shots."

Joe Ferris said, "May be he's just tired of shooting and killing."

"Old fellow, it requires all kinds of moral and physical qualities to be a good hunter. It requires good judgment and cool courage. On the hunt, by custom and repeated exercise of self-mastery and will power, a man must get his nerves and his nerve thoroughly under control. Otherwise we all have buck fever sometimes, don't you know."

"Sir, I expect it's a long time since Dutch had buck fever," said Joe Ferris. "It's not buck fever just because he's seen too much blood."

"Ah, Joe, I don't know what you mean by that. D'you know—one day I want to go back to Africa, south of where I went before, and hunt the greatest game on the earth—rhinoceros, elephant, Cape buffalo, the mighty lion. By Godfrey, I've never even *seen* a lion! Doesn't the idea make your blood rush?"

"Can't say as it does, sir."

There was a bleached buffalo skull. Sight of them was still common on the plains. They found nothing else that day, to Joe's relief, and they made camp by twilight in a fairly open section of Bad Lands where a low butte was crowned with rusty-red clay evidence that an old coal fire had consumed a surface lignite vein.

Roosevelt sat cleaning his favorite rifle. He did it mostly with one hand, still favoring the arm he had injured. The rifle was an 1876 Winchester in .45-75 caliber; he'd had the lever-action weapon custom-engraved for him with likenesses of buffalo, antelope and deer. His arsenal also included the bird shotguns—a Thomas ten and a Kennedy sixteen hammerless—and back in the ranch house for general round-the-meadow shots he owned a three-barrelled gun with twin shotgun bores above a .40-70 rifle tube. And in addition to all that he wore a .45 Frontier Colt single-action revolver, plated with both gold and silver and engraved with elaborate scrolls; raised on its ivory handles were his initials and the lugubrious head of a buffalo, in commemoration of the one he had shot last year and danced around.

He was a dandy dude for certain but Joe knew how that could fool people into underestimating him. From last year's experience Joe recalled how well Roosevelt knew his equipment and its uses. In his taxidermy kit, for example, were knives, arsenic, cotton wads, brushes, surgical shears, needle and thread. He would skin his prizes with great patient care. He didn't smell too good after he got done, but the job would be top class.

Roosevelt finished cleaning the rifle. He put it away. "I remember my first gun. My father gave it to me when I was thirteen. A 23-gauge Lefaucheux double."

"You may need some of those guns on two-legged game before too long," Joe observed. "What are you going to do about the Markee?"

"Do about him?" Roosevelt blinked behind the glasses. "Why, nothing. Unless he forces an issue, I've no reason to be concerned with him. Live and let live, old fellow."

"I get the feeling the Markee don't think the same way you do about that. He thinks you're a Jew, and he thinks Jews ought to be 'dealt with.' That's how I heard him put it."

"He's mistaken on both counts, then," Roosevelt said with his stubborn equanimity. Then he disappeared into the bushes again, sick with the colic. It seemed to Joe Ferris that the dude was always sick with something or other; and it had not ceased to amaze him that Roosevelt never seemed to give in to his constant ailments or to complain about them. Did he never feel despair?

In the morning Joe heard the sad rich cadence of a meadowlark's song. It was very loud and urgent. By the cock of Roosevelt's square head Joe realized the dude had heard it as well.

Roosevelt was quick to identify birds but he still hadn't learned what their songs could signify. Joe put his hand on his Remington revolver and looked all around.

A moment later sure enough he saw a small party of Indians emerge from behind a knoll and canter effortlessly away on their tough many-colored ponies.

Roosevelt's eyes squinted behind the glasses as the Indians rode away. He looked at Joe—at Joe's hand on the revolver—and said accusingly, "You knew they were there. Before we saw them—you knew."

"Yes sir."

"How?"

"Meadowlark didn't make that loud racket for no reason."

"I see." Roosevelt slowly smiled. "I see! Thank you, old fellow." He stretched higher in the saddle and braced the high plains wind: his teeth glittered with the urgent desire to be driving forward.

Joe ranged his horse alongside the New Yorker's. With absolute certainty that his wish would be obeyed, Roosevelt said, "Find me buffalo."

It made Joe uneasy and a bit angry with himself; he had the

strong feeling Roosevelt understood perfectly well that he did not like hunting at all—that he went along grudgingly—but the dude seemed to have an uncanny appreciation that he did his job well and conscientiously, and seemed altogether confident of Joe's ability to produce, however reluctantly, whatever was asked of him. No matter how much Joe might dislike the work, it was difficult not to feel flattered.

The wagon rattled along behind them. They went onto the flat prairie. In the afternoon they came upon a middle-distant herd of blacktail.

"Good targets for you, sir," Joe murmured.

Roosevelt dismounted and, his arm still being too weak for long-range shooting, aimed by resting his rifle across Manitou's saddle. He fired.

A moment passed. Then, astonishingly, two bucks collapsed.

Joe paced off the distance with his benefactor. "Four hundred yards, I make it."

Roosevelt was staring at the two deer. The single bullet had killed both of them.

Joe said, "I've heard of accidents like that. Never seen one before."

Roosevelt's eyes didn't move. "Accident? Old fellow, that's the best shot I've ever made."

Joe thought, *More like a miracle*. Roosevelt was at best a mediocre marksman.

But it was the sort of story a man might brag on for the rest of his life.

Nearly a week out, on a sullen humid day with a damp taste of coming rain on the wind, they went up into a range of timbered hills and came upon a track remarkably like the footprint of a giant human, and a b'ar tree claw-stripped of its bark up to an alarming height of eleven or twelve feet.

Joe had a look around. From this elevation the land swept away to the tiny saw teeth of a far blue horizon, and nothing stirred anywhere; but Dutch Reuter was alert for the first time—wary as an elk—and Joe Ferris said softly to the New Yorker, "Sir, please keep in mind you can't outrun a grizzly. Some men have tried. I never heard where any of them lived. If you can't shoot the bear down, climb high up a tree—and hang on, for he'll try to shake you out of the branches."

"What if there's no tree to climb?"

"Then there likely won't be a bear. They like the woods."

It was not until after Joe had spoken that it occurred to him that, with his arm in its painful weakened condition, it must have been beyond Roosevelt's capabilities to climb a tree.

The same point might have occurred to Roosevelt as well. But he said nothing of it. He did not seem deterred in the least from his eager purpose.

In any event they didn't find a bear just then; all they found was rain. It was wet and dismally chill and Joe was miserable, especially when Roosevelt made such a point of how he was enjoying it all.

"Just remember Trollope's precept: 'It's dogged as does it.'"

"Whatever you say, sir."

The fire's livid coals turned their faces Indian-dark. Crickets made a din in the night and Joe heard the tremulous call of a little owl. A tethered horse scratched its neck against the tree. All the animals were nervous.

Joe hunkered under his tarp and watched water drip off the trough of his hatbrim. He cleared his throat. "Say, Mr. Roosevelt?"

"What is it, Joe?"

"Why do you have to kill that bear?"

"I have never shot a grizzly. Do you know what a rare privilege it is to be in this country, so close on his track?"

"Bear never did nothing against me or you, sir. Why not leave him be?"

"We test our courage by standing and facing such magnificent killer beasts."

"Bear's got no rifle to shoot back at us."

"What on earth has got into you of late, old fellow?"

"I just don't see where it improves us to be killing creatures that never did us harm."

"It's the robust challenge of sport, my friend—and the requirements of modern science. Have you any idea how little is know about the grizzly bear? If we find this beast I shall learn a great deal from him."

"Like what his meat tastes like?" Joe was in an exceptionally sour mood; perhaps it was the rain.

Roosevelt did not take offense. "Yes, by Godfrey. I shall learn that, and I shall take his measurements. I shall examine the contents of his stomach, to learn about his diet, and I shall try to determine his age. I shall mount his head and cure his hide, study his skeleton and his organs, examine his teeth and touch the texture of his fur. I shall fill my notebooks and publish the results of my studies, so that naturalistic science may be advanced."

"Yes sir. And what'll we do with the half-ton of meat we can't eat?"

"It will feed someone. Indians if we can find them. If we can't, then coyotes and wolves and vultures."

"If every man who comes west with a rifle shoots him a grizzly bear," Joe said dismally, "pretty soon there won't be anything but bear ghosts."

Roosevelt scoffed. "Don't exaggerate so."

"Happened to the buffalo, didn't it. You used to see millions on these plains. How many we seen in the past week?"

Roosevelt—for one of the few times in Joe's recollection—said nothing at all. He only peered at the fire through his wet eyeglasses. Beyond him, beneath the wagon, Dutch Reuter snored loudly.

Theodore Roosevelt stood face to face with the great grizzly. The wind, plucking at its glossy brown coat, made its fur ripple like tall grass. Roosevelt aimed the rifle across the crook of his bad arm. As the bear lowered its head to charge, Joe began to lift his own rifle, but then Roosevelt fired.

The report of the gunshot echoed out across the hills with such reverberation that it seemed never to end.

Joe was ready to shoot but it wasn't necessary; the single bullet had killed the bear instantly: square between the eyes. It tumbled forward, however, and dropped only a few yards in front of the New Yorker.

Roosevelt didn't even take a step back.

It had been an act of considerable bravery. You had to admit that, Joe thought.

Roosevelt walked forward happily.

Joe looked down at the mountainous bear and said dryly, "You want to rassle the next one barehanded or will it satisfy you to use a Bowie knife?"

"I don't believe that brag of Mister De Morès's. Do you?"

Joe only shook his head. In truth he didn't care.

Roosevelt reached down to touch the bear's throat. The animal didn't stir. It was a magnificent beast. "Feel this coat, Joe. Like fine silk."

"They are proud animals," Joe said in a dull voice. "They like to keep themselves clean."

Roosevelt stood up. "You may as well have Dutch bring the wagon up. We've a hard day's work on this bounty."

"Yes sir."

As Joe turned away he heard his employer's voice again, unusually quiet:

"Old fellow, by Godfrey you've infected me with an evil spirit."

"What?"

"I don't feel the thrill in this that I ought to."

A lone buffalo browsed on a yellow-grass slope. A huge specimen—truly his "great bison bull." Roosevelt got off his horse, settled the rifle and steadied his aim. Joe looked away. The air was cool, the breeze fresh. A flight of Canadian geese went over, southbound. Joe waited for the sound of the shot. He made a face; he felt sick, as if he'd had too much rot-gut tonsil paint the night before.

After a very long time he turned on his heel to see what was wrong.

The buffalo was there as before—hardly two hundred yards distant; an easy shot. Roosevelt was still down on one knee, still sighting the rifle. But now he eased the hammer down and stood, shook his head slowly and rammed the rifle back into its saddle scabbard. He looked at Joe.

"Damn you, Joe."

Joe began to smile. "Be that as it may."

Roosevelt did not return his smile. He was quite grave. He said, as if it were an idea that had just occurred to him, "Old fellow, it's one thing to hunt an animal for meat and sport and leather and science—it is another to exterminate a species. God gave us no right to do that." He gripped the saddlehorn in his good hand and hauled himself into the saddle.

They rode away. Behind them the solitary buffalo continued to graze.

Next morning they loaded the wagon with bearskin, deer antlers, stuffed birds, full-racked elk and the head of the magnificent grizzly. It was time to go home.

Twelve

Bill Sewall came in out of the grey weather, bearing a burlap sack full of coal. They had dug the lumps off the buttes by hand. "I wish it'd make up its mind to rain or snow or clear up."

Wil Dow watched his uncle Bill take a match from the tin holder and go round lighting the kerosene lamps on the walls. Uncle Bill said, "I have got to get to the tonsorial place, get some dentisting—need to get my grinders put in order." He went through the ritual of packing and lighting his pipe. "And I want to find out what stockings are worth."

Sewall went to a window to glower up at the bluffs, fading now into early dusk. From where Wil Dow sat mending tack he could see the glow on a distant mound to the northwest where lightning had struck and a stubborn strip of soft lignite coal had caught fire in a clay hillside. In the cool days the vein smoked like a little volcano. Every night it glowed red, like twilight. These winter evenings were long; even Wil Dow felt low.

Uncle Bill said, "It's a great resort for thieves and cutthroats. Cowboy work—the cattle torture. I shall never like this country for a home."

"Oh, Uncle Bill."

"A man that could come here from New England and like it better than at home must have a depraved idear of life or hate himself or both."

"Well I don't hate myself and I don't feel depraved."

Mr. Roosevelt came in removing his heavy coat. Between painful coughs he said with great vehemence, "It's a wild arcadian romance, the wonderful charm of this region. In Dakota we are geographically in the exact middle of the North American continent, did you know that?"

His asthma was acting up. He sprawled wheezing in his rocking chair, tired and grimy from the long day's labors, and pulled out a volume of Swinburne from the row of books that stood fading on the south-facing windowsill. It democratically supported everything from the Bible to Ike Marvel. That ended the conversation for the moment. On the sill were Hawthorne and Lowell, Parkman and Bonner, Macon and Cooper, Keats and Tennyson, Craddock and Irving. They all were Roosevelt's old friends. Wil Dow had been endeavoring to sample them but there was never time enough; he would begin to read after supper but his lids would droop and he would sleep after only a page or two—often as Roosevelt was only getting started for the evening, writing industriously in his journals under the yellow cone of the whale-oil table lamp. He was still writing that book.

He was keeping up his correspondence too. There were frequent letters from back East, some of them in what looked like female handwriting—more hands than one, from what Wil glimpsed. Roosevelt wrote regularly to his sister but there was someone else as well. When he read those scented notes there was a quality of thoughtfulness in his concentration that led Wil's mind into varieties of interesting speculations.

Roosevelt cleaned his teeth and shaved every morning whether there was company or not. He washed his own clothes and took his turn feeding the horses, although it was true he rarely swamped the stables; that was left to Wil, as if he were the youngest—or perhaps it was just to remind them who was boss here.

Roosevelt sometimes spent part of an evening in the dark cellar developing his glass-plate photographs. Then, mildly stinking of chemicals, he would get into the rubber bathtub and soak, after which he would select a book and sit reading in his rocking chair while Dutch cooked up something to eat—often game of their own killing: grouse or ducks, deer or antelope. Roosevelt sometimes would make a remark about something he found in his book; he and Sewall would get into philosophical and intellectual arguments and Roosevelt would rock all around the room as he debated vehemently. Wil Dow, cleaning up after the meal, would listen with hungry interest. Uncle Bill was a rough man but not an ignorant one; he couldn't spell—neither could Roosevelt—but you had to admire the breadth of his keen mind: when Roosevelt said something complimentary about the diplomatic skills of Talleyrand, Sewall was quick to scoff. "Tallyrand was a hypocrite and a liar. If that's what a man requires for diplomacy then I want no part of it." Then in the morning Wil would have to go to a book surreptitiously to look up "Tallyrand."

Wil spent many a dull glum winter afternoon working cattle down the coulees toward fresh stands of curly buffalo grass—the staple winter feed of the Bad Lands. If there was an exceptionally weak animal he would take it, in the Mackinaw boat or across his saddle depending which side of the river he came from, into the barn and feed it hay.

All the while he was aware that Dutch Reuter was everywhere—mending fence, doctoring cattle, braiding leather, chopping wood. Dutch worked so hard that for a while he seemed to forget himself: the restless look went out of his eyes.

Then they had a visit from Pierce Bolan. The thick-chested yellow-haired Texan stood before the fire batting his hands together and said, "I have found a lot of dead sheep."

Roosevelt said, "We've seen them too."

Dutch Reuter said, "For Dakota, wrong kind of sheep."

"You got that right for certain, Dutch," said Pierce Bolan. "Merinos can't survive this climate. But forget the sheep. They're dead. It don't matter. What does matter—they keep crowding in cattle all the time. Especially the Marquis. In a short time they will eat us all out. You notice how the Marquis's cows graze one place down until food gets scarce and then they drive their cattle to where it is good without regard to whose range they're eating out."

Bill Sewall agreed. "I've had to chouse two, three dozen De Morès cattle off our ground just lately." He pulled at his red beard.

"I'm afraid the boss was led to believe there was more money in this than he will ever see."

Roosevelt said cheerfully, "I shall prove you dead wrong about that, old chap." He turned to Pierce Bolan. "It's cold and it's late. You'll share our supper and spend the night, of course."

At the break of day Pierce Bolan was first to leave the house—and first to return. "You folks got visitors. May want to arm yourselves."

Roosevelt was finishing his breakfast. "What's this?"

Wil Dow went to the window. He heard Bolan say, "Johnny Goodall and a crew. They're turnin' out a lot of cows. *Lot* of cows."

A thin crust of frost crunched under their boots when the five men walked upriver. Roosevelt had distributed rifles and shotguns; Wil Dow felt the ominous weight of the over-and-under three-barrel gun. He bounced it nervously in the circle of his fist as he walked.

At the foot of Blacktail Creek—nearly at Roosevelt's doorstep—half a dozen riders were dispersing cattle onto the bottoms. Pierce Bolan had not exaggerated. Wil Dow could not begin to count the animals. There was a sea of them.

He followed the boss's lead. They walked down there straight up. No hesitation. Mr. Roosevelt made up in grit what he lacked in size. Wil Dow waited to see him go off like a rocket.

Johnny Goodall reined his horse expertly through a clump of cattle and came forward with his hands wide and empty save for the reins. He had the courtesy to dismount, so as to give the five men his eyes at a level—more or less; Johnny was taller than any of them.

Roosevelt said, "You've quite a number of cattle with you, Johnny."

"Fifteen hundred head, sir."

"I'll ask you to keep moving them until they're off my land."

"I've got orders to fatten them here, sir."

That was it, then. Wil Dow felt it like a fist in his belly. The glove had been thrown down: the challenge was here. He laid the gun across his forearm and eased his body a quarter-turn away so that the muzzle was lined up on Johnny Goodall.

Johnny gave him a glance, shook his head slightly, and paid him no further attention.

Roosevelt said in a surprisingly mild voice, "I suppose I'm to take this to mean Mr. De Morès is affronted by my continuing to employ Mr. Reuter."

Uncle Bill Sewall thrust his beard toward Johnny Goodall. "You can't climb the old man just because that French fool and his ambushers threw down on him."

"I'm not climbing anybody, Bill. I've got no quarrel with Dutch."

"Your boss surely thinks he does."

"I herd cattle, Bill. That's all I'm here for."

In a voice that failed to conceal tautness behind its pretended calm, Pierce Bolan said, "Say, Johnny—this wouldn't have anything to do with that letter to the judge, would it now?"

Johnny had nothing to say to that.

Bill Sewall said, "What letter?"

"There's talk Judge Bateman got a letter asking him to swear out a warrant on the Markee for murderin' Riley Luffsey. Talk is, the letter's signed by Mr. Theodore Roosevelt."

"I wrote no such letter. I know of no such letter."

Bolan muttered, "Better tell that to the Markee, then, before he—"

"If Mr. De Morès wants to ask me any questions, let him ask them to my face." He turned to Johnny Goodall, who had listened to it all without any change of expression. "Well?"

"There's been a warrant sworn," Johnny conceded. "The lawyers are dealing with it. That's between the Marquis and the law—it's nothing to do with these cows. I've got orders to turn them out on these bottom grasses. Fatten them for winter slaughter."

"Not on my land, Mr. Goodall. Not today nor any other day."

"This isn't your land, Mr. Roosevelt. I'm sorry, sir, but you never filed claim to it."

"Neither did anyone else. It's open range—I've told you that before."

"The Marquis owns it, sir."

"I don't take backwater from any one. I shall put up a stout fight. You'll be gone with your cattle by daylight, Johnny, or we'll move them for you."

"I've got my orders, sir." And that was all Johnny had to say.

* * *

In the barn Roosevelt cinched his saddle on Manitou. Dutch Reuter said, "I come along."

Bill Sewall said, "Better not. Nothing the Markee'd like better than to see you in some dark alley on your back with your eyes open wide. Better you stay here."

"I agree. Look after the ranch," Roosevelt said to Dutch. "Don't tangle with Johnny or his men."

"I just let them cows the house eat down?"

"Look after our own stock. Ignore theirs. There's more than enough work here. Stay out of their sight—give them wide berth and pray don't give them any excuse to do you violence. Those cattle and their drovers will be out of here within thirty-six hours—you may count on that."

Dutch was too angry to keep still. "They try trouble to make, I some cowboys sure shoot—"

"That's quite enough, Dutch. You'll shoot no one. Those cowboys are earning their pay—doing their jobs with honor, and in the face of great possible risk. They're to be admired. We have no quarrel with them. Are you listening, Dutch? If you work for me, you will do as I ask. This is for everyone's good—it's best for you and for us as well."

"Yah, yah," Dutch growled in disgust. He stomped out.

Pierce Bolan said, "If I'm not needed—"

"Pierce, thank you very much for your help. You'd better hasten forward quickly"—there was a quick flashing smile—"get home and tend your own flock."

"Flock? That's a word we don't use much around here, sir," Bolan said dryly. "I'll take it you meant it in the Biblical sense." He climbed aboard and ducked his head to clear the barn door's header beam, and rode away at an insolently slow clip, watched by two or three of the De Morès cowboys. Johnny Goodall was down there, giving instructions. Roosevelt said, "I'll say again, for clarity, that our quarrel isn't with Johnny. No one's to choose a fight with him—is that understood?"

Wil Dow said, "Yes sir." He was relieved to hear it. He liked Johnny.

Bill Sewall's squint showed his displeasure. "Johnny knows who he works for. He takes the man's pay—he ought to stand the consequences."

"If it weren't for Johnny," Roosevelt replied, "things might be a good deal worse. He sets an example of true American courtesy for the edification of our visiting pretender to the throne of France. Without Johnny, I fear this territory might well be in flames."

Wil Dow was privileged to ride with Roosevelt and Uncle Bill Sewall toward town.

There had been dry weather for more than a week. As soon as they were away from the frosty river bottoms, the trail lofted a great raveling cloud-banner behind the travelers because there was nothing to hold the dust down. They passed a cliff where reddish-brown strata had bled down over the white stripes beneath them; it looked like dripping rust—or blood. Wil Dow wondered if it was an omen.

By the Lord, he thought, *this is surely some adventure*. Keyed up with a half-shaped anticipation of battle glory, he grinned at Uncle Bill, who scowled back at him with dismal bleakness.

They made a fast ride of it and there was little talk. Not long after the early sundown they came out of the canyon where the road tilted down to reveal the scattered display of the town's lights and the well-illuminated sprawl of tin peaked roofs beneath the glow at the top of the towering slaughterhouse smokestack. Beyond, higher up across the embankment on the promontory to the left of Graveyard Butte, lamps winked a mile away; that was Château De Morès. Down on the river the Marquis's crews were still chopping ice for storage in the ice-house against next summer's refrigerator-car needs.

Bill Sewall took the right-hand fork—the one that led toward the château—but Roosevelt called him back and went the other way, toward the ford. "We must think in military terms, Bill. It would be foolish to ride up there in the dark without scouting the lay of things first."

They splashed across the icy river into town. McKenzie was open late, forging a new iron rim for the wheel of a stagecoach; they turned their horses over to him with a request that they be dried, brushed and fed. Wil Dow felt the strike of the smith's heavy eyes as they swiveled past him, past Uncle Bill, and settled on Roosevelt; Wil remembered hearing how there'd been some sort of dust-up between them—the boss had knocked the blacksmith down, according to what he'd heard—but McKenzie's eyes shifted away now and he took the reins of the three horses while Roosevelt said, "Thank you, Mr. McKenzie," and led them away.

The De Morès offices were in a long two-story business building that looked as if four houses had been nailed together end-to-end. There was a big shade tree at the corner, near the front door. Roosevelt knocked loudly at the door. There was no reply. The windows were dark.

Bill Sewall said, "Nobody here. Not even Van Driesche." Van Driesche managed the offices for De Morès. Despite his name Van Driesche was very British: originally, it seemed, he had been De Morès's valet and butler. Van Driesche was an exceptionally private man and no one knew much about him, or cared to; he looked like a skeleton with white hair pasted on top, and invited no affection.

At any rate neither Van Driesche nor his employer was about. They went on toward Joe Ferris's store. Wil Dow ducked his face against the frigid wind; the temperature was dropping sharply.

Joe let them in. Roosevelt said, "I hope we're not intruding?"

"No sir. Always happy to see you." Joe took them through to the rear of the store and added lumps of lignite to the fire. The isinglass window of the cannon stove glowed furiously but it wasn't enough to keep out the blasts of winter that came in through chinks in the boards.

Then again, Wil Dow thought, winter was at worst a mixed curse, for at least it held at bay the smell of the abattoir.

Uncle Bill Sewall was examining the stock of boots on the shelf. He complained, "You know I can't get any boots here that will wear at all. Ten- or twelve-dollar boots don't last much more than two months. Sometimes not more than one."

"It's rough country on footwear," Joe Ferris agreed. "I buy the best quality I can obtain. I'm trying to find a better supplier."

Roosevelt said, "Is Mr. De Morès in town, do you know?"

"Afraid I don't keep tabs on him. We're not exactly made of the same leather."

"I ask because no one ever seems to know when he may be at home. He has a mighty restlessness, that fellow—it seems at any moment he may be off impatiently rushing to Helena or Miles City or Chicago—"

"Pursuing his visionary dreams," said Arthur Packard, entering and slamming the door behind him against the bitter wind. "The Marquis is at home—I saw him an hour ago. Why?"

"He's trying to seize possession of my ranch."

"Now there's a surprise," said Joe Ferris, showing no surprise but plenty of irony, and fixing his glare on Packard.

Wil Dow was confused; he had thought the two men to be friends.

Joe turned his attention back to Roosevelt. "Sir, where you're concerned you may as well know the Markee has got a hate that won't go away—like the stink of something that died under the floor of the house."

"Joe!" snapped Pack. "Mind your tongue."

"They've got a right to know what's going on." Joe's eyes were crowded with a bright blue tension. He said to Roosevelt, "The Markee's lawyers are throwing every delay they can think up, but it's plain sooner or later he's going to stand trial for murdering Luffsey. He blames you for the arrest warrant, even though it's common knowledge the letter to Judge Bateman must've been writ by Huidekoper or Eaton. And meantime Luffsey's Irish friends are talking high and heavy against the Markee, and that includes Redhead Finnegan and Frank O'Donnell running around loose—and Dutch Reuter out on your ranch. All in all it does seem to make the Markee see red, doesn't it, Pack."

"They're riffraff. Low dogs. They deserve what comes to them—they endangered Madame's life," said Arthur Packard. He seemed to be watching to see how Roosevelt would react to that, but the New Yorker took another route:

"You may put it in your newspaper that Dutch Reuter was not one of the riflemen who shot up Mr. De Morès's house."

"How do you know that?"

"I asked him. I have his word on it."

"And you believe it?"

"I have every reason to place my faith in Dutch's honesty."

"There are some who'd say you were a fool, then."

Roosevelt removed his glasses, polished them and put them back on, hooking them over one ear at a time. Then he looked Arthur Packard straight in the eye. "Are you one of those?"

"I'm a newspaperman. I'm impartial. But I'll say this much—I know Dutch well enough to know he'll lie when he wants to." He pointed an accusing finger toward Joe Ferris. "You know that better than anyone. You rode with him."

"I did," said Joe Ferris, "and I know him to be a man who would not shoot from ambush."

Arthur Packard shrugged. "As I say, I must remain objective."

Wil Dow made a face. The damned editor was a weasel—a fence-sitter.

Roosevelt said to Joe Ferris, "It appears Mr. De Morès has done a rash thing—he's thrown fifteen hundred head of cattle onto my ranch. He must have known it would bring me straight to his lair. I should like to know as much as I can about his frame of mind. Is he susceptible to reason? Or is he too angry for that? I realize his temper must have been rising because some of his vaunted business ventures have been collapsing. His sheep have been dying by thousands— "

Joe Ferris said with marked displeasure, "Seven thousand dead Merinos out there, sir. Come spring the buzzards will have a banquet. I hear some mutton-packer filed an enormous suit against him for breach of contract and you're right, it hasn't sweetened his temper any. The Markee even hauled Jerry Paddock on the carpet but Jerry knows how to curry favor with him . . ."

"To coin a phrase," said Arthur Packard dryly.

Joe ignored it. "It was Jerry convinced him there was money in raising sheep and once he decided, he was too stubborn to admit he'd made a mistake. He believed he'd bought fifteen thousand head but I think Jerry only brought in about seven thousand—they took a turn around the mountain during the tally—"

Roosevelt said, "Meaning they were counted twice?"

"Yes sir. In any case they were the wrong breed for the climate and they've all been winter-killed. Naturally Jerry Paddock won't admit that. He's been claiming Finnegan and Reuter and the boys have been murdering the sheep out of spite."

"I believe he's right about that," said Arthur Packard.

Bill Sewall snorted. "There isn't that much ammunition in all Dakota."

Arthur Packard said, "Nobody wants to make excuses for Jerry Paddock's petty soulless tyranny. But he's a hard worker. He manages a store and a saloon and several other enterprises. You can hardly accuse him of indolence. And it's quite possible he made an honest mistake about those sheep. He's never raised sheep, any more than the Marquis has. If what you say about Merinos has any truth in it, I'd be inclined to believe they both were misled."

Joe Ferris pinched his lips together and kicked the stove repeatedly until the fire glowed brighter. "You want to know about business ventures ready to fall down? The Markee's sunk a fortune in that damn fool Deadwood stagecoach line and it's got no future at all."

"On the contrary," said Packard. "It provides a vital link between Deadwood and the railroad, and it will increase the commerce through this town threefold within the next year. The line will have a United States Mail contract by summer, and—"

"It won't last half that long." Joe Ferris said it without exceptional heat—he was smiling at Pack with a kind of amusement that suggested a private ongoing joke between them—but his words were uncompromising. "The stagecoach line will fail because the Markee has put his stupid faith in Jerry Paddock, and Jerry's milking the scheme for all he can. The Markee paid him good money to buy trained teams. Jerry bought wild horses and put the difference in his pocket."

"Prove it! Prove it!"

"When they start their runs to Deadwood, I wouldn't care to predict the kind of safety record they'll chalk up. There sure as hell won't be any mail contract, Pack." Joe flapped a hand at the editor in arch dismissal. He went on: "And his cattle business is not what he says it is. I have had the word from businessmen down the line—people I buy drygoods from. Nobody is buying De Morès beef. Of course the Markee makes excuses for that. He claims his cars keep getting shunted off the main line and held aside until the ice melts inside them and the meat spoils. He says the railroad's in cahoots with the Jews on the Chicago Beef Trust—"

"Swift and Armour?" interjected Roosevelt.

Arthur Packard said, "The blasted meat-packing cartels."

Roosevelt said, "It was Gustavus Swift who developed the insulated refrigerator car and ice-harvesting facilities and the shipment of refrigerated dressed meat to New York and the other cities around the country. Surely Mr. De Morès cannot deny the man the fruits of his own inventions?"

Joe Ferris said, "All I know from the people I talk to in Minneapolis is that every time they see the Markee he's lost another shipment of beef and he's yelling against the Chicago meat-packing Jews and the New York Wall Street Jews."

"Of whom apparently he believes I am one," said Roosevelt.

Packard said, "Why can't you fellows concede he may know what he's talking about? Maybe it's true that the Jews resent his youth, his foreignness, his energy. He's constantly engaged by obstacles designed to thwart him. The railroads give better rates to shippers whose business is far smaller than his. The butchers are intimidated from handling his meat. He issued stock in his National Consumers Meat Company at ten dollars a share but no one bought it because people in the market were frightened off by pressures from the Chicago packers. The Marquis has reason to believe the Jews have sent the message out that he is to be destroyed. Well he shall not be destroyed. He has promised that, and I believe it."

Joe Ferris shook his head with an expression that blended pity and disgust. "He was a fool from the beginning to think he could run a year-round meat packing business. Cattle here in the winter are nothing but skin and bones, and it's all they can do to survive at all. You slaughter them, you get nothing but gristle and bone. The plain truth is, *any* time of year these range-fed beef of his just simply don't taste as good as cattle that have fattened on grain in the Chicago yards. The Chicago packers produce better meat than the Markee does—that's all there is to it. That's why nobody buys his beef. Pack, when are you going to see the Markee's as crazy as the Lunatic was? What are you—a moon circling his planet?"

"Allow me to point out that not only has the Marquis De Morès stimulated the region's economic growth with his capital, but he has a great sense of civic duty. He's built the brick church and the school. Why, he and Lady Medora even pay the schoolteacher's salary. He's organized the fire brigade and donated a park and seen generously to the welfare of everyone who needs help. And he—"

"*I've* never been invited to dine at the château," Joe Ferris retorted, "nor any other ordinary mortals. He only invites you because you keep writing him up as the Messiah come to Dakota.

Only the elite aristocracy are welcomed at that house up there, from which the mighty king of the mountain can look down on *his* village and *his* employees." Then Joe looked down at his feet. "I am mortally tired of that man. But he's not going to stop. You know his father-in-law? Baron Von Hoffman's bank in New York—second in importance only to Drexel Morgan. If the Markee makes a mess of one venture he can afford to just buy into another."

"Then Baron Von Hoffman ought to be aware of the nature of his son-in-law's folly," Roosevelt replied. "Now I shouldn't wish to keep you up. We've business to do and then if it's not too much imposition on your hospitality we'd like to stay the night in your room upstairs. I refuse to put up at De Morès's hotel."

Bill Sewall said to Wil, "Anyway who'd want to pay the Markee's prices? You know he charges two dollars a night? Highway robbery."

Joe Ferris said, "Welcome to the upstairs. You know how to find it. The ticks are new. Shouldn't be too much livestock in them. Pump's out back if you want to wash. You going up to the château now?"

"Yes."

"I'll go with you."

"I'm grateful. But it isn't your affair, old fellow."

"I wouldn't miss it for the world."

Wil Dow was impatient with himself, for the flesh of his belly trembled as they approached the château's verandah.

Someone had seen them coming: they had seen a man's shadow run toward the house when they were but half way up the bluff. Now post lamps exposed them; anything might be hidden in the darkness beyond; he was damp with sweat even in the deep chill.

They were five; the editor Packard had insisted on accompanying them—"for my newspaper, and who knows, perhaps for history"—and Wil Dow made a point of placing himself on the opposite flank of the five-man line from the miserable toady. Roosevelt plunged forward resolutely between Ferris and Sewall. Wil Dow and his uncle carried rifles; Roosevelt had no weapon in his hand but the engraved Colt revolver was in his holster and it had not escaped Wil Dow's notice that the boss had stripped off his glove.

Four abreast, with the editor off to one side now, they approached the house. Breath steamed from their open mouths; they all were a little winded after the climb.

They were still several yards from the step when the door slammed open. Wil Dow stopped in his tracks. His fists tightened on the rifle. The others to his right had stopped as well.

Up on the porch the Marquis De Morès moved forward into the light—a bamboo stick in his hand and two revolvers thrust through his sash. He was hatless; lamplight gleamed on his wet-down hair.

Roosevelt said, "Mr. De Morès, I want your cattle off my land."

"Are they on your land, Mr. Roosevelt? I was unaware you owned any land."

"If the cattle are on my ranch twenty-four hours from now I shall take appropriate measures."

"That would not be wise. I hold title to that land."

"By Valentine Scrip? Show me the document that gives you title to that precise portion of land."

"It is not necessary. I hold prior right to the land in any case, because my stock were there first."

Roosevelt smiled: he actually smiled. "All I can see out there that belongs to you is a littering of dead sheep."

Joe Ferris was looking down toward the far end of the verandah. It was deep in shadow, but something had alerted Joe; he said, "All right. Come on out here where we can all see you," and after a moment there was a stirring—Jerry Paddock moved forward into a pool of light that fell out through the window. He carried a rifle under his arm.

Wil tried to watch everything at once. There was a thudding in his ears. The Marquis's arctic gaze was fixed on Roosevelt—enough to chill a block of ice.

Let's get this done—let's make a fight of it, by damnation!

De Morès played with his lead-filled bamboo stick. Without taking his eyes off Roosevelt he said, "Arthur, what are you doing with these gentlemen?"

Packard had to clear his throat before he could reply. "Reporting the facts."

Joe Ferris said, "Then may be you want to absent yourself from the line of fire." He kept his eyes on Jerry Paddock, who stood on the porch like a vulture.

Paddock's lip curled. He said to the newspaper man, "And take the crazy half-pint dude with you, while you're at it. Ain't nobody here got any use for him or his stupid big words."

Roosevelt did not grant Paddock so much as a glance. He said, "Mr. De Morès, in this democracy you have not been authorized by divine right to make your own laws or to change ours. Listen to me, sir—if we have to move your herd, there's bound to be shooting."

Arthur Packard eased away, off to one side. Wil Dow took note of the movement without turning his eyes or his head.

The Marquis said in a chilly voice, "Perhaps there is room to compromise."

"I will not compromise with a man when he is plainly in the wrong."

The Marquis smiled, sleepy-eyed, silken. "If I remove the cattle, then you shall remove Mr. Reuter from the land."

"No." Roosevelt chopped the word off; it seemed to reverberate afterward.

The Marquis's smile hardened. "Then I'll slaughter him where he stands."

"Try that, sir, and I'll see you hang for certain," Roosevelt said in a controlled voice that gave each word its full due.

Wil Dow thought there was nothing left to do now but wait for it to explode: the fuse was lit.

Jerry Paddock stirred: the rifle barrel glinted. His abrupt movement made Will realize how still Paddock had remained until now. It was a measure of the apprehension in Paddock.

The Marquis De Morès looked away toward the lights of town. After a moment he spoke in a different voice:

"A compromise then, as I said before. Shall we put it at one thousand dollars—no, make that a thousand five hundred dollars, or one dollar per head, to let them graze on the bottoms for a few weeks until they get up to proper weight? Then I shall bring them to the abattoir and they'll be out of your way."

Wil Dow was astounded by the Marquis's retreat. He looked at Roosevelt. It was a lot of money.

Roosevelt said, "I appreciate your willingness to discuss the matter. But how am I to know when 'a few weeks' is to end? No, Mr. De Morès. I can't back down from you, not for any sum of money. I want your cattle off my land by sunset tomorrow or I'll slaughter them where they stand."

Wil Dow heard Arthur Packard's abrupt intake of breath.

Surely it was bluff, Wil thought; Roosevelt wasn't a wanton slaughterer of steers. All it needed was a banging of tin pans and gunshots; the herd would remove itself soon enough. It wasn't the cattle that posed a threat; it was Johnny Goodall and the De Morès crew.

Just then Madame la Marquise appeared in the doorway. The Marquis heard her step; he glanced around at her. She did not speak. Her husband held her glance a moment and then turned to face the five men below him. With a strange conciliation the Marquis said, "I'm sorry you cannot accommodate me in this favor. Very well. We shall remove the cattle from the land, as you ask."

In a gesture to Jerry Paddock, the Marquis flapped a slack hand as if throwing something away. Paddock strolled to the steps, tucked the rifle under his arm, dropped off the verandah and walked away into the night, stroking his beard.

The Marquis turned on his heel—a smart military about-face—and took his wife by the arm and steered her inside. She looked back briefly; Wil could not tell at whom she was looking, but he saw Arthur Packard frown furiously and then De Morès had disappeared and the door closed, and it occurred to Wil that the Marquis may have broken off the confrontation out of respect for his wife's safety. It was the only thing he could think of that could explain De Morès's sudden decision to back down.

He felt savagely dissatisfied even though clearly this was not the last of it. Things could not remain this highly charged. There would be more, he thought, and it was likely there would be powder smoke and blood.

At Elkhorn, Dutch Reuter picked a path through the clutter of dry antlers on the piazza and walked down the meadow in such obvious desolation that Wil Dow was on the point of following anxiously behind him. But he respected Dutch's privacy; he only watched as Dutch went down the bank and tossed a stone into Blacktail Creek. Dutch hunkered there a long time.

It was cold, and finally Wil went back inside the house, where Roosevelt was writing a letter—probably to his sister Bamie back in New York. Or to his other faithful correspondent: almost certainly a woman, but what sort of woman? In what way connected to him? It was a bafflement to Wil.

Dutch did not come in for supper. He did not appear at all that night, and in the morning his horse and saddle were gone from the stable; gone too was his kit. He had lit out, it seemed, for parts unknown. Wil Dow could imagine his thoughts: *To bring any more trouble on Mr. Roosevelt I do not wish. Good to me he is.*

Or perhaps Dutch was only following his urge to wander—like a cloud's shadow across the ground.

Thirteen

This meeting at Eaton's Custer Trail Ranch was charged with expectation. A chinook howled around the house, bringing wind and rain and muddy thaw; it also had brought a powerful visitor from across the line—Montana baron Granville Stuart, who sat at the head of the Eaton table as if he owned it.

A.C. Huidekoper listened for the music in Granville Stuart's deep voice and heard none; the voice was a tuneless rasp. One could not escape the feeling there would be a similar sound if Stuart were to scrape his hand across the edge of his jaw: he was the sort who would need to shave more than once a day to keep beard-shadow from coarsening his sun-browned skin.

At every encounter with Granville Stuart, Huidekoper found himself endeavoring to dislike the man, but failing in the endeavor. Stuart—hardened pioneer—had brought one of the first herds of cattle up the trail all the way from Doan's Store in Texas to the Montana wilderness back in the war-charred days when blackleg renegades made any cattle drive a gantlet of danger, when Comanche and Cheyenne were still a deadly threat on the southern and central plains—even before Custer's army challenged the Sioux in the north; Granville Stuart had braved it all and established his cattle kingdom in the new world of Montana. He had blazed the way and earned fame and honor on the frontier, and along with it a portion of fear and distaste, for it was common knowledge that his methods of protecting his empire sometimes had much in common with the methods of the more ruthless medieval lords of the Inquisition.

It could be said politely that Granville Stuart tended not to err on the genteel side. Huidekoper often had found occasion to deplore his appalling attitudes. Yet Stuart in spite of all remained ingratiating, even likeable. There was something childlike about his innocent faith in the infallibility of righteous institutions, the simplicity of all questions, the rectitude of all answers and the propriety of brutality in a good cause.

Granville Stuart personified the legendary Texican attitude toward lawbreakers: whether they might be heinous felons or casual miscreants, whether their victims be murdered, maimed or merely inconvenienced, his answer remained the same; it adhered always to the same Old Testament simplicity:

Hang him.

Not surprisingly the news of his presence at Eaton's had drawn a sizable gathering tonight. Among the stockmen on hand were J.N. Simpson, Henry S. Boice, Gregor Lang, H.R. Tarbell, Pierce Bolan, J.L. Truscott, the unavoidable Deacon W.P. Osterhaut and half a dozen more, and of course Eaton. *And y'r ob't s'v't*, Huidekoper thought, out of respect for his sense of the precise.

Off by himself, according to his habit, stood Johnny Goodall, representing the Marquis De Morès, who was again in the East doing something that had to do with finance—something doubtless devious and sinister, of which no good would come.

They awaited the arrival of Theodore Roosevelt, who had the farthest to ride—his Elkhorn Ranch was nearly fifty miles from here. In the meantime there was desultory conversation about the end-of-winter weather and about the confused reports and rumors of an expanding bloody provincial rebellion just over the border of Canada. Several conversations buzzed in Huidekoper's ears. The gathering of men had the superficial air of a social evening but the ladies were absent and the Eaton bar was closed—sure indications of serious business at hand.

"A lot of wasted time," Huidekoper heard Granville Stuart bark.

"Save the Territory a lot of trouble and hang those two boys that ambushed the Marquis."

Howard Eaton said, "Seems to be some dispute as to who ambushed whom."

"Why, those boys are trying to put a saddle on you, Howard," scoffed Stuart. "You know as well as I do, a man with blue blood flowing in his veins doesn't go out to bushwhack those ring-toters from a dry gulch. What I hear about them, good men go wide around them as if they were a swamp. Now I can't honestly see the Marquis dirtying his hands on the likes of those, can you?"

The discussion was interrupted when Theodore Roosevelt entered, looking surprisingly fit in his trim buckskin suit. Granville Stuart accorded him the courtesy of rising from his chair, since Roosevelt was something of a foreigner and allegedly high-born as well.

Stuart was tall, wide, muscular, imposing as an outsized marble statue of a general. He offered his handshake. Roosevelt showed a definite constraint before accepting it.

Huidekoper did not know what Roosevelt might have heard about Stuart that caused such hesitation; but he had observed often enough in his lifetime that such little things could lead from the smallest start to the bitterest quarrels: they stung a man's pride and made him lose face, and eventually the memory of the little thing could be the chancre that turned the man savage.

And he was acquainted well enough with Granville Stuart to know it might not take very much to transform him into just that state.

Roosevelt turned away from Stuart almost immediately and, strangely, addressed himself to Johnny Goodall: "Well, Johnny. How do you find things?"

"That kind of depends on how you lost them." As usual Johnny did not smile; but his voice expressed an offhand amusement and it elicited Roosevelt's soft chuckle.

Huidekoper saw the way Roosevelt nodded his square sandy head. He found it extraordinary that Johnny and Roosevelt should be enjoying colloquy on such informal terms. The two men could not have been less alike—they might have been from different species—yet there appeared to be something positively warm between them, something in the easy way their eyes met and then drifted off to examine the rest of the crowd, something that suggested a camaraderie, a respect for each other and even perhaps an affection for which Huidekoper could think of no plausible explanation.

Granville Stuart was bending Eaton's ear. Huidekoper caught a portion of it: "—the little young fellow from New York over there?"

"He's proved himself on round-up and on the range."

"Understand he's been quarreling with my friend the Marquis."

"He's had his provocations, I believe."

"The very thought of Jerry Paddock makes me feel positively warm toward Judas Iscariot," Deacon Osterhaut was saying to Pierce Bolan. "Paddock's a mendacious scoundrel."

Bolan said, "A what?"

But at that moment Deacon Osterhaut espied Huidekoper and reached for him. Huidekoper could not escape. The Deacon's handshake was like a Bible drummer's: he gripped Huidekoper's right hand in his own, folded his left over them both, stared Huidekoper unctuously in the eye and, standing a foot too close, spoke in his treacly Southern accent with foul-breathed earnestness: "I've lost four head to wolves. It is an unholy tragedy. Now you bring your hounds to my place at the earliest convenience, y'hear?"

Huidekoper extracted himself as quickly as he could from the clutches of the dour pumpkin roller.

Huidekoper was taken aback when he saw the glint of Roosevelt's eyes, the flash of his teeth in comical zest. Roosevelt said *sotto voce*, "One might suspect the Deacon suffereth from mental carbuncles and dyspepsia."

Huidekoper took the New Yorker away from the fireplace. In the corner past the window he said, "There'll be a vote tonight, on the Association."

"I know."

"I wanted to sound you out privately."

"About what?"

Huidekoper said, "About the Marquis De Morès."

"What about him?"

"If the Association were in your hands—what would you do about him?"

Roosevelt blinked, his eyes artificially large behind the lenses. "I should seek to insure that the laws be enforced—and I should be prepared to journey to Bismarck or if need be to Washington to make sure they were carried out properly and vigorously. But I can't support or condone the employment of lawlessness to fight lawlessness."

Huidekoper said, "Then you've changed your mind?"

"Not about vigilantes."

"About taking a hand here. If your name is put forward for the chair, you'll accept it?"

"Let's wait and see whose names are put forward, shall we?"

Roosevelt gave him a quick flash of a smile and a friendly gentle punch on the bicep, and turned to contend with a question from Pierce Bolan.

Huidekoper stood alone for a moment, pleased. He felt that in some fashion—perhaps soon to make itself more clear—his judgment had been vindicated. His early instinct had been astute: Roosevelt, for all his initial reluctance, could yet be the salvation of them. Huidekoper held what he had no difficulty admitting to himself was a nearly superstitious conviction that Roosevelt—because he was on a level with De Morès in matters not only of class and wealth but of will, acumen, leadership, *spirit*—Roosevelt, in spite of all the dubious attributes that made him seem ludicrous and outlandish, could be the one man who had any chance of marshaling the Forces of Good successfully against the Marquis De Morès and his ever so formidable Forces of Evil. The victory would require no less than a Crusade, Huidekoper knew, and no less a knight to lead it than the outwardly absurd Theodore Roosevelt.

Granville Stuart's voice grated painfully on Huidekoper's ears: "A.C.—I hear you don't like the way the country's developing."

Huidekoper pulled out a chair and adjusted himself on it; the actions gave him time to compose his thoughts. "As I see it, the country has got limitations no one wants to acknowledge. Too many have made the mistake of allowing themselves to be caught up in this cattle craze. The Marquis De Morès keeps increasing his herds at a mad rate, and at the same time it seems as if every week another Texan arrives with as many cattle as he's got left from the twelve-hundred-mile drive from the Red. We've got an alarming invasion on our hands—they're increasing the number of beeves in the Bad Lands far beyond the capacity of our grasses to support them. We'll soon be entirely overgrazed. As for such fodder as remains, I reckon horses are best adapted to it."

Deacon Osterhaut said, "Crying wolf again, A.C.? They more than three million acres of grass on the Little Missouri. Three *million*. You're irresponsible, forever fueling fears."

Was the Deacon's alliteration deliberate? Surely not. He hadn't the ear.

Howard Eaton said, "I happen to agree with A.C. Too many folks seem to look at Dakota as a place to make a killing but not a living. They don't see it as a place to settle and stay. They've all got plans to go 'home.'"

Huidekoper said, "To me this *is* home."

Eaton said, "What about you, Theodore? Is this country home?"

"It is for now," said Roosevelt. "I've no idea what the future holds. But at this time the Bad Lands are my home, and this country has my undivided regard."

Granville Stuart glanced unpleasantly at Roosevelt, making a show of his dislike. Huidekoper thought immediately that Stuart was not at all the sort of man who ever could apprehend the value of the little New Yorker; Stuart probably did not like Roosevelt's cocksuredness and most likely regarded Roosevelt as no more than a nuisance that had to be tolerated—a small bull who, wherever he went, brought his own china shop with him. That was Roosevelt's reputation. Old Four Eyes. Storm Windows. Dude Roosenfelder. But Huidekoper felt confident that his expectations of the Cyclone Assemblyman had been met. All but one, which—now that he had Roosevelt's encouragement in the matter—he had every hope of accomplishing this very night.

Unlike the Montana baron, Roosevelt did not have a big voice but he seemed to have learned to make his limited vocal range effective by enunciating precisely and biting off words with sharp attention-commanding clicks of his teeth. He said to Howard Eaton, "What you've said has merit. We're all beginning to feel crowded. As long as we have tolerable weather we can get by with fifteen acres per head of cattle, but should there be drought we'd need twice as much, and we're nearly at that density now. It isn't only the newcomers. We all depend on cooperation in the cattle trade—without it, there'd be no round-ups and indeed no trade at all. Now we seem to be at a point where when one outfit overstocks its range, it is not only that outfit's cattle that suffer—it's the cattle of everyone along the river who finds his grass consumed by visiting herds that happen to have wandered by for a bite."

He was looking at Johnny Goodall when he spoke. Johnny said mildly, "If anybody breaks a law, I expect he ought to be held to book for it."

Huidekoper inserted himself angrily. "Where's there no effective law enforcement, there are still certain unwritten laws that civilized men recognize. Your employer seems to have chosen to disregard those. Let me put it plain to you, Johnny—some of us are tired of being intimidated by the roughshod tactics of the Northern Pacific Refrigerator Car Company. I for one won't stand for more of it. If your cattle are pushed onto my range I'll have no hesitation. And if that doesn't put it clear enough, it's my opinion the Marquis has as much moral code as a water trough."

Feeling Johnny's immediate brittle stare, Huidekoper clasped his hands behind him and thrust his chest out while privately he wondered, *What is in me that will not let me leave well enough alone?*

Granville Stuart said, "It's all very well to stand at the end of your chain barking, but if I was you I'd be careful the Marquis doesn't slip the chain."

The sarcastic outburst gave Johnny time to think it over and fortunately the heat went out of his eyes. He said, "Take that up with my boss, Mr. Huidekoper, not with me."

Huidekoper resumed breathing, realizing only then that he had stopped doing so. Johnny Goodall was a decent man, he thought charitably, but nevertheless it was deuced difficult to feel any warmth toward the Texan. Brutally practical, Johnny chose his friends by their usefulness or their toughness, and was loyal to his hire simply because it was his hire, with no evident concern for the moral quality of his employer.

Granville Stuart said, "I understand the Marquis owns his grazing lands. Bought them and paid for them. No man here can say as much. You're a bold man to talk of *your* range, Mr. Huidekoper."

Huidekoper said, "The Marquis may be a friend of yours, Mr. Stuart, but he's no friend of mine. Nor of these other men here, whether they know it or not."

Howard Eaton spoke quickly in an all too obvious effort to head off strife. "We're here to try and organize a stockmen's association. Let's try to keep it to that, gents. Now Mr. Granville Stuart's been kind enough to come clear over from Montana to give us the benefit of his advice—as some of you know, Mr. Stuart's chairman of the Montana Stock Growers' Association—and I for one am interested to hear what he has to say."

"We sure can use somebody's help," Pierce Bolan said. "Things around here are a God-damned panorama."

"Mind your blaspheming tongue, Pierce," said Deacon Osterhaut.

Granville Stuart pushed his chair back. He crossed one leg over the other and tipped his head forward to light a cigar. He turned it in the match flame until he had it going to his satisfaction and then, having concluded that careful ritual and gained everyone's expectant attention, he spoke:

"Last week my range foreman came on an old lumber camp, found more than two hundred horses penned up. Whoever put them there must have fled when they heard my men coming, for there was no one about. Every one of those two hundred animals had its brand obliterated—likely by a red-hot frying pan. Do you take my point?"

It struck Huidekoper now that despite his unpleasant voice, Granville Stuart was possessed of a gift for suasion. The Montanan went on, speaking in his deep unhurried manner. "Either we give up or we declare war on horse and cattle thieves, both on my side of the Montana-Dakota line and on yours. Apprehend them or drive them out of the country. Now I am not speaking for range war. We don't want another Lincoln County catastrophe up here. It might cost lives on our own side—anyhow if you go openly to kill thieves, you can be held by the authorities for murder. So I'd surely recommend against open war." He smiled, however, in such a way that it was clear he had no compunctions against the waging of a *secret* war against the thieves.

Roosevelt said, "Except in matters of immediate self-defense or the protection of our property from present endangerment, I don't believe we have the right to take it upon ourselves to define or enforce the law."

Granville Stuart watched him unblinkingly. "Mr. Roosevelt,

there's a federal marshal two hundred miles south of you, and a sheriff a hundred and fifty miles east of you, but there's no authority that's seen fit to look into your difficulties with thieves. If you delegate responsibility to a government that won't accept it or exercise it, then your only choice is to take it back into your own hands."

"The instinct may be natural," Roosevelt replied, "but I put it to you, sir, that the mark of a civilized man jolly well is his ability to control his instincts and set aside his savage impulses. By Godfrey, it wasn't for the benefit of lynchers that our forefathers founded this republic."

"We're not in the republic now," said Stuart. "Your friends asked my advice. I'm giving it. Form a committee of safety—or live with the consequences."

"The important matters are not stock-poaching and petty thievery," Roosevelt argued—addressing himself not directly to Stuart but to the gathering at large—"and I don't believe the important matters can be solved by forming ourselves into a wild band of night-riding avengers. Our serious concerns are with the proper division of range and the restriction of new immigration, so that no one is crowded out, and with such other matters as may affect our common interest. I had understood we were meeting tonight to form a ranchmen's association, and with all due respect to our visitor from Montana I submit that any such association should restrict itself by charter and by unanimous consent to the pursuit of proper legal ends by proper legal means."

Granville Stuart squinted complacently through his cigar's smoke. "Appears to me you and Huidekoper make a fine pair. You both have an uncommon fondness for empty talk."

At that moment Johnny Goodall did an astonishing thing. He said, "I move we form a Little Missouri Stockmen's Association, and I move we elect Theodore Roosevelt chairman."

Amid the hubbub—men waving their arms, shouting, proposing names of other candidates—Granville Stuart stalked outside in an evident huff; and Roosevelt buttonholed Johnny Goodall. Huidekoper, fascinated, pushed his way near enough to hear. Roosevelt was saying: "I pray you, don't let this be put to a vote. I don't care to be the cause of quarrels among my neighbors. I'm grateful for your splendid courtesy but I'd count it a favor if you'd withdraw my name."

Huidekoper plunged in boldly. "Nonsense. Let it go forward. You'll win hands down." In a compartment of his mind he found himself amazed to be on the same side of things as the Marquis's man.

"No, old man. Not here." Roosevelt's eyes darted everywhere—as if seeking a place to hide—and suddenly Huidekoper understood: Roosevelt had lost his political confidence.

Johnny Goodall aimed his weathered squint down at Roosevelt. "Not a man here who saw you work on round-up will vote against you."

Huidekoper gripped Roosevelt's coat—to the New Yorker's evident displeasure; Huidekoper released it quickly but spoke with undiminished urgency: "Johnny's right. You've got it in the palm of your hand, Theodore."

"Great Scott, man—can't you see I don't want public office!" Roosevelt wheeled away in what seemed to be an effort to prevent their seeing the moisture in his eyes but he wasn't quick enough. It astounded Huidekoper to realize the man was so afraid.

Names were being shouted across the room. "Nominate Howard Eaton!" "My vote's for Gregor Lang!" "Move we elect A.C. Huidekoper!"

That last was Howard Eaton's voice. What a princely gesture. Huidekoper beamed at him but couldn't catch Eaton's eye.

Deacon Osterhaut's voice scratched: "Second that nomination—in favor of A.C. Huidekoper!"

The man was shameless. He'd perform *any* act of cajolery or flattery to make his way up the social ladder by gaining the benediction that came with the loan of Huidekoper's pack of hounds.

Huidekoper lifted his hands in the air. "Let me have your attention. Gentlemen! Please!"

He bellowed it. The bedlam dwindled. Huidekoper said, "By the standard rules of order, before other nominations can be entertained, the motion is before the chair to form a Little Missouri Stockmen's Association, and to elect Theodore Roosevelt chairman. The motion has been seconded."

Roosevelt said, "Those are two distinct matters. They should be

Medora von Hoffman Vallombrosa, Marquise De Morès

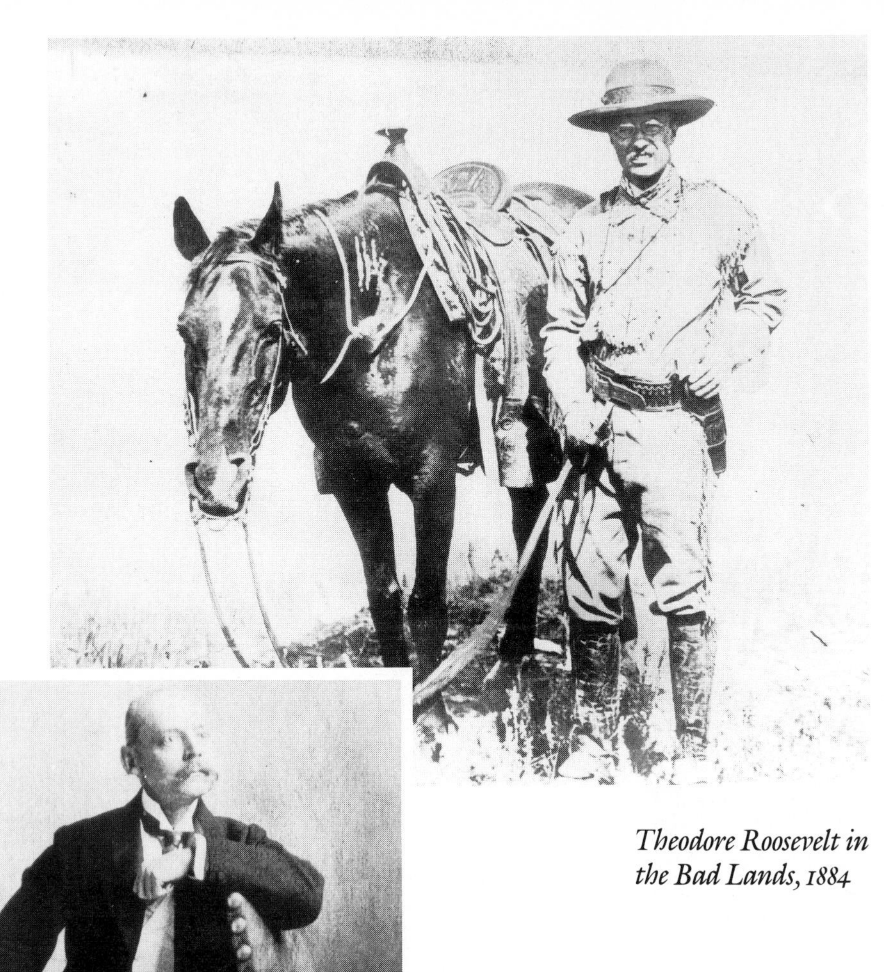

Theodore Roosevelt in the Bad Lands, 1884

A.C. Huidekoper

Marquis De Morès in the Bad Lands, 1884

Theodore Roosevelt in his new buckskin suit

Arthur T. "Pack" Packard

Joe Ferris

Theodore Roosevelt on his horse Manitou

Most emphatically I am not your enemy; if I were you would know it, for I would be an open one, and would not have asked you to my house nor gone to yours. As your final words however seem to imply a threat it is due to myself to say that the statement is not made through any fear of possible consequences to me; I too, as you know, am always on hand, and ever ready to hold myself accountable in any way for anything I have said or done.

Yours very truly

Theodore Roosevelt

Letter from Theodore Roosevelt to Marquis De Morès

LEFT TO RIGHT:
Wilmot Dow, Theodore Roosevelt, Bill Sewall

Theodore Roosevelt captures boat thieves
(PHOTO BY THEODORE ROOSEVELT)

Theodore Roosevelt, ranchman

put forward as two separate motions. The chair must exist before you can put forward candidates to fill it."

There was a rising mutter of voices. Huidekoper waved his arms again. "Mr. Roosevelt is correct in reminding us of our parliamentary duties, of course. Which is precisely why his presence is so important. A vote for the establishment of an association should not imply a vote for any particular leader. Mr. Goodall, would you care to withdraw your motion and replace it?"

"Sure."

After a moment, when it became evident the Texan had nothing further to say, there was a ripple of laughter.

Howard Eaton said, "You've got to say it, Johnny. Do you move we form a Stockmen's Association?"

"I sure do."

"Then I second the motion."

Huidekoper said, "All in favor? Show of hands." Hands went up. "Opposed?" The hands went down. "Seems to have carried unanimously. Now I guess there's nothing further to prevent us entertaining motions for the election of a chairman, is there, Theodore?"

"Technically you ought to elect a chairman pro tem in order to conduct the proceedings and supervise the balloting."

Huidekoper grinned. "Anyone want to nominate A.C. Huidekoper for that job?"

Howard Eaton shouted, "So moved!"

Someone seconded. Huidekoper said, "Chair will entertain motions . . ."

Johnny Goodall opened his mouth to speak. Roosevelt stared at him with such desperate gravity that the very force of his expression seemed to draw Johnny's eyes and make Johnny hesitate. Roosevelt shook his head back and forth—beseeching. Johnny's squint narrowed and Huidekoper thought, *Do it, Johnny. You've got to. If you let him get away from this, he may never have the nerve to face another election.*

And, he thought dryly, *we'll lose our best gladiator against De Morès.*

Johnny's chest deflated. Huidekoper realized there was a chance the courteous Texan would do what Roosevelt wanted him to do.

Huidekoper gripped Roosevelt's arm roughly. The New Yorker's head came around. There was an increasing impatient discord of talk in the room. Huidekoper pitched his voice to reach no farther than Roosevelt's ears: "If anything, it's more important to you than it is to us."

"You need a local man," Roosevelt said.

"It's no good clutching at straws, Theodore."

"Damn it, man—I came out here to be on my own. Not to run for public office. My political career has been destroyed for all time—and I'm the last one who needs reminding of that. All I want is to be left alone!"

Huidekoper said quickly, "If you don't risk anything, Theodore, you can hardly win anything worth the winning."

Roosevelt snorted. "I don't want to 'win' this. There's nothing to be won but drudging hard work. I've had enough of the thanklessness of voters. Let them find someone else to be their trammeled serf."

Johnny Goodall said, "For a man wants to be alone, you did a fair job of running things on your part of the round-up. Mr. Roosevelt, if I didn't believe you're the best man for this job, I wouldn't have said your name. Now I am aiming to nominate you again unless you tell me different right now."

Roosevelt met Johnny's eyes. The Texan's slow smile was guileless; there was honest respect in it. Clearly he was being more than just polite; he was being truthful.

Roosevelt drew a long unsteady breath. He coughed, stifled it, swallowed, wiped a palm across his mustache and finally said, "I suppose I ought to be grateful to you both for reminding me that I can't spend the rest of my life afraid I might lose a few votes."

"All right then," said Johnny. He lifted his head. He had a great big voice when he chose to employ it. The overtones rang—quite literally rang—against the ceiling beams. "Nominate Mr. Theodore Roosevelt for chairman of the Stockmen's Association!"

"Second." That was Pierce Bolan.

Huidekoper said, "Nominations are open. Who's next?"

No one spoke.

The silence was baffling.

Huidekoper felt exasperated. "Come on. Don't be shy."

Howard Eaton said, "Want me to nominate you, A.C.?"

"Thank you, Howard, but my vote's for Roosevelt. Come on, the rest of you—cat got your tongues?"

Again no one seemed to have anything to say. After a moment Pierce Bolan said, "Quit wasting time, A.C. Let's elect the man and get on about our business."

"Is the chair to understand there are no opposing nominations?"

"Well," Pierce Bolan said in a very dry voice, "anybody want to nominate the Markee?"

There was a shocked moment of dead quiet and then a cloudburst of laughter.

Someone went outdoors to find Granville Stuart. He was gone. One of the wranglers reported that the Montanan had departed in evident displeasure, announcing with some vehemence that he would spend the night in town at the De Morès Hotel.

The meeting lasted well into the night, with new Chairman Roosevelt guiding things briskly from one topic of concern to the next; now that Roosevelt had been installed by the grace of a near-unanimous majority, he seemed eager to press forward without ever looking back. Huidekoper was surprised not by the obvious pleasure but by the efficiency with which the New Yorker covered a great deal of ground in a short period of time. Nevertheless he felt a restive sense of anticlimax.

When the formal caucus adjourned, Johnny Goodall was first to say his good-nights. He went to the door and Huidekoper overheard Roosevelt say to him, "You'd make a capital politician, old fellow . . ."

Howard Eaton took Huidekoper aside. "I have a suspicion."

"And?"

"Granville Stuart couldn't wait to be off to the De Morès side of town. Don't be plumb surprised if our royal friend gets himself unofficially appointed chief of the Dakota branch of the Granville Stuart Montana Regulators."

Roosevelt, having heard, joined them. Huidekoper said, "The idea would seem to be true enough to De Morès's spirit of romantic recklessness."

"If he does it—will you join him?"

"Join De Morès?" Huidekoper was shocked.

Eaton said, "You're the one who keeps agitating for a committee of safety."

"De Morès is interested in no one's safety but his own."

Roosevelt said, "All the same, if Howard's right, you'll get your vigilantes."

"Not *my* vigilantes. This is not the way I wished it, Theodore."

"I'm reassured to hear that," said Roosevelt, "for I fear if Mr. De Morès assembles a party of vigilantes, it will be not so much for the purpose of ridding us of thieves as it will be for the purpose of driving the small ranchers off the land Mr. De Morès claims for himself. And don't be surprised, by Godfrey, if he doesn't mind whether he drives us off alive or dead."

Fourteen

The news Pack relayed in *The Bad Lands Cow Boy* was distressing because it came from nearby. Open warfare had broken out just to the north across the border in Canada: the Riel forces had risen in armed rebellion against what they said was the Ottawa government's indifference to the Western provinces; they had set up their own unrecognized government and the army had sent troops west on the not-yet-completed Canadian Pacific Railway to do battle with the rebels at Batoche.

There was no question what would happen to Louis Riel if the Canadian army caught him. He would be hanged for treason. In the meantime half way around the globe Khartoum had fallen to the Mahdi; Chinese Gordon and his entire garrison had been massacred—just hours before the British relief column arrived. Clearly there had been a Divine error, for such catastrophes simply did *not* befall Her Victorian Majesty's forces anywhere in the Empire. Assuredly it must mean the end of Gladstone's prime ministry. No matter where on the globe you looked, it seemed order was capitulating to chaos.

To lighten the front page Pack printed one further item from the telegraph:

"A woman is only a woman, but a good Cigar is a Smoke."

—*From the new poem "The Betrothed" by Rudyard Kipling.*

He put the paper to bed and it was late when he left the office but the night was mild and he needed to stretch his legs. It would soon be baseball season—none too soon, he thought. The weekly games seemed to keep tempers in check and just now God knew the Bad Lands wanted calming.

Against his nostrils a thick current of whiskey and beer and tobacco smoke rolled out of Jerry Paddock's place as he approached it. He heard from the forge the clang of Dan McKenzie's hammer upon the anvil; the hour was late but McKenzie was still putting the Marquis's second-hand stagecoaches in order for the rough mountain run to Deadwood.

Pack heard the voices of Jerry Paddock and his sometime wife, quarreling bitterly. He heard Paddock's dangerous growl: "You listen to me!"

And Little Casino's hoarse reply: "I listened to you one time before. Didn't pay then, won't pay now."

Little Casino's voice climbed to a shrill screech until Paddock burst out onto the street, face aflame, and stopped to regard the door venomously before he plunged half-running toward Bob Roberts's place, a need for whiskey visibly howling through him. When Paddock slammed past, Pack felt the ill will in the rogue's scowl. Pack stifled his smile of amusement until Jerry Paddock was gone.

Very faintly on the wind he heard the crisp notes of Lady Medora's piano from the hilltop. Liszt, he thought. Beautiful dexterity.

He went into Bob Roberts's place. Currents of smoke swirled under the low ceiling and stung his eyes. He saw Pierce Bolan at one of the four tables, eating a late supper. Along the bar stood a light scattering of after-dark diehards—merchants, Dr. Stickney, overnighting cattlemen from the Bad Lands, unemployed hunters. The latter group was missing two of its more notorious members; Finnegan and O'Donnell had been lying low since the killing of Riley Luffsey. As for Dutch Reuter, no one had any idea where he had drifted off to.

Also notable by their absence from Roberts's bar were Johnny Goodall's cow hands and butchers—indeed, any of De Morès's employees. These days they did their drinking exclusively at Paddock's. The town had divided sharply and dangerously into factions; whenever one group met another you never knew when something might ignite the tinder.

Pack did not care for beer tonight. He risked a whiskey, took a sip and felt the sharp burn of it on tongue and palate and throat. It heated his chest as it went down. He closed his eyes tight for a long moment and opened them to see Sewall and Dow enter.

Sewall planted his feet in the middle of the narrow room. Graven-faced, he turned his gaze slowly until men began to look at him in curiosity. When he had most everybody's attention he said in a flat angry voice, "Jim Hayden's dead."

There was the scrape of bootheels as men turned to look at Sewall. Bob Roberts said, "Who shot him?"

Wil Dow said, "He wasn't shot."

Pierce Bolan said, "Drank too much bad whiskey, then?"

"No," said Sewall.

"Then I guess he can't be dead. That's the only two ways people die around here."

A ripple of laughter rolled around the group until Bill Sewall said, "Jim was hanged."

Everyone went absolutely still. A hush—in fairness Pack had to think of it as a hush—fell over the saloon.

Wil Dow said, "We found a paper nailed on his door. Skull and crossbones, and one word. 'Vacate.'"

Bob Roberts heaved a great sigh. His deep voice rolled out like lumps of coal down a metal chute. "They've come over from Montana, then."

Pack said, "'They?'"

"Vigilantes. Give some of the boys a speedy trial under the cottonwoods."

He felt a rush of excitement. His nose twitched. "Who are they?"

"Had hoods over their faces," said Bill Sewall. "Could've been anybody."

"Masked riders," Roberts said. "Then it's likely stockmen, fed up with outlaw thieves. Word I hear, Granville Stuart's called for a big desperado round-up."

"Brave enough to kill—but not to show their faces," Bill Sewall growled.

Wil Dow said stoutly, "No mercy, nor any real justice either."

Bob Roberts said, "They've been saying Granville Stuart's vigilantes over in Montana are Texas boys—saying he's brought in gunmen from the Panhandle. Saying he pays them a dollar a day to clean up the range."

"Now, those are rumors," Pack said. "Where are some facts?"

"The *fact* is Jim Hayden," Bill Sewall said, "hanged by the neck until dead." He made a gesture of confusion and helplessness, extending his arms out as if to embrace the room. "Cowboys. May the Lord save us. I do fear they'll find it is a good piece harder to get injustice back into the bottle than it was to let it out."

Pack said, "Now let's not jump to confusions. Maybe Jim Hayden moonlighted the wrong man's calf. Maybe it was bound to happen. Everybody knows Jim had too much talent with a running iron. I wouldn't be surprised if one of his neighbors caught him in the act and thought to throw the fear of God into other thieves by making it look like the work of an army."

Bill Sewall said, "I am sorry to dispute you, Mr. Packard, but there's an army sure enough. At least twenty riders."

"More like thirty," Wil Dow said.

"How do you know that?"

"We have seen them, I'm telling you. Wil and I swang off to one side. Otherwise they'd've run us down."

Pack took out his notebook. "Tell me what you saw."

Dutch Reuter combed the kinks out of both horses on the bank of a tributary creek before he broke camp. It was nearly two hours after sunrise, Dutch being in no particular hurry today, and after he loaded all his worldly goods on the pack horse he stood by his saddle mount and considered the various horizons.

It was a stirring in his loins that finally decided him, against his better judgment, to turn east and head down through the gullies toward the river. He knew of a convenient ford near Bolan's ranch and from there it would be not too many hours' ride up out of the Bad Lands to the woman's dugout soddy on the plateau. Dutch felt sufficiently at peace today to put up, in exchange for the exercise of conjugal rights, with her righteous female harangues.

He passed the rotting maggoty skeletons of a few winter-killed sheep that had been picked over by coyotes and vultures and ants; not quite sure whether to express his scorn with laughter or a snarl, he did neither, since nobody was watching, but simply continued on his way down a long brush-studded coulee. It would serve the swine-hound of a Marquis right to worry himself into an early grave with all his grand ambitions. The swine-hounds were stupid. What could possibly be the value of it when all a man needed for the enjoyment of life was easy free passage through open country with the prospect of hot food and a woman's moist warmth at the end of the day?

His mood was so docile he refused to allow the intrusion of any thoughts about the sharpness of the woman's tongue.

Dutch leaned back in the saddle to ease the horse's downhill passage and tipped his tattered hat back to expose his face to the warm sun. A taste of early spring; it would be a fine afternoon on the prairie. With luck he might shoot a brace of grouse or partridge to bring to the house as a peace offering to the woman.

At the bottom of the river gorge was a wide stretch of tree-shaded flats. He threaded through the groves, enjoying the shade, listening to the birds. Sound and scent of the rippling river quickened the horses' gaits. Dutch gave them their heads. They trotted to the bank; Dutch stepped down and let them drink their fill from an eddying pool that looped out to one side from the main flow of the Little Missouri. He washed his face and drank. It was fresh and cold the way he liked it—melted snow off the Black Hills, warmed by the spring sun in its shallow journey across the plains; in another week or two, unless there was a new cold spell, the melt would fill the river with a torrent. But not yet. Just now the level was only middle-high.

Dutch filled his canteens and walked out on the rocks as far as he could in order to squint at the ford a hundred meters downriver.

It looked all right; the splashes of white foam were there to indicate that the bottom lay close to the surface. It was always sensible to examine such places before plunging into them because you never knew when a floating log might come along and smash a deep cut through what once had been a pleasant stirrup-high walk across.

He was leading the horses toward the crossing when he spied a strange phenomenon coming toward him from the trees at the base of a rainbow-striped butte to his left: a man afoot.

After a moment it became clear the pedestrian was Pierce Bolan. Dutch stopped and waited with a knowing grin while the Texan trudged forward.

Pierce Bolan was sweaty and limping, and empty-handed; he had his hat, clothes, boots and holstered revolver but that was all.

"Listen, you old Dutchman, you don't need to look so pleased at a man's misfortune."

As always, Dutch had to filter the words through the dictionary of his mind, converting them one at a time into German before he could make sense of them. One time the stout *frau*, in exasperation, had wailed about how he had been in North America for damn near half his life and he still couldn't speak or understand English worth a damn. Why, she demanded, did she have to go and pick the only man, red or white, on the plains who had absolutely no calling for languages?

"Horse you throw?"

"Naw. I didn't get pitched off. Stopped to take a squat, forgot I was riding a half-broke Indian mare, left her hitched to a twig, and the next thing I know she's spooked by a butterfly and half way to the next county. I don't mind the horse and I don't even mind the walk home but that was my good Winchester rifle and my second-best double-rig saddle. You come across a spotted blue mare with my rig and rifle on a Mandan saddle blanket, I'll be obliged for the return of same. Spread the word for me, will you?"

"Yah. That I do," Dutch agreed, knowing as well as Pierce did what the chances were of having the goods returned in this sort of country. "But come on, Pierce, we can double ride. How long ago horse spook? We catch."

"Last I saw she was on the dead run for Montana and that was three hours ago. No chance of catching up now, but I'm obliged for the thought."

It was a few miles from here up a draw to Pierce's ranch. It would make a pleasant ride in the unusually warm sun. Dutch said, "Come on, then, get up—I you home take."

Pierce smiled. "Much obliged." Then something caught his attention past Dutch's shoulder. The way Pierce froze made Dutch turn and look that way.

They were coming downriver, visible at intervals between clumps of intervening trees; they were half a thousand meters away, riding bunched up in a solid-packed column of threes, about two dozen horsemen cantering forward at a businesslike clip. There wasn't much dust right along the river where they were riding and even from here Dutch had no trouble seeing the hoods they wore over their heads.

In a calm voice Pierce Bolan said, "Dutch, get the hell out of here."

"Both of us. Come on—you up climb."

"I'm respectable, Dutch. They don't want me. It's you they're after. They still think you shot up the Markee's house—they've put the word out on you. Listen, get out of here. I'll flag them down and palaver, give you a little jump on 'em. Maybe I can talk sense to them. Go on—on the run now."

The riders had seen them now; they were lifting their horses to a menacing gallop and Dutch didn't have to do much translating in his head in order to appreciate the wisdom in Pierce's judgment. Dutch flashed a grin of gratitude at the young Texan, grabbed up the pack horse's reins, leaped aboard the saddle animal and spurred urgently toward the ford.

He skewed among trees, splashed across, came heaving up out of the river and as he went up into the cottonwoods on the east bank he hipped around in the saddle to look back.

Half the crowd flowed around Pierce Bolan in a closing circle. The rest were coming straight for the ford on the dead run. They had guns up and there was no more time for contemplation: Dutch rammed his horses into the trees, ducked to keep from being decapitated by a low branch and galloped recklessly ahead, bent low over the saddle, dragging the pack animal at full gallop.

He had a good lead when he came out of the trees and ran up the dry creekbed of a tributary coulee; it curled around an acute bend to the northeast and he knew he would be out of sight of the pursuit for at least a little while; the knowledge steadied him enough to allow him to reason ahead. When he had climbed six or seven hundred meters into the coulee with a cresting rib of sloping ground on either side he took the risk of slowing the pace long enough to take a good look down the backtrail.

Gott im Himmel.

They were coming—at least ten of them, thundering up the creekbed.

One of them lifted a rifle one-handed and Dutch saw smoke puff from its muzzle; a moment later he heard the faint crack of the gunshot.

He had no idea where the bullet went but it left no doubt of the hooded horsemen's intention.

Dutch hauled his two steeds to the right, spurred frantically and yanked on the tow-reins, urging them up over the hump of land that separated this canyon from its neighbor. They went half-sliding over the sloping rim, hoofs scrabbling for purchase against clay and shrubs. He lost his hat and heard more gunfire before he was over the crest; two or three bullets ricochetted off objects close enough to make him flinch from the noise.

Out of their sight-line he fled down into a tangle of shallow gullies where artesian pressure had encouraged the growth of scrubby trees that stood twice as high as a man—a considerable stretch of forest for these parts, and a Godsend to Dutch. The pursuers would expect him to continue eastward for the high ground and try to out-run them across the flats of the high plateau; so he whipped the pack horse savagely away uphill, fired two shots in the air that helped propel the frightened beast on its way toward the crest and turned his own mount sharply downslope—west: back down toward the river.

He trotted through the trees; it was cool in here away from the sun. He chose a meandering aimless-seeming path that would leave tracks like those of a riderless horse that was following its natural inclination to wander toward the smell of fresh water.

And pray to God it would fool the pursuing swine into following the wrong set of tracks.

He continued downhill, reining in his nerves and his horse, forcing himself to keep the pace to a mild haphazard trot. The trees were too thick to permit a view of anything more than a few meters away. He stopped twice to blow the horse and let it graze; he turned his head slowly in every direction in an effort to pick up any telltale sounds against the flats of his eardrums. There were various distant sounds—hoofs clattering on rock, men's shouts, a spirited whinny—but none of it gave useful evidence whether the pursuit was proceeding east or west.

Dutch pushed his lips tight together and gigged the horse downhill at a faster clip; anyone who followed this far would not give up before catching the "riderless" horse, so there was no point continuing the deception any longer and he lifted the beast to a canter, moving as quickly as he could without raising too much sound.

He was nearly down to the river when he heard the sharp clanging chip of horseshoe on rock—behind him and not far at all. He stopped and listened.

No question those were hoof-falls, approaching steadily. Several horses—three or more.

Dutch spoke a curse in his mind. They must have split up the party to follow both sets of tracks.

He had never killed anybody that he knew of but the extreme circumstances of the moment made him think seriously about lying up by the trail with his rifle and picking them off as they approached.

A cooler second consideration made him think better of it. He might get a good shot or two but he probably wouldn't be able to knock down all of them, and the noise of shooting would draw the rest of them. Not much future in that.

Not much future in anything right now, he thought, but there was no point quitting before you were caught.

He rode toward the river, draping the reins over the horse's withers so they wouldn't trail and trip the poor animal. He slipped his rifle out of the scabbard and clutched it tight in his fist, and when he came past a litter of volcanic boulders he slipped off the wrong side of the horse and teetered on the rocks, slapping the horse with the rifle's buttstock. It continued to amble downhill toward the river.

Dutch made his way afoot across the sharp rocks, making little leaps from one to another; the important thing was not to touch any soft ground where he might leave a footprint.

Moving in that manner he came to a patch where there were no rocks. But by good fortune there was a good stout deadfall. He crawled across roots and trunk and a firm fallen tree-limb—made his way to the next string of stones and finally brought himself to the river's edge.

The water ran several feet deep along the curve, birling against an exposed root system where it had undercut the clay bank.

It was going to be cold but it looked good enough; anyway it would have to do. Dutch slipped into the stream, sucked in his breath at the sudden frigid cold and lowered himself all the way into the water, clutching a root overhead, propping the rifle above him with his free hand; he slipped under the tangle of roots and came up beneath the cutbank.

He had to turn the rifle and swap hands to pull it lengthwise through the overhanging roots. There was no way to keep the rifle completely dry but he did his best—pressed it against the roots above his head and suspended it there with one hand until the arm got tired; then he traded hands and waited and shivered while the eddying water lapped around his throat.

He was inside a cave; his view of the world was restricted by a great many gnarled roots and he couldn't hear a damn thing over the rush of the river but he was alive and, he hoped, invisible.

Nothing to do but figure on waiting it out here until they rode off—if he could stand the cold that long.

It was no good predicting. Either he would be lucky or he wouldn't

It wasn't long before he glimpsed movement on the opposite bank and moved his head forward to get a better view between roots. By shifting his face from side to side he could command a fair view of the area, a bit at a time, and it wasn't so far away; he had a clear enough perception of what transpired then—clearer than he'd have preferred.

A dozen horsemen were gathered, all of them hooded. Several dismounted now. One dragged a man forward at the end of a lasso and Dutch saw it was Pierce Bolan. Pierce was yelling at his captors but they weren't paying any attention. Dutch couldn't hear what anybody said over there; all he caught was the raging high timbre of Pierce's voice.

Dutch had to clench his teeth to keep them from chattering. It was mostly the icy cold of the water but he knew what was going to happen and he watched, because there was no point in not watching.

They tied Pierce Bolan's hands behind him and it took four of them to boost him up on one of the saddle horses. Pierce struggled and yelled all the way but it had no effect.

Several horsemen entered the creek from this side, upstream not far from Dutch; one of them was leading Dutch's saddle horse. So they'd found it. Presumably half a dozen others were still up on the rim chasing the pack horse.

Across the river the new bunch, leading Dutch's horse, joined the rest. They were all wearing hoods, various colors and patterns of cloth— bandannas, bedsheets, old shirts; probably whatever makeshifts had come to hand—with big torn-out eyeholes. Dutch wondered why they continued to wear the masks when, so far as they knew, there was nobody around to recognize any of them. Maybe they were afraid someone would chance upon them; or maybe they didn't know each other? That made a kind of gruesome sense: if you didn't know who your fellow-murderer was, you couldn't testify against him.

A thin man tossed a line over a tree-limb and knotted the noose around Pierce's neck. A short man stood at the head of the horse, holding it, and a burly man, who seemed to be the leader, stood like a hunchback, hands buried in the pockets of the long coat that flapped against his ankles; that one made an indicative show of sincere regret—Dutch had to fight down the impulse to shoot the swine and to hell with consequences—and then the swine threw his head back and said something to Pierce Bolan.

Pierce shouted back at the swine, raging at him.

Dutch changed hands on the rifle, shivered in the chill water and specified to himself with dismal clear logic why there would be no good served by his interfering. They would still lynch Pierce Bolan, and they would kill Dutch himself in the bargain. It was better to live and fight again another day, Gott damn it.

The hooded swine turned away and made a sharp gesture with a swinging arm; they slapped the horse out from under Pierce Bolan and he fell slantwise and was brought up hard before he could hit the ground—brought up by a snap that whipped his head hard to one side as if it had been hit by a buffalo-gun bullet.

Dutch thought it was a wonder it didn't rip his head clear off.

Pack broke off his labors in the office of *The Bad Lands Cow Boy* to go outdoors and clear his head. The words were not coming properly—he wasn't sure what to say about the events he was reporting.

The morning sun was bright but the breeze was cool enough to make him turn his coat collar up. He saw Sewall and Dow in front of Joe's store lashing their purchases down across their pack animals. Joe stood on the porch chewing the cud with them. Pack waved them all a hesitant good morning and was thinking about joining them when the noise of a disruption drew his attention toward the embankment.

Several men were running—in pursuit of a lone man afoot.

Pack caught Joe Ferris's eye. It took no more than that; in a flash the two were off, racing through the side street on a course designed to intercept those men. After a moment Pack heard the drum of hoofbeats behind him and assumed it was Sewall and Dow, coming along out of curiosity.

Another foot chase; it reminded him, as he puffed along, of the pursuit of the Lunatic. The poor bewildered soul was in the asylum now.

At the edge of the river the fugitive tried to run under the bridge but two of his pursuers were there first. The man backed out into the sun; the two pursuers came forward with revolvers in their hands and Pack recognized them as clerks who worked for Jerry Paddock in the De Morès Hotel. The rest of the crowd caught up—some of Paddock's hangers-on: two bartenders, a stable hostler, several workers from the abattoir crews.

One of the hotel clerks said, "All right, Calamity. I guess that's it."

Pack had heard the name "Calamity" once or twice. He associated it with a reputed hardscrabble horse-rustler and petty thief but he'd never seen the man.

The former fugitive stood surrounded by Paddock's well-armed men. He looked a bit of a calamity sure enough—lanky and filthy, dark-skinned with shaggy black hair, a full bird's-nest beard and eyes set very close together. If he'd had a hat he must have lost it running. He looked as if he hadn't had a meal in days; his clothes were ragged and he was not armed.

Calamity stood with his feet splayed wide in weariness. He puffed. He shifted his bleak glance from one face to another and the crowd slowly pushed forward, closing the circle around him.

One man shifted his rifle into his left hand and reached out to grip Calamity's arm. "You all finished here, boy."

Water fretted against the pilings of the railroad bridge. Pack glanced at Joe Ferris beside him. Joe's face was glum. His hand lay on the butt of the Remington revolver in his holster but he did not draw it out. He was looking off downriver.

Pack looked that way and saw, of all people, Redhead Finnegan and Frank O'Donnell coming up horseback from the ford, their stirrups still dripping. The two hunters halted their horses, still fifty or sixty feet away.

They seemed to have picked a rather spectacular time to have emerged from their seclusion.

More horses came up from behind. Pack looked around and, as he expected, saw Sewall and Dow; but then came Jerry Paddock, who rode straight past them without a glance and walked his horse straight into the crowd. His men parted to make way.

The gaunt Calamity looked up at Jerry and his face went carefully blank.

The hotel clerk said to Jerry Paddock, "Upstairs in a customer's room. He was going through a man's luggage."

"Search him."

The man with the rifle continued to hold Calamity's arm while the hotel clerk went gingerly through Calamity's pockets.

On their horses, Sewall and Dow watched. The older man was scowling; the younger looked eager and excited.

A little distance away, Finnegan and O'Donnell sat with their rifles across their saddlebows. They didn't stir. Several of Paddock's boys were watching them, narrow-eyed and ready for trouble, and Pack muttered to Joe Ferris, "I would just as soon be somewhere else just now."

By way of reply he heard Joe's long exhalation of breath: a sound of unhappy resignation.

The clerk's search produced a small metal shaving mirror and a golden watch and chain.

From high on horseback Jerry Paddock said, "What'd you want the shaving mirror for, Calamity? To admire your pretty face?"

"It's my mirror. It's my own. Belongs to me," Calamity said.

"Come again, you long-whiskered sinner. You haven't shaved in ten years."

The clerk was examining the watch front and back. He squinted at it up close and said, "Initials CJW."

"What's Calamity's name? Anybody know?"

Calamity said quickly, "Christopher J. Williams, that's my name." His voice was hardly more than a whisper.

"Hell," said the clerk, "his name's Bill Smith. But they's a guest registered in the hotel under the name of Clarence Worth, I think it is—anyways it was his room Calamity come runnin' out of."

Jerry Paddock said, "May as well hang him."

Pack closed his eyes for half a second and then lifted his voice sternly. "Now, hold on."

Paddock swiveled in the saddle to regard him with disdain.

Pack said, "If you lynch that man in front of all these witnesses, you'll have to go to trial for it. Now, I'm not saying you'll be convicted, but why invite the trouble?"

Joe Ferris said, "Put him in the Bastille overnight and I'll take him over to Dickinson for trial tomorrow. That watch is evidence enough—he'll go to prison."

Watchful and insolent, Jerry Paddock touched each of them with his sliding glance. It lingered on Finnegan and O'Donnell. Pack couldn't tell whether it was their presence that made him hesitate.

Bill Sewall said, "Hang him and you'll have to hang quite a few of us, else we'll be obliged to testify to what your lynch-party does here."

For the first time anger glowed in Jerry Paddock's deep-set eyes. "Who asked you to shove your Jew-loving nose in?"

From downriver Redhead Finnegan yelled, "Why don't you go ahead and lynch the poor son of a bitch? Same as you been doing to all them good boys up and down the Bad Lands."

Jerry Paddock's muderous glare swiveled back toward the two hunters. "Red, if I want to kill a man, I kill him standing up and facing him. I don't put a mask on and ride up on him in the middle of the night—"

"You mean like you shot Riley Luffsey? Was that standing up and facing him?"

In that moment of distraction Pack saw Calamity grab his captor's rifle.

Pack, keyed to a twang-taut pitch as it was, jumped a foot at the *bang* of its discharge—it must have been cocked; it went off into the air—and for a moment Pack wasn't clearly sure what was going on. He thought he heard Calamity say, "Make room—make room—I'm goin'!" and he had an impression of several men backing away from Calamity's wildly swinging rifle. . . . He thought Calamity tried to run for it, toward the dubious sanctuary afforded by Finnegan and O'Donnell, but the path must have brought him tangentially toward Jerry Paddock because when Calamity looked up, Paddock's under-shoulder revolver was out and cocked and leveled at him.

Pack blinked and tried to breathe. His attention steadied. There were guns up, all over the place, and he prepared to throw himself flat on the ground. He felt the distress in Joe Ferris and knew Joe probably was ready to do the same.

But there was a broken frozen instant of time in which nothing stirred, nothing at all.

Pack saw clearly the twisted sneer under Jerry Paddock's Chinese mustache and the steadiness of Paddock's cocked revolver, aimed straight at Calamity's face. He saw too that Calamity's rifle was not pointed anywhere near Jerry Paddock.

He heard Joe Ferris say, "For God's sake, Calamity, don't fight the drop."

Pack could not believe his eyes then, for against all reason Calamity was swiveling the rifle, making his try—a wild fury distorting his face out of shape, a half-strangled sound escaping from his throat—and without compunction Jerry Paddock fired immediately.

The gunshot so close to its ear spooked Jerry Paddock's horse. Jerry sawed at the reins and stood up in the stirrups, leaning hard to one side as the horse wheeled.

Pack saw that Calamity had fallen limp to the ground. An immediate stink lifted from him and drove men back—even these men whose nostrils were inured to the abattoir.

Pack peered through, ducking from side to side to get a view. Calamity was most certainly dead. Part of his face was gone, red and glutinous. Pack looked away and tried to stifle his nausea. He had never seen a man shot dead in front of him before. *And I want never to see another.*

* * *

The Concord was drawn up awaiting departure for Deadwood. Despite nay-sayers the stage line was in operation. The four coaches had been running since the thaw began. Like the others this handsome vehicle was painted black and gold, with the Vallombrosa coat-of-arms and a bold legend: U.S. MAIL—MEDORA STATE AND FORWARDING CO. Admittedly that was a bit premature, as the Marquis had not yet been awarded a mail contract, but of course it was merely a matter of time.

Two passengers—drummers by the look of their travel-worn suits and threadbare carpetbags—got aboard. There didn't seem to be much freight. The driver cracked his whip and yelled.

The coach rocked forward, drawn by four skittish teams. Pale dust smoked from its wheels.

It was mildly cool; there was an easy breeze. Huidekoper and Joe Ferris came across the intersection from the store to Pack's place. With an air of urgency Joe said, "Mind if we come inside?"

Pack looked at him, not altogether in surprise. He went back into the *Cow Boy* office. The two men followed and Huidekoper looked out both ways along the street before he closed the door. His movements were somehow conspiratorial.

Pack said, "What is it?" although he already knew.

"Want to talk to you about what's going on out in the hills," said Joe.

Huidekoper said, "These are hard times for principles. Some people don't seem able to afford them. We have got to rekindle a sense of proper morality in the populace. Your newspaper must be part of the effort. It's a vital element."

Pack said, "Now, I assume you're talking about the Stranglers. Grim sort of proceedings, I know. But sometimes—"

"The hell," Joe said. "They're murderers, Pack. No excuses."

Pack found it hard to keep his mind focused on what they were saying. He still felt lightheaded and a trifle nauseous. It had been two days but he hadn't been able to rid the sight and stink of Calamity's sudden corpse from the front page of his vision.

Huidekoper was talking. "In isolated camps and coulee cabins up and down the river, the Stranglers are going about their awful business with a relentless eagerness."

He talks in paragraphs, Pack thought.

Huidekoper went on, his voice nearly accusing: "Do you know how many they've slaughtered?"

"No. Do you?"

"At least half a dozen," Joe said. "May be more."

"Not to mention," Huidekoper mentioned, "that it's becoming increasingly apparent they are not entirely averse to the lures of plunder."

Just now Pack was having difficulty in stirring up much interest in the subject of Huidekoper's crusade. "Some say they are cleaning up the territory."

"And that it's long overdue," Huidekoper said. "I know. I've seen your remarks in the paper."

"I don't know why you're badgering me, A.C. I thought you were all in favor of setting up a safety committee."

"Please don't throw that back in my face. I'm tired of it. I've never advocated lynch law."

Joe was looking around the room. "Speaking of cleaning up the territory—you ought to clean this place up, Pack. How can you find anything in this mess?"

Huidekoper said, "I'm sure he knows where every tiny thing is."

Pack knew it always took the bald-headed windbag forever to get to the point, but now Joe was beating about the bush with equal reluctance. What were they up to?

Joe said, "Don't know if you heard. Day before yesterday they nearly hanged Dutch Reuter."

"Nearly?"

Huidekoper said, "Fortunately he had a fast horse."

Pack said, "Now, Dutch Reuter doesn't salivate my sympathies. He's a cowardly ambusher—let him look out for himself."

Joe's eyes showed anger for the first time. "You're spouting the Markee's geyser again. Dutch never ambushed anybody."

"I was there, Joe, when the bullets came through the walls."

"And I suppose you saw Dutch's face out there in the middle of the night whilst you were belly-down and trying to dig a hole in the floor?"

Huidekoper said, "Joe—Arthur—please. To return to the subject at hand—Granville Stuart's raiders. Can we not agree they are an abomination upon the land? They're like the Four Horsemen of the Apocalypse, tenfold. Every day I hear more about their vigilante-ing after what they call horse-thieves. I'm compelled to tell you that Theodore Roosevelt foresaw it right—they seem to be attacking any small rancher in the Bad Lands."

Huidekoper talked and talked. Pack wondered irritably if the man had ever had an unexpressed thought.

It was a moment after Huidekoper said it before the impact of his words caught up with Pack:

"They found Pierce Bolan afoot, so they assumed he intended to steal a horse, and they hanged him."

A shock of alarm grenaded into Pack. "Pierce Bolan? They hanged *Pierce Bolan?*"

He was still trying to absorb it. Huidekoper's talk ran on and on:

"Dutch Reuter saw it. Saw the whole thing. Hooded masked men. They gave Pierce no chance—hanged him from a tree, broke his neck and rode away as if they'd done a fine work of justice."

"Did Dutch Reuter tell you this? How did you find this out?" Pack asked.

"I'd rather not say," Huidekoper replied, but it seemed obvious the only way he'd have known so much so soon would be by having spoken personally with Dutch Reuter.

Pack said, "I wouldn't take Dutch's word for anything. Where is he now?"

"I've no idea," Huidekoper said. "Making himself invisible, I should imagine. The point is, Pierce Bolan was an honest man. There was no evidence, beyond the slenderest thread of stupid suspicion, that he had any intention of stealing a horse, and even if there had been, the intent to steal a horse is hardly a capital crime. But such is the arrogance of mobs when you put ropes in their hands."

"That is damned raw," Pack said. Outrage grew in him. "Who did it?"

"Conveniently no one has seen their faces—or at least cares to admit having seen them. You know, of course, that De Morès is backing them. He may take advice from Granville Stuart, but it's De Morès who's the force behind the Stranglers in the Bad Lands. He hopes they'll drive all the small ranchers out for him."

Pack felt dizzy; it was too much, coming at him too fast. Calamity and then Pierce Bolan and now this talk about De Morès.

He said, "I don't know that at all. And I don't think you do either. You're just seizing at anything that'll abet your campaign against the Marquis. I certainly don't intend to print such allegations unless you can show me proof."

"Why, hell, Arthur," Huidekoper said with a mild and uncharacteristic show of humor, "I never knew that to stop you before."

Pack wrestled with it for a day and a night. He did not sleep. He interrogated everyone he could find who might have a scrap of information. Finally at half-past ten in the morning, feeling ashamed of the cowardly way he had lingered over breakfast in the cafe, he drew himself up and reared back on his dignity and tramped resolutely to the De Morès offices.

He was kept waiting for ten minutes until Johnny Goodall came jingling out of the private office. Van Driesche, the skeletal secretary with the British accent, admitted Pack to the Marquis's presence. The Marquis owned a desk but it was rarely his habit to sit at it; he tended to pace around the room when confined to an office and Pack was lucky to have found him here at all, for the Marquis rarely set foot in the place.

This morning he wore a black silk shirt and a white neck scarf. His pointed longhorn mustache bristled. "Ah, Arthur. You've come just in time to rescue me from a Purgatory of paperwork."

"I'm not here on a happy errand, I'm afraid."

"What is it? Has someone died?"

"Yes, as a matter of fact."

"Who?"

"Half a dozen men or more. Including Pierce Bolan."

"Ah. The Regulators."

"The Stranglers, they're calling them."

The Marquis's left eyebrow lifted. It was a talent Pack had tried to cultivate, thus far without success—the ability to elevate one eyebrow.

The Marquis said, "The Stranglers. I rather like that. Yes, the Stranglers. It has a suitably ominous sound. Perhaps it will throw the fear of God into the outlaws. What do you think?"

"It already has." Pack took a deep breath. "And into some others as well. Pierce Bolan was no outlaw."

"I'm not sure I knew the man. I recognize the name . . ."

"Place on Beaver Creek."

"Yes. Well there are dozens of outlaw cabins in that district, aren't there."

"Now, Pierce Bolan was a hard-working man. I don't believe he ever stole."

"Arthur—why talk this way to me?"

"Because there are people here, people not without distinction and importance, who believe you're the leader of the Stranglers."

This time both eyebrows went up. The Marquis said, "Indeed. Can you picture me riding my horse all over the Bad Lands by day and by night, hanging outlaws from trees, and still having time to be here at my very busy duties every single day, and to entertain our visitors each evening as well?"

"No one's said you ride with them. You've been identified as the force behind them."

"Identified. By whom?"

"By men who can't be ignored."

"Their names?"

Pack had gone too far too stop. "Names? What are the names of the Stranglers?"

"I've no idea, Arthur."

Pack hesitated. He believed the Marquis, as he always had; but he understood that good men could have evil impulses. He said, "Now, you do know what the vigilantes are doing."

"Doesn't everyone?" The Marquis was nearly purring. A little smile hovered beneath his mustaches.

Pack said, "The outlaws need to be cleaned out—I've always agreed with you about that. You've created wealth here, and that always attracts the low element—they've descended on the Bad Lands like moths to a flame. I've got no sympathy for criminals. And I've got no patience with so-called law officers like Harmon who leave us no choice but to find our own way to defend ourselves. My newspaper supports that position without reservation."

"Then we are in agreement. Why are you here?"

"Because Pierce Bolan has been lynched, and Dutch Reuter was nearly hanged, and some of our best citizens have come to believe things have gone too far."

"I don't know anything about Mr. Bolan. As for Reuter, you

know my feelings about that man, but if someone tried to lynch him, I still don't understand why you've come to me. If it's because of the ridiculous rumors that Mr. Paddock rides with the Regulators, I can assure you there's no truth in them. Mr. Paddock has no more time for such activities than I do."

"I believe that. Now, I've come because I'm obliged to tell you that if I don't publish the suspicions of these citizens, I'm sure they'll turn up in the newspapers in Dickinson and Mandan and Bismarck. It would be better all around if you could head it off now."

"And how may I do that? What do you want to do, Arthur—print a story that says, 'Marquis denies lynching Pierce Bolan'? Do you believe that would dissolve the suspicions of my enemies?"

"If I could simply print your side of the story—"

The Marquis looked out the window and looked back at Pack, and said, "I shall be happy to tell you my 'side,' as you put it—I shall candidly take you into my confidence—but you may not print a word of it. Is that agreed?"

"I don't—"

"When I've explained, you'll understand why. I must have your word."

"Now, in conscience I don't believe I can—"

"Then we shall compromise. I always believe in the opportunities of compromise, as you know. Let's say I shall leave it to your conscience, but you'll at least agree to keep an open mind until I've finished. Agreed?"

"That's certainly fair enough."

"Sit down, Arthur."

Pack chose the corner chair, so that he wouldn't have to look at the Marquis in silhouette against the window.

The Marquis paced. "You've stumbled onto part of the truth. When you understand the whole of it, you'll comprehend the vital need to keep it secret. It's true my friend Granville Stuart began the movement, but each posse operates independently, and knows nothing of the membership of the others. I myself know none of the names of the Regulators in the Bad Lands posse, even though in a sense you are correct in believing I am its leader. My leadership is indirect, and mainly takes a financial form—I pay the wages and expenses of the possemen. Their actual leader is a man named W.H. Springfield. Do you know him?"

"No."

"Have you ever heard of him?"

"No."

"Good." The Marquis lifted his weighted bamboo stick from the desktop and began thrusting it out to arm's length and holding it there for prolonged intervals. "In some ways I would prefer not to know him myself. He has an evil temper. He's an agent of the Pinkerton National Detective Agency in Chicago. I assume you have heard of *them*?"

"'We Never Sleep,'" said Pack, quoting the detective agency's famous slogan. A picture leaped immediately into his mind of the advertisements with their enormous single wide-open eye.

"Precisely. In Chicago I consulted with Mr. Allan Pinkerton personally. He assigned Mr. Springfield as the best man for this task."

Pack felt a rising prickle of excitement. He leaned forward.

The Marquis shifted the stick to his left hand and resumed exercising. "Mr. Pinkerton gave me fair warning that I should not find Springfield personally to my liking, and he was more than correct in that anticipation. But Springfield is doing the job to which he was assigned. His mission was to move through the Territory in the guise of a tough—to establish himself as a thief in order to infiltrate the rustler crowd to find out who they all were."

The Marquis held the stick out again, then lowered it for a moment's rest. "I know it sounds like a pot of penny-dreadful drivel, Arthur. I can't help that. I promised you the full truth."

"Go on."

The Marquis extended the stick again. "When first I met Mr. Springfield he was sewing his papers into the lining of his coat, in case he should be arrested. He needs to be able to identify himself to officers of the law—he has what I suppose is a natural fear that by mistake one day he may be thrown into a cell in company with deadly villains whose arrest he may have caused. His fears may be well grounded, for according to Mr. Pinkerton he's had an astounding record of successes."

"Then I'm surprised I've never heard of him."

"It's a good thing for him you haven't. Of course Springfield is his real name, and as you may imagine, he does not go by that name when he's working undercover, as he is now. I don't even know what name he's using here in the Bad Lands."

The Marquis grasped the stick in both hands now, and held it straight out in front of him, then slowly lifted it directly overhead and lowered it forward again.

"He's a strikingly ugly man, our Mr. Springfield. The sort I should imagine I would feel a kinship to if I were a horse-thief. In the past few weeks he's played poker and pool with toughs in every town and outlaw camp within a hundred miles' radius of us. I'm happy to tell you he's gained the confidence of the thieves, at least to the extent that he was able to identify and arrest a cattle-thief named Lepage."

"I've heard that name. But I didn't know he was hanged."

"He wasn't. Lepage is in Canada, so far as I know. Springfield offered him one hundred dollars and the promise of freedom in Canada, in return for the names of all the thieves in the Bad Lands. Lepage was agreeable to that arrangement. He gave Springfield a list of names. Springfield has given me that list, and I can tell you as a result that things are even worse than we had believed. The rustling ring is full of thieves and murderers—scores of them, including several whose names would surprise you mightily, even as they surprised me. Pierce Bolan's was one of them, and in fact Springfield tells me he found the hides of several stolen cattle buried in Bolan's compost heap. These little—what do they call them?—shoestring ranchers—have a way when they are hungry of assuming the right to slaughter their neighbor's cattle in lieu of their own, so as to save their own for more profitable use in the marketplace. In any event we have the information now. I authorized agent Springfield to organize a posse and round up all the rustlers whose names are on the Lepage list. They are to be driven out of the Territory, and if they offer resistance, they are to be hanged, as an example to the others."

The Marquis stopped pacing. "The operation is businesslike, methodical and backed by evidence. It's not a haphazard series of raids by wild murderers, as the rumors would have it. If we had reasonable law enforcement here, it would not be necessary, but in the circumstances, Mr. Springfield is the nearest thing we've got to a duly licensed officer and he is under strict instructions to give every suspected person the benefit of the doubt. There's no lynch-mob fever here—you must understand that."

The Marquis loomed above Pack's chair. Pack said nothing. He was impressed by the trust with which the Marquis had granted his confidence.

The Marquis said, "You understand now, perhaps, why the matter can't be described in the newspaper. It would jeopardize Springfield's life, it would endanger the success of the enterprise and it would provide aid and comfort to some of our most influential enemies."

"Now, I want desperately to see that list," Pack said.

"I'm sure you do, and perhaps one day I shall show it to you."

"Tell me one thing, at least. Is Theodore Roosevelt's name on it?"

"No names, Arthur. I've put a great deal of trust in you today. I ask for a bit of faith in return."

When Pack left the Marquis's presence he wandered through the town in a dull haze of uncertainty. Things were exploding at him from all directions. He no longer knew what to think. There was rectitude in the Marquis's position, no question of it; nevertheless—Pierce Bolan? Pack had spent quite a few hours in friendly colloquy with that bright and amiable Texan. They had played cards; they had broken bread together. *I'd have staked a good deal on his honesty.*

It made a man begin to wonder if he was as good a judge of character as he thought he was.

He pulled himself together. The important thing to remember at all times was that he was a newspaperman, dedicated to impartial objectivity. His own feelings did not matter. The only thing that mattered was truth.

Fifteen

With spring came somehow an increase in the intensity of Uncle Bill Sewall's complaints. True the frost was out of the ground, but it seemed the chinook must have blown the tops off all the buttes for dust had curled everywhere; and being made of heavy clay it sank into clothing, well-water, food—everything.

Then there was rain. It came in all directions—slantways, sideways, upside down—and it fueled the mighty onslaught of the melting ice pack. The river rushed and boiled. Here at its confluence with Blacktail Creek the Little Missouri, tortured into a narrow chute, crashed around the bend with great twisting leaps of froth. There was one particularly nasty morning when the flood nearly reached the barn.

On the opposite bank, scattered along the hillsides, Wil Dow saw great dark chunks of rock that looked like cattle—he had to stare at them a while to see if they moved. If they did, the Elkhorn riders had to swim their horses across the foaming muddy torrent and hope to survive.

After a week the boiling river became impossible to ford at all. They had to use the skiff—ferry their saddles across and then attempt, on the west bank, to catch horses that had been running wild all winter.

It all turned the earth to mud and Bill Sewall's mood to something even worse. But Wil Dow loved all of it. When Uncle Bill's pumpkin-rolling became too strident he cheerfully interrupted: "Come on, Uncle, you know if it hadn't been for Mr. Roosevelt we never would have got to see this Wild West."

That always provoked Uncle Bill to a fit of caterwauling about how he had never wanted to see the filthy Wild West and hoped never to see it again.

On the far bank the horses were fresh and frisky in the morning. They had to be gentled and retrained for use before spring round-up could begin.

Wil picked out a roan and, with Uncle Bill holding its head down, climbed into the saddle and settled his boots in the stirrups. "All right. Turn him loose."

Uncle Bill let go of the bit and backed away. Wil waited. The roan stood bolt still. Wil pulled his hat down tight and experimentally gigged his small blunt spurs into the roan's flanks.

The horse burst forward. Ears down, it unwrapped like a loosed steel spring. A thin tight spasm of pain shot through Wil's spine and he saw Uncle Bill's lips turn white. He felt his backbone try to break up through his head. The roan swapped ends and started pile-driving on four stiff legs; it wheeled and reared, humped and uncoiled, headed for a tree to scrape him off, changed its mind at the last minute and went to more hammer-bucking. It slammed down on all fours with an impact that snapped Wil's head forward on his neck. The sun whipped up and around; clots and damp wisps of clay roiled, choking Wil's nostrils. He grinned, and stayed glued to the reeling saddle while his vision dimmed and filmed over with a red haze and he tasted blood. His grip started to loosen; he knew he was going over—and then the roan quit fighting. It subsided into a few perfunctory pitches, did one more music-hall turn, trotted spitefully back and forth and finally stood still, head down. Its ears moved forward, cocked up, a gesture of surrender.

Uncle Bill said in a very dry voice, "Ride him, cowboy."

He accompanied his uncle Bill on a swath through a rough section of ravines, past rainbow-colored shale strata, heading up toward the short grass country. Everything that grew in the Bad

Lands seemed dwarfed, with the exception of some ashes and cottonwoods that grew to a fair height in sheltered clusters against high cutbanks near the river. Above on the steep rough slopes clung red cedar and juniper and all manner of scrub brush.

Sometimes it was necessary to throw a riata noose around bogged cattle and pull them out before they sank into the gumbo and died. Sometimes horses needed rescuing as well. Sometimes you didn't get to them until it was too late.

They prowled the forty-mile width of the Bad Lands. The strata were so clearly defined, so sharply contrasting in colors that they looked like painted ribbons. There was a chalky blue Bentonitic clay in a few of the parallel lines. The rain had made it run like inkstains.

By happenstance on an afternoon that might have been a Wednesday or a Friday they crossed paths with Mr. Roosevelt himself. Riding his favorite horse Manitou he came out of a coulee with a pleased look and reined in beside them. The wind drove bursts of rain in under his hatbrim so that he had to keep removing his spectacles and wiping them. "I love the wild desolate grandeur of the solitude. Sometimes you feel certain to the rock-bottom of your soul that no one's ever been there before you, no human eye ever seen what you're seeing."

Sewall said, "You'd generally be wrong. Every time I make up my mind I'm where no human man ever traveled I run on a tobacco tag or a beer bottle."

Wil Dow thought: *William Wingate Sewall, philosopher on horseback.*

At first glance, despite Uncle Bill's dour predictions, the herd looked pretty good. The Elkhorn seemed to be prospering. "Long as we can keep from getting lynched," Uncle Bill grumbled.

In intervals between downpours the occasional rider passed by from upstream, bringing news from the world beyond the Elkhorn. After the first flurry of lynchings, mostly the word was unexciting: the Marquis's lawyers continued to win delays in court, and most folks believed he never would stand trial for the Luffsey murder.

Roosevelt asked every rider for news of Dutch Reuter—who would be one of the key witnesses against the Marquis if it ever came to trial—but no one knew a thing. Wil Dow told the boss, "At least we can take heart from not hearing he got hanged."

After a few weeks' respite the news from upriver turned

downright bad again—the Stranglers were riding in force and purportedly had strung up more than a dozen "outlaws" and, as a result, a good many men had taken flight from their small outfits in the Bad Lands.

"Good riddance," said Uncle Bill. "They must have guilty consciences."

Wil Dow retorted, "Maybe they're just scared of getting lynched by mistake."

"It's all right to listen to the boss, Wil, but you don't need to swallow every word he says as Gospel truth. There's all too many stock-thieves hidden out in these Bad Lands and they're by no means the innocent band of independent ranchers Mr. Roosevelt makes them out to be. He's inclined to take too much on faith."

"They're innocent," Wil Dow said, "until proven guilty. So say I."

"Aagh," Uncle Bill growled in disgust.

In any event each of them traveled well-armed wherever he went, even if was only from the house to the barn.

Stranglers or no, the commerce of the prairie must go on. Spring round-up, with its attendant sorting out and branding of the season's calf crop, could not await the whim of night-riding vigilantes.

Roosevelt left a hired man to look after things at the Elkhorn while the boss took his two New Englanders south with their cavvy to join round-up headquarters. The temporary caretaker they left behind was a cowboy recommended by Eaton's foreman; he had injured his Achilles tendon and Eaton wanted to spare the man the rigors of round-up.

By general consent Johnny Goodall once again was elected round-up manager. Wil found the first two days in the headquarters camp near Custer Trail given up mostly to re-educating remuda ponies that were grass-fed, unshod and frisky. That first campfire evening was a delight to Wil Dow even though his bones ached so from bucking that no matter how he lay down he could not find a tolerable position. But bruises and aches could be forgotten in the swapping of good-natured lies. The Stranglers were not forgotten; but here in the heavily populated camp they could be set to one side while the ranch hands played cards and checkers, braided rawhide riatas and spun tall tales.

Even Roosevelt had learned to yarn. He said, "I chased that horse so far this afternoon I ran right into a Sioux Indian camp and got into conversation with an old red gentleman whose name I didn't catch, but we had quite a spirited discourse. When I scolded the old chief for his polygamous marriages and told him he must give up all but one wife if he hoped to be a Christian, the chief directed my attention at the several women and replied, 'Very good, sir. You tell *them* which one!'" Roosevelt laughed loudly at his own joke.

Sewall squirmed against the hard earth, trying to make depressions for hip and shoulder, and said, "Strikes me the man who first called it 'Bad Lands' hit it about right."

Howard Eaton said, "I understand that was a Frenchman, Boneval, one of Astor's old fur men."

This was at least the dozenth explanation Wil had heard; nonetheless he attended with interest.

Eaton went on: "They'd done some trading, filled three or four wagonloads of pelts. They were trying to get away from some Indians and they came on the Little Missouri. Couldn't find game of any kind, and the weather so dry and hot the wagons came to pieces. Provisions ran short and they had a hard time getting through. So Boneval named the country Malpais, which is Bad Lands in French."

Johnny Goodall said, "I heard that story and sixteen others. Lakota Indi'ns say they been calling this country Bad Lands for a thousand years."

Sewall said, "You ever meet an Indian didn't like to spin a lie? A thousand years ago there weren't any Lakota around here. This whole place was the bottom of an ocean, as a man can plainly tell on account of you pull up dead brush to make your fire on top of any high bluff around here, you find clamshells in the dirt."

Wil Dow said, "Maybe the Indians had gills in those days."

"Well you could be right about that. Maybe they had steamboats too."

Huidekoper rode in and unsaddled. He dampened down the evening: "Jerry Paddock and his boys are riding the district. I recommend you gentlemen watch out they don't gulch you."

Bill Sewall said, "Jerry Paddock is a creature I can stand to be near only if the wind happens to be right."

Wil Dow said, "For sure he's tied up with the Stranglers."

"I wouldn't be surprised," agreed Huidekoper. "Wherever there are underhanded doings, I always expect to find Jerry Paddock up to his chin. I don't believe he rides with the vigilantes but I certainly would not put it past him to be passing information to them."

The subject put a chill on things. Everyone turned in quickly; there was no more conversation.

In the morning Wil thought he was first awake and first to the coffee but he found Roosevelt wrapped in a blanket by the fire reading his book—Washington Irving. The boss lowered the book and put his grave glance upon Wil Dow. "You know these months have been my first experience in living among what I suppose my family would call the common folk. Working and riding among these ordinary men of the West—I find it a privilege. They're bully men."

"Yes sir."

All that morning Wil Dow saw Roosevelt try to prove he belonged among the common folk by continuing to ride horses too rugged for him; they kept bruising his bones. Hadn't he broken enough bones already? The boss was pushing himself, asking too much of his mortal skeleton; he must have known that but he kept pushing.

In noontime dinner camp Wil Dow said, "Uncle Bill, we have to find a way to persuade him he doesn't need to prove he's man enough to get killed by some outlaw horse."

Bill Sewall gave it thought. After a moment he carried his tin dish across to where the boss was cooking up a brace of quail he had shot. Wil trailed after him.

Roosevelt was using his engraved hunting knife to push the meat around the black frying pan that sat directly on the fire. Quail made good round-up eating, for they did not need to be plucked; it was a quick matter to pull off the skin, cut off head and feet, take out the insides, salt, roll in flour and fry hot and fast.

Uncle Bill said to Mr. Roosevelt, "Cowboying isn't a religion."

"Whatever do you mean by that?"

"It takes more than faith—more than devotion. It's no reflection on a man if he doesn't happen to be the best bronco-buster in the country."

"Why, Bill, I'm a second-rate horseman and I've never laid claim to better. You know that."

"You admit it cheerful enough. What you won't admit is that you're as scared of horses as I am. That's not unreasonable. But it's not smart to be too proud to give in to it."

Had it come from anyone else it might have provoked fiery argument. Bill Sewall was one of the few men alive from whom Roosevelt would tolerate that sort of comment without retort.

When Wil looked up he saw Johnny Goodall gazing at them. He was sure Johnny had overheard; but Johnny said nothing. He walked away. Apparently Roosevelt had not seen him; the boss was occupied trying to remove his pan from the fire without burning his hands too badly.

They helped themselves. The first bite burned the roof of Wil's mouth but he found it delicious. Roosevelt was saying to Uncle Bill, "Any man would be a fool not to own a healthy respect for the power of a half-ton beast with sharp hoofs and sharper teeth, Bill, but I don't intend to back away from any horse, and that's all I care to say on the subject, except that I'd certainly feel better all around if I were free to ride no other horse than good old Manitou. He's a steam engine—I trust *that* beast never to let me down. Truly a horse without compare."

"Well you do cook up an eatable dinner, for a New Yorker," said Uncle Bill.

At dark an unexpected traveler dropped in: Jerry Paddock, looking decidedly out of place in his black suit. He helped himself to a cup of coffee. "Just out doing a little spot-checking for the Marquis De Morès so we can work up a rough preliminary tally."

Roosevelt's jaw crept forward to lie in a pugnacious line. "I should have thought that would be Mr. Goodall's province."

Bill Sewall said, "I had the idea you'd prefer the nighttime for your kind of business."

Jerry Paddock gave him a dangerous look. "Say what you mean, Sewall."

"Mean what I say. No more, no less. I wouldn't be surprised, that's all, if one night the boys find you messing with a branded steer. Now that you've run out of sheep to slaughter."

"You could get hurt real bad talking that way," Jerry Paddock said.

"I might. But I doubt you're man enough to be the one to do it. Not face to face anyways."

Wil Dow was getting used to the rough threats these Westerners flung at one another. He'd heard the rumors about Paddock—that he'd killed several men, most recently young Riley Luffsey from ambush and that fellow Calamity in town. The man was an evil-tempered killer. When he'd ridden away Wil said to his uncle, "I wouldn't ignore his bluster."

"I would," Sewall replied, and granted Wil one of his rare and precious smiles.

Johnny Goodall came from another fire and squatted down between Wil Dow and Roosevelt. Johnny said, "Seems the cattle winter-drifted quite a ways. Our brands have been seen as far away as the Yellowstone and down along the Indian Reservation. We're sending representatives to our other round-ups."

"Capital idea."

"Huidekoper's got a gentle way with animals and Indians and all, so I've asked him to take a man with him and ride down along the Reservation for us. He's consented. Now I want to ask if you'd be willing to represent the Little Missouri brands over on the Yellowstone round-up."

"I'm honored you'd trust me with so considerable a responsibility."

"It takes a man of judgment, Mr. Roosevelt. I trust yours."

"Thank you, Mr. Goodall. I accept."

"Take one man with you," Johnny said. In the next moment without further palaver he was up and riding away, loose in the saddle with that cowboy's ease that even Wil Dow never could match, though he tried hard.

Johnny had the reputation of being a hard strict man. Wil thought, *He is a kind man too*, and wondered how many men were aware of that streak in the tall Texan.

Roosevelt peered at Bill Sewall, then at Wil Dow.

Sewall said, "Take Wil, if it's all the same to you, sir."

"You mean that, Uncle Bill?"

"Why not? Myself, I've got no hankering to ride a thousand miles of boring prairie."

"Whoopee!"

And so in the morning Wil set off for the far West with Theodore Roosevelt.

They drove their sixteen-horse remuda at alternating canter and trot, tiring them out enough so that the horses would not be inclined to stray during the night; otherwise it would be too much work for two men to hobble eighteen horses each evening.

The rich smell of the recent rains lifted from the damp earth. Wil Dow could not contain his excitement. He kept throwing his hat in the air. When he looked at Roosevelt he saw the boss grinning at him with wide pleasure.

They stopped briefly in the afternoon for a cold meal of smoked beef and hard biscuits. Roosevelt said, "I wish I could fathom what excellence Mr. De Morès must own that commands unwavering loyalty from a man as fine as John Goodall."

So the truth about Johnny Goodall's kindness had not escaped him after all. In spite of his obtuse-seeming ways there wasn't much, Wil thought, that escaped Roosevelt's awareness. The cowboys still regarded the boss as something of a buffoon—he'd proved himself among the men and they were no longer stringing the tenderfoot but echoes of "Hasten forward quickly there" would reverberate through the Bad Lands as long as there were horsemen. Wil felt privileged to be among the rare few who knew how good and astute a man existed behind the surface of that buffoonery.

The trek west toward the Tetons was a journey of endless fascination for Wil. Roosevelt talked a great deal, mostly contributing to Wil's education about terrain and wild animals and the history of the land; he also read three or four books a day. And he read and re-read those letters he had from the East.

There were two women who wrote to him with great frequency. One was his sister Bamie. The other—Bill Sewall had been so bold as to ask: Roosevelt had replied only, "An old friend, Bill. A very old and valued friend."

Finally they raised a lonely light far across the vast darkness. Homing on it, they found a camp of cattlemen gathered around a fire. They turned in their horses to the night wranglers and Roosevelt took out his eleven branding irons and led the way into the camp, where he walked directly to the sulky-looking cook and said, "We're from the Little Missouri round-up."

"My God, now they're sendin' us a dude four-eyes." The cook pushed spite at them. "I suppose you want grub to eat?"

Roosevelt said quickly, "We're not hungry. We'll wait for breakfast." It wasn't true but it was the expected thing to say.

A short wide fellow brought himself across to have a look at the pilgrims. "What brands you represent?"

"Are you the wagon boss?"

"Aeah."

Roosevelt knew enough to say nothing further; he merely handed his collection of irons to the man, who examined their ends with concentrated deliberation before he handed them back. "Pick yourselves a spot and bed down where you ain't in the way. We break out at three in the morning, and I want your bedding rolled and corded. If it ain't, cook'll leave it here and you'll go without for the rest of the round-up."

The wagon boss turned away. He hadn't introduced himself; he hadn't said good night. But that was customary. If you were a stranger you had to prove yourself.

In the present case that was no great difficulty, as Roosevelt's good reputation had preceded him among some of the cow hands and it spread swiftly throughout the round-up after their arrival. Wil Dow was pleased that his own name was known a bit too, as that of a Down-Easter who had learned cowboying faster than anyone in known history.

And if they needed any further means of cementing themselves in the good graces of the Yellowstone cattlemen they achieved it on the second day by shooting two antelope and delivering them to camp for dinner.

The country had an enormous majesty and that week was an idyll for Wil until an afternoon when clouds rolled forward over the high jagged peaks. Upon the prairie an unsteady wind stirred the tall grass in slashing green waves.

There was an uneasy quiet in camp that evening. Then somewhere around midnight there was a sharp blow in Wil's ribs and he awakened to hear the cook growl: "On your horses, gents. Everybody out."

Wil sat up, grinding knuckles into eye-sockets. "What is it?"

"Stompede weather. Wagon boss want all hands on deck tonight."

Thunder rolled in the distance. Voices drifted in the dark still air and he heard a rattle of hoofbeats. Beyond the fire's circle of illumination he could see nothing. He saw Roosevelt groping to saddle his horse and the boss's strange clumsy movements made Wil say, "Are you all right, sir?"

"Fine as can be, thank you. You'll find if you keep your eyes shut around the fire, you'll be able to see better in the dark once you're away."

"Wouldn't care if I kept my eyes shut all night," Wil said.

"Never mind, Wil. Nobody ever gets enough sleep on a round-up."

The wagon boss's voice carried softly across the camp: "Wranglers—I want double spare ponies on halters and rope-tie. We won't have time to fish for them if the sky breaks—and I ain't fixing to find these cows dispersed over half of Wyoming when the sun comes up. Got better things to do than gather these same cows all over again. Now everybody ride an easy circle and keep gentling those critters. If, God help us, things do bust loose, try to head 'em east so they'll bunch against the river. Otherwise, they run west, we'll spend all summer combing them out of those mountains."

At first the slow circling line of soft-singing horsemen kept fragile control. Three thousand uneasy cattle stayed put even when lightning flickered over the plains to the south and thunder carved its long ragged tearing slits through the thick damp fabric of the air.

Wil Dow kept licking rain off his lips. He could see hardly a thing in the clouded night—now and then the hint of a steer's horn alarmingly close to his knee—but in the increasingly frequent artillery flashes of lightning he managed to keep himself oriented with regard to the herd.

He tried to keep from laughing at the extraordinary sound of Roosevelt's attempts to sing "Oh, bury me not on the lone prairie." *If anything will start a stampede*, Wil thought wryly—and never had the chance to finish the thought, for an earsplitting crash all but opened his skull while a blinding many-forked snake's tongue of light split the sky so close as to awe Wil and strike him half-blind.

The horse shuddered, squealed and bolted. Wil grabbed the saddlehorn and flailed. He swayed precariously—tried to firm his feet in the stirrups and knew he was riding for his very life.

Stampede.

The world was revealed to him in sudden flashes—battlefields must be like this. The noise was awful: as if the earth itself were in collapse. The horse galloped flat-out, head down, ears back, and only barely kept up with the heaving surf of lifted tails and longhorns; Wil was in the middle of the stampede and if he should fall, or his horse stumble, he would be minced under a thousand cloven hoofs.

Another flash—and ahead he saw *nothing*: the great seething ocean of dark forms crested and disappeared.

A cliff?

In the darkness his eyes went wide with terror.

The horse ran and ran. Wil prayed for a lightning bolt and heard nothing but a continuation of the horrible deafening rattle of the stampede.

Somewhere right around here, it must be . . .

He held his breath, locked his legs against the horse's flanks and felt the saddle tumble away from him when the horse went over the edge but he had an iron grip on the pommel and somehow the horse still had purchase—its hoofs were scrambling at a steep slope and Wil slammed hard down onto the leather and reared far back to give the horse balance and then with a juddering jar the horse's front feet hit flat ground just as a flash of lightning revealed this new world and Wil saw the river of cattle flowing pellmell through the wide shallow gully and up the steepening pitch of its far bank, and over the top—and in the midst of it all he saw a solitary horseman above the backs of the cows like a centaur: by the shape of shoulders and hat, unmistakably Theodore Roosevelt.

The boss—alive and riding the stampede.

It cheered Wil. His mount staggered but ran on, mane streaming. Wil said, "Good boy. Good boy," and found resource enough to let go of the saddle with one hand and pat the horse on the neck.

He rode blind again, galloping, guiding the horse by lightning bursts to his left to try and get out past the edge of the running herd. He remembered the wagon boss's stricture to head them east but by now he was entirely turned around and had no idea what direction lay before him. To get out of this alive would be achievement enough.

He heard the squeal of an animal going down; the saddle shook under him when the horse took a dip and recovered; his hands kept slipping—soaking wet and he had no idea if it was sweat or rain.

It was the noise, he thought desperately—the deadly pounding of thousands of hoofs in this total blind blackness—that was what truly terrified a man because it stopped him from hearing, it stopped him from *thinking* . . .

He knew if he lived beyond tonight he would never forget the horror of this.

Then in the faint glimmer from a distant splash of lightning he saw that he had escaped the worst of it: he was out of the stampede, running along at the side of it. He pulled the horse more sharply away to the left and rode in that direction until the dread noise diminished with distance. Then he slowed the horse to a walk and finally stopped altogether and allowed the poor animal's quivering and quaking to subside.

He talked all the while. "All right. Easy now. It's all right. Gentle down. Easy now." Talking as much to himself as to the horse.

Got to get on. Got to stay with the herd. Can't let them get away. Stay alongside—keep them bunched. At least that way they'll still be in one crowd at daylight.

He waited the next flash of lightning. It was a while coming; the storm was moving away or petering out. He saw the black rolling flow of cattle, oriented himself and ran at an oblique course, aiming to intercept, guiding by sound. Lifted the horse to a tentative gallop and went over an easy little rise of a hill and felt the most God-awful startling blow—a sickening thud of muffled sound as he slammed forward and something sharp raked at him and then he felt the horse go down and he just managed to jerk his legs out from under.

When everything settled down he examined the horse, familiarized himself with his surroundings, appraised his circumstances and said aloud, "A fine thing. For shame." And saw nothing left to do except go to sleep.

At dawn he was trudging afoot with his saddle and bridle across his shoulder, soaked with rain, feet splashing in his boots, backtracking the herd across the rolling plain.

God knew how many miles they had run last night. It was going to be a long walk back to the wagon camp, assuming it had not been moved—

Miraculously Roosevelt was here, riding up behind him, full of good cheer, driving thirty or forty head of exhausted cattle. "What happened to your horse?"

"Ran full gallop straight into a tree. Only tree on the whole prairie and I managed to hit it dead-center. I owe some poor stockman a good horse."

"Some may have suffered far worse losses than that. Well I am happy to see you alive and healthy, Wil."

"And I you, sir."

"I do believe last night brought me as close to death as I ever hope to come," replied the boss. "Climb up behind me. We can ride double if we go easy. These cattle are too tired to mind."

The herd had scattered into little bunches but by good fortune the main direction of its flight had been eastward. Penned by the great loop of the river, the cattle were not beyond recall—if they could be recaptured quickly enough.

The rain had stopped by midmorning and most of the hands were accounted for. After a quick meal they fanned out on fresh horses.

By the time the herd was recaptured, Wil Dow and Roosevelt had each ridden forty straight hours and worn out five mounts.

There followed the harrowing intrusion of burials: three men had been stomped to death.

By the end of that spring's round-up, Wil observed, Roosevelt had just about completed an astonishing metamorphosis from sickly dude to robust outdoorsman. He wasn't a pretty rider but he could stay on his horse and do his job as well as any man. He had barreled out with thirty pounds of new muscle; he was weathered and brown and rugged. There was no question about the respect in which he was held amongst the ranchmen. He was still chairman of the Stockmen. But it seemed to Wil Dow that Roosevelt, for all his brilliance and his wholehearted endeavor, never would be attached to this earth the way Huidekoper and some of the others were.

Strung out in its long line the culled Elkhorn herd filed onto the grass of the home ranch. Wil and Roosevelt, leading the way, found the hired man heating a slender iron in a hasty fire. An unbranded calf lay on its side kicking ineffectually, its feet tied together with piggin' strings. A long-spined cow, ribs showing, stood nearby with her head lowered suspiciously. The hired hand was preparing to put the Elkhorn brand on the calf.

Roosevelt stepped down. "There's the mother cow. You can see plainly it's not my brand."

Wil Dow said, "It's De Morès's brand, sir."

The hired hand said, "I know what I'm doing here—I know who I work for." He had a big hat, rusty spurs and a sly confidential smile.

Roosevelt said, "Put down that iron. I'll give you your time. You're fired."

The hired man reared back on his haunches. "I always look out for my boss's interests. What's wrong in that?"

"By George, a man who will steal *for* me will steal *from* me. We don't need your kind here."

After they had distributed the cattle among the greening pasture lands there was one more halfhearted storm. Huidekoper loomed through the rain. "They scared out George Medlock, Bill Roberts and Jim Monroe. Three good men by my reckoning. They heard the Stranglers were coming, and they rode out of the country."

"I am sorry to hear it," said Roosevelt.

"The Stranglers went on down Beaver Creek and yesterday they hanged Tom Allen. He stood up against his house with a cocked rifle and taunted them—I hear he winged one before they knocked him down. They put a rope around his neck and demanded information, and when he didn't tell them anything, they hanged him."

Wil Dow said, "I heard Tom Allen had a habit of branding cattle that weren't his, that he acquired in ways that wouldn't stand up to research."

"He couldn't stand up to a lynching," Uncle Bill Sewall said.

Roosevelt stood with Sewall and Dow on the covered piazza. "For Heaven's sake step down and come in—don't sit there drowning."

"No thank you. I won't stop. I'm on my way to the Killdeers. But I felt I had to warn you about the Stranglers. They don't leave room for doubt, these boys. They give every suspect the benefit of the noose."

Wil Dow said, "Seems to be having the desired effect. I haven't heard anyone complain of stock theft just lately."

Huidekoper let it go by. "I don't mean to alarm you, Theodore. But the Stranglers are vigilante-ing in force. Your small outfit is a very possible victim, especially since you've sided against De Morès more than once." Huidekoper took a long breath. "They have killed more than twenty men."

"*Twenty?*"

"Including more than one through carelessness and mistakes. One of the masked fellows went to a new widow last week and admitted a slight mistake had been made when they hanged her husband. They tell me the fellow in the mask said, 'Madam, the joke is on us.'"

"You made that up."

"I'm afraid I didn't," Huidekoper said. "I've heard this also—that two of the so-called rustlers were found shot dead by exploding bullets. I know only one man on this range who uses such things."

"A serious accusation requires more than hearsay evidence. You know that."

"Of course I do. But I've been gathering facts, and some of them are of uncommon peculiarity. For example the lynchings seem to be directed entirely against permanent settlers—men with houses or at least cabins. Doesn't one ordinarily think of horse-thieves as migratory transients? If so, why are all the victims men who live in their own houses? Also I put forth for your attention the singular fact that, in spite of twenty-odd killings, and in spite of their having frightened and driven scores of squatters out of the country, not one stolen horse or cow has been recovered." He lifted the reins. "Not one."

The rain left with him.

Bill Sewall went about grumbling in his beard but Roosevelt refused to allow his spirits to be daunted. "Right, lads. Bring out the tally sheets if you please."

Having consulted the round-up records they concluded they had lost no more than twenty-five head all winter from cold, wolves, bogs and illness. "They seem in admirable shape," Roosevelt said. "We've got thirty-three hundred and fifty head of cattle, market value about eleven thousand dollars, and it appears our cows have dropped eleven hundred and forty calves this season. I'm certain now—I shall make this my regular business. Old fellows, I count us a resounding success!"

Bill Sewall said, "Give or take a Strangler or two."

The boss gave him a tough square look and, after a moment, reluctantly nodded.

Sixteen

From *The Bad Lands Cow Boy:*

> We neglected in our last issue to mention the minstrel entertainment given by home talent at the rink on the evening of the Twenty-sixth of June. The variety part of the entertainment would have been a complete success if we had brought our guns along and killed all the performers at the beginning of the first act. The orchestra led by Mose de Spice was simply indescribable. To escape a popular uprising Mose fled the next morning for the Pacific Coast.
>
> Several men have been hung for horse-stealing, most recently Modesty Carter, but the plague of outlawry still goes on. We wish to be placed on record as believing that the only way to cure horse-stealing is to hang the thief wherever caught.

Pack took a running start to trundle his wheelbarrow-load of papers up the embankment to the depot platform. The train chuffed to a halt and Pack handed the newspapers up to a porter, an armload at a time. While the porter stacked them in a corner of the vestibule, Joe Ferris came out of the car past him and stepped down off the train.

Pack said, "I wondered where you were. Another buying trip to Bismarck?"

"Just so." Joe picked up one of the copies of *The Bad Lands Cow Boy* and glanced through it, stepping aside to allow a handful of passengers to climb aboard. Joe looked up and Pack saw his head rear back; Joe blinked rapidly, then gripped Pack's elbow and steered him rapidly away from the train steps.

Pack said, "What's wrong?"

"You see who just got on the train?"

"No, I didn't notice. Why?"

"The fellow in the Mexican hat? That was Modesty Carter."

"What of it?"

Joe folded the newspaper and pushed it in front of Pack's face. "Read your own column. Modesty Carter got hanged for horse stealing, did he?"

"Now, I had it on the best authority," Pack muttered, while he allowed Joe Ferris to haul him away from the embankment.

"If he picks up that newspaper," Joe said, "you'll be explaining things to him down the business end of a six-shooter. You had better arm yourself."

"I never carry a gun."

Joe regarded him with narrowing suspicion. "This best authority of yours. Did it tell you Modesty Carter was dead—or was *going* to be hanged?"

Pack turned a palm upwards. "It was three days ago. I assumed by now they'd have had the job done."

On the Fourth of July Pack dressed in his good suit and groomed himself appropriately for the speakers' platform and went outside with a stern scowl on his face to indicate his disapproval of the bursts of shooting that cluttered the morning. The boys never seemed to think about the fact that when bullets were fired into the air they had to come down somewhere. Last Christmas McKenzie's mule had been killed outright by a shot that appeared to have been fired straight down into the top of its head. McKenzie was still upset about it and whenever the subject came up it still caused uproars of laughter from Redhead Finnegan and that irresponsible short-sighted crowd of Irish hunters.

Joe Ferris emerged from the store, locked up and joined him. Joe had a sour reluctant expression on his round face. "You heard they took Modesty Carter off the train and killed him."

"Did they. Too bad he didn't read the *Cow Boy.*"

"Too bad for him he couldn't read at all. So now lynching's the price of illiteracy, is it?"

"The man was a horse-thief, Joe. I even heard him brag about it one night."

"When he was drunk."

"*In vino veritas.*"

"What about the *veritas* in your God-damn newspaper?" Joe said, not masking his disgust. Then he walked away. Pack stared after him, affronted.

The sunlight thrashed Pack. Flies swarmed incessantly and he tried to ignore the suffocating blood stink of the abattoir. It was closed for the holiday but the heat and the motionless air had trapped its spoor.

None of that seemed to discourage the celebration. In one street the heavy traffic of pedestrians had made way for a whooping horse race. It kicked up a great thunderhead of powder dust. In another street eight men in their trapdoors ran a frantic foot race. Pack thought, *Riley Luffsey would have distanced them all.* But poor young Luffsey had chosen the wrong course and had paid for his race. It continued to amaze Pack that such a clear lesson in the fruits of evil seemed to have made no difference in the behavior of Finnegan, O'Donnell and the jackanapes pack, not excepting such unfortunates as the late and unlamented Modesty Carter.

High across the river a group of ladies was gathered under parasols and Lady Medora was amusing them with her target practice. She fired from a kneeling position toward a target against the backstop of the bluff. Pack knew she was a crack shot—better than her husband. The Diana of the Bad Lands.

It made Pack slightly uneasy; he preferred to think of this woman of exquisite delicacy painting beneath her parasol or playing Verdi on the piano in her southwest room.

The last time he had seen her at close range, a week ago, she had looked positively gaunt, and Pack had felt a savage bafflement: was she Innocent? Or was she trapped in a painful limbo between secret love and outward loyalty?

He made his way toward the depot. This morning in town the shooting was especially promiscuous and annoying. When Pack elbowed through the crowd and climbed onto the speakers' platform to join Huidekoper and Roosevelt and the others he was of a mind to put as much distance between himself and Roosevelt as he could. He sat down at the far edge of the platform beside Deacon Osterhaut while the noisy formalities commenced with a parade that included the Dickinson Silver Cornet Band, the members of Fort Sumter Post G.A.R., and from Montana the Onward Lodge R.R.B.

There was a rolling mighty display of farming and reaping machinery and it was followed by citizens in carriages, on horseback and finally on foot.

Bill Sewall stood just below the edge of the platform. He beckoned and, when Pack bent over, remarked in his ear, "Trouble with it is, everybody in five hundred miles is so enthusiastic they had to get in on the procession there, so there's nobody left to watch it except you and me and those gents over there who appear to be too drunk to see a thing."

Sewall by now was widely known for his fundamentalist disapproval of the heavy drinking of the Bad Landers. It would have made him a laughingstock if he had been a less formidable man.

The parading seemed endless in the heat but finally it was over and Howard Eaton mounted the platform and recited the Declaration of Independence very loudly. The band struck up an overture and the entire crowd joined in singing "America." Deacon Osterhaut offered up an interminable prayer.

Sewall looked at Huidekoper's bald head. "Old A.C. ain't careful he'll get the sunburn on his beaver slide there."

Pack's turn came. He took out his printed speech and read it aloud with as much fervor as he could manage in the wilting heat. His message to the throng was one of good tidings—Progress!—and when he concluded his remarks he was pleased by the length and enthusiasm of the applause, liquored up though it may have been.

Then he glanced to his right and announced as briefly and brusquely as decency permitted, "And now it is my privilege to give you former Minority Leader of the New York State Assembly, prominent Bad Lands citizen and chairman of the Little Missouri Stockmen's Association—Theodore Roosevelt."

There was too much applause to suit Pack. After prolonged yelling and whistling and the firing of far too many gunshots, Roosevelt smiled at Pack without visible rancor as he rose to speak. He had put on a healthy amount of muscle-weight in the past year but to Pack he seemed owlish and foolish. He spoke without notes. His voice was reedy but it had a penetrating whine. Admittedly he spoke with precise clarity; Pack, who sat clear of Huidekoper where no one would jostle his arms while he wrote down his notes, had no trouble understanding him.

Roosevelt said, "My fellow citizens of Dakota, we—ranchmen and cowboys alike—have opened a new land. This is our land—all of us. Let us be reminded that the Lord made the earth for us all, and not for just a few who may have been chosen by their purple bloodlines. We all are the pioneers, and we know that the first comers in a land can, by their individual efforts, do far more to channel out the course in which its history is to run than can those who come after them. Their labors, whether exercised on the side of evil or on the side of good, are far more effective than if they had remained in old settled communities. So it is particularly incumbent on us here today to act so as to leave our children a heritage for which we will receive their blessing and not their curse."

Roosevelt went on. Ebullient and histrionic, he gathered energy until he was declaiming with intense galvanic explosions of sound and crazed facial contortions. Yet he held them in thrall. You had to grant it to him. His bombastic rhetoric would have wrung tears from a statue of General Sherman.

Showing his whole mouthful of huge tombstone teeth he enlisted their emotions: "Rampant barbarism must be countered by clarity and courage!"

A clear enough reference to the Stranglers. So foolish. Roosevelt's maniacal bravado in the name of justice—his naive fastidiousness regarding due process—these things could bring him down, Pack thought. There were exceptional occasions when the ends justified the means; you had to acknowledge that, or you had no decent contact with reality.

"I do not undervalue for a moment our material prosperity," the dude went on. "Like all Americans I like big things: big prairies, big forests and mountains, big wheat-fields, railroads—and herds of cattle, too—big factories, steamboats, and everything else. But it is not what we have that will make us a great nation; it is the way in which we use it. We must keep in mind that no people were ever yet benefited by riches if their prosperity corrupted their virtue. It is of more importance that we should show ourselves honest, brave, truthful and intelligent, than that we should own all the railways and grain elevators in the world."

After Roosevelt took his seat and the shouting and applause and gunfire were done, the crowd flowed away toward the picnic tables and the kegs and jugs.

Pack cornered Roosevelt on his way off the platform. "Now, does this speech presage your return to active political life?"

"It jolly well does not. I'm a ranchman, pure and simple."

On the contrary, Pack thought. There was nothing either pure or simple about the pompous dude from New York. You never could tell what devious schemes were being hatched behind the protective reflection of those flashing eyeglasses.

Jerry Paddock loomed before Roosevelt like a woolly mastodon. "You talk real loud."

Roosevelt faced him. "Mr. Paddock, I've heard that you boasted you'd shoot me on sight. Perhaps I've been misinformed. If it's true, I'm at your disposal. Now's the time for you to get at it."

Roosevelt pulled his coat back to show that he was indeed armed.

Jerry Paddock looked at Roosevelt's gunbelt, then at his face. Jerry let a while go by, and Pack wondered what he was thinking. Finally Jerry said, "I must have been misquoted. Had a few drinks, maybe. You know how it is."

"Then we understand each other." Roosevelt did not conceal his scorn. He turned his back and walked away.

Jerry was in an easygoing mood, Pack observed; but then Jerry was invariably in whatever mood he wanted or needed to be in.

A moment later when Pack climbed down he glimpsed Roosevelt behind the platform—bent over, coughing violently.

Pack turned away and strode toward the punch bowl but Bill Sewall was there. Sewall said, "You see he's no longer the greenhorn."

Pack said, "He needs to grow up. Some of his remarks were all too transparently aimed at the Marquis, who is the bread and butter of this community. Your employer seems to enjoy throwing raw meat on the floor. He is headstrong and aggressive."

"Being headstrong and aggressive—now and then that's not such a bad thing. You know he is always trying to make the world better instead of worse, and that's a rare virtue now-a-days. I reckon it may be a failing in him that he sees everything and has an opinion on everything and he is not remarkably cautious about expressing said opinion, but he wants instantly to set everything to rights, and maybe he never will grow up if by that you mean learning that things are not fair, but he has got more heart and more will power than—"

"Will power, is it? Or rabid lunacy?" Pack was impatient. "What about his own tragedies, then? What's fair about the deaths of his mother and his wife?"

"He's put those behind him. He pretends they never happened."

"Now, how in hell can he do that?"

"It takes strength," Sewall said. He looked at Pack. "I don't guess I understand you, Mr. Packard. Seems to me you would have to hate Mr. Roosevelt a whole lot to keep from loving him."

Somewhat drunk, Pack looked up across the river in time to see the light wink out in Madame's bedroom window. He had found out that when Madame la Marquise prepared for bed, two of her maids helped her dress for the night and got out the two large hairbrushes from her silver-decorated toilet set. One maid would take the left-handed brush, the other the right-handed brush, and they would work on Madame's long auburn-red hair. The loose hair was kept in a brown sack and when the sack was half full the hair would be removed from it and braided into plaits so that Madame could wear it as part of one elaborate hairdo or another; it always matched perfectly because, of course, it was her own hair. After brushing her out, the two maids would prop several pillows behind her so that Medora could sleep sitting up in the French canopied bed. Her parents believed that sleeping in a fully recumbent position could cause the lungs to collapse.

Pack sighed. She certainly added more than a touch of charm to the Bad Lands.

* * *

In the dream Pack was climbing a dirt trail along a cliffside. It became ever narrower. He knew he'd walked it before but this time he couldn't: fear wouldn't let him. Someone was shooting at him from a distance; he could hear the popping of gunfire. He got down and crawled, belly flat. He still couldn't make it to the top. He began to try to inch backwards, but the trail started to crumble. He called for help but no one came.

Startled, Pack came awake from the rubbish and rubble of his dreams.

He sat up and made himself smile by remembering last Saturday's baseball game. They had soundly thrashed Joe Ferris's boys. What a game it had been.

Recalling it, inning by inning, helped keep his mind off the death he had seen before his eyes—that of the man called Calamity—and those he hadn't seen: Pierce Bolan's and Modesty Carter's and another thirty or so, most of whose names he had known, some of whose faces he had known, a few of whom had shared drinks and conversation with him.

He made his way outdoors on this morning of July fifth. Drunks lay around in crowds. Sewall came tramping out of Joe's store and climbed across a pair of fallen bodies and harrumphed. "Look at them. Like poisoned flies, dropped wherever the paralysis took them. Your Western whiskey's worse than gunfire. Why, this whole misbegotten town could be taken today by three sober men."

Pack moved on quickly without giving Sewall time to trot out his dubious opinions about the cattle business.

Outside Bob Roberts's saloon Frank O'Donnell stood squinting, evidently sober. He and Finnegan and that lot hadn't been doing much drinking of late, Pack had noticed. Possibly they were afraid a crowd of Stranglers might come upon them when they were drunk.

O'Donnell's shirt, half undone in the heat, showed the weathered bronze of his chest. He was tossing a nickel until he missed his catch. The coin fell into the dust of the street, sinking and disappearing as if into murky water. O'Donnell's pitted face was still, a study in stoicism.

Beneath the bluff along the river Pack heard the boom of grouse cocks and the merry warbling gossip of snow buntings. He needed to be away from the smell of town; he walked across the railroad bridge to the left bank and climbed the slope below the château and came upon two bonneted maids pushing the babies around in their landau-hooded prams. On the hillside nearby the lady Medora was painting, working under a parasol umbrella whose long pointed stake was jammed into the earth beside her. At that moment, apparently unaware of Pack's presence between junipers, Theodore Roosevelt came up, riding the blasted horse Manitou about which he never stopped boasting, and addressed himself to the nearer of the maids: "Be so kind as to commend me to your mistress."

Pack listened dispiritedly to the loud racket of grasshoppers. It was a terrible time for black flies and mosquitoes and midges. He watched the maid speak to Lady Medora; her mistress looked up with a smile. As the horseman approached she watched him with what appeared to Pack to be a slanting vitality that could not help but incite him.

"Well, madame, by George I am dee-lighted to be at your service."

The astonishing hubris of the cad!

She rose to meet him, her clothes rustling, and as Pack watched the dazzlement he felt ruddy blood rise in his cheeks.

He knew he should step forward and announce himself..

She wore a trim burgundy habit and a jaunty eagle feather in her hat. He wanted to kiss her eyelids.

There was a melody always in her; it was softly in her voice when she spoke to Roosevelt. "How good to see you. Do you mind the heat awfully?"

It was abundantly clear they were absorbed in each other, so much so that Pack felt forcefully excluded. He turned and walked away.

At the bridge Joe Ferris stood with Huidekoper. They were looking uphill past Pack. Joe was saying, "—the Markee's pampered pathetic concubine."

Huidekoper replied, "The way you talk, you'd think the poor woman were a Temptation—part of the arsenal of evil with which the satanic De Morès is attempting to subvert and corrupt the good Roosevelt. Why Joe, you're even more suspicious than I am!" He looked up. "Morning, Arthur."

Pack snapped, "Gentlemen, I surely pity you, for you obviously can't tell who is subverting whom."

They laughed at him. It was no use. Blasted by the malevolent purgatorial sun, Pack took refuge in the shade of his office and mixed a Seidlitz powder for his hangover.

On the tenth of July the thermometer in the shade of the porch of *The Bad Lands Cow Boy* registered 125 degrees and the strong hot wind seemed to be killing almost every green thing in the country. Two crows on a branch outside the *Cow Boy* shack argued with considerably less raucousness than usual. There had been no rain since April—no growing season for grass; the great range meadows were bone dry. On his rides out of town in search of news and gossip, Pack found the grass brown and wilted, the atmosphere dismal amongst the Bad Landers. Sagebrush had roots deeper than grass, so it would survive where grass would not; but even those clumps had gone a dry chalky blue color. Here and there he saw sickly green leaves on some of the willows and cottonwoods that grew where the subsoil was moist. Fall's colors had arrived three months early. Junipers had gone grey and the ash trees were moulting leaves that went burn-brown without ever turning gold; and even in the sheltered coulees the graze had nearly all been killed by the hot winds.

It was a dismal summer all around. Too hot even for baseball. The abattoir made the town virtually uninhabitable but miraculously the Marquis, harried and beset by enemies, only seemed to keep going faster and faster.

Among other things the Marquis was livid because his stagecoach line had been the victim of obvious calculated sabotage. Two months ago the Northern Pacific Railroad had designated the town of Dickinson—not Medora—as its terminus for Deadwood freight. The churlish railroad lackeys claimed that Dickinson was closer to the Black Hills and the route easier. "Lies," the Marquis trumpeted. "The Beef Trust is undermining my business everywhere. They're behind the Dickinson coach line—my men in the East are investigating information I've received that the Chicago Jews bribed the Postmaster to award the mail contract to the Dickinson line."

The fact remained: after only seven months of operations and a loss of a great deal of money, the Medora-Deadwood line was defunct. The stagecoaches were sold and the thirteen way-stations abandoned.

There was much speculation as to how much money the Marquis had lost.

It was a dreadful shame, Pack said to his supper companion in the cafe.

Joe Ferris gave him a wry look and a bleak shake of the head. "You poor blind idiot. The stage route sank in the gumbo slough because the Marquis is a puffed-up fool. I didn't know anybody who'd travel on those coaches. You ever poke your newspaper nose into their safety record?"

"They never had a single fatality. The Marquis is very proud of that."

"He had plenty fatalities if you count the poor horses. He had bad roads, loads too big to carry—"

"You can't blame him for foul weather."

"He should have taken it into account. Not to mention Jerry Paddock stole so much there wasn't enough left to provide decent service."

"Now, where's your evidence of that?"

"Everybody knows Jerry Paddock bought disintegrating harness for the price of new, and untrained horses for the price of broke ones."

"Now, one trouble around here," Pack railed, "is that there are altogether too many things that 'everybody knows'—if I were to listen to you, I'd believe Jerry Paddock shot a man for breakfast every morning."

"If he doesn't, it's not for lack of the urge to."

"It's fortunate for you I'm a tolerant man and I understand when you keep blaming all the problems of the world on Paddock and the Marquis. I suppose you'd like to find a way to blame this drought on them too. It's only natural, what with the suspicion that Paddock's the villain who emptied the store and drove Swede Nelson from town, you'd have a score to settle with Paddock. Now, I'm tolerant again because I know you are beholden to Theodore Roosevelt—"

Joe growled, "Be that as it may, gratitude's one thing. Right and wrong's another."

"—and you notice I haven't badgered you too much just because you've taken to wearing that Remington revolver all the time now, even though I know what 'everybody knows' about how you've been hiding out Dutch Reuter so you can be sure to deliver him alive to testify at the Marquis's trial. Incidentally tell me—isn't Dutch getting pretty restless, what with the legal delays persisting?"

"There'll be a trial," Joe said. "Before the end of the year."

"How do you know that?"

"You have my word on it."

"Are you the one who keeps writing letters all over the place, stirring things up?"

"Me? No. I'm not much on writing letters."

Pack said, "Then who is it? Roosevelt? Huidekoper?"

"There'll be a murder trail, that's all I can tell you."

"Nothing will come of it. The Marquis has the Allen brothers on his side—foremost lawyers." Pack pushed his chair back. "Where's Dutch Reuter?"

"Why? So you can publish it in the *Cow Boy* and next week we can find his carcass hanging from a cottonwood?"

Pack stood up, filled with anger. He pushed the cafe door open. The hot wind blasted in fitfully, reeking of slaughter. Joe tipped his head back and smiled beatifically. "You can put *this* in your newspaper—you can tell the Markee that he can scheme and plan all he wants, and he can send out all the Stranglers in the world, but before the end of the year he'll be on trial for murder and old Dutch Reuter will be on that witness stand to tell what really happened out on that road where Riley Luffsey was murdered."

Seventeen

The months began to run together in exhaustion for Wil Dow. At the conclusion of fall round-up, with its distressingly small tally, Uncle Bill said, "I call it the abomination of desolation. It makes me pretty fierce to think of the green forest back home in Maine."

Wil was not quite willing to say so aloud but he was ready to agree with Uncle Bill's assessment. The heat seemed to have no end. Mr. Roosevelt was the only one who didn't seem to mind it. He went on with unflagging drive.

Wil felt very low. He saw that Uncle Bill had been right after all. In this drought each steer needed as much as thirty acres. The Bad Lands were crowded together thicker than that now. Beef prices were falling every day and yet just last week another Texas fool had brought in six thousand head from the south.

Then again, Wil sometimes thought, drought really wasn't much of a threat if there was no one left alive to suffer from it. The Stranglers had killed more than forty men. Seemed as if they were burning another ranch every day—or maybe it was the poor starving Indians hungry for red meat. They had been setting grass fires to cover their thievery and, some said, to get revenge against the whites because the Stranglers had murdered three or four of them. Every stockman had been injured by the scorched-earth behavior of the infuriated Indians. Wil and Uncle Bill and Roosevelt had worked heroically to extinguish several grass fires. They would slaughter a steer, split and splay it bloody-side down, and rope-drag it forward, smothering the line of flames, fighting their fire-maddened horses at every step. In that manner the ranchmen had contended with blazes day after day—as if the miserable round-up hadn't been discouraging enough, with its dying cattle and panting horses.

Yet Roosevelt remained in high spirits and Wil felt shamed that he too had fallen behind, unable to match the boss's inexhaustible energy. On top of it all, Roosevelt was writing again, working on a biography of Thomas Hart Benton, the Missouri Senator; his previous book had just been published—*Hunting Trips of a Ranchman*—and Wil had been admiring the leather-bound edition and hoping to find time to read it. He had glanced through it and been gratified to see that someone had fixed the boss's spelling.

By November Huidekoper and his hounds and huntsmen had wiped out the last of the grey wolves who had preyed on the stockmen's livestock. "They've driven the species to extinction in the Bad Lands," Roosevelt growled, "and I believe if the Stranglers are left to run wild much longer they'll accomplish the same end with the human inhabitants."

By this time the Stranglers were said to have murdered more than half a hundred men. Bill Sewall said, "I believe we're the only inhabited outfit left in a ten-mile radius. Six months ago there were eight including Pierce Bolan, who is a man I still miss. A prudent fellow would think about pulling up stakes."

"No one would count you a coward if you did that," Roosevelt said with surprising equanimity.

Wil said, "That's what they want us to do—De Morès and his vigilantes. They want us to go. I say we should take the fight to *him*."

Roosevelt looked at them both in turn. "Speaking for myself, I shall not run, and I shall not be alarmed into attacking a man against whom I have no proof."

Uncle Bill was exasperated. "Then what the blazes do you aim to do?"

"By Godfrey, I will stand my ground!" Roosevelt's eyes and teeth glittered ferociously.

Wil drew himself up. "Well then," he said, "I expect my uncle and I will stand it with you, sir. If the Stranglers want us, then by Godfrey let them come and try!"

There was a ferocious rainstorm—far too late to be of any service; all it accomplished was to wash away tons of caked dry earth and fill the rivers with clay silt. The downpour lasted two days. In the middle of the following week on a bitter evening Mrs. Reuter came down Blacktail Creek riding sidesaddle with a matted buffalo coat over her divided buckskin riding habit. Wil helped her dismount in the barn and began to unsaddle her horse but the stout woman would have none of that. She took care of her own animal—it looked to Wil as if it had endured a lengthy wearying journey—and, once it had been watered and curried and stalled and grained, Mrs. Reuter accompanied Wil up to the house. Roosevelt welcomed her with a big pleased grin and gave her a seat by the fire.

She said, "Well look at you. I shall have to let out that suit again—you're coming through the seams."

"This wonderful country has built me up, by George. I'm ready to go fifteen rounds with any man in Dakota."

"You look it."

Uncle Bill pulled on his pipe, Wil boiled coffee and Mrs. Reuter said in a different voice, "There'll be no more trouble with Indians setting grass fires."

"How so?"

She accepted a tin cup of coffee from Wil Dow, smiled a tired sad thank-you, blew across the steaming surface and said, "I saw a line of riders the other night. They turned east to give my house wide berth, which is not usual, and I wouldn't have known they were there at all if my horses hadn't started acting up. I climbed the hill and saw them circling past the place—a large number of white men, at least forty of them, strung out single-file and they rode with no talk at all. Such silent stealth that I knew they'd been up to something monstrous evil. So I saddled up and backtracked them."

"In the middle of the night?" Sewall said, astonished.

"Well that's when it was," she replied.

Wil Dow said, "Did you recognize any of them?"

"Not at that distance in the dark. But I know who they were."

Roosevelt said, "The Stranglers."

"Well of course."

Mrs. Reuter tasted the coffee and approved it. "They've been using one of the game trails near my soddy as a regular route these past months. I've seen them go by at least a dozen times but usually there's talk and crude laughing—you know the way a mob of men will get."

Roosevelt said, "You didn't inform anyone of this?"

"I keep my own counsel, Mr. Roosevelt, and I have good reason for doing so."

Wil Dow felt a keen stab of realization. "It's Dutch. You've been hiding him out."

Mrs. Reuter's head whipped around. Her eyes were wide. "How on earth did you know that?"

"A guess, that's all. Sorry, ma'am."

Roosevelt said, "Evidently an astute one. Is Dutch well?"

"Well as can be expected of a restless man who must confine himself to the root cellar whenever there's a hint of movement on the horizon." Mrs. Reuter looked over her shoulder as if in fear of eavesdroppers. "I beg you— don't breathe a word of this to anyone."

Uncle Bill said, "Nobody will find out from us. We're Dutch's friends."

"I know that. I'd have told you long ago, but Dutch is so scared he made me promise not to tell a soul in the world except Joe Ferris. Joe's been kind enough to falsify his sales records so nobody can see I've been buying twice as many provisions as I used to."

Roosevelt said, "I'm tickled pink to know Dutch is in good hands. You were saying—you saw the Stranglers in the night, and you backtracked them . . ."

"I did, until I found they had covered their trace deliberately in some of the Malpais creeks north of here. But I had my suspicions by then. I knew the Indians had their hunting camp up beyond the Killdeers. That's where they'd been raiding from—stealing meat and setting those grass fires."

"Ah yes. The Indians. We're back to them."

"They'd been moving camp a few miles each night but holding to the same district—close to the Canada line where they could get across if anybody spotted them."

"You knew where they were," Roosevelt said, "and you told no one?"

"She didn't want to bring attention on herself," Wil said. "For Dutch's sake."

"Is that right, madame?"

"I'm obliged, Mr. Wil, but I don't need defending. I've been friends with the Indians since before most whites came into this country. It's their grass, what's left of it after the sheep and cattle and horses you all poured in—I reckon they can set fire to their own land if they see fit."

"It isn't 'their' land, it is everyone's land."

"I make no apology, Mr. Roosevelt. It would have pleased me if they had wiped out every last head of the rotten Markee's stock."

"Were their depredations directed against the Marquis? If so, they seem to have gone about it rather indiscriminately, for we all suffered from it."

"To an Indian we're all the same," Mrs. Reuter said. "They can't see any difference between the Markee and you."

"For the moment let it pass," said Roosevelt. "You rode to their camp, I presume, and what did they say that makes you believe they'll set no more grass fires?"

"They didn't say anything. They're dead."

It took Wil Dow a moment to hear what she had said. He felt his forehead wrinkle and he was about to speak when Roosevelt broke the silence:

"Dead? How?"

"By murder, I should imagine."

Uncle Bill said, "How many?"

"I counted forty-three mounds of fresh-dug earth. There probably are more that I didn't find. Those men did their best to hide the evidence of their grisly work. I did not have the stomach to dig them up, but there were two dozen lodgepoles scattered around and I saw groups of ponies running loose. And coyotes pawing at the mounds."

Uncle Bill said, "What about their tent skins?"

"Possibly the murderers buried the tepees with the bodies—to hide the evidence of their crime. There's nothing but travois poles and of course those don't prove a thing. I was caught there by a hard rain that lasted two days—"

"We had the same storm," Wil said.

"—and it stirred the topsoil together so completely there's no sign of those graves now."

Uncle Bill said, "So the murderers have that massacre on their consciences as well."

"What consciences?" snapped Mrs. Reuter. She finished her coffee. "It soon will be over, I pray. The Markee's lawyers have exhausted their delays. Next week he is traveling to Bismarck to stand trial. The Markee and Jerry Paddock."

"Not a moment too soon," growled Uncle Bill.

In the morning, like some omen, came the early onset of winter—a bitter dry cold that froze the water in the bucket on the piazza and chilled everything to the marrow.

Mrs. Reuter said, "I know no one has a shred of proof to tie the Markee to the Stranglers. But when he and Paddock go to prison—you can bank on it, that will put an end to the night-riding, then and there."

Uncle Bill said, "I would surely like to be there to see the Markee get his comeuppance."

Wil Dow looked out at snowflakes drifting through the dawn. "You go, then, Uncle. Not me. I'd sooner be out here in the wild country than in some city courtroom having to smell cigar smoke."

Roosevelt said, "Then we'll hire a good man to keep you company in looking after the home ranch and keeping an eye peeled for vigilantes, while your uncle and I escort Mrs. Reuter and her good husband to the capital. For by Godfrey I wouldn't miss this trial for the world."

Eighteen

Pack looked out his hotel window. On lantern-lit Rosser Street barkers shouted the praises of crib girls while the big-voiced macs showed off the salient attractions of their painted powdered sporting women who gave gents the benedictions of their professional smiles and awaited escort to their cubicles on the Row behind the saloons.

There were a good many armed men abroad in the night who had never previously graced the streets of Bismarck with their presence. Tempers were short; cool reason was scarce; danger quivered in the town.

Pack returned his attention to the notebook on the desk. He turned up the lamp's wick and resumed writing:

> He is a gentleman of capital whose works are of incalculable benefit to Dakota, and it should be a travesty were Bad Lands desperadoes to have their way in the forthcoming Trial. Outlaws must not be permitted to swagger through the Territory insulting and terrorizing good citizens. It is criminal to persecute a man simply because he happens to be a Marquis. We find it an utter

outrage and disgrace that he is being held in a jail cell like a common criminal during the period of the Trial.

When he realized he was hungry he put on his suit coat and went downstairs. It was late and a good many people must have finished supping long ago but the big ornate dining room was crowded to its capacity. He was not surprised to see so many familiar faces. Both factions were represented by strong turnouts. There were, he thought, no neutral parties; you were for the Marquis or you were against him, and in some ways the outcome of this Trial was bound to seal the fates of those on both sides, for it would determine whether the Marquis was to be allowed control over his own empire and a voice in the guidance of its inhabitants.

If there was any justice, he kept telling his friends, the Trial would give the Marquis the benediction of a resounding vindication, and once and for all would silence the disorderly drunken tongues of the Irish louts and the thieving Bad Lands "ranchers" who were so precious to the foolish sentimentalities of Roosevelt, Huidekoper and their soft-hearted ilk.

Still, he was startled to see both sides so strongly represented in this very room. Around an oversized table in the near corner Madame la Marquise sat in conference with the heavy-set Allen brothers and their four co-counsel. They had their heads together and Pack did not wish to disturb what might be a conference of strategic importance so he made his way toward a small table at the side.

The air was perfumed with strains of chamber music from a string quartet in the anteroom. The woodwork was ornate and polished to a gleam; the tablecloths were of excellent linen, the service crystal and sterling. How extraordinarily civilized it all was.

As Pack sat down he saw Joe Ferris at a table in the middle of the room. Joe was dressed in his good grey suit and appeared to have finished his meal; he was sitting back toying with an empty brandy snifter. His choice of company made Pack scowl furiously, for Joe sat—evidently at ease and happy to be seen with them—between Theodore Roosevelt and Dutch Reuter's wife.

There were three others in the company: Huidekoper, Eaton and a man whom Pack believed he recognized as the editor of a Chicago newspaper. Roosevelt was holding forth in his unpleasant squeaking voice. Pack couldn't make out the words. He sniffed, allowed a scowl to settle appropriately on his face, and examined the bill of fare.

A moment later he was startled when Joe Ferris said from immediately above him, "When you get done marveling at the prices let me recommend the beefsteak. Real prime bull-cheese."

"Kind of you."

Pack felt awkward, for everything in the past year and a half had been building toward this event, and he found it disquieting that of all the people with whom he might be conversing in a public place on the eve of such a decisive Monday, he should be seen in the company of a man who made no secret of the fact that he would be testifying for the opposing side.

Joe said dryly, "It's all right, Pack. I haven't contaminated the kitchen. Look over there—you see all the big fat defense lawyers he's got on his team? Enough legal talent to make the sidewalk groan with their weight. Did you know the District Attorney applied to the commissioners for one or two lawyers to help him? I guess the Markee's boys got to the commissioners first, because they turned him down. He's going in there all alone."

Pack had little sympathy to spare. "Poor Ted Long, left all alone in such a den of thieves and criminals as Bismarck."

"You see Frank Allen there? The fattest one. With the burnsides. Funny thing, but it seems he just happened to serve as Judge Francis's clerk when the good judge was practicing law back in Newark, New Jersey. That was before President Arthur appointed his political friend Mr. Francis to the bench out here in the Territories."

"You're clutching at straws if you try to make something sinister of that."

"I guess I must be. Not that there's any collusion here, of course," Joe said. "All the same it won't matter. The truth will out."

"It most certainly will," Pack said. Indeed that was exactly what he hoped for.

Joe said, "They're clowns, all of 'em. I hear the Marquis made the mistake of giving friend Paddock several thousand dollars he was supposed to distribute here and there to make sure the right witnesses showed up. Of course Jerry forgot to distribute it. Maybe it felt too good in his pocket."

"That's nonsense. The matter doesn't need bribery or coercion. Everybody knows the Marquis has always stood ready to clean up the matter then and there."

"'Everybody knows,' hey?" Joe grinned at him.

Pack felt a warm flush. "I hate a man who'll throw my own words back at me."

"Hate away. What're you going to eat?"

"Maybe chicken," Pack said defiantly.

"That's right," Joe said, "I'd stay away from the beefsteak if I were you. It may be De Morès beef and you might break a tooth on it."

Pack looked past Joe at the table where Roosevelt was talking with the Chicago editor. Mrs. Reuter sat in a more or less civilized costume—it had puffed sleeves—and a hat that looked rather like a small overturned milk bucket, or at least Pack assumed it must be a hat because she wore it on her head. She looked prim and grim. Pack said to Joe, "Tell me. Where have you got Dutch?"

"Who says I've got him?"

"'Everybody.'" Pack grinned at him. "You know it really wasn't necessary to go to such shenanigans to keep him alive. O'Donnell hasn't been murdered, has he. And he's primed to tell the same lies as Dutch Reuter's. Dutch is safe enough. Where'd you hide him?"

"You can search my room if you like," Joe said. "You won't find him there. Let's just say I have a feeling Dutch is lying low where he'll be safe until it's his turn to testify. May be you're right he'd have been left alone, and may be you're not. The Markee can handle one eyewitness against him. I don't believe he can handle two."

"Then as usual you underestimate him," Pack said with confidence. "I'll have the beefsteak."

When he returned to his room he unfolded the documents he had obtained four hours earlier from the court clerk. On top was the list of jurors' names: Edick, Frisby, Gage, Griffin, McKinney, Moorehouse, Northrup, Ronass, Wahl, Watson, Williams, Young.

Not one Irish name among the twelve. Luffsey's death had infuriated every Irishman in the Territory.

There were notes regarding various legal documents. The Allens had kept filing motions for dismissal—quite rightly pounding home the fact that nobody could know who killed Riley Luffsey, and that nobody could even be sure who started the shooting, and therefore in the event of a long and costly courtroom hearing the only possible outcome was predetermined, for the issue of reasonable doubt was the overriding consideration. The case should never have come to trial.

That was the long and the short of it.

But if it hadn't come to trial—would we ever have a chance of finding the truth?

It was a quandary for sure.

District Attorney Theodore K. Long, who had made no secret of his longstanding friendship with A.C. Huidekoper and who seemed to hate the Marquis with a virulent and all too obvious passion, had refused to drop the case even when the Marquis's attorneys had succeeded in achieving a change of venue from Mandan to Bismarck. Long had ridiculed that effort.

Pack had been astonished to read the report of District Attorney Long's frothing vituperation in the Mandan newspaper.

> "I shouldn't think Bismarck would need the glory of such an infamous trial," avers our righteous Mr. Long. "The entire matter is a gigantic burlesque. Bismarck. Bismarck! We all know the character of Bismarck! Bismarck is a city that chose its very name in a cold-blooded effort to gain investment from the Chancellor of Prussia! Bismarck is the home of more dishonesty, skulduggery, rascality, scoundrelism, fraud, perjury, subornation of perjury, bribing of juries, corruption in public and private places than any other city of the same size on the face of the globe!"

Pack turned a page. He couldn't help thinking when he glanced through the Indictment that its author must have been three sheets to the wind.

District Court Sixth Judicial District

INDICTMENT

Territory of Dakota, ss: County of Morton The Territory of Dakota, vs. Antonnie de Vallombrosa, Marquis de Mores, and E.G. Paddock.

The Grand Jurors of the Territory of Dakota in and for the Second Subdivision of the Sixth Judicial District, upon their oaths, present:

That heretore, to-wit: On the 26th day of June, in the year of our Lord one thousand eight hundred and eighty-three in the county of Billings in said Territory of Dakota, Antonnie de Vallombrosa, Marquis de Mores, and E.G. Paddock, did commit the crime of Murder, committed as follows, and did in the county of Billings (said county being attached to the county of Morton for Judicial purposes) without the authority of law, willfully, unflawfully, feloniously and with premidated design to effect the death of William R. Luffsey, then and there kill and murder him, the said William R. Luffsey by then and there shooting him with Winchester rifles, loaded with poweder and balls, which Winchester rifles, loaded with powder and balls, the said Antonnie and E.G. then and there in their hands held and discharged said balls, taking effect in the body of said William R. Luffsey, causing then and there certain mortal injuries (a description whereof is to the Jurors unknown) to said William R. Luffsey of which said mortal injuries he then and there immediately died. This contrary to the form of the Statute in such case made and provided, and against the Peace and Dignity of the Territory of Dakota.

Dated Aug. 19th, 1885.

(Signed) James R. Clark, Foreman of the Grand Jury.

Monday morning despite the cold the streets of Bismarck were alive with pedestrians; you'd have thought there was going to be a holiday parade. The air was rich with smells of cooksmoke and offal.

The mob outside the brand-new Burleigh County courthouse

had an audibly Irish accent and seemed to have lynching on its mind. Pack stood on the top step surveying the scene and was alarmed by the size of the crowd and the growling sound that seemed to pulsate from it, like a warning rumble from deep inside the throat of a predatory beast.

An elaborate phaeton coach was drawn up in front of the courthouse. Eight shotgun men on horseback surrounded the coach, keeping the crowd back away from it.

From alongside the building the Marquis De Morès, escorted by four barrel-shaped deputies, walked around into sight.

The crowd's growl became a roar.

Ignoring it, the Marquis went directly to the coach. The lady Medora was inside, breathtakingly beautiful, looking out. She did not emerge. The Marquis bowed over her hand and kissed it. There were yells, catcalls, and—from somewhere off to the left—an outburst of whistling and applause.

Pack looked that way and saw at least a dozen men on horseback, all of them applauding fervidly while their elbows clutched ready rifles against their coats. He recognized several of them—men who worked in the abattoir.

When the Marquis straightened he gave the crowd another baleful look and ascended the stairs. "Good morning, Arthur."

Pack felt the restorative power in the Marquis's flashing eyes.

The Marquis lifted his head to face the crowd down. His costume was no more subdued than ever; as always he wore the widest sombrero and the wildest scarf. He watched them with scorn.

"Well gentlemen, if you have the rope ready, here I am."

No one spoke; no one moved.

Craven lily-hearts!

The Marquis's lip curled. He went inside.

As Pack joined the retinue he looked back and saw the coach wheeling away. She would spend the day, and the next day, and however long it might take, sequestered in her borrowed rooms; she would not attend court, and the force of proper decency in this age was such that her fair name would never be permitted to be mentioned in the Trial.

Shoving past Pack, Jerry Paddock, in the shabby elegance of his worn suit, was escorted into court by two deputies. He walked with the swagger of a sailor prowling the deck in rough seas.

The theater—for that was its actual purpose, Pack thought; this was more melodrama than actual trial—was filled beyond its capacity and reminded him in an ominous way of a wedding gone awry, for the room was plainly divided into two sides, with partisans of the Marquis turning their angry faces frequently toward Luffsey's friends and toward those who, for whatever reasons, felt they were supporting law and order. He saw rich and poor on either side.

Pack found no seat left unoccupied. He was forced to stand at the back of the room and try to take notes under the baleful eye of an armed deputy whose attitude toward everyone in attendance was one of profound anger and suspicion.

Among the spectators in the seats before him Pack recognized a good many familiar heads and backs. Roosevelt was down there of course, with Joe Ferris and Huidekoper and the others. Mrs. Reuter did not seem to be with them this morning.

On the other side of the room were Granville Stuart and a crowd of important ranchers from central Dakota and eastern Montana—quite a few with their bonnetted wives, for the Trial had become one of the social events of the season.

In the rows behind the ruling families were clusters of De Morès men. Johnny Goodall was not among them; Pack recalled that Johnny had elected to remain in Medora and look after the De Morès cattle interests. Johnny had better learn to get off the fence and choose sides, or he might soon find himself looking for new employment.

Pack's view of the spectators was limited to an aspect of the backs of their heads; but he had a clear vista of the theater's stage. The prosecutor, District Attorney Theodore K. Long of Mandan, stood examining a sheaf of papers. Alone behind the Prosecution's long wooden table, he was a tall Lincolnesque figure—he seemed very young and gawky, and Pack felt affronted; he trusted the prosecutor would not play upon the illusion of his own frailty in a cheap effort to gain the jury's sympathy.

Defending De Morès and Paddock at the opposite table were the half dozen heavy-set city men he'd seen in the dining room last night. He recognized in profile Frank B. Allen and his brother

Edward S. Allen of Allen & Allen, Bismarck. In their midst sat co-defendant Jerry Paddock, hatless and slick, and—a considerable distance from their chairs—the Marquis, sultry-eyed and scornful, gripping his massive silver-headed stick with both slender hands, putting on a magnificent display of his rock-solid Wagnerian belief in his own manifest destiny.

The clerk said in a loud squeak, "All rise!"

There was a clatter of thuddings and scrapings. When everyone was upright the judge walked in, robes flowing behind him: Presiding Judge William H. Francis—a dark-skinned man, bald on top with a monk's fringe of dark hair around the back and sides of his head. He had a deep and suitably judicious voice. He called the court to order.

"The clerk will call the jury in the case of Territory against Antoine de Vallombrosa, Marquis de Morès, and Eldredge G. Paddock."

Pack found the first day of the trial to be anteclimactic in the literal sense and anticlimactic in the figurative, as it was given over largely to dry recitations of facts by Sheriff Harmon, Dr. Stickney and other non-participants most of whom responded in droning voices as if delivering themselves of lessons memorized in a schoolroom—and, Pack thought, that probably was not far from the truth, for it was all but certain that the zealous caddish Ted Long must have rehearsed his witnesses into the wee hours to make sure their answers would be exactly what he wanted them to be. Pack took pleasure in observing that there was an ironic possibility that Long's carefully prepared scheme appeared to be flying back in his own face, for the witnesses seemed to have been so over-rehearsed that all the spontaneity had gone out of them. *If I were on the jury they certainly shouldn't make much of an impression on me.*

There were testimonies as to the discovery of the body of Riley Luffsey, the determination that it was in fact dead, the doctor's statements about the bullet wounds inflicted upon Dutch Reuter and Frank O'Donnell, the observation that O'Donnell's rifle (Territory's Exhibit B) had been smashed beyond use by the impact of a forceful missile, the testification that three horses had been shot dead and the bullets removed from their carcasses and preserved (Territory's Exhibits C, D, E), the analysis of bullet holes in

Luffsey's clothing (Territory's Exhibits F, G, H), the finding that the cause of Luffsey's death was a bullet wound in the neck, and Sheriff Harmon's claim—which came as a total surprise to Pack, and caused an audible gasp in the audience—that investigation of the scene of violence had produced a slightly flattened lead slug that was without doubt the bullet that had killed Luffsey (Territory's Exhibit A).

Ted Long, clearly knowing he had scored a crucial point with audience and jury alike, waited until silence had settled upon the courtroom. Then he said, in a quiet voice that made everyone lean forward, "Now Sheriff Harmon, I ask how you know this is the specific bullet that caused the demise of the decedent. Was it found inside the body?"

"No sir."

"Where was it found?"

"In a cutbank twenty-eight feet from the corpse."

"You measured that distance?"

"Yes sir."

"There were, I take it, numerous slugs imbedded in that same cutbank?"

"Yes sir."

"How many?"

"Approximately sixty, sir."

"Then what singled this one out for your attention?"

"It had visible traces of blood and flesh on it, sir, and a piece of human bone about an eighth of an inch by a quarter of an inch."

There was a reaction from the audience—a sort of collective gathering of breath. Long held up an envelope to the sheriff. "Now will you look in this envelope and identify its contents, please?" To the judge he said, "Territory's Exhibit I, marked for identification."

"These are my initials on the envelope," Sheriff Harmon said. He opened it and made a show of peering inside. "Yes sir. This is the chip of bone in question."

"The one you found adhering to the bullet that was found in the cutbank near Luffsey's body?"

"Yes sir."

Long said, "Now with regard to this chip of bone and the blood and flesh you mentioned earlier, did you determine whether or not these evidences of human injury were related to the decedent's wounds?"

"We did. The chip of bone is an exact match for an indentation in Luffsey's fourth spinal cervical vertebra."

This caused a good deal of noise from the anti-Marquis faction. It was put down only with a forceful pounding of Judge Francis's gavel.

Ted Long was smiling at his witness. "And did you make any further determinations about this bullet, Sheriff Harmon?"

"We did, sir."

"What were they?"

"It's a 150-grain slug, .38 caliber, most likely fired either from a .38-40 or a .38-56 weapon."

"Would that be a rifle or a handgun, Sheriff?"

"Well, your .38-56 is strictly a rifle cartridge, on account of its great length and the powerful recoil. Your .38-40 on the other hand is a shorter cartridge with considerably less powder in it, and it is fired by both rifles and revolvers."

"Now, have you had occasion to examine the arsenals of weapons owned by defendants in this case?"

Edward Allen said, "Objection." He put both palms on the table and heaved himself to his feet. "Defense objects to use of the word 'arsenals.'"

"Sustained," said Judge Francis. "The term is clearly inflammatory."

The gangly District Attorney glared with suspicion at the judge, then at the defense table. Finally he returned to his witness.

"Did you take a look at whatever weapons may have belonged to defendants?"

"I did."

"And what did you find?"

"Mr. Paddock owns four handguns, two shotguns and three rifles. One of the rifles is a Springfield long-range .38-56. We confiscated it for evidence."

"Territory's Exhibit J, marked for evidence," Long said to the clerk.

The sheriff continued: "The Marquis De Morès owns a great many firearms—I can't give you an exact number because he has so many offices and residences, but in the château outside Medora and in his office in the De Morès building in Medora we counted more than forty firearms. One of them is a Colt 1873 Frontier model revolver, caliber .38-40."

"Territory's Exhibit K, marked for evidence."

Sheriff Harmon added in a loud voice, "I'd sure call it an arsenal."

"Objection!"

"Sustained. The witness will refrain from gratuitous commentary. Sheriff, you know the behavior that's expected of you in this court, and I'll tolerate no further reckless inflammatory statements."

Long returned to the witness. "Had either weapon been fired recently at the time of your investigation?"

"Sir, both weapons had been freshly cleaned and oiled prior to our examination."

"Indicating, perhaps, an attempt to cover up evidence of guilt?"

Both Allen brothers were on their feet shouting: "Objection! Objection!"

The judge pounded his gavel and leveled his withering gaze at District Attorney Long. "Sir, you know better than that!"

"I withdraw the question, Your Honor."

"Strike it from the record," said the judge.

Long shoved his hands in his pockets and regarded the jury for a few moments until the room settled down. Then in a leisurely voice he said, "Sheriff Harmon, I ask you now to describe whatever facts may have been disclosed by your investigation of the injuries that killed the three horses— those belonging to Mr. O'Donnell, Mr. Reuter and decedent Luffsey."

"Yes sir. They all had a lot of bullets in them."

"By 'a lot' what do you mean?"

"We counted twenty-three bullet wounds in Luffsey's horse. Somewhat fewer in the other two, but there were at least fifty bullets fired into those three horses."

"Somebody must have had a powerful dislike toward those horses," Long observed.

There was a titter somewhere in the audience. It provoked an outburst of laughter throughout the room. The judge pounded his gavel for order.

Pack sniffed. What a cheap trick that had been, to break the tension with such a poor joke.

Ted Long strolled half way across the stage and turned, scratching his chin, to regard his witness with a cool demeanor that indicated he now intended to be deadly serious. "Sheriff, would you describe for us in further detail the condition of the scene as you found it, with regard to the horses, the cutbank, the slugs you found, and any tracks in the earth or other physical evidence that may have a bearing on these proceedings?"

"Yes sir. The cutbank faces the Little Missouri River from a distance of about a hundred feet at that point, and—"

"That is, it's about a hundred feet from the bank of the river across a relatively flat or gently sloping patch of ground to the foot of the steep slope?"

"Yes sir, that's right. There's some brush along the bank there, but it's low scrub. Mostly it's just bare clay along there. The road runs right along the foot of the cutbank, and it's some feet higher than the high-water mark of the river."

"How far is it, approximately, to the opposite bank of the river?"

"About three hundred yards."

"Go on, please."

"Yes sir. Up the road toward town about fifty yards there's some trees. Under those trees the ground tends to be moist and kind of soft, and we found evidence of quite a lot of horse traffic—"

"By 'evidence' you mean tracks?"

"Yes sir, horse tracks. And we found the indentations of a pair of boots. Heels and toes, and one place where we had a left heel and a right toe behind one another, suggesting that a person had kneeled down on one knee."

"In the position one would naturally assume in order to fire a rifle?"

"Objection. Calls for a conclusion on the part of the witness."

Ted Long said, "Your Honor, Sheriff Harmon certainly must be accepted as a qualified expert on such matters."

"Mr. Long, I shall not permit the record of this trial to be cluttered with the miscellaneous ramblings and opinions of witnesses. Confine your questions to the facts, please."

Long was evidently displeased but after a moment he regained his composure and addressed himself to the sheriff. "Did you have occasion to measure these boot tracks and to try to match them to anyone's boots?"

"We did, sir. They were a perfect fit for the boots worn that day by the Marquis De Morès. And there were particles of that clay on the boots."

Frank Allen stood up. "May the Court please. Defense willingly stipulates that defendant Vallombrosa, Marquis de Morès, was at that place at that time. No one is denying his presence there. The Prosecution is belaboring the issue in a manner prejudicial to the Defense."

"I agree," said Judge Francis. "Mr. Long, you've more than made your point. Please get on to another line of questioning."

"Yes, Your Honor. Sheriff, let's return to the cutbank and the dead horses. You were about to describe that scene in more detail."

"Well, the marks left by the three horses indicated they'd dropped athwart the road, three abreast more or less, forming a sort of bulwark facing the trees, with the cutbank behind them. Most of the bullets we found in the carcasses indicated, by the angle of entry and the position of the wounds, that they had been fired into the horses after they were knocked down."

"That would be consistent, would it not, with the idea that a considerable amount of gunfire was being aimed at the three innocent hunters—"

"Objection!"

"Sustained."

"Sheriff, the voluminous gunfire you've described—it penetrated the horses and, above and behind them, the cutbank?"

"Yes sir, that's right."

"From what angles did this gunfire arrive?"

"From at least two different angles. It came from the direction of the trees where we found the boot prints, and it came from off to the right, that is, the direction of the river."

"Now, what was the caliber of the slugs fired from the latter direction?"

"Those were the .38 caliber slugs, sir."

"And the bullets that came from the direction of the trees?"

"That's kind of hard to say, Mr. Long."

"Why?"

"Because those bullets mostly disintegrated into pieces."

"You mean they were smashed beyond recognition?"

"No sir. Not smashed. Exploded into pieces."

"And there was no way to make a determination as to their caliber?"

"We were able to make a rough judgment, by measuring the curvature of some of the fragments and imputing a radius. They certainly were not small-caliber bullets. They were at least .38 or .40 caliber, and possibly as large as .44 or .45."

"And these exploded bullets were found both in the horse carcasses and in the cutbank?"

"Yes sir."

"And how about the unexploded .38 caliber slugs that had been fired from the direction of the river?"

"Most of them were in the cutbank up behind the horses. Two or three were found in the horses."

"What conclusion can we draw from that distribution of bullets, Sheriff?"

"The man who fired the .38 caliber bullets was shooting from the opposite side of the river."

"How did you determine that?"

"Well, if the shooter had been on the near bank he'd probably have dropped a lot more ammunition into those horses, assuming he was shooting at people barricaded behind the dead horses. On the other hand, if the shooter was across the river laid up in the brush there, then he wouldn't have been able to see much of the horses, because the brush on the near side of the river would have obstructed the lower part of his view, and all he'd have been able to see would be over the tops of the dead horses."

Edward Allen said, "Your Honor, the Defense has listened with great patience to this litany of guesswork, and we feel obliged to object to the extensive expression of opinion on the part of the Prosecution's witness."

Ted Long said angrily, "May the Court please, the witness is merely testifying to the only possible interpretation that can be put upon the physical evidence he has described."

Judge Francis studied both lawyers. After a moment he said, "I'm going to sustain the objection, Mr. Long, for reasons stated earlier. We're interested in discovering facts here. It's up to the jury to render the opinions. The questions and answers will be stricken from the record, regarding Sheriff Harmon's opinions about where certain bullets may have been fired from."

Ted Long said in pained exasperation, "Your Honor!"

"Proceed, Mr. Long."

"I must register objection to this high-handed and arbitrary exclusion of vital evidence!"

"Mr. Long, you may proceed or you may depart."

"Very well," Long said through gritted teeth. He returned to his witness but the momentum clearly had gone out of his charge. "Sheriff, I take it you examined the weapons, if any, possessed by the Decedent and his companions?"

"In two cases I did. Two of the men, both injured, surrendered themselves immediately after the incident to the custody of Mr. Ferris, who kept possession of their weapons until my brother and I arrived on the train. In the third case I was unable to locate the man, Mr. Reuter, so I was unable to investigate the condition of his weapons, or indeed, to determine whether he had any."

"In the two cases that you did examine, what did you find?"

"Mr. Luffsey possessed a rifle and a revolver. Both were fully loaded, and neither appeared to have been fired."

There were rumblings and growls throughout the audience. Pack sat up straight. He was thinking: *That's not the way I heard it*. But he hadn't actually seen Luffsey's weapons . . .

"And Mr. O'Donnell?"

"He had a rifle. It had been fired once, with the empty cartridge case still in the chamber. The magazine was fully loaded."

The crowd's voice became a roar. Opposing men yelled at each other. Bedlam broke loose.

Throughout the Trial's early testimony the Marquis's main show of emotion was one of arrogant disdain, but he must have been chagrined to hear some of the reports, even though it ought to have been obvious to any dolt that crucial portions of the evidence must have been manufactured as part of the overzealous effort by Sheriff Harmon and District Attorney Long to bring about the Marquis's downfall by framing him: whether the Marquis was innocent or not, any right-thinking observer could see his enemies were creating evidence right and left to bolster their case.

Nevertheless, whether true or contrived, the physical evidence that had been mustered by the District Attorney was more imposing than Pack had been led to expect. Throughout the first three days Long cleverly amassed his facts and lies, pounding home again and again evidence contrived to support the Prosecution's contention that the Marquis and Paddock had conspired to ambush the three "innocent hunters."

At the end of the third day's proceedings Pack was granted a brief audience with the Marquis in his cell. Madame Medora was there of course. She said, "Antoine and I want you to know how deeply we appreciate your support in these difficult times."

The Marquis said, "Roosevelt has been in the same seat every day."

"Yes, I've seen him."

"You know, don't you, Arthur, that he has financed the opposition."

"I've tried to find evidence of that."

"Roosevelt and the other Jews. I have heard some spectators behind me express their wonder at what one of them called 'the strange courtship between the New York dude and his aristocratic enemy.' There is of course no mystery in it at all. Roosevelt is there hoping to see me fall. But he is the one who is doomed."

"Doomed to disappointment, you mean."

The Marquis smiled. Even here, Pack thought—even in this dismal cell, with nothing before him but the prospect of a long solitary night and tomorrow's continuing discomfort in court—even now the Marquis's composure was uncracked, his smile cheerful. What an extraordinary man!

Pack said, "These have been dark hours for you both, I know. But you have the support of a great many good people, and the Defense will begin soon. I've every confidence you'll make a shambles of the Prosecution's trumped-up case."

"Don't give it another thought, Arthur. Just continue to honor us with your good wishes."

His heart pounding, Pack offered to escort Madame la Marquise back to her lodgings. To his amazement she accepted. He gave her his arm and she came along with determined stride, skirt billowing and one hand holding the wide sombrero on to her head.

Theodore Roosevelt came around the corner and nearly blundered into the lady. He stopped, lifted his hat, showed his big square teeth and gave Pack barely a glance before he said to the Madame, "At least it's a mild evening."

"The weather has been very kind." Her voice gave away not a thing. Pack thought sometimes that Medora would die as she had lived—with well-mannered seemliness and unfailing etiquette. But her eyes—they were another thing entirely. When she regarded Roosevelt the look of unrequited longing in her eyes was so intense it frightened Pack.

His suspicions were inflamed to the point of absolute conviction. He saw the way they looked at each other. Feelings were bright in the burning of their eyes: he saw the hot instincts rising in both of them.

And yet—and yet Madame Medora only gave Roosevelt the benefaction of a tiny curtsy. "Will you walk with us?"

"Dee-lighted."

During the remainder of the evening's walk she said not a single further word to either of them.

La belle dame sans merci.

But then at the door of the sumptuous house in which she was staying as a guest of one of the city's leading families she turned to face the New Yorker. Seemingly ignoring Pack's presence altogether, she stood with her head cocked a bit to the side and slowly smiled at Roosevelt. Pack felt shocked clear down to his boots: it was nothing if not a suggestive smile. She said in a soft and silky voice, "I do hope to see much more of you in future, Theodore."

"A sentiment I share in abundance, madame." Roosevelt touched his hatbrim, gave Pack his brisk nod and big grin, and strode away with his choppy stride.

Medora said, "Despite my husband's opinion, I must say Theodore is truly a remarkable man, don't you think, Arthur?"

Pack felt incapable of suppressing his anger. Turning away, he thought savagely, *Go inside, madame—or I'll take you for another kind of woman.*

Lurking in the shadows outside the hotel Pack saw a familiar figure. It was Jerry Paddock's wife, Little Casino, having made her way to Mandan to ply her occupation in the dark. She stepped forward into the lamplight but then she recognized Pack and the false smile dropped away from her face. Pack said, "Don't worry. I know things look bad but the Defense hasn't started its case yet. Tomorrow you'll see a different play altogether."

Laughing like an angry crow, Little Casino said, "Sweetie, I ain't worried at all."

"Well good night to you, then."

Somewhere not far away a baby wailed; Pack heard a woman's weary plea: "Please don't cry. Please don't." He approached the hotel. Dan McKenzie was coming out. The blacksmith looked around, spied Little Casino and strode straight toward her. Pack made as if to go inside, but lurked at the corner of the doorway, interested in McKenzie's movements because something about the man had always puzzled him and, during the past several days in Bismarck, he had observed McKenzie gambling, spending a lot of money, living very well. So when he saw McKenzie approach Little Casino he listened in on the conversation.

"I want to borrow five hundred dollars."

Paddock's wife gave the smith a filthy look.

McKenzie grinned fearlessly. "I feel my memory getting poor. On the other hand I'm remembering some other things that could maybe cost you a thousand or ten thousand."

Little Casino scribbled a note, folded it in half and slipped it to McKenzie. "Five hundred ought to do for now. Take that to the paymaster." She added in a dry voice, "Don't be surprised if you're the first witness they call—before you bleed them to death."

Well it was, after all, only the sort of thing you would suspect of a man of Jerry Paddock's caliber.

He entered the hotel and considered going up to his room to revise his notes but weariness drove him into the saloon bar. There was a crowd. Men were bellied up and more men stood three-deep behind them, eating prairie oysters and drinking grain whiskey. Pack heard Huidekoper say, "The judge is plainly on the wrong side. It's an uproarious exercise in corruption and double-dealing on all sides. It's a fiasco."

When Dan McKenzie came in behind him Pack glanced that way, then managed to get a bartender's eye and order a drink; but all the time he had Redhead Finnegan placed in the corner of his vision. Finnegan was amply present—the primitive untamed atavist from Bitter Creek, his red hair long and snarled, his skin greasy and filthy. He stood at the end of the bar defiantly hoisting drinks with Frank O'Donnell, whose stubborn dead-on stare challenged any and every man in the room to call him a liar.

Finnegan snarled, "He ain't no more titled than I am. Markee hell. He made it up. Who's to dispute him? He made it up, so he could spit on the equality of men here."

Pack heard Dan McKenzie say, "Hobble your lip, Red. You've got a leaky mouth. No telling who might be in here." McKenzie never looked at Pack but he knew McKenzie felt his presence. It disgusted Pack to hear the smith's talk; McKenzie now was pretending to be a friend of Finnegan's. Clearly the man had no conscience whatever. He was playing both sides for advantage.

Fury shook A.C. Huidekoper. He plunged past Pack without recognition, then belatedly turned and acknowledged him. "Somebody ought to tell Finnegan to quit drinking."

"Everybody's got to kill his own snakes," said Pack.

"The city's a box of tinder just waiting for a matchstick. A loudmouth in a packed bar room—it doesn't take any more than this."

"Yes—I see—you're right, I suppose." Pack gave the man a distracted nod and gulped down the remainder of his drink and hurried out, suddenly unnerved by the close pressure of the crowd and a curious confusion that ran rampant through his mind.

There was still a light under Joe Ferris's door. Pack knocked and was admitted. Joe was in shirtsleeves; he had been reading—it was Roosevelt's book about his adventures in the Wild West, mostly a pack of exaggerations and outright lies as far as Pack was concerned. He said, "I thought you didn't care for hunting. Why read about it?"

"Because I am mentioned in the book," Joe said proudly. "How are you enjoying the proceedings? Appears to me the Prosecution's leading the De Morès gang by thirty or forty to nothing, and only a couple innings left."

"Don't count the Marquis out," Pack said. "He's going to win this, you know."

"I doubt it. Not after Dutch Reuter takes the stand. Still, I grant you anything's possible, the way the Marquis's boys have been spreading money around." Joe added in a wry tone, "But of course it's only to encourage witnesses to tell the whole truth and nothing but the truth."

Pack said, "They're only fighting fire with fire. Do you think the Prosecution's lily-white in all this? They're the ones who started buying witnesses."

Joe gave him a moment's grave look. "Be that as it may. What are we to you, Pack? No more than actors on a stage that's lit by the presence of the Marquis De Morès?"

It was unclear what excuse Ted Long had used in persuading the court to allow the Prosecution to withhold two witnesses until after the Defense presented its case. Reuter and O'Donnell were scheduled to appear no earlier than Friday. It didn't make sense to Pack but he was unable to learn anything useful; the decision had been made in chambers.

On the fourth day of the trial Ted Long made every effort to press Jerry Paddock to admit that the Marquis had plotted with him the night before the fact to murder the three hunters. But Paddock refused to be shaken; he never admitted a thing.

Then the Marquis himself faced the jury, head up, unblinking. The very picture, Pack thought, of gallantry under fire.

"Luffsey and O'Donnell fired their rifles until they were empty," said the Marquis in a tone of studied equanimity, "and then commenced to discharge their revolvers."

District Attorney Long leaped to his feet. "I object to this perjury on the part of the witness! Previous witness, Sheriff Harmon, has testified that the weapons of Luffsey were oiled and fully loaded, and O'Donnell's rifle had been fired only once, with the empty cartridge case still in the chamber!"

Judge Francis gaveled him down. "The District Attorney, having been present throughout the discourse of the past four days in this courtroom, must know full well by this time that testimony has been contradictory as to a great many matters, beginning indeed with who actually started the shooting. Former witnesses have been allowed to testify to the full, and this witness will be accorded the same courtesy. I rule in favor of the Defense. Objection overruled."

It made Ted Long's dike burst. He bounced upon his feet, hollering objections over the measured pound of the gavel until Judge Francis bellowed back at him: "Sir, if you do not shut up and sit down, you will be held in contempt of court!"

Smiles broadened on the faces of the portly Messrs. Allen.

Pack caught a glimpse of Theodore Roosevelt's face as it turned toward his neighbor. A vein throbbed visibly at his neck; Roosevelt was furious.

Long pounded toward the bench, waving his fists. Astounded by the District Attorney's outlandish behavior, Pack listened with disbelief to Long's raving shouts:

"The Court cannot rap me down with a gavel! I am the representative of The People, and I am here to see a fair and impartial trial—to assist the court in the enforcement of substantial justice. Instead of the Court extending to me that aid and support to which I am entitled under the law, the Court has uniformly during this whole trial sought to tie the hands of the Prosecution and has openly aided the Defense; the Court has shown by its action in this case that it is determined to aid the acquittal of the defendant and that it will not leave a stone unturned in the accomplishment of such acquittal; the animus of the Court throughout has shown a most marked feeling in favor of the defendant and against the Prosecution; the Court has sought at every point to embarrass the Prosecution and to aid in the acquittal of the defendant; the judge has insulted me personally and has handicapped me officially."

Having listened to it all with a demeanor of infinite patience, Judge Francis smiled before he said, "Sir, you may continue prosecuting the case if and when you purge yourself of contempt. If, out of respect to the institution of this Court rather than the person of the judge, you will state for the public record that you bear the burden of guilt for your contempt, and if you will apologize to this Court, then this Court will relieve you of all odium and reinstate you."

"An apology, sir, would stultify my sense of manhood. I am nothing if not a friend of this Court, but I have been trampled by the remarks of this judge. You have abused me personally and insulted me repeatedly professionally. You have acted in a manner unbecoming the office of a judge and provoked me to say all that was said. I have done nothing to regret. I have only tried to perform my official duty and I will not apologize."

Judge Francis again was all smiles. "In that case let me point out that your refusal to acknowledge your guilt of contempt serves to increase the severity of that contempt. I direct the sheriff to remand this prisoner to jail."

Pack saw, not without a certain glee, that Theodore Roosevelt looked ready to throttle the judge.

"And I shall stay there until I am ordered out," Long shouted. "No apology!"

While Dutch snored, Joe Ferris drew his Remington revolver and cocked the hammer: he heard footsteps outside. More than one person.

When the footsteps grew louder, with no attempt at stealth, Joe lowered the hammer gently; and when he heard the code knock he holstered the Remington and opened the door.

It was Roosevelt and Mrs. Reuter. Joe put his head out and looked both ways along the quiet street; saw nothing in the silent dusk, withdrew and closed the door.

Dutch was sitting up; Mrs. Reuter settled on the edge of the bunk and murmured to him.

"We came the long way. I don't think anyone followed us." Roosevelt was carrying a small case, the kind of valise in which lawyers or commercial men toted their papers. He opened it upon the splintery plank table and took out a packet of food and several bottles of beer.

Dutch looked wretched: gaunt, scabrous, pale from his months of hiding indoors. He had no spirit left. He reached for a beer bottle. "Tomorrow? I in court tomorrow talk?"

"Not tomorrow," Roosevelt said. "You are scheduled for today—if the District Attorney gets out of jail." The muscles of his face jerked in a sequence of rictus grimaces. "I understand his feelings but by George the man's an utter fool for affronting the judge so blatantly. He's allowing the judge not only to try his case but, by all indications, to lose it for him by default in the bargain."

Joe went to the window and peered out. "Why, I thought it looked pretty good for a conviction. The judge ain't the jury, thank God."

"In the end I don't think they're going to convict De Morès," Roosevelt said. "Nor Paddock either, for that matter."

"Why not?"

"If justice is to be served, then it will come down to the question of reasonable doubt. They're probably guilty—but 'probably' isn't sufficient in a court of law. Nor should it be. The District Attorney can harangue all he wants; if he hasn't got absolute proof then he hasn't got a case. But that's not a good enough reason for abdicating as he did yesterday."

"Hell," Joe said, "whose side are you on?"

"I try to be on the side of justice and truth, as we all should try to do," said Roosevelt. "In any event I feel obliged to visit the jail and see if I can't persuade Mr. Lang to recant his outburst and return to the arena."

Dutch said in a pinched voice that sounded nearly strangled, "We this finish pronto or I myself outburst get."

Mrs. Reuter said, "I can't see what excuse the judge had for not putting Dutch on the witness stand two days ago. We should have had it done with by now. It's cruel."

Her concern was for what remained of Dutch's soul. The man was about as dispirited and dejected as you could be and keep on breathing.

Joe stood at the window surveying the street; he said over his shoulder, "I expect the Markee's boys persuaded him to postpone Dutch's testimony as long as possible to give the boys every chance to find us."

"An uncharitable speculation," Roosevelt said, "but, under the circumstances, a plausible one. And yet another reason why I must make it my business to convince the District Attorney that he must get back into the fray. He may still have a chance, if he can place O'Donnell and Dutch on the stand this afternoon and present their case forcefully enough."

"Looks like we may be in a little bit of a fray ourselves," Joe said. "Here comes Dan McKenzie with a pack of De Morès boys—armed to the teeth."

They were moving up the street without hurry, stopping at each house to knock at the door.

Roosevelt crossed to the window with four quick strides. It took him only a glance to see what was transpiring. "House-to-house search, is it? Then we'd better get you out of here, Dutch. Out the back way—on the run now."

Dutch's face went a shade whiter. He turned toward the back, then reached out with a certain defiance to clutch a fresh bottle of beer before he allowed Mrs. Reuter to steer him away. It was the only moment of spirit he had evinced. Just about all the sand seemed to have drained out of Dutch these past several months.

Roosevelt began to go with them; then Joe heard his voice:

"Joe? Are you coming?"

"Guess I'll just wait here a bit."

"To do what?"

"May be throw them off the trail. May be slow them down a little."

The dude shook his head emphatically. "You're spoiling for a fight, old fellow. This isn't a suitable time or place. Come on, then."

Reluctantly Joe allowed Roosevelt to pull him away from the window. "Where'll we take him?"

"Back streets and alleys," Roosevelt said as he slid through the door. "Up to Mr. Long's office. I've no doubt they've already searched there. Then you can keep watch over Dutch while I go and try to persuade our overly emotional District Attorney to mend his fences."

There was said to be a good deal of maneuvering; Pack was not privy to it but he heard that Roosevelt had visited Long in jail and that pressures had been brought to bear on the judge from both sides, all parties being desirous of bringing the conflict to a speedy conclusion. In any event, when the recess ended, Judge Francis fined District Attorney Long $250 for contempt; Long signed a check for that amount and the judge allowed the trial to proceed.

The interruption, Pack thought, had done great harm to the Prosecution's case and great good to the Marquis's, for Long had betrayed himself indelibly as a man of rash misjudgment.

There ran through the crowd a sudden ripple of excited shouting. Pack saw people crushing toward the door. Something was happening outside. Pack saw legions of the curious pressing toward the doors and, since there was no possibility of getting through that way, he sprinted up the stairs onto the gallery, from which he was able to look out through the window.

They came forward on foot down the dusty center of Rosser Street, walking abreast, rifles in the crooks of their arms: Joe Ferris, Bill Sewall and Theodore Roosevelt, with Dutch Reuter unarmed among them. Dutch was furiously smoking a quirly and looking straight ahead with the rigidity of a man who expected a bullet in the back at any instant.

Below Pack's window the sidewalk filled to overflowing with excited spectators. Dan McKenzie and a sizable group of De Morès men moved out onto the street, spreading wide enough to cover nearly the entire width of the thoroughfare, and Pack saw Dutch Reuter's pace falter. Sewall gripped Dutch's elbow and propelled him forward. The four men advanced steadily; McKenzie and the boys formed their line of skirmish, blocking the way to the courthouse door, and it occurred to Pack that from this high angle of view it rather resembled the movements of toy soldiers on a game board. Only toy soldiers didn't carry loaded Winchesters.

It was Roosevelt who spoke, while still walking forward; Pack had no trouble hearing the clipped high-pitched words:

"Stand aside, gentlemen, if you please. We have lawful business before the court."

It was foregone, really; none of the boys was prepared to start anything raw in front of dozens of witnesses in broad daylight. McKenzie must have realized that quickly enough, for he stepped aside without a word and Roosevelt's party marched up the courthouse steps without pause.

Pack wheeled back to the gallery rail to look down into the courtroom.

Bill Sewall remained near the door with his rifle across his chest while Dutch, in semblance of suit and cravat, walked down the aisle between Theodore Roosevelt and Joe Ferris. The two guardians stopped at the railing where Roosevelt aggressively met the Marquis's stony scowl while Dutch Reuter ascended the stand to testify. Roosevelt and Ferris went back to their seats. Mrs. Reuter was there, beaming infuriatingly at everyone around her.

As Dutch sat down in the witness chair he glared malevolently at the Marquis. The Marquis was royally dressed and, Pack thought, royally annoyed.

District Attorney Long aimed a savage glance of triumph toward the Defense table and when the babbling roar of the crowd finally calmed down he commenced to question the old German.

The Marquis had waited under the trees until the three hunters approached, and then had held their attention with insults while, from ambush across the river, someone—probably Jerry Paddock—had drawn a bead on the nearest of the three, who happened to be Riley Luffsey, and had shot him out of the saddle without warning, after which both the Marquis and the hidden gunman across the river had exhausted considerable supplies of ammunition in a vain attempt to wipe out Dutch Reuter and Frank O'Donnell, who had saved their own lives only by flattening themselves behind the bloody corpses of their horses and firing two or three blind shots in the air to discourage approach by their attackers.

This was the story Dutch told; it was the same story Frank O'Donnell had just finished telling, earlier on that same Friday morning.

Dutch's broken English was no aid to comprehension, but Long patiently took him through his testimony time and again, so that there might be no confusion as to his statements.

The whole affair, Pack thought, was a shameful circus, inasmuch as it was patently obvious there wasn't a whole lot of truth in the two outlaws' bleatings.

On cross-examination the Allens made valiant attempts to discredit the stories of O'Donnell and Reuter. But aside from a variety of minor discrepancies they failed to "break" either witness. That was hardly surprising, Pack thought, in view of the fact that if either of them admitted the whole yarn was a pack of lies, they'd go up for perjury and most likely they'd be lynched before sunset by the outraged citizenry. So they had no choice but to remain glued forever to their pathetic tissue of scandalous falsehoods.

And now it was Pack's turn to testify. He felt his pulse rumble. Stage fright, he thought. When he took the witness chair he smiled nervously at the judge and tried to recall if he had remembered to comb his beard this morning.

Frank Allen took him cursorily through the events of the morning in question. It was no time for misgivings or doubts; Pack related the facts as he knew them. Then Frank Allen said, "Please describe to the jury the character of the witness Frank O'Donnell, as you know him."

Pack said, "Mr. O'Donnell is a very rough fellow and reputedly a late associate of Jesse James. I recall being in the presence of Luffsey and O'Donnell on an occasion when I heard O'Donnell say, 'Damn the Marquis or any of his men. If that son of a bitch of a Marquis or any of his men go near my ranch I will put a bullet into them.' Later I asked Luffsey why O'Donnell had said such a thing, and Luffsey replied that 'he had no use for the French son of a bitch.' And upon another occasion I heard O'Donnell say to a crowd, 'I tore down the son of a bitch's fence and will do it again; if anyone thinks I won't shoot the Marquis, let him step out here.'"

Frank Allen smiled. "May we remind the Court that there's been ample testimony to show that the hunters were never seen to enter town unless they were armed to the teeth. In view of that testimony, as now reinforced by the word of this honorable and respected newspaper publisher, may we suggest to the Court that it is ever more obviously an outrage for the eminent prosecutor to refer to these outlaws, as he has done repeatedly during this trial, as 'poor professional hunters' and 'peaceable citizens.' By mendaciously accusing the Marquis of murder, these vagrants of the Little Missouri have tried to bring down the Marquis's fences and to bring an end to what they mistakenly regard as French colonialism in the Bad Lands. Clearly, Your Honor, we have before us a classic case of insufficient evidence and reasonable doubt. Once again we ask for a directed verdict of Not Guilty."

Judge Francis returned Frank Allen's friendly smile in kind. He opened his mouth to speak. *About time, too*, Pack thought.

That was when there was a disturbance in the spectator rows. A man had stood up.

It was Theodore Roosevelt. He did not speak. He only stood to his full height—such as it was—and gazed across the intervening distance, staring the judge in the face.

Judge Francis brooded at the upstart. Like everyone in the courtroom he knew very well who Roosevelt was.

The judge considered what he had been about to say. Then he sat back. "I'm sorry, Mr. Allen, but this case will go to the jury."

Never saying a word, Roosevelt sat down.

Pack did not understand why his own first involuntary reaction was to smile.

Nineteen

Joe Ferris finished cleaning his Remington revolver and replaced the heavy cartridges in the cylinder. He thought a while about the things he had seen and heard this week, and finally he went upstairs and down the length of the carpeted hall and knocked at the door of Theodore Roosevelt's suite.

"Come in."

The moment Joe entered the room his searching glance found Bill Sewall's face and sought information in it. Lamplight threw hard shadows across Sewall's deepset eyes. He smiled briefly.

Seeing nothing alarming there, Joe turned to regard Roosevelt, who sat writing at the side table. A fire leaped on the hearth behind him. Joe said, "There's talk against you, sir. Some of the men who support the Markee. They're saying you and I bribed witnesses to testify against him."

"Don't be alarmed, old fellow. Once the verdict is in, however it's decided, all this will die down."

Joe heard a step behind him. He turned to look at the man who had entered through the open doorway.

"Theodore," Huidekoper said, in a voice Joe didn't recognize at all.

"What is it, old chap?"

Huidekoper, hands shaking, withdrew a half-curled note, folded in half, from the sleeve of his greatcoat. "De Morès has written you a letter from his cell. The deputy asked me to deliver it."

"What's in it?"

"A gentleman doesn't read another gentleman's mail. But I can guess."

Joe Ferris thought, *So can I.*

Roosevelt accepted the letter from Huidekoper. He unfolded it and read the single sheet. Then he sat heavily, head down, elbows on the table, fingers interlaced, forehead on knuckles.

Huidekoper placed his hat on a hook with the careful doleful precision of a mourner. Joe looked at Bill Sewall and saw nothing but stillness upon the woodsman's red-bearded cheeks.

Finally Roosevelt spoke. "For a long time Mr. De Morès has incubated hate. During the trial he has been kept in jail with nothing to do but brood. Now the trial approaches its climax and he does not know for certain which way it will go. I suppose it's strange that I should have more faith in his good luck than he has, but that seems to be the case. I'm sure they'll find him not guilty, by reason of insufficient evidence. Any reasonable man on the jury must concur there's doubt as to his guilt. But he doesn't seem to have much faith in our system of justice. I suppose he has worked himself into some sort of frenzy of suspicion and rage."

He pushed himself upright in the chair and used his index finger to prod the unfolded letter across the table. "I think you all probably would like to know what it says. Please read it."

> My Dear Roosevelt,
>
> My principle is to take the bull by the horns. Joe Ferris is very active against me and has been instrumental in getting me indicted by furnishing money to witnesses and hunting them up. The papers also publish very stupid accounts of our quarreling—I sent you the paper to N.Y. Is this done by your orders? I thought you my friend. If you are my enemy I want to know it. I am always on hand as you know, and between gentlemen it is easy to settle matters of that sort directly.

Your very truly,
Morès.

I hear the people want to organize the county. I am opposed to it for one year more at least.

Joe took his turn after Huidekoper and Sewall. When he had read the letter he understood why neither of them had said a word.

Bill Sewall was watching Roosevelt with narrowed uncertainty. Huidekoper turned to Joe Ferris in a transparent effort to avert crisis: "Were you really instrumental in getting him indicted by furnishing money to witnesses and hunting them up?"

"I thought it was you," Joe replied. "Writing letters to Washington and all."

Huidekoper turned. "Was it you, Theodore?"

"No. I do not write letters behind people's backs."

Bill Sewall said, "It may have been Mrs. Reuter." He stood facing Roosevelt. With vexation tempered by fondness, Sewall spoke softly, bringing them all back to what they were trying to evade. "The Marquis was trained at St. Cyr. They say there isn't his equal as a swordsman in any country."

"I'm sure that's a vast exaggeration. I've seen him fence with Wibaux—I thought him only adequate. He might have killed Wibaux but that's because Wibaux is nearly as clumsy with a sword as I am. In any event I certainly wouldn't think of engaging De Morès in swordplay. Why play into his hands? As the challenged party I have the choice of weapons. My choice would be the rifle."

"He's a dead shot," said Huidekoper, "and he loads his ammunition with exploding bullets."

Roosevelt said calmly, "By George, if he needs to use exploding bullets then he jolly well can't be all that much of a dead shot, can he. Recall, if you will, how much ammunition he seems to have poured wastefully into the carcasses of those poor dead horses in the road."

Joe said, "My Remington and I are at your disposal, sir."

"Thank you, old fellow. It won't be necessary." Roosevelt sighed. "Really, you know, my friends, I do not approve of duelling. It's barbarism."

Huidekoper said, "No man in his right mind would dignify this rot with a reply of any kind. Look at the postscript. Clearly he's on the verge of lunacy. First he challenges you to an affair of honor and then he gives you his advice about county government. Ample evidence, it seems to me, that he's deranged. No one will think any less of you for ignoring the fool."

Roosevelt examined the letter again. "I'm afraid the words and their meaning are clear. The postscript may be open to interpretation but the challenge is not. In the circumstances he gives me no choice. I shall not back down and I shall not be seen to back down from Mr. De Morès." He removed his glasses and bent his large blue eyes close to the paper as he wrote.

Huidekoper said in alarm, "What are you doing?"

"Writing back an acceptance of the challenge."

Joe said, "And you ought to demand an apology."

"An apology is worthless if you have to ask for it."

"Your idealism is as demented as it is magnificent," said Huidekoper. "It's appalling."

Roosevelt said, "Sensible men since ancient times have realized that courage is not the only virtue but that it is the virtue without which the others are meaningless. Conversely, of course, courage alone may be insufficient. You may find it in men of evil character. Without a sense of duty and responsibility—without cool judgment and moral strength—a man counts for very little. Reputation be damned. For my own sake I cannot play the coward."

Huidekoper muttered, "Pardon my scoffing—but one would think you were the first man ever to have discovered the Ten Commandments."

"Your cautionary objections are noted," Roosevelt told him, and handed his own two-page note to Sewall. Joe went around behind him to read it unabashedly over his shoulder—Roosevelt would stop him if he didn't want Joe reading it, and Roosevelt said nothing so Joe squinted and tried to read in the poor light but by then Sewall had put the first page behind the second and Joe only was able to read the last part of the letter. It was enough:

> Most emphatically I am not your enemy; if I were you would know it, for I would be an open one, and would not have asked you to my house nor gone to yours. As your final words however seem to Imply a threat it is due to myself to say that the statement is not made through any

fear of possible consequences to me; I too, as you know, am always on hand, and ever ready to hold myself accountable in any way for anything I have said or done.

Yours very truly,
Theodore Roosevelt

Roosevelt gave Joe a dry look—*If you're quite finished now*?—and said, "Bill, if you'll be so kind as to act as my second, please inform Mr. De Morès's second that I have chosen Winchester rifles and that I choose to have the distance arranged at twelve paces. My eyesight is weak as you know and I don't consider myself an especially good shot—therefore I must be near enough so that I can hit. We will shoot and advance until one or the other is satisfied."

"Maybe they'll convict him. Then you won't have to fight."

"Yes. Well we shall see whether they convict him," Roosevelt said with a dryness that was not typical of him. "Perhaps they will, after all."

Joe replied, "You may have been a great politician but you're a bad liar."

Twenty

Pack dreamed he saw the Marquis De Morès riding toward him, galloping at the head of an army of French soldiers, all of them shooting: in the dream he saw vividly the orange muzzle-flashes. He tried to hide; there was no place. He tried to run; his feet were gripped immobile in clay. The thundering army galloped upon him, and he awoke.

Perplexed, Pack remained in his seat to scribble quick notes. The crowd was filing toward the exits.

The trial had lasted a week. After closing arguments the jury retired at 2:40 P.M. for deliberations. They were out only ten minutes. The jammed courtroom hadn't even emptied yet. Now Pack saw the crowd reverse itself. He squeezed his elbows together to make room.

On the stage of the theater the Marquis sat bolt upright. Nearby, but ignored by the Marquis, sat Jerry Paddock, arms folded.

The judge was brooding in Roosevelt's direction. Roosevelt met his glance; there was a brief display of teeth. Then Roosevelt swung his gaze boldly toward the Marquis, but the Marquis was looking elsewhere. Roosevelt's eyes then came around in this direction and

Pack felt the force of them behind the lenses of the metal-frame glasses.

He's got nerve, Pack had to admit.

The jury filed in and sat down; the foreman presented a folded piece of paper to the clerk. The room was quite still. "All rise."

The clerk unfolded the verdict and read slowly aloud:

"We, the jury, find defendants not guilty."

District Attorney Theodore K. Long shot to his feet and shouted, "I demand the jury be polled!"

The clerk addressed the jury. Pack watched with grim satisfaction as each man in turn answered that he had voted "Not guilty."

Pack joined Granville Stuart and a weighty group of substantial citizens in vociferously applauding the verdict.

Finnegan's hooligans booed and hissed.

Ted Long yelled, "This courtroom is a den of iniquity! I am of a mind to give this judge Sir William the Second a good cowhiding!" And stalked from the court, near apoplexy.

The judge, busy pounding his gavel, may not have heard the prosecutorial fulminations. When the racket eventually subsided the judge said, "Prisoners are discharged on finding of Not Guilty. Court is adjourned."

The Marquis bowed graciously to the judge, then turned on both heels and stared into the audience.

Roosevelt was there, in his seat, unmoving as the crowd milled about him. Pack saw him meet the Marquis's gaze with a bleak stare of his own.

Joe reached for the notepad that lay open on Pack's desk. Without asking permission Joe sat down, picked it up and read aloud:

"The Marquis has always had the sympathies of the better class of people. He is to be congratulated on the result and every true friend of the West will rejoice in his acquittal. There is no man in Dakota who has done more to develop the West than he, and a conviction in this case would have been a calamity."

Joe said, "You're a worse stuffed shirt than Roosevelt, d'you know that? You're a snob."

Pack stood at the window. Cold air blasted in at him but he had the window open so he could look out at the celebration along

Rosser Street. There was a fair chance that some of tonight's quarrels might lead to murders, he feared; the Irish and their friends were not good losers.

When Joe finished reading the paragraph aloud, Pack said irritably, "You might have asked."

"You're going to print it in the newspaper right out in front of God and everybody, aren't you?"

"All the same."

"Don't be sour now. You've won, haven't you?"

"It's not my victory, Joe. It's a victory for justice. Even your friend Roosevelt agrees with that. There was no real evidence against the Marquis."

"So now the Markee's free to go back and destroy what's left of the Bad Lands," Joe said in a sour voice, "just as soon as he comes back from his urgent business in the East and gets done shooting Theodore Roosevelt to pieces. Bill Sewall went looking for De Morès and Van Driesche after the trial and it turns out they'd left town on the New York train. Did you know that?"

"Business before pleasure."

"Or may be the Markee isn't exactly the brave hero you think he is."

"You may accuse him of a lot of things but cowardice is hardly one of them. He's fought duels to the death."

"With men who were unquestionably his inferiors in training and strength."

"Like the grizzly bear he rassled?"

Joe said, "That's a lie about the grizzly. I thought you knew that."

"It's not a lie."

"The taxidermist is in Mandan. Go there. Ask him. The Markee stabbed his knife into a hole that was already there. He'd shot the bear from a safe distance. The taxidermist kept the pieces of lead as a souvenir. Exploding bullet."

"I don't believe that."

"Then ask the taxidermist, God damn it!"

"He's probably an Irishman!"

Joe said, "The Markee's a bully and a coward in my view. He didn't expect Roosevelt to accept his challenge. So he's run off east to think it over. He'll come back because he's got to put a good face on things. If Roosevelt hasn't left the country by then the Markee'll go through with the duel because he knows he's better at those things by a mile. But he'll be a little nervous because he didn't expect Roosevelt to show this kind of courage. Roosevelt will show him a few more surprises too. He's always tougher than anybody expects him to be. But listen, Pack—be that as it may, I don't want to see him killed. I don't think you do either."

Pack retrieved his notebook, snapped it shut and slapped it down on the desk.

With the toe of his boot Joe hooked a rung of the chair beside him and slid it out toward Pack. "Sit yourself."

Pack felt obstinate. He stood fast. "Why?"

"Because I've got to make up my mind whether I'm willing to be your friend any more."

"That's up to you."

"And because you're at the point where you have to choose between pursuing your own life and being a satellite."

"You're wrong. I'm my own man." He wouldn't have thought Joe's lexicon would have included such a word as "satellite." Joe was a man of constant surprises.

"Your trouble, Pack, you doubt the wrong people and you seem to know everyone's business but your own. For God's sake it is time for you to see the light and realize that the true hero of the Bad Lands is not that strutting bastard De Morès at all."

"All right, Joe, I know you don't like his walk or his talk. It's not your style. He's got no skill at blending. It's not in him to go unnoticed. He can't ape the mannerisms of pedestrian men. That's because he dreams mighty dreams. He bestrides this land like a Colossus. He inspires—"

"He inspires nobody but you, Pack. Hell, De Morès's real followers—loyal supporters—are just about nonexistent. There's his wife who adores him with blind faith and there's Johnny Goodall, who rides his own trail, and there's you. Other than that there's only opportunists like Jerry Paddock and Dan McKenzie."

"Not to mention a few no-accounts like Granville Stuart and—"

"The rich folks from Bismarck and from over in Montana? They side with him, sure. Why not? They fawn on the titled son of a bitch. They'd admire to be just like him—filthy rich and frivolous. They live off to one side, they don't live *under* him where you find out for sure what it really means when De Morès says he believes in the divine right of kings. He makes no secret he means to become a king himself. He believes his blue blood gives him the right to make laws in our Territory—well this isn't France. I don't care about Granville Stuart, Pack. Granville Stuart lives in Montana—it's no skin off him what happens in the Bad Lands. Where I live, nobody except you trusts the Marquis. Some take his pay and keep quiet, but they all know his promises are about as durable as snow on a hot griddle."

Pack said in a low voice, "He has never broken his word to me."

"May be the occasion didn't come up. Good Jesus, the Stranglers have killed more than sixty men. Sixty men, Pack."

"No one's laid that at the Marquis's doorstep. God knows you've tried, but there's no shred of evidence. He has told me, confidentially, that he doesn't know any of the Stranglers by name or by sight."

"He doesn't need to know their names to be their paymaster. He's the boss, Pack. Without him there'd be no Stranglers."

Pack walked back and forth with his hands rammed deep in his pockets. Head down, not looking at his friend, he said, "Huidekoper and the others saw what a man of imagination and vision could do in this wilderness, and they hate him for having shown them up. They try to blame him for everything that happens. Sour grapes."

"He's a foul-tempered childish fool. He killed Luffsey—I don't care what the trial says—and he'll murder Theodore Roosevelt however he can. If this duel takes place it'll mean Roosevelt's life. He's toughened up and he's got grit enough for ten, I guess, but be that as it may, I've spent plenty days hunting with the man and I can testify, you put a rifle in Roosevelt's hands and two times out of three he couldn't hit the broad side of a barn from inside the barn."

An enormous weariness dragged Pack down into the chair. His eyelids drooped. "The death of Theodore Roosevelt might not be a significant loss to the world, Joe. The death of the Marquis De Morès, on the other hand—"

"That's an unforgivable thing to say. God help you."

Pack blinked. He felt listless.

Joe said, "He won't ever be king of France, I agree. But he's a better man by a country mile than the Markee. Remember how he handled the Lunatic? He cared, even about that poor useless creature. He has got no vindictiveness. None."

When Pack made no reply, Joe murmured, "What's eating at you?"

"Now, I am a newspaperman. My duty is to be objective—to see the truth as it is, and not as you would have it be."

Joe went to the door. "Hell, Pack, you wouldn't know the truth if it shot you between the eyes." He went out. The door closed not with an angry slam but with a quiet reproachful click.

Twenty-one

Wil Dow was happy Mr. Roosevelt and Uncle Bill had come home safely; at last he could dismiss the useless hired man and get some sleep instead of leaping awake at odd intervals to keen the night for creeping Stranglers.

So he welcomed them home with unfeigned enthusiasm. But coming home did not brighten Uncle Bill Sewall's outlook. He put a bleak half-lidded stare upon the tortured waste of ice-rimmed thorns and vulture-picked bones and pronounced it harrowing and merciless.

"Uncle, doesn't it give you a lift to come home?"

"Home? This ain't my home. Anyhow we have got bigger things to worry on. They turned the Marquis loose—and now he aims to kill the boss."

Then Sewall told Wil of the impending duel between Mr. Roosevelt and the Marquis De Morès. The Marquis was in the East attending to urgent business matters that were overdue but he would be back in Medora by the arrival of the new year and would place himself at Mr. Roosevelt's disposal upon the road below the railroad bridge on the fifteenth of January at 3 P.M.

"He chose that hour for a reason. You watch," said Uncle Bill to

Roosevelt. "He'll be west of you, facing east, and you'll have the sun in your eyes."

"Perhaps it will be a cloudy day," said Mr. Roosevelt without heat.

Wil said, "I'd be proud to go in your place, sir."

"Thank you, Wil. It won't be necessary. Now please tell me—are the Stranglers still about?"

"I'm not pleased to report it but they are." Four days ago, Wil told them, four travelers had found a lifeless body swinging from the limb of a cottonwood not six miles from the Elkhorn house, and nearby—probably not dropped accidentally—they had found a torn scrap of paper bearing the names of eighteen or twenty men. They had come by: strangers who claimed they were not Stranglers, and while Wil held his cocked three-barrel gun ready they had shown him the list and he had found fifteen of the names legible. In the past several days since word got out that the list had been found, at least a dozen men seemed to have scattered and disappeared in a great hurry.

Mr. Roosevelt inquired, "Was any of our names on the list?"

"No sir. I believe I would have mentioned that."

"That's the first good news I have heard in a month," growled Uncle Bill.

"Dutch Reuter's name was on the list. So were Finnegan and O'Donnell."

Uncle Bill said, "Then the Stranglers are out to avenge the honor of De Morès. Any idea where Dutch went?"

"Haven't see him," Wil said. "Haven't heard a thing."

"God help him. It was a brave thing he did, testifying in court."

Mr. Roosevelt said, "It was his duty."

Wil coaxed higher flames from the fireplace logs and went to peer through the frost-grimed windowpane. A dozen scrawny cattle stood huddled against the windbreak of the cottonwoods, pawing and gnawing at the earth. A steer lurched into the yard, lame on swollen frozen feet. Several bulls had lain down to die. There was nothing to be done about it.

They hadn't been to town for mail or supplies in more than two weeks. One morning the thermometer showed 25 degrees below zero. It was the coldest winter Wil Dow had experienced. After tossing feed to the stock in the barns he hurried inside, beating his gloved numbed hands together, in time to hear Sewall say, "Not likely any of us be suffering from the heat for a while."

There were two deer hanging from the piazza roof. It was Uncle Bill's idea to keep two or three carcasses ahead, so as to be provisioned for blizzards. As it turned out, not much hunting was required, as the deer had come down off the slopes into the shelter of the bottomland trees—it was a simple matter for two men to beat the bushes while the third waited for the animals to come out.

In the evening a current of frigid air rolled down the coulees. Treetops were tossing in the wind. Sewall said, "A real snorter tonight." Breath steamed from his mouth. He hung his saddle on its rail in the barn and batted his gloved hands together and glared at Wil Dow. "Look at me—a cow puncher! What's dignified in that? I am about ready to go home. I always said I should never live here longer than I was obliged. Right from the start I saw a good many drawbacks to this country. Just as soon as I get enough money you will see me go back to Island Falls, the quicker the better."

"Well, Uncle Bill, it costs like fury to get a train ticket."

They walked up to the house. Wil bent to peer at the Fahrenheit thermometer on the piazza. It was 32 degrees below zero.

Mr. Roosevelt came up from the stable. He tore the gold-rimmed spectacles from his face. They brought bits of skin with them. Bundled in skins you could get along all right with your back to the wind but there was no comfort if you had to face it. Still, the boss seemed to delight in the hardships and dangers and even the pain of it.

The water bucket was frozen solid, top to bottom. A hard wind shook the house and howled through the bare trees. Roosevelt was suffering from asthma and cholera morbus, and writing in his biography of Thomas Hart Benton.

Wil said, "At least it can't get any worse. It can only get easier after this."

"I wouldn't count on that," said Uncle Bill.

He was right. It became the most ferocious winter in Dakota history. In the snow-clad iron desolation the white river stood solid and motionless as granite. A rubble of shattered icebergs heaped itself nearly to the piazza of the house. They endured blizzard upon blizzard. Footing became ever more treacherous. The coulees filled almost level. The snow melted, froze, melted and froze again, higher and higher until the slick hard drifts were impassable.

Cattle weren't able to get through to the grass beneath; and in any case there was precious little grass at all, after the preceding season's overgrazing and fires. Even now there was a growing number of dead cattle to be found everywhere. It was certain there would be heavy losses. When spring came they'd find out the extent.

In the meantime it was necessary to tie a rope to the corner of the house and to wade blindly, bucking the drifts, to find the barn; once this was done Wil tied the riata to the barn and they had a lifeline between the buildings. But there were three consecutive days when they couldn't use it, for the temperature dropped to 60 degrees below zero.

"Everything comes to an end," said Mr. Roosevelt with satisfaction. He stood on the piazza in shirtsleeves. There were chunks of ice on the river; the chinook was blowing and there must have been a very warm thaw upstream to the south, for a flood kept pressing upon the high dams of thick ice until they burst. These explosions heaped great crags of ice in piles along the river; there was a tremendous crashing and roaring.

It couldn't help remind Wil of the advancing date for the duel. He couldn't fathom the way Roosevelt seemed to regard it. He was neither in a dither nor in a blithe pretense; he neither worried it nor ignored it. He spoke of De Morès without particular rancor and he mentioned the duel occasionally and lightly, as if it were nothing more than another occasion in his calendar—a dinner to attend, a speech to deliver.

The threat of it may not have bothered the boss but it hung over Bill Sewall like a huge black cloud and there were whole days when it dampened Wil's spirits as well; he couldn't get the spectral anticipation out of his mind.

One morning Wil exploded. "Doesn't it ever get you down?"

"You can't allow those things to get you down, old fellow. When the time comes, I shall confront Mr. De Morès, and hope I can talk him out of this foolishness. That failing, I suppose I shall have to shoot him, or be shot by him. I shall endeavor to wound him as lightly as possible, and still dissuade him from continuing. What more can I do? In the meantime it's no use brooding, is it. Now you may have forgotten, but I have not, the four deer that we shot weeks ago and hung from a tree to keep the coyotes from them. With this thaw we shall have to rescue that meat right now or it will spoil. Are you with me?"

"Best we all go together," said Uncle Bill. "And keep both eyes open for Stranglers. They could easy have it in mind to save the Marquis some trouble. He wouldn't have too rough a time duelling with you after you got hung."

The three men used their Mackinaw skiff to get across; Wil bent his back to the oars. It was harrowing to go into the rough current just ahead of the ice dam but they kept dry and pulled the boat high up the bank and walked inland on Indian-style snowshoes.

They set out on foot, traveled two hours, arrived at the tree and found a few bones, nothing more.

Mr. Roosevelt examined the tracks. "Mountain lion," he judged. "Not long ago. Bully! Let's go after it."

They spent the rest of the day hunting lion, with no success, and returned in a rising gale to make their perilous way back across the river. They took the boat out of the water and hitched it securely to a tree high on the bank before they hurried inside.

Mr. Roosevelt was determined that in the morning they should continue the cougar hunt. Uncle Bill was not cheered by the prospect.

In the morning the boat was gone.

Wil said in a hushed voice, "Indians!"

Uncle Bill had a look at the rope. It had been cut. "You may be right. But I didn't know they used any kind of boat except canoes."

Then Wil espied a dark object on the bank below. He scrambled for it and picked it up. A man's glove. "Look here!"

Mr. Roosevelt said, "I don't recognize it. Do you, Bill?"

"No. But I expect it's a white man's glove. Indians don't use them, do they?"

Mr. Roosevelt made fists. "Scoundrels!"

"Scoundrels with nerve," Uncle Bill observed, "to go out into those ice packs in an open boat."

"By Godfrey, let's saddle up, Bill. We can overtake them."

"Think again. Half the ground's frozen stiff and the other half overflowed. Anyway all they need to do's keep on the opposite side of the river. We try to reach them, they can pick us off. The river's so high it'll probably kill them anyway. Howard Eaton told me only two parties ever tried to go down this stream in boats, and they neither of them ever made it. One boat got swamped in the rapids and the other party was on a portage, got killed by a grizzly."

"We will pursue the thieves, Bill."

"No sir. Anyhow by now the boat's probably kindling and they're probably drowned or froze to death."

"We will pursue them, by thunder! It's a matter of defending principle. To submit tamely and meekly to theft is to reward evil and encourage repetition of the offense. Great Scott, man!"

Uncle Bill flinched before the outburst. "That may be as you say. But there's a power of white water on this river."

"I know that, but you two are used to this kind of navigation in Maine. You're so accomplished at handling boats in rough water I always suspected you had webbed feet."

Wil Dow said, "We can't ride and we can't walk and we have no boat, so I don't rightly see how we can pursue them."

"We shall simply have to build a boat," said Roosevelt.

They fashioned a boat by stripping lumber from the ranch house. They nailed it together and caulked it with pitch. Wil Dow gave it a little run on a slack eddy in the river and with dubious faith pronounced it serviceable.

"They've got a mighty jump on us," grumbled Uncle Bill. "No chance to catch them now."

"We may fail," Roosevelt replied, "but it won't be for want of trying. We'll go now. By George, old fellows, this will be a grand adventure!"

Uncle Bill caught Wil's attention. Then he rolled his eyes toward the sky.

They loaded provisions and Roosevelt's camera and a knapsack full of books, armed themselves and gave chase.

With Uncle Bill in the bow steering and Wil aft at the oars and Roosevelt athwart the boat with his rifle at the ready they made slow advance through great slabs of broken ice that had tumbled over one another in wild confusion. The chinook had scoured the hills and left them bare and grey, scarred by washouts where the clay was still dark from melted snow that had run off and swollen the river.

The temperature kept dropping. Uncle Bill sat forward, hands on gunwales, swaying his body-weight to balance the boat as it breasted ridges of white water.

The wind in Wil's face was ice-cold and he said, "Likely have this breeze in our faces all day."

"That would have to be the crookedest wind in history," Uncle Bill replied.

Along one stretch a coal vein was on fire high above them. It burned for more than a quarter of a mile, at the end of which a great boulder tipped ominously from a precarious overhang; sure enough it did tumble into the river and they had scarcely gone past it at the time. The plunging rock made a tidal wave that lifted the boat ten feet and nearly swamped it.

They came around a bend into a gale blowing straight upstream. Funneled into a howling rush by the narrowing cliffs it roiled the water into a froth that stood higher than Wil could believe. He heard Uncle Bill say, "That looks pretty saucy."

Wil said, "We can weather it if we lay the boat about right."

"Give it your all, boys!" Roosevelt's voice, and subsequent coughing fit, were all but lost in the racket as the strong wind met the current hard enough to make a vertical wall of water. The boat met the bared teeth of the gale; knifed into the white wall and rocked and shuddered. Foam soaked Wil's every pore. The home-made skiff took on more water than he believed she could hold; but she came through the roil without striking rock and when they wheeled into the lee of the cliffs they were still afloat and it was time to start bailing with their hats.

Sewall said calmly, "I believe that is the swiftest run I've ever had."

The boss said, "By Godfrey, that was fun!"

They camped at dark with no sign that the fugitives were within reach. Wil and his uncle put up the tent. The three of them huddled inside under the post lantern. Roosevelt kept busy reading *Anna Karenina* with keen interest and writing for energetic hours in his Benton biography. Wil shivered and thought that after all, much as he hated to admit it, Uncle Bill was right. This cowboying was not a pleasant sort of life. It was time to get back to a civilized country where you could trust the climate and the animals and the human creatures as well.

Roosevelt put away his writing box. He grinned at Wil. "Self-reliance is a quality I deem fundamental."

Wil thought, *I shall hit him with my fist if I hear one more "By Godfrey this is fun!"*

On the third day they found the stolen Mackinaw boat.

It was tethered to a rock near a clump of undersized cottonwoods. The ferocious current nearly carried them past it but they made a landing.

Roosevelt was first ashore, as they all leaped from the boat brandishing rifles and revolvers. Campfire smoke curled up from the lee of the cottonwoods. Uncle Bill had a quick look at the Mackinaw boat and nodded his head, pronouncing it sound. Roosevelt pointed toward the cooksmoke. Then he jabbed his rifle first to the right, then to the left, indicating that he wanted them to disperse and converge upon the camp. They separated to move inland. Feeling the beat of his pulse, Wil cocked both hammers of his ten-gauge Parker. There were sixteen buckshot in each cartridge—enough to mince a man.

He crept among the bushes.

When his hands were ready to fall off in ice splinters he heard Roosevelt's loud high-pitched cry: "Put up your hands!"

Hurrying around from behind the cottonwoods Wil caught the sorry sight of Dutch Reuter at the campfire, hands in the air quivering.

Roosevelt's voice ran forward out of the trees: "Are you alone here?"

"Right now I am."

"Dutch, what on earth are you doing here?"

"To get warm trying."

"Well old fellow, I advise you to offer no resistance."

"Yah. All right."

Dutch seemed sheepish, and in a way glad to see them. Uncle Bill ventured out of the woods. When his appearance drew no fire he advanced into the camp.

"You look underfed, Dutch."

"Not much food. Three weeks on the run I have been."

Wil came out. Roosevelt said to Dutch, "We are going to have to take your weapons," and when there was no objection Wil helped his uncle disarm Dutch—two holster guns, a pocket pepperbox, a big knife and a little knife and a rifle leaning against a stump.

Roosevelt kneeled down to put wood on the fire and said, "Dutch, you are a blue-rumped ape. I had not hoped to meet you again in circumstances such as these."

Dutch rolled a smoke and accepted the chastisement without comment.

Uncle Bill said, "It ever occur to you about the irony in stealing a boat that belongs to the very man who saved your life more than once just lately?"

Dutch said, "Shut up, Bill."

"The devil I will. Who's with you?"

"Red and Frank." That would be Finnegan and O'Donnell.

"And I guess you'd be on the run from the Stranglers?"

"Yah," said Dutch. "They us on the list put."

"That's no justification for stealing a boat that isn't your property," said Roosevelt.

"Yes sir." Dutch offered no argument.

Wil said, "Finnegan and O'Donnell. Where are they?"

"Hunting. Food."

Uncle Bill said, "Keep the fire burning. They'll be back."

They waited in ambush. The chinook had died; the air was still and cold. There was no sound except the lash of the river and a grinding of pack ice.

Tight with strain Wil listened for sounds and kept thinking of the things that could go wrong. He mistrusted the silence; he strained his ears against it and half a dozen times thought he heard things but there was nothing and then suddenly without warning Redhead Finnegan was there, looming in the twilight as apparitious as if he were hanging from a gallows.

Frank O'Donnell was right behind Finnegan.

They walked silently into the camp. Finnegan carried a snowshoe rabbit by its hind feet. They weren't expecting trouble; they hadn't seen anything to alarm them. Dutch sat morosely by the fire and did not look up.

Roosevelt said, “Hold up.”

“Guns all around you, boys,” said Uncle Bill.

Wil said, “Over here too.”

O’Donnell stood motionless. Finnegan, rifle across his left forearm, seemed undecided.

Roosevelt stepped into sight. Wil followed suit and he saw Uncle Bill step forward from the trees.

O’Donnell said to Roosevelt, “Doing the Stranglers’ job for them now, are you.” But upon Uncle Bill’s gesture he dropped his rifle readily enough.

Finnegan stood at the focal point, near the fire. He had not relinquished his rifle. After a long interval he said with pathetic bravado, “Hell, a man’s got to die sometime.”

“We are prepared to shoot you down if you offer trouble.” Roosevelt’s teeth flashed—a white rectangle across his weather-darkened face.

Finnegan took his right off the grip of his rifle. He dragged his hand over his face, rubbing hard, as if to scrub his features away. He looked over his shoulder. “Frank . . .”

Frank O’Donnell gave a haggard little wave from down by his hip to indicate that he meant to stay out of it.

Redhead Finnegan’s head swung heavily from side to side. His darkly matted hair swung back and forth under his hat. Wil caught the hard killer glint in his gaze. The stretching moment was taut with uncertainty.

Uncle Bill said mildly, “Red, maybe you remember how we all saw how that fellow Calamity tried to fight the drop and died for his trouble? I still kind of remember how slippery the ground got underfoot with his blood. Is that a mistake you care to imitate?”

Finnegan brooded more and at the end uttered a deep hollow sigh. “I guess not,” he murmured, and let the rifle slide to the ground.

They searched the two thieves and relieved them of an arsenal. Uncle Bill borrowed Wil’s double-barrel and Wil said, “If you’re going to use that to cover them, be careful with it. The right-hand barrel goes off when you don’t mean it to.”

“If it happens to go off it’ll make more difference to them than to me," Uncle Bill replied. He turned his head toward Roosevelt. "Now we've got them. What'll we do with them?"

"What do you suggest?"

Cautiously Uncle Bill muttered, "Some might say why not just shoot them down *ley fuga?*"

"Because we are not murderers," Roosevelt said. "Wil—your suggestion?"

"Well I suppose they ought to be hanged, sir, but I don't know."

"What makes you hesitate?"

"Well Dutch has been a friend of ours and all."

"And that makes him less guilty than if he were a stranger?"

"Well I guess not, sir."

"And so?"

"I don't like the idea of hanging people, Mr. Roosevelt. There's got to be some kind of difference between us and the Stranglers."

"Bully. Bully for you. You have grown up a great deal, Wil. You're absolutely right. Now there'll be no more talk of shooting or lynching—unless they should be so foolish as to make a break for it. I assume everyone understands me clearly? We'll take these three in with us and surrender them to the lawfully constituted authorities and they'll be prosecuted in a court of law."

"So's the Stranglers can hang us proper," said Finnegan.

Roosevelt said, "You have our protection against the Stranglers, Mr. Finnegan."

That made Finnegan laugh aloud.

Before they lost the light entirely Roosevelt set up his glass-plate camera and had Wil and Uncle Bill take pictures of Roosevelt holding the three boat thieves at rifle-point. The capture of the thieves, Roosevelt said, would make a good chapter for his new book about the West.

Handling the prisoners was not as difficult as Wil had at first feared. O'Donnell did as he was told. Dutch was eager to oblige—anything Roosevelt wanted of him. As for Finnegan he ignored the proceedings; he seemed disgusted with himself.

That evening the temperature dropped to around zero. Wil supervised while the prisoners gathered firewood. It was too cold to tie their hands; they'd have got the frost. Roosevelt took their boots away from them and put the three prisoners on the far side of the fire and told them not to come across it or they'd be shot. The prisoners rolled up in buffalo robes and did not look eager to bolt barefoot through the frozen spiny wilderness, but all the same, by Roosevelt's decree, the three captors took turns standing night-guard.

That first night Wil watched until midnight, then Roosevelt until daybreak; next night Uncle Bill would take the first watch, then Wil; so forth. In that manner every third night one of them would get to sleep all the way through. Except that Roosevelt never slept very much anyway. He was always reading a book or writing one. Or keeping up with his correspondence with his sister and Miss Carow—for, Wil had learned, that was the name of Roosevelt's constant correspondent in New York. Miss Edith Carow. Must be a warm and tender romance there, judging by the ever increasing frequency and thickness of the letters they exchanged. Wil wondered what she was like, this Edith Carow.

In the morning they assembled at the roaring bank. Bill Sewall contemplated the heaving froth. "What now?"

"Downriver, old fellow. No choice."

"Nobody knows where this river goes. Where we are right now—the map says the river's fifteen miles from here. Nobody has done a survey. It's guesswork. We could hit a hundred-foot waterfall around any bend."

"Then keep your ears open, that's a good chap." Roosevelt's grin was luminous.

They headed downstream in both boats. Almost immediately they ran into an enormous ice jam that held them back for hours. All they could do was follow it at its own petty pace. "Maybe we'll get a warmer thaw," Wil suggested.

"And maybe if my aunt had wheels she'd be a buckboard," Uncle Bill said.

Each time they touched shore Frank O'Donnell would think about trying to make a break; sometimes he actually tried. He never got more than three or four paces before a loud word would bring him up short. Dutch Reuter was ashamed of himself and tried nothing. Redhead Finnegan, oddly, seemed remorseful and sad—evidently not because he felt guilty of any crime but because he was disgusted with himself for having got caught.

They made only two miles the first few days. It was icy bitter tedium. Roosevelt had ample opportunity to finish reading his Tolstoy. It was fortunate they had found several books amongst the prisoners' booty; it seemed Finnegan and his friends had looted a few ranches along the way to their escape, and had come away with several bottles of liquor as well as some magazines and books, of which the most appropriate seemed to be *The History of the James Brothers*. Roosevelt set about reading it with avid interest. It prompted him to ask Frank O'Donnell if it was true, as mentioned in the trial of the Marquis, that he had actually ridden with Frank and Jesse James. O'Donnell only glared at him without reply.

Roosevelt began to write a letter and Wil was prompted rashly to say, "Writing to your lady friend, sir?"

"My very good lady friend, yes indeed. My sweetheart from years ago, and if you're not careful, Wil, I shall bore you to tears with exultations about her."

"Guess you saw her when you went back East last trip?"

"You may recall I broke a bone when I was East? Miss Carow, angel of mercy that she is, helped nurse me back to health. We had an opportunity to rediscover the things we'd seen in each other in the first place. Though between you and me, I can hardly credit that she sees much in a little four-eyed dude like me."

"What sort of lady is she, sir?"

"Very fine, very lovely—and deserving of far better than the likes of your obedient servant."

"I don't believe that, sir. Sounds like you are to be congratulated."

"That would be premature, old fellow. But I do hope the time will come." Roosevelt's lips peeled back from the big teeth. He was in a splendid mood.

Downriver behind the slow-moving ice they had to guard the prisoners every minute; none of the three was to be trusted, and as the days passed Finnegan seemed to revive himself with the aid of rising anger: even more than O'Donnell, Finnegan especially seemed to be on the lookout for a chance to redeem himself by escape or by surprise attack.

They traveled on into the unknown and untested reaches of the river—in all no more than twenty miles as the crow flies, but more like a hundred because of the oxbow bends and double loops of the river.

And now they were out of provisions. Wil cooked up a last batch of biscuits, as muddy as the water he had to use in preparing them.

Uncle Bill said, "That's it, then. We'll have to kill them or let them go, since we can't feed them."

"No," said Roosevelt. "We're not suffering any worse punishment than they are."

"It won't serve justice much if we all die out here."

"If it comes to that we can die just as quickly with these prisoners as without them," Roosevelt pointed out, and Wil saw no way to refute that.

Uncle Bill said, "You are always the last one to quit." He didn't sound pleased to say it.

It was then that they saw cattle on the slopes above the river on the opposite bank. Wil got out his rifle, eager to shoot one, but Uncle Bill said, "It's risky business to kill other folks' cattle."

"We are not thieves," Roosevelt said.

"Then that's that," said Uncle Bill. There was no question of fighting Mr. Roosevelt. His will, and his swashbuckling approach to this, were such red-hot things that they simply wilted whatever resistance tried to form objections within his companions.

And so, Wil thought, we will starve to death in this blasted Wild West.

They found a wagon road, so they left the boats in the ice jam and made their way on foot—a journey the bootless prisoners did not enjoy—to a small ranch. Its house was no more than a hovel. A wagon stood off to the side and there were horses in the corral. Roosevelt said, "What place is this?"

"Don't know," said Uncle Bill.

Finnegan said, "The C Diamond." He seemed pleased.

The owner, an old frontiersman, came out squinting and said, "Finnegan, by God, what have you done now?"

"Guess I have made a fool of myself again."

Wil was not happy to see the friendliness with which Redhead Finnegan shook hands with the old frontiersman.

They spent the night. Roosevelt sat up with his back against the door and his rifle across his lap. As far as Wil could tell, he must have stayed up reading and writing all night.

In the morning Roosevelt bought provisions from the old man and hired his wagon and team. "Now you two," Roosevelt said to Wil and his uncle, "can do me the fine favor of taking the two boats downstream to the mouth of the river, where they can be recovered. I myself shall put the three captives in the wagon. This old gentleman will drive it. We'll take them overland into town, following the plateau rather than going down into the Bad Lands."

Uncle Bill protested vigorously. He took Roosevelt by the elbow and tried to steer him off out of the old frontiersman's hearing but Roosevelt shook him off.

Uncle Bill said in a forceful whisper, "It's a fifty-mile trip all alone with three killers for company, not to mention that old fellow, whose allegiance you might describe as dubious at best."

Roosevelt said, "There are two boats, and there are two of you. I can't see one man handling that enterprise. Can you?"

"Leave the damned boats."

"Damned if I will! After all the trouble we've taken to secure them?" Roosevelt laughed. "Never mind, old fellow. I shall be all right."

"All alone with these four bad men?" Wil Dow said.

"It shouldn't be hard to persuade them they are safer in my hands than in those of the Stranglers. They'll be tame as kittens, I warrant."

"Don't count on that," said Uncle Bill. "You're talking about a long lonely trip. The ground's still frozen on the plateau and I don't like the look of that sky."

"By George, I shall enjoy it."

"And what if all five of you end up at the end of the vigilantes' lynch ropes? I don't like this idea."

"It's not an idea. It's a decision, and I've taken it. I'm truly touched by your concern, Bill. I shall be fine."

"Don't do it."

"Your advice is noted. And now I think you've run out of things to say on the subject."

After slow consideration Sewall uttered a grudging sigh. "You are the boss and we take orders from you."

"Yes," Roosevelt said quietly.

Wil shared his uncle's dour view. But what were they to do? Forbid Roosevelt at gunpoint?

Wil helped Roosevelt heave provisions into the bed of the wagon. The boss kept stopping to wipe off his glasses. They had steamed up from the heat of his exertions.

"Very well. Let's go." Roosevelt picked up his rifle to supervise the loading of the four men.

Wil was not near enough to prevent anything. He saw it clearly when Dutch, climbing onto the wagon, had his chance to jump Roosevelt.

Dutch saw it too. There was that moment of hesitation . . . Then he climbed over the sideboard and settled onto the wagon bed.

Redhead Finnegan was furious. He made no effort to keep his voice down. "You could've fallen back on top of him there."

"Shut up, Red. Always Roosevelt me square treated."

"Aagh!"

Frank O'Donnell said quietly, "Well it's a hell of a long walk to Medora." He grinned without mirth.

Twenty-two

A hard jagged wind rushed against them. The dark spread of clouds unrolled until it covered the sky. Flickering snowflakes boiled between earth and cloud. Tiny hailstones began to sting the ranchman's exposed cheeks. Walking forward steadily behind the wagon he tucked the rifle under his arm for a moment, tied his bandanna over his hat and under his chin, wiped his glasses with a gloved finger, pulled the flannel muffler up over his nose, batted his hands together and resumed his ready grip on the Winchester.

It was awkward holding the rifle because the gloved forefinger hardly fit in the trigger guard. If the need to shoot should arise, it would be a matter of thumbing the hammer back and letting it slip—hardly a recipe for deadly accuracy.

O'Donnell and Finnegan doubtless were aware of those shortcomings.

Still—a rifle bullet meant certain trouble and possible death; they knew that too.

The wind ran along the plains with a howling echo that lifted and fell in tortured fury: it pounded him like a boxer's fist. Suddenly the whole pressure of it was upon him, making him question his bearings and squint through raised hands. He ran forward, stumbled, caught the tailgate of the wagon and clung to it.

He hoped the storm hadn't taken Sewall and Wil by surprise. This kind of weather could blind a man on the river. He didn't want to think of the two boats battered to matchsticks after all this effort—nor the two Maine woodsmen thrown into the freezing torrent.

Really there wasn't much likelihood of that. Sewall was a canny fellow and Wil had sand. Neither of them would be fooled by Nature. They'd be sitting it out, most probably, in one of those natural caves at the foot of the cliffs—waiting for the blizzard to journey on.

Nonetheless he had a moment of concern about them as the storm filled the world with its sudden misery. He gripped the tailboard and kept pace with the slow-moving wagon. Through the swirling blow he saw O'Donnell and Finnegan—both of them twisting around on the high seat to blink at him. They were grinning. In the wagon bed Dutch Reuter huddled under his poncho, a figure of chilled misery.

The old frontiersman had no gumption left. He drove hunched over, flapping his reins ineffectually; the wagon crawled forward, its wheel rims sucking gumbo in slithery ruts.

The ranchman thought about leaping into the shallow bed of the wagon but it was no good letting them come close to him; that would give the four men an easy chance to jump him and so he stayed behind the rattling vehicle, left hand gripping the tailboard, right hand gripping the rifle.

A good hike—healthy exercise.

The driven hail never seemed to reach the earth: it slanted past him in horizontal planes, skimming the ground and bouncing away like pebbles thrown by children. The storm pummeled him, sliced at his clothes, made his ears sting; the cold felt its way up his sleeves and pried itself inside his clothing and the wind leaned against him with such force that the ground seemed to tilt and whirl under his feet.

He couldn't trust his sense of direction. Some large object spun violently past him—tree branch? Clump of brush?—and he began to hear bigger hailstones crash and rattle against the wagon.

He saw it dimly when the two Irish rascals looked back again.

Their faces were covered with cloth now but their eyes were filled with a secret amusement—and then they were whipped from sight when his foot caught on something and his grip was wrenched from the tailboard and he tipped, fell, rolled, sprawled . . .

He got up on one knee and swiveled his head from side to side—and couldn't see anything beyond arm's length.

The wagon was gone. It might as well have been a hundred miles away.

There was a hollow moment in his chest. Panic.

He shouted. The force of the gale whipped the words away; he couldn't even hear his own voice.

Where was the wagon? He could see nothing: nothing at all except roiling whiteness. He lurched around on both knees, turned a full circle and found nothing more substantial than the wheeling snow.

The storm shrieked. He stood up and went down again, unable to keep his balance against the relentless pressure of the driving wind. Bits of ice trickled down inside the back of his collar.

A fit of coughing took him.

He thought, *A fellow could die quickly enough out here if he didn't keep his wits about him.*

He groped for the rifle, found it, felt at the earth with his hand.

Think now. West wind—it was at the right shoulder. Keep it there. Feel the contour of this ground again . . .

The road was deeply rutted—various thaws must have rendered the clay into soft muck and it had been channeled deep by the few wagons that had passed. Then the gumbo ruts had frozen, hard as granite. Not likely the wagon could have turned out of the ruts. Not likely, for that matter, that they even knew he was no longer at the tailgate.

Catch up, then. Come on—*move.*

Knees bent low he waddled forward, leaning to one side against the callous-hard palm of the wind, dragging one foot to keep to the line of the ruts.

It was slow going—treacherous. He tripped, fell down, realized by the sudden stinging that he had bruised his nose. He wedged his feet under him, stood up and proceeded.

He was thinking, in a deliberate and reasonable fashion, that there was a very short limit on the length of time a man could survive weather like this.

Bullets of ice whacked his coat. He heard their muffled but audible slaps. This day was harsh beyond anything in his experience.

The metal eyeglasses hurt like fire. He removed them carefully, folded the stems, slipped them gently into the coat pocket; in this day-turned-night they were useless anyhow.

With eyes all but shut, goaded by desperation, he fought the blast and lurched forward, seldom confident whether he was going uphill or down. All he knew was the cold, the wind and the rutted clay.

At best he would get out of this bruised and half-frozen. At worst . . . *Oh, my darling Edith* . . . At worst he might—

No earthly use dwelling on that. One step after the other. Keep to the ruts. Keep moving.

Impossible to reckon time. Doubts grew in his mind: suppose the wind had shifted course? Suppose he was going the wrong way—back away from the wagon?

The storm bucked and pitched like the devil's own broncho. *Well I have ridden those. I shall ride this one too.* He grinned into the bared teeth of the savage animal.

He flinched from the ice-stones; batted his arms across his chest and struggled on. Feeling drowsy now. Clung to a dreamlike sort of half-wakefulness in which a part of his mind knew the other part was drifting. Necessary, the first part told the second part, to fight for sentience.

He plowed into a knee-high pile of snow wedged against a scrub plant and it was a moment before he realized that was wrong: must have lost the road. Felt behind him with a toe and backed up and prodded the earth with his hand until he knew the ruts were there. Which way now—left or right?

It was a sign of the dangerous deterioration of his mind that it took quite a while to remember that the wind needed to be at the right shoulder.

Exhaustion and frostbite. With senses slowly disintegrating he recognized the dangers. He felt the ache in his legs as they began to turn numb; he stamped his feet hard as he walked. Tucked the rifle under his arm and whacked his hands together with powerful beating strokes.

Don't worry, my darling Edith. I shan't stop fighting back. Nothing will keep me from our lovely nuptial appointment.

Must feel like this to be blind.

He groped ahead of him, hand splayed . . .

Abruptly his hand banged into something hard; he stubbed his finger.

He felt at it. Flat vertical surface. Wall? Ridiculous. Couldn't be a building in the middle of the road.

Maybe this wasn't the road.

Or maybe it wasn't the *same* road.

Had there been a fork in the road? Had he taken the wrong turn? Walked into a farmer's yard?

He slid his hand across the surface and found its boundaries.

The wagon tailboard.

It wasn't moving.

He heard, or felt, something; he bent down and dimly saw the huddled lump beneath the dubious shelter of the wagon bed: four men; ferociously flapping blankets and ponchos. He caught the dim glimmer of a pair of yellow eyes. O'Donnell or Finnegan? Whichever—there was the threat of death in those bleak eyes.

They saw him at the same moment he saw them. A hand reached for his ankle—pulled him down. Tumbling, he nearly lost his grip on the rifle. There were hands against him in earnest—pawing at his face, scrambling for the weapon. He could smell their rank breath. It was Finnegan's burly arm that slammed the side of his head and encircled his neck.

It was all a terrifying confusion then.

They were pulling him to them—tugging him under the wagon—it was hard to sort out, in his mind, what was transpiring; Finnegan had a headlock on him and O'Donnell was slithering around, trying for purchase, and he saw Dutch Reuter just beyond them—Dutch was wide-eyed, watching with his mouth agape, not moving, not taking any action, not making any choice or decision but simply watching to see how it was going to come out . . .

Finnegan roared, louder than the storm. There was a red haze;

there was a drumming thunder in his ears where Finnegan's heavy arm was ready to crush his skull . . .

"By thunder you haven't whipped me yet!"

He stood up—stood up on his hind legs with such an immense effort that he not only dragged the Irishmen with him *but also lifted the back of the wagon on his bent shoulders.*

It squeezed Finnegan's arm against the wagonbed, hard enough to bring a grunt of pain from the man; and then the ranchman swung the rifle, hard, and had the satisfaction of hearing the barrel smack noisily against flesh and bone. There was an outcry—O'Donnell—and then the ranchman was stumbling back, crouched over, weaving for balance, sucking air, trying to find his bearings.

Finnegan hurled himself forward, scrambling, trying to reach him. The ranchman fired a sudden shot into the ground. The bullet sprayed frozen mud in Finnegan's face; the abrupt explosive noise seemed to stun them all to motionlessness.

In that broken interval of time the ranchman slapped the rifle's forestock into his palm, yanked the hammer back and laid his aim hard and steady against the Irishman's face not two feet away.

"Hold!"

Finnegan stared at him. The rage of murder in his eyes slowly cooled.

The frigid air sawed in and out of the ranchman's lungs. He coughed hard.

Finnegan held—silent and still.

The wind seemed to have dropped; everything had gone quiet; and the ranchman said resolutely, "Very well then. You've had your chance. It didn't work. Now get back!"

When Finnegan began to crawl back under the wagon the ranchman let the hammer down slowly but he kept the rifle trained on his adversaries.

He moved forward, shooing Finnegan back, until he had all four men huddled tight against the singletree. He crouched under the tailboard and sat crosslegged, aiming the rifle at them, and sat without a word to await the end of the storm.

Soon enough it passed by—as quickly and as mysteriously as it had begun. By early afternoon it was possible to see miles across the high plain. The sky was lead-grey. A warm soft rush of south wind brought such an emphatic thaw that even the larger hailstones underfoot were transformed to slush within less than an hour after they had fallen; the temperature climbed so rapidly that the ranchman, heated from the exertion of walking behind the wagon, removed his coat and tossed it in the flatbed and made do comfortably in buckskin shirt and fringed waistcoat.

Dutch Reuter, after half an hour's battering in the lurching wagon bed, asked permission to get out and walk.

"I have your word you won't jump me?"

"Yah. My word you got. No trouble—my word on that."

"Then get down and walk. Beside the wagon, where I can see you."

The two Irishmen shot malign glares at Dutch.

The muzzle of the ranchman's rifle stirred. "Turn your faces forward, please."

They glanced at each other, grinned unpleasantly and presented their backs to him.

Dutch said plaintively, "You me can trust."

"I'm sorry, Dutch, but I'm not sure I can. I don't think you know yourself whose side you're on."

Dutch went alongside the wagon without further complaint.

Walking along behind the procession, the ranchman opened his copy of *Anna Karenina* and resumed reading where he had left off last night.

He sat with his back braced against the wagon wheel, notebook on his upraised knees, rifle across his lap; at intervals he looked up at the four men beyond the fire. The two Irishmen and the old frontiersman lay close together; Finnegan and O'Donnell were talking in low tones. Dutch Reuter slept off to one side, by himself, thoroughly shamed.

At a guess there were another thirty miles or so left to travel. Barring another storm they could make it that far by tomorrow evening.

The four pairs of boots were piled beside the ranchman. He adjusted the blanket around his shoulders and continued to write in his notebook. After a while the mutter of the two Irishmen's voices began to annoy him. He said, "Please be quiet now. You may as well get your sleep. You'll need it for tomorrow."

"What about you, dude? Need your sleep too, I expect." Finnegan heaved his head up and leered. "Sleep tight—if you can."

"Go to sleep," O'Donnell said, "and maybe you won't ever wake up." But there wasn't any conviction in it. They'd been licked and, he thought, they knew it. The rest was no more than hollow boasting.

"No more talk now," said the ranchman. He dipped his pen in the inkwell.

The fire dwindled. He fed it and poked it up. A fitful racket of snoring rumbled beyond the fire. It was around three o'clock. Abruptly Finnegan sat bolt upright and glared at him.

The ranchman laid his hand on the grip of the rifle.

Finnegan smiled slowly.

The ranchman said, "Test me again and I may have to tie your hands, Red."

Without argument the rogue lay back.

Well it will be a long night and a longer day. But it will come to an end.

Dutch moved closer to the fire, held his palms out to warm them and said, "Without help maybe all this you cannot do."

"I think I can."

"Man got to sleep."

"Plenty of time for that after we get to Medora."

"Something you try prove?"

"What?

"You trying prove? Something?"

"I'm not *trying* to prove *any*thing, Dutch. I'm demonstrating that it's against the law to steal a man's boat, and if you break that law, you will be held accountable. That's what the rules of civilization mean."

"Maybe the Markee and the Stranglers a different rules of civilzation they got."

"The rules apply to them too—whether they know it or not."

"I to the Markee that will say. 'Markee,' I will say, 'the rules of civilzation you got to obey.' This I will say right after you he shoot dead."

"He hasn't shot me dead yet, Dutch."

"And when he does?"

The ranchman said, "Everyone has to die, sooner or later. But no one has to run away."

"Ever you scared get?"

"Certainly I get scared."

"Right now?"

"I don't know about right now. I don't think your friends are going to make any further trouble."

"How about the Markee you duel fight?"

"We'll see—we'll see."

After that the silence stretched a long time until Dutch Reuter said softly, "I you like. But you one crazy dude."

"Good night, then, Dutch."

In the morning he watched the old frontiersman settle his team into the traces and he held the rifle across the crook of his elbow while the four men climbed onto the wagon. Finnegan looked down at him. "Dutch is right, you know. You're one crazy bastard."

"Got *cojones* to spare," O'Donnell agreed. "You going to walk us all the way to the railroad? Can't be much less than thirty miles—and plenty of swollen streams between."

"We'll get there."

"Know something?" said O'Donnell. "I think you will, too."

Finnegan growled, "Let's go if we're going. Jail's got to be warmer than this."

Dutch Reuter looked at his two Irish companions in obvious surprise. Then he turned a growing smile toward the ranchman and drew himself up like a pigeon.

The ranchman knew he might have their respect at last but it didn't count for much. There was a long gloomy walk ahead.

The ranchman wiggled his toes in his boots. He felt the swollen blisters and said, "Let's go."

Twenty-three

Pushing his wheelbarrow with its teetering tower of newspapers Pack trudged over the snow past Joe Ferris's store, boots crunching loudly. Joe was inside at the window looking out. Pack saw him look away—make a *point* of looking away. Pack continued on his errand.

It was truly a season of damnation. Only three weeks ago a train had been snowbound in the station for days. Starving cattle had drifted into Medora, smashed their heads in through windows and eaten the tarpaper off several lean-tos and shacks. A sodbuster couple had gone out to try and feed the cattle in their barn, and had frozen to death within fifty feet of the house. And a horse rancher had shot himself to death, or so it was claimed; there were suspicions it might have been the Stranglers, although Pack was fairly certain they'd disbanded and dispersed. He had put the question to the Marquis and the Marquis had not denied it.

As he reached the depot platform he encountered an astounding sight. It was something out of a fevered dream. There came lurching a battered wagon with four men on it and, walking behind the tailboard, bedraggled, mudcaked, scratched, black-and-blue, a skeletal apparition that was identifiable only by its teeth and eyeglasses.

"Just the man I want to see," Roosevelt croaked. "We need the key to the jail."

The wheelbarrow nearly capitulated when Pack set it down.

Roosevelt stumbled, then grinned. "Come along, Mr. Packard."

"What in God's name is all this?"

Redhead Finnegan, on the wagon—for Finnegan it was indeed, Pack determined after a closer look—thrust his face over the sideboard and glared at Roosevelt. "This dude's trying to railroad us, Pack. He and his crew ambushed us in the Bad Lands. He'll tell you any old pack of lies. Don't believe a word he says. You can see he's plumb crazy."

Roosevelt leveled his rifle—a ghost as determined as a bulldog. To Pack he said, "Come along."

"Well I don't know. Their word against yours—"

Dutch Reuter jumped down off the wagon, startling Roosevelt whose rifle swung tentatively toward him but Reuter ignored it. He had bits of brown grass and twigs in his beard. He clutched Pack's coat. Pack shrank back. Reuter's breath was foul. "His boat we steal. Behind the wagon all the way with his Winchester he walk. Fifty miles. Two days. Fifty miles. *Fifty miles!* His eyes he never close. Twenty foot back walking, and all the time that book he's reading. 'Keep going there—keep going.' Big storm. Him they jump—Red and Frank, they jump. And he fight 'em off! That wagon and two men, on his back he lift! Bejesus out of them two tough boys he scare. And the river. Dead cows. Take apart the wagon, he makes us. Pieces across we carry. Put back together. That water God-damn cold."

It wasn't easy trying to put the German's words back together and make any sort of sense out of them. Pack tried to review what Dutch Reuter was saying. It began to come clear.

Reuter said in awe, "No man so God-damn brave I ever seen. No man. No sir."

Pack slammed the Bastille door shut upon Finnegan and O'Donnell. They were bellowing.

Dutch Reuter remained outside. Roosevelt said to him, "Go on, Dutch. Get out of here—get out of the country before someone hurts you. Don't stay around here, for you're a fool. You haven't got enough sense to take care of yourself."

"*Mein Gott, Herr Roosevelt*—such kind and generous—how can I you thank? *Gott im Himmel*—a hundred thanks, a thousand thanks . . ."

Roosevelt looked at Pack in amusement and said, "By Godfrey, it's the first time a man ever thanked me for calling him a fool."

Pack gaped at the fiendish filthy spectral wraith before him. Roosevelt was so tired his every muscle quivered visibly.

Roosevelt said, "Be on your way now, Dutch."

Dutch Reuter stumbled away.

Pack stood a foot from Roosevelt and yelled at him: "Do you have any idea what you look like?"

"I don't know how I look," Roosevelt replied with a wide grin, "but I feel first-rate!"

"You've got to see the doctor. Right now." Pack steered him away from the jail. "Is that story true? Fifty miles? Three days all alone? My God, it's no good talking about Reuter—*you're* the fool. Biggest damn fool I've ever heard of. Why on earth did you do this?"

"Why, they stole my boat."

"Did they now. Well why in hell didn't you just hang them on the spot and save yourself all this trouble?"

Roosevelt said, "We are civilized men, thank God—not vigilantes. It was my duty to bring them to book, not to murder them."

Pack tried to offer an arm but Roosevelt shook him off and stumbled into town on his own.

His awe somewhat dampened by the little dude's damnable posturings, Pack trudged beside him, fearful the New Yorker would slip on the hard-packed snow.

Roosevelt seemed too weary to initiate conversation. The silence made Pack feel awkward. To dispel it he said, "We've been wondering if you'd show up today."

"Wondering?"

"For the duel? Between you and the Marquis?"

"Good Lord. What's the date, then?"

"Fourteenth of January."

"Is it. Fancy that. Well then—by George, I am at his disposal," Roosevelt whispered. He turned his face toward Pack with the most dreadful livid mask of an expression. Undoubtedly it was intended to be a grin but, undoubtedly as well, Roosevelt had utterly no idea what it did to his appearance.

They went past Geng's Furnishings & Notions and into the nearest provider of refreshment. It happened to be Jerry Paddock's saloon. There were a dozen men in the place. The hand-lettered sign on boards advertised EVERY THING FROM COW BOY BITTERS TO DUDE SODA. Roosevelt nearly fell into the nearest chair.

Pack said, "We've got to get you to the doctor."

"Nonsense. I'm fine."

Pack shoved the table a bit to one side and sat down beside him.

"Coffee," Roosevelt croaked. He tipped the rifle against the wall behind him.

Jerry Paddock, shifty-eyed and seedy, had been drinking; he looked wickedly cheerful. "Well well. Looky who showed up. Just in time to give the Markee his target practice."

"The man's tired and thirsty," Joe said. "Coffee for both of us, Jerry. Your very best."

"In a pig's eye." Paddock came swinging past the bar and rolled two revolvers out of his shoulders holsters. The Mandarin mustache drooped past his sharp-pointed jaw and his rough grinning glance swung hard from Roosevelt to Pack and back again. He was quite drunk and very pleased with himself. He had been insufferable ever since the court had acquitted him; he was a man who not only liked to be on the winning side but took great pleasure in rubbing everyone's nose in it.

Jerry Paddock cocked his two revolvers one at a time with melodramatic deliberation.

Pack said, "For God's sake, Jerry—"

The earsplitting blast of a gunshot cut him off and left his head reeling. There was another explosion. Pack blinked. He found he had jerked back in his chair hard enough to drive it back against the wall.

Jerry Paddock had shot holes in his own floor. He wagged the guns in Roosevelt's face, taunting him.

One of the butchers at the bar said, "Look at old Jerry. Thinks he's Wild Bill Hiccup."

Jerry Paddock said in a very quiet dangerous voice, "Four Eyes is going to treat." He moved forward and planted his feet, so that he stood leaning over Roosevelt, a gun in each hand. "Four Eyes made a damn fool of himself over in that courthouse and now he's gonna pay for it. Come on then, you yellow-livered son of a mangy bitch. Let's see the mint of your money. Set up the drinks, you God-damned puny little peckerwood."

There was an audience here; and reputation was a very important thing to a man like Paddock. It would be impossible for him to back down. Pack wondered if Roosevelt knew that. Despite his conviction that the New Yorker's discomfort was not altogether undeserved, Pack found himself obliged to intrude. "By God, Jerry, if I were armed—"

"Set up the drinks," Jerry Paddock said stubbornly to Roosevelt. His eyes, quite drunk, blinked with a dull yellow gleam that was full of mortal danger.

Then he fired again: left, right, left, right. The explosions rocked Pack's head back; he felt dizzy and deaf.

Roosevelt said with a tired sigh of resignation, "Well, if I've got to, I've got to," and rose, looking past Paddock toward the bar. And still coming up out of the chair he used all his rising weight to plunge his right fist straight up into the brittle point of Paddock's jaw.

Both revolvers exploded—possibly from involuntary convulsions of Paddock's hands, for the bullets went into the floor and by that time Paddock was toppling backward like an axed tree.

Pack was paralyzed with astonishment.

The back of Jerry Paddock's head struck the bar a sickening thump not six inches to one side of where the butcher was standing.

Paddock tumbled to the floor and Roosevelt was upon him in an instant, twisting the revolvers from Paddock's limp fists.

Then Roosevelt stumbled back to his chair. It lay on its back as though it had drunk too much and passed out. Roosevelt righted it, collapsed into it and dropped the two revolvers on the table. His exhaustion was obvious.

"Jesus Christ in Tarnation," exploded the butcher. "Knocked him out cold with a single punch to the jaw!"

Roosevelt said, "He made the mistake of standing to close to me with his heels too close together."

Pack said, "I don't believe what I just saw."

"Then you're a foolishly overskeptical man, aren't you." Roosevelt's toothsome grin flashed at him. "I told you, didn't I, that I used to be a boxer at Harvard?"

"I knew that," Pack said sourly. "I looked into it, you know. I found out you fought more than a dozen matches—and never won a single one."

"There's always a first time. And a second as well. You may recall I acquitted myself similarly with Mr. McKenzie last year."

Nothing daunted Roosevelt's infuriating good cheer. Pack, shaking his head in exasperation, went behind the bar to pour coffee.

On the next day—January fifteenth, the day fixed for the armed confrontation between Theodore Roosevelt and the Marquis De Morès—Pack knocked at the door of Joe Ferris's store before he walked in. He closed the door behind him against the cold.

Joe said, "Since when have you been knocking at that door?" He stood behind the cash counter in his flour-dusted apron.

"Seems to be a need of formality, somehow." Feeling a warm pink wash in his cheeks, Pack helped himself to a soda cracker. "He awake yet?"

"No, and he won't be for another four days unless somebody sets off a pound of blasting powder next to his ear."

"He's got two hours."

"Be that as it may, you think may be the Marquis might extend the schedule a day or two?"

"Now, you know he won't."

"And so do you know it. Which kind of sums up the Markee, may be. Now what are we going to do about this fellow upstairs?"

"I'm thinking of telling the Marquis he can't fight today. Unless you have an alternative to suggest. And incidentally let's not have any penny-dreadful heroics. You are not going to fight the duel in his place."

Joe said, "Never had any such intention. But at least you and I agree the duel should not take place today?"

"We do, certainly. The Marquis can be too much the man of honor sometimes—too rigid by half. Nobody denies that. It happens also that he has a business appointment in Chicago that requires him to catch today's train."

"Even if he has to step over a dead body to do it."

"That's up to Roosevelt, isn't it? He doesn't have to turn up, you know."

"He can't *not* turn up," Joe Ferris said. "He's not gaited that way and you know it."

"I might have argued that point with you once upon a time, but after the way he decked Jerry Paddock yesterday—I saw it with my own eyes and I still can't believe it. He may be a fool but he's brave enough. No, I don't expect him to back off."

Joe said, "There's one thing we could try. But it would have to come from you, not me. They have some regard for you up there in the château. They won't let me in the door."

Pack was suspicious. "Now, what d'you have in mind?"

"That acquittal on the murder charges hasn't prevented his enterprises from collapsing faster than he could try to save them. Seems to me the spirit's gone out of him. I think he can be reasoned with—if it comes from the right quarter."

"Which quarter's that?"

"Talk to his wife, Pack. She's the only one with any influence over the madman."

Pack scowled. "He's not a madman. He's a visionary."

"Have it your way. Just talk to her."

"Well it's a thought, I admit. Not only does the Marquis listen to Madame—she'd plead Roosevelt's case more earnestly than anyone else."

"You're wrong about that, you know."

"What?"

"You think there's something between them. Around behind the Markee's back."

"Now, I've seen them together."

"You've seen one thing and thought another. I'll tell you something, Pack. You keep thinking Roosevelt's secretly in love with her. It's not Roosevelt who's weak in the upper story over her, you damn fool—it's you."

"I for one, certainly . . . I'm hardly the only one . . . Every man in town—"

"Every man in town, mostly, knows a lot of things about her that you don't seem to know. Surely she can take a man's breath—but she's spoiled rotten. Her every whim's attended by one of twenty servants and if you know Mr. Roosevelt at all you've got to see how her life must look to him—all frivolous and downright decadent. The women in his own family may be used to having a few servants around but they damn well know how to fend for themselves. This girl Medora, she's got no independence—no life of her own at all, except what the Marquis allows her. She's well born, well bred, well trained, but she does what she's told. That's not Mr. Roosevelt's kind of woman. He's been polite and considerate to her because I reckon he feels sorry for her, and I expect may be he admires her loyalty to the Markee, but—"

"Now, Joe, she's not stupid! You make her sound vacuous. She's got more talents and skills than most of the grown men in this Territory."

"All right. Be that as it may. Roosevelt's been writing to his lady friend in New York, hasn't he now."

"How would you know that?"

"I'm postmaster, ain't I."

"You spied on him?"

"I'm no spy, Pack. You know better. I can read an address as well as the next man, and when he keeps sending letters every chance he gets to a Miss Edith Carow who clearly isn't his sister—"

"She could be a maiden aunt."

"And I could be Christopher Columbus. Hell, Pack, if you've got to know, I asked him one day and he told me. He said, 'That is Miss Edith Carow, the sweetheart of my childhood, and we intend to be married in London in the spring.'"

Theodore Roosevelt said, "An event to which I look forward with the most avid pleasure," and came down the stairs.

Pack wondered with alarm how much he had heard.

Roosevelt had done his best to clean up his outfit. He had shaved and some of the bruises had gone down and he looked nearly presentable.

And he was toting his Winchester.

He jacked it empty on the counter, picked up the cartridges, counted and examined them, and reloaded the magazine carefully.

His voice had a dull flat listlessness; it was unlike him. "In the absence of Mr. Sewall, I wonder if you, Joe, would be so good as to act as my second, and convey to the Marquis the information that I am available at his convenience."

Pack said, "If I may be so bold. Joe and I don't think this is the best time for you to go engaging in a duel."

Roosevelt blinked behind his eyeglasses. They were, Pack noticed, sparkling clean. Roosevelt said, "Is there such a thing as a good time for a duel?"

"Now, I believe there's a chance this one can be averted until you're feeling stronger."

He waited for Roosevelt to argue with him. The New Yorker said, "By all means. What do you have in mind?"

"I don't suppose you'd be willing to back away?"

"I don't suppose I can."

Joe Ferris said, "But if the Markee was to back away, you wouldn't force the issue, would you?"

"Old fellow, I should be a very happy man indeed if the Marquis should choose to withdraw his challenge. I've no desire to kill him, nor be killed by him."

Pack drew a deep breath and closed his eyes for an instant, and opened them. He looked Roosevelt in the eye. "Not much chance this will do any good, but will you object if I go to talk with the Marquis?"

"Why certainly not."

"And have you strenuous objection to my speaking with Madame Medora as part of the effort to change the Marquis's mind?"

"None whatever. For all I care you may speak with the Devil himself, if it will help restore peace and tranquillity to our town."

The Marquis De Morès was ready to climb into the carriage. He had already handed Madame up onto the seat. Facing Pack he stood with feet braced apart and whapped the weighted bamboo stick into his open palm.

Pack said, "Roosevelt has had a gruelling adventure—"

"Yes. Arthur, don't you find it a wonderful irony that he should be the man to arrest Dutch Reuter? Think of the trouble he could have saved himself if he'd simply let me have the old fool to begin with."

Madame Medora said, "Antoine, you must see that Arthur's right. It wouldn't be fair to take advantage of his weakened condition."

"If he says he's prepared to meet me, then I assume he has come prepared to decide the matter."

Madame la Marquise leaned over, reached out and touched a palm to her husband's cheek.

Pack watched her with an altogether new fascination.

Most women were realists, he had found—much more so than men were. A thing that fascinated him about Medora was that unlike most women she was not such a realist. No matter how accomplished, she was not practical; she was a romantic.

Whatever her feelings about Roosevelt might be, she was indeed in love with the Marquis. She wasn't blind to his arrogance and prejudices, any more than Pack was; she was able to ignore them because the great shining light of her romantic faith washed away all the shadows from her picture of him. Soft as she was, she had the will not to see things if they were unimportant by comparison with the man's true greatness.

Pack was able to recognize those qualities in her because he shared some of them.

"Antoine—if Theodore were to be killed in the Bad Lands, by you, I'm rather afraid there might be repercussions throughout New York Society."

She said no more than that; and Pack did not understand why her words made the Marquis stop dropping the heavy stick into his palm.

The Marquis looked away from her and met Pack's inquiring stare. A sort of snarl curled one corner of the lip beneath the meticulously pointed mustache. The Marquis lifted his Winchester out of the carriage, jacked it half open to see the cartridge in the chamber, made a grunting sound in his throat that Pack couldn't decipher at all, climbed up onto the seat and tapped the driver's shoulder with the muzzle of the rifle. "Let's go."

Roosevelt threaded the crowd to climb onto the platform with his rifle in hand. Joe Ferris watched with a scowl. "You shouldn't be here. If he sees you he won't have any choice but to fight."

"On the contrary—there is a choice, and it's his to make."

"Sir, begging to differ. Look at the size of the crowd watching here. In my experience it's always better to let the other chap keep his dignity intact."

"I shan't impugn his dignity. I shall say nothing inflammatory to him. But I am here, and here I shall stay. You may as well give up the argument, old fellow."

Joe opened his mouth to speak again but thought better of it; there was too much steel in Roosevelt's eye.

They hadn't long to wait. The eastbound train pulled in with a good deal of steamy chuffing—and the Marquis and Marquise arrived in their surrey. Arthur Packard came puffing along behind them, on foot.

The crowd made way. The Marquis stepped down. He carried his stick in one hand and a rifle in the other. He handed the stick up to Medora. The weight of it brought her arms down to the seat.

The Marquis kept his rifle in one hand, aimed at the ground. He faced Theodore Roosevelt. The crowd hung back, fascinated; no one made a sound. Joe recognized all the familiar faces—Johnny Goodall, Dan McKenzie, Eaton, Huidekoper, Deacon Osterhaut, Bob Roberts, dozens of others; and over at the edge with his two guns protruding from their shoulder holsters stood Jerry Paddock. Joe put his hand on his Remington revolver and made sure Jerry Paddock knew he was watching him. Jerry's expression did not change but his hands dropped to his sides and that was enough to provoke Joe Ferris's tight cool smile.

"Well, then," said the Marquis, "here we are."

Roosevelt nodded. His eyeglasses were sparkling clean, Joe noted. He must have washed them yet again.

There was a long run of silence—long enough to make sweat stand out on Pack's brow. Joe kept one eye on Jerry Paddock the whole time. He heard restless stirrings amid the crowd.

Roosevelt stood rock-steady, jaw jutting. The rifle was in his hand; his thumb was curled over its hammer.

The Marquis looked at that, and at Roosevelt's face. Then his faithless glance wandered toward the tops of the bluffs.

Roosevelt's grasp whitened on the rifle and the Marquis said, "May I pass?"

Theodore Roosevelt breathed deep. "The platform is open to any one. It's a free country, sir."

There was something like a low moan from the collective throats of the crowd.

The Marquis still didn't look Roosevelt in the face. He was

looking across the river, uphill toward the château. "I am going east on business. Then my wife will join me in New York and we intend to go home to Paris for a season of civilized amusements."

"Paris is at its best in the spring," Roosevelt said.

"Yes. Quite." The Marquis turned, finally met Roosevelt's eye and said, "I'm glad you agree there are always ways by which gentlemen can settle their differences amicably."

"However you prefer it, Mr. De Morès."

The Marquis said to Pack, "You may put it in your newspaper that I will return in the summer. I am a Dakotan—I have come to stay."

Pack wrote it down and Joe Ferris had the feeling they never would see the Marquis De Morès again.

The crowd stirred, uncertain. The Marquis boarded the train. The driver carried his luggage across the platform and then returned to the carriage; he lifted the reins but Madame stayed him. She watched the train until it pulled out; she waved, and the Marquis's colorfully sleeved arm waved back from the departing window.

Madame regarded Theodore Roosevelt with unhurried gravity.

The ranchman returned her glance; he smiled and bowed low. It was, Joe realized, a gesture of gratitude and respect.

Madame nodded graciously, acknowledging it. Then she gave Pack a warm smile—Joe was amused to see how it nearly melted Pack to a puddle. She prodded the driver with her husband's heavy stick, and the surrey pulled away.

Jerry Paddock uttered a loud clear obscenity before he wheeled away.

That was the signal for the crowd to disperse. Joe let his hand fall away from the revolver's handle. When he sucked in a long ragged lungful of wind he realized he had not been breathing at all.

Roosevelt said, "Thank you, Arthur. I'm deeply grateful. It's quite possible I owe you my life."

"I've been objective and non-partisan. I'm pleased if my efforts have helped to keep the peace."

"You can't remain aloof under the pretense of objectivity, you know. You must commit your soul to the values in which you believe. Defend them, and be damned to noncommittal dispassion.

You must have a firmly defined public spirit if you're to be one of the governing class. It's your plain duty—as it is mine. And now if you don't mind I think I'll repair upstairs and read for a bit."

When the New Yorker had gone to his room Joe said, "He'll sleep a week now."

"Public spirit," said Pack. He scowled at Joe. "He's always making speeches, like a stuffed-shirt schoolmaster."

"Seems to me his speeches make pretty good sense."

Pack was irritable. "I didn't expect the Marquis to back down."

"A lot of folks didn't. Maybe they see now the kind of bully he is. Only fights when he knows he's got the advantage."

"That's not a fair judgment. There were a lot of factors," Pack said. "But I admit too many things have taken me by surprise today. One was when Madame agreed so readily to talk to him."

"What did she say to the Markee?"

Pack consulted his notebook. "'*Antoine—if Theodore were to be killed in the Bad Lands, by you, I'm rather afraid there might be repercussions throughout New York Society.*'"

"New York Society," Joe said. "That means her father the banker—who happens to be the source of the Markee's fortune. Well you said she wasn't stupid and you were right. I guess she saw right away—and she reminded the Marquis that a duel might have killed more than Theodore Roosevelt. So you see, Pack, the Marquis didn't withdraw out of the goodness of his heart. More like greedy cowardice."

Pack said, "You'll have a hard time proving that to me." He turned to go, and then stopped abruptly; he swung back with surprise all over his face. "Now, you've run another confidence game, haven't you. This time on *me*."

Joe said with wide-eyed guilelessness, "What're you talking about?"

"When you asked me to intercede with Madame. It wasn't your idea at all. It was *his*."

Joe grinned. "What ever makes you say that?"

"If it had come from him—if he'd been the one to ask me, I wouldn't have done it. He put you up to it. He used you, Joe. He knew I trusted your friendship and he used us both."

"Ah, well, then, may be," said Joe Ferris. "Be that as it may, do you really feel ill-used?"

* * *

There were distressing reports from the hills as the cattlemen went out with the spring round-up. For two weeks Pack waited while they scoured the Bad Lands, finding no cattle, growing to believe the storms must have drifted the main herds pretty far from their home ranges. They found a few steers, most of which they killed for food. They ranged farther and wider, and to his disbelieving consternation Pack learned in the end that the terrible winter had wiped out the greater part of every herd in the Bad Lands—ironically, with the sole exception of the De Morès herd; the Marquis's tough Dakota-bred three-year-olds had survived, and Johnny Goodall had the unhappy duty of selling them off to settle a small portion of the Marquis's massive debts.

The only blessing was that the Stranglers were gone. Evaporated with the snows. With the departure of the Marquis their payroll likewise departed—and therefore so did they. Pack supposed the ugly Mr. W.H. Springfield had returned to Chicago to take a new assignment for his employers at the Pinkerton Detective Agency. As for the identities of the men who had ridden in the noose-party posses, no one had found any further clue to those, and he doubted anyone ever would. It was certain Jerry Paddock knew more about them than he was admitting—it was Jerry who had slipped Pack the embarrassingly premature information about the hanging of Modesty Carter—but Jerry had very little to say to anyone about anything these days. Little Casino had not returned with him from Bismarck; apparently she had found a high-roller there who suited her temper better and she had run off with him to the East, while Jerry took solace in lugubrious portions of whiskey abetted by profits from his multifarious shady schemes.

At the end of the round-up, seventy men rode into Medora driving one limping steer. When Pack interviewed Theodore Roosevelt, the ranchman said he had ridden across his entire home range and not found a single live steer.

Neither Sewall nor Huidekoper had the ill manners to say "I told you so."

Roosevelt's ranch was a casualty—but Roosevelt was not. On that final day he came to the train station wearing a derby hat, in defiance of local custom. No one knocked it off; no one fired a shot. Huidekoper was there, and Eaton and Joe Ferris and even McKenzie; there were a score of well-wishers, most of them long-faced because of the dreadful winter kill.

Jerry Paddock, perhaps still nursing his sore jaw, was noticeably absent.

Before he followed Dow and Sewall aboard the Express, Roosevelt said, "You see, Arthur, I intend to wear any hat I please." He lifted the derby off his head and held it high, grinned at the onlookers and replaced the hat square across his eyes.

A.C. Huidekoper stepped forward to shake his hand and Roosevelt said, "The land will recover, and you with it. You're a capital fellow."

"Yes, it takes more than a few blizzards to get rid of a long-winded geezer like me. Good luck to you, Theodore."

Pack said, "Have you a parting quote for the *Cow Boy?*"

Roosevelt squinted through his glasses at the towering bluffs. He looked all around. "I came to the hills of this fair Territory in great despair, and it has blown the cobwebs from my eyes. This great and glorious West has made me strong and whole, and ready as well as eager to return to my spirited career of honorably stirring up the hack politicians of the Empire State." At that last bit he flashed his brash many-toothed mischievous grin.

"What are you going to do?"

"My good lady Edith is waiting in New York to marry me and I have a little daughter whom I haven't seen in far too long a time. And after such experiences as those we have enjoyed with the royalist Mr. De Morès I am resolved to plunge myself back into politics, for it seems more than ever important to me that the ideals of our precious democracy be defended. I've decided to run for the office of Mayor of New York."

"Well good luck to you, Theodore."

For it was true: Pack had been admitted to the circle of those permitted to address Roosevelt by his first name.

He still was not certain it was a circle to which he cared to belong.

Roosevelt pointed to the precarious stack of newspapers in the wheelbarrow behind Pack, and said offhandedly, "Why don't you tie those in bales so they won't get away from you?"

As the train departed, Pack wondered, *Why didn't* I *ever think of that?*

That night, by pure accident, *The Bad Lands Cow Boy* burned to the ground.

Epilogue

June 1903

A considerable crowd had gathered in the ghost town. Several hundred people waited by the embankment for the eastbound flyer. Looking out the window of the train, Pack saw women and old men in the uniform of the Grand Army of the Republic and children and young men in the ragtag outfits of the Cuban campaign. Many of them were too young to remember this town when it had been alive; but Pack recognized some who had been cow hands here.

He saw dozens of men draw sidearms and check their loads.

The train, preceded by the howl of its whistle, slowed a-clatter across the Little Missouri River bridge. The President and his party were aboard, including Pack, having joined the train five miles west at Huidekoper's loading pens; it wasn't for the local celebrants to know that Colonel Roosevelt and his hand-picked cronies had spent the night at the site of his old Elkhorn ranch swapping ebullient yarns about the old days in the Wild West.

Not that those days were so far gone. Pack saw dozens of arms lift above the hats of the crowd. Each hand had a gun in it.

One of them was Jerry Paddock's.

Joe Ferris saw him too. When the train stopped Joe was out first, moving fast despite his considerable girth. Pack followed him into the crowd but when they reached the point where Paddock had been standing, the villain was nowhere to be seen.

"Come on," Joe said. "We've got to find him."

Pack knew what was in the front of Joe's mind. Roosevelt was President only because of the assassin's bullet that had killed McKinley; Jerry Paddock was just crazy enough to want to replicate that bit of history—and there was no question Jerry Paddock had a score to settle with Theodore Roosevelt.

Pack and Joe jumped up on the platform and swiveled, trying to peer in all directions at once. The crowd swayed maddeningly; it was difficult to see anyone clearly. A blustery wind—buff-colored from the sand it carried—stung Pack's eyes and lashed his coat against his knees and made it difficult to see; he squinted and once he thought he saw Paddock and he reached out to tug at Joe Ferris's sleeve but it wasn't Paddock at all.

Paddock was somewhere else—out of sight, working up his rage, perhaps drawing his two guns even now.

When he stepped out onto the rear vestibule President Theodore Roosevelt was clearly pleased by the size of the crowd, by the earsplitting shout of welcome and by the racketing fusillade of gunshots that roared overhead.

"By Godfrey, a true Bad Lands reception." The President laughed with magnificent vitality. His wide face shone in the sun—that famous broad cartoon of huge teeth, shaggy mustache, glittering eyeglasses. "Thank you all, my fine friends! My goodness—this must be the entire population of the Bad Lands down to the smallest baby. What a fine day!"

His autograph was much in demand. He bent over the railing to receive books and papers, signed them and handed them back. Then after a short time—short enough to prevent the crowd from growing restive—he removed his rough hat and held it up in one hand while from the platform at the back of his private railroad car he obliged the multitude with a torrent of talk.

The election campaign was still a year away but the President was taking no chances; this tour of the West was unabashedly designed to mend old fences and build new ones. There was the issue of Roosevelt's unelected Presidency: he had not been voted into the office; he had inherited it, and those who disapproved of his politics resented that. And there was also the fact that in the last election large portions of the West had voted for William Jennings Bryan—and against the McKinley-Roosevelt ticket—on the free-silver proposition, which was an issue both sides of which still bestirred great wrath among Westerners. It seemed transparent to Pack that Roosevelt was trying to repeal the free-silver sentiment by exploiting his close ties to the region.

The Bryan partisans had not folded their tents. Quite the contrary; they had risen to the challenge with the fervor of zealous fanatics. Pack knew that earlier whistle-stops on this journey had been enlivened vividly by several hostile audiences. A few had broken into serious mob riots.

"Even discounting Jerry Paddock, there may be trouble here too, from the malcontents," Huidekoper had said to Pack just ten minutes ago. And sure enough he heard the angry murmuring sounds of discontent rumbling from several quarters of the crowd as Roosevelt plunged into his hearty speech.

Trying to watch everyone at once, Pack stood under flailing shadows as the great restless rolling buffalo of a man (when he was orating you didn't notice how short he was) thrashed his powerful arms, peppering the air with spirited high-pitched exclamation.

Roosevelt engaged the crowd with what some of them wanted to hear: he talked of his new designations of National Wildlife Refuges; he talked of San Juan Hill and of his intention to send the Navy to the Isthmus of Panama to protect the proposed canal route against resistance from what he called "those homicidal corruptionists of Colombia."

Much of the President's harangue had the hollow ring of campaign malarkey. Yet the man actually meant what he said. The President could spout bombast and bluster but he was no fool. The world, Pack thought, had seldom known such a contradictory array of conflicting qualities in one man.

There were boos and hisses now—catcalls; a segment of the crowd was turning unruly. Pack heard the rallying cry "Cross of gold!" and there was a nasty growl from a dozen throats.

That was when the gaunt two-gun pushed forward through the crowd. *Jerry Paddock!*

Joe Ferris reached under his coat.

Jerry Paddock smiled his wicked saturnine smile and shook his head at Joe Ferris.

Joe's Remington lifted.

The President watched—silent for a change—for a brief moment while Jerry Paddock waved a hand at Joe Ferris and, keeping his hands in plain sight, climbed onto the train and stood facing the crowd, a gun on each hip, his arms folded, whipping his stare instantly toward anyone in the crowd who showed any signal of disapproval.

Pack was stunned. Jerry Paddock turned gravely and offered his right hand, and Theodore Roosevelt with a flash of his brilliant grin clutched the offered handshake and then Paddock like a trained dog stepped back behind the President and that was that.

After that the hecklers kept their peace. The rest of the crowd kept interrupting Roosevelt with applause. The President waited it out with a big smile. There were no more boos or hisses; Jerry Paddock's malevolent two-gun glare silenced them immediately.

The speech reached its bully climax:

"I got a Spaniard or two. Bullets everywhere. Well some of you remember how I told the boys who enlisted with me in '98 it would be no picnic—and the place of honor was the post of danger, and we each must expect to die!"

A great roar went up.

At the President's shoulder A.C. Huidekoper said, "You see they all feel you're their man, sir."

"They're all my old friends," said the President. Pack saw again the fabled grin when Roosevelt looked back to Jerry Paddock the two-gun man: "Even the ones who tried to kill me."

The murderer smiled. "At your service, Mr. President." He touched a finger to his hatbrim in obeisance.

And then the train was ready to leave; the President turned as if to go inside but then he stopped at the railing and peered uphill. When Pack followed the line of his glance he saw smoke rising from the chimney of the château.

A.C. Huidekoper said, "That'll be the last of the servants. They're about to leave for good. You missed Madame by about six weeks, Mr. President. She came out with two of her grown children to close up the place and take some of the furnishings back to France."

"Is she in good health and spirits?"

"Very good indeed, and as beautiful as ever."

"Chère Madame," said the President. "She's not had a happy life. I do wish her well."

Pack got Roosevelt's ear momentarily. "Sometimes when I think back on the Marquis and the Stranglers and all that, I still ask myself if now and then the Marquis may have been right, according to his own lights. Do you ever ask yourself about those days—if sometimes maybe the ends do justify the means?"

"No, Pack. You can't tailor your code to fit the needs of the moment. Right and wrong exist. One need not apologize for espousing absolutes. Permit me, old fellow, to remind you that Moses did not come down off the mountain with The Ten Suggestions. The Marquis was wrong—dead wrong, and that's all there was to it."

With that and a flashing grin of his great tombstone teeth the President stepped inside. A moment later the train was away.

The crowd dispersed. Pack stood fast, watching the train dwindle.

Pack said to Joe Ferris, "Now wasn't that singular—what Jerry Paddock did?"

"I guess may be Jerry's always hankered to be on the winning side. That little show he put on—do wonders for public opinion. I wouldn't be surprised he ran for public office one day soon. Why, they'll probably name a creek after him."

Pack said, "The thought makes me shudder."

"Well hell, Pack, there's nobody left around here except hermits and wild goats. Jerry Paddock can get himself elected sheriff of all that if it's what he wants."

A.C. Huidekoper pressed the reins of a saddle horse into Pack's hand and Pack heard him say dryly, "Perhaps after all this time you can begin to admit that it was the ridiculous four-eyed dude there, and not the magnificent Marquis, who, by his example if not his manner, taught you what it really means to be an honorable man."

"That is true," Pack admitted—finally. "He was the better man, wasn't he. And I was wrong in believing otherwise. And I'm prepared to buy you gentlemen a drink to that discovery."

Joe Ferris said, "I have observed that it takes some people a mighty long time to grow up." Pack felt the firm clasp of Joe's arm around his shoulders. It made him smile. It was good to be among friends—and to know who one's real friends were.

Postscript

The business ventures of the Marquis de Morès suffered their final collapse in 1886 and he departed for France in the fall of that year, having lost more than a million of his father-in-law's dollars in an age when the value of the dollar could be measured by the fact that the average annual wage—a comfortable living wage—was $250. He said he would return to Dakota but he never did.

After he left the United States, De Morès went to India and hunted tigers. His fortunes were dissipated; his father-in-law refused to support his ventures any further. Nevertheless, increasingly paranoiac, he resumed his vain and somewhat absurd attempts to restore the French monarchy and ascend the throne. Perhaps the most extreme public bigot of his day, he stood for a Paris council seat on the "Pure Anti-Semite" ticket, killed at least one Jewish army officer in a duel and—curiously—helped stir up a scandal of charges of rampant corruption in connection with the financing of Suez Canal builder Ferdinand De Lesseps's celebrated attempt to build a canal across the Isthmus of Panama. De Morès's plots against De Lesseps and Clemenceau brought final destruction to the French attempt to build a Panama Canal—thereby opening the way for Theodore Roosevelt to complete the Canal two decades later.

De Morès served several months in prison for inciting a crowd to riot, and was instrumental in provoking the anti-Semitic frenzy that led to the infamous Dreyfus case that inflamed Zola to write *J'Accuse*.

In 1896, in a mirror-reversal of the ambush that killed Riley Luffsey, the Marquis was himself ambushed. At age thirty-eight, Antoine Amédée Marie Vincent Manca de Vallombrosa, Marquis De Morès, was murdered in the Tunisian desert by Tuaregs, who hacked him limb from limb. He had gone to North Africa to lead a preposterous expedition whose objective was to form a Franco-Islamic alliance against the Jews and the British.

His widow Medora, faithful to the end, posted a reward for the capture of his killers. She saw them brought to justice and executed. They were reported to have been bandits but more likely they were hired assassins in the pay of the French government, to whom De Morès had become an embarrassment too vast to be tolerated.

De Morès had been in line to succeed his father as Duc de Vallombrosa but, as things worked out, his father survived him by a decade.

One suspects De Morès would not be amused to know that today his birthplace, a sturdy 250-year-old manor, serves as the Paris Embassy of the USSR.

Nearly all his evil schemes were frustrated; he saw himself as a tragic hero but the mustache-twisting Marquis, like other great evildoers, remains as absurdly and malevolently comical as Wile E. Coyote in a *Roadrunner* cartoon.

I know of no evidence of any communication between Theodore Roosevelt and the lady Medora, Marquise De Morès, at any time after their Dakota adventures. It is a fact, however, that Madame De Morès paid her last visit to the town of Medora in 1903 not long before President Roosevelt made his pre-campaign swing through the West. On that final visit to Dakota, Madame De Morès was accompanied by her grown son Louis and daughter Athenais; she stayed six weeks and closed up the château, which had remained unchanged from seventeen years earlier—the De Morès servants had kept it intact, just as it had been on the day of the family's departure in 1886.

Later, during the First World War, Lady Medora maintained the Vallombrosa family mansion in Paris as a hospital for wounded men. She ministered tirelessly to their injuries; she was wounded by a German shell when the house was bombarded. In March 1921, as a result of that wound, she died at the age of sixty-three; she had outlived Theodore Roosevelt by two years.

Medora and her husband are buried side-by-side in Cannes. They were survived by three children: the two abovementioned, born in America, and son Paul, born later in France.

Arthur T. Packard remained a newspaperman throughout his life. The last issue of his *Bad Lands Cow Boy* was published on December 23, 1887; the next day, the building where Pack and his new bride lived, and where the *Cow Boy* was published, burned down. (In 1970 publication of the *Cow Boy* was resumed by Clayton C. Bartz and David C. Bartz, as a historical journal.) Pack remained in the West and in the newspaper game, carving out a long journalistic career in the region between Chicago and Montana. As late as 1912 he was a prominent supporter of Roosevelt's independent Progressive Party ("Bull Moose") attempt to regain the Presidency.

In Chicago in 1931, Arthur T. Packard died; he was seventy.

William Wingate Sewall published a memoir shortly after Roosevelt's death, and died a decade later at eighty-four, in March 1930. His nephew Wilmot Dow had died earlier of acute Bright's Disease in Island Falls, Maine, at the age of thirty-six in 1891.

Joe Ferris joined Theodore Roosevelt's campaign for the Vice Presidency in 1900, and traveled with Roosevelt through North Dakota and Montana. Long before that, Joe had sold his store and moved to Montana. Roosevelt kept in touch with him for many years. In 1912 Joe, like his friend Pack, was a delegate to Roosevelt's Bull Moose convention.

Howard Eaton, the first dude rancher, ran his tourist outfit at Custer Trail until 1904, when with his brothers he moved to the Big Horn country—Wolf, Wyoming, where the famous Eaton Ranch still operates today. Meanwhile the Eaton brothers' original Custer Trail Ranch near Medora has become a Bible camp operated by the Lutheran Church.

A.C. Huidekoper was one of the few ranchers to remain in the Bad Lands and keep faith in the region. As the foregoing story shows, he was still living there when Roosevelt visited in 1903. Huidekoper raised horses there, quite successfully, until he retired in 1906, at which time according to memoirist Lincoln Lang, "his herd numbered . . . approximately five thousand head of equine blue bloods, constituting perhaps the grandest, most distinctive single herd of horses the world ever knew, . . . ranging from full-blooded Percherons to polo ponies from a cross between thoroughbred racing stock and the best Indian pony mares obtainable. The latter were, in fact, the pick of Sitting Bull's war ponies."

Roosevelt wrote dryly in his *Ranch Life and the Hunting-Trail*, "One committee of vigilantes in eastern Montana shot or hung nearly sixty—not, however, with the best judgment in all cases." Ironically the founder of the Montana Stock Growers Association and clandestine leader of the neighboring state's vigilantes, Granville Stuart, according to Roosevelt's *Autobiography* "was afterwards appointed Minister by [President Grover] Cleveland, I think to the Argentine."

As for Theodore Roosevelt (*magna cum laude* and Phi Beta Kappa, Harvard 1880), by 1886 he was revitalized and as mature as he was going to become. He returned east to marry Edith Carow (she later described her husband the President fondly as "a six-year-old boy") and to plunge back into the political life. He lost his bid for election to the office of Mayor of New York but that failure did not daunt him. Soon after, he was appointed Police Commissioner of New York City; he went on to higher offices.

He recruited many Rough Riders in the Spanish-American War from amongst the Bad Lands cowboys with whom he had worked during his ranching days.

Throughout his adventurous life as New York Police Commissioner, Colonel of Rough Riders, Governor of New York State, Vice President of the United States, two-term (1901-1908) President of the United States (the twenty-sixth, and the youngest ever to be inaugurated), builder of the Panama Canal, first American winner of the Nobel Peace Prize, candidate in the ill-fated 1912 Bull Moose election campaign, world traveler, hunter, naturalist, author of three dozen books and uncounted articles and essays and at least 150,000 letters—some 20 million words in all (he read as many as three books a day throughout most of his life)—and leader of the gruelling Amazon River explorations: as for Roosevelt, right up to his death at sixty in 1919 he kept up running correspondences and frequent reunions with old friends like Joe Ferris and Bill Sewall. Several of them (particularly Sewall, still a woodsman and guide) were frequent honored guests in the Roosevelt White House.

It was Theodore Roosevelt who—even before he became President—guided, expanded and protected the National Park system in time to preserve the great Yellowstone wilderness. Later, as President and as the leading conservationist of his era, he created the Forest Service and quadrupled the holdings of the National Forests to nearly 200 million acres; and he established numerous wildlife refuges, signed the Act that allowed the President to proclaim National Monuments and National Parks, and created by proclamation 23 such areas.

Today the Marquis De Morès's weighted bamboo stick is in the collection housed in the splendidly preserved De Morès Château on the bluff ("Graveyard Butte") overlooking the town of Medora, North Dakota. The property was given by Louis Vallombrosa (eldest son of the Marquis) to the State of North Dakota, and is administered by the State Historical Society. Its restoration began in 1936; the work was performed by a WPA crew whose labors were fueled and made happy by thousands of intact bottles of wine they found in the cellar beneath the lady Medora's kitchen.

Thanks to contributions made by the De Morès heirs and by other benefactors, the château contains a fascinating collection of possessions from the 1880s including quite a few of the couple's hunting trophies, furnishings, decorations, books, clothes, weapons, utensils and art works, the latter including a small watercolor that Madame la Marquise painted of the château—slightly impressionistic, very pleasing; Medora had a good eye for color and design.

In the visitor center near the château stands one of the four Concord coaches used by De Morès's ill-fated Deadwood stage line.

The portrait of Madame la Marquise that is the most popular likeness was painted by the artist Charles Jalabert in New York City when she was still Medora Von Hoffman; reproductions are all over the town that was named after her—even on the place-mats of local cafes. The original painting hangs in Bismarck.

Medora town, now restored and developed as a tourist attraction, is much as it was in the 1880s. Harold Schafer, founder of the Gold Seal Company in Bismarck, and his wife were the architects of the town's restoration. Among the revived town's attractions are Joe Ferris's store—still operating as a general store—the rebuilt *Bad Lands Cow Boy* shack, the railroad depot, the little brick church that Madame la Marquise caused to be built, and the onetime De Morès Hotel (now, with wonderful irony, called the "Rough Riders"—De Morès would have shrieked).

The great abattoir-slaughterhouse burned down on March 17, 1907, but the foundations and the awesomely tall chimney remain to mark the site.

The railroad is still in use across the unpredictable Little Missouri, and Riley Luffsey's grave is on the butte; take a walk along the embankments on a certain sort of Bad Lands day and it seems not much of a stretch to imagine the footprints of the Lunatic and those who pursued him.

Among the best preserved and least Disneyfied of the restored "ghost towns" of the Old West, Medora brims over with artifacts and scenery that bring to life the Roosevelt-De Morès era.

The town is gateway to the spectacular Bad Lands of the 70,000-acre Theodore Roosevelt National Park, given federal protection in 1947 and National Park status in 1978. For anyone interested in the real West and its history and its morality fables, a visit is virtually mandatory. (The site of Roosevelt's Elkhorn Ranch is approximately in the middle of the Park.)

Roosevelt actually had two Dakota ranches—the Maltese Cross seven miles south of Medora and the Elkhorn thirty-four miles north of town. The cabin that stands today at the headquarters of the South Unit of the Theodore Roosevelt National Park (just at the edge of Medora town) was Roosevelt's original Maltese Cross ranch house. No buildings from the Elkhorn have survived, although the site of the ranch is still accessible by foot trail from a nearby park road, once the traveler obtains permission from the rancher whose land provides access to it.

* * *

It has been suggested, not without justification, that the image of the Wild West that prevailed during a good part of the twentieth century was to a surprising extent due to the activities of three men: Frederic Remington, who painted it; Owen Wister, who wrote about it (*The Virginian*); and Theodore Roosevelt, the American Winston Churchill, who not only wrote about the West in its heyday of adventure but created a good part of The Myth by living it in the Bad Lands.

The three men—all Ivy Leaguers (Harvard and Yale), all contemporaries—were close friends. The portrait of the West in the works of Remington and Wister was based in part on the experiences of their friend Roosevelt. Therefore it may not be too surprising that some of the set-piece conventions that became familiar in pulp fictions and "B" movies are to be found unabashedly in the real life of that astonishing unique American hero, Theodore Roosevelt.

Acknowledgments

It gives me pleasure to acknowledge, with great gratitude, the invaluable assistance provided by Todd Strand and the other archivists who keep track of the Roosevelt and De Morès collections at the State Historical Society of North Dakota, North Dakota Heritage Center, Bismarck; by the people of Medora, North Dakota; by the staff of the De Morès château; by the Rangers of the Theodore Roosevelt National Park, including Denise Heidecker of the National Park Service who indulged my foolishness by agreeing to take a picture of me in front of Theodore Roosevelt's cabin; all the memoirists, acquaintances, reporters, historians and biographers (see Bibliography) who made my work possible by writing in such extensive detail about Theodore Roosevelt and his days in Dakota Territory; and—indispensibly and most generously—by Dr. John Gable, director of the Theodore Roosevelt Association at Sagamore Hill, Oyster Bay, Long Island, New York.

For help in preparing the manuscript I am happy to thank Bina Garfield, Jane Cushman, Sara Ann Freed and Otto Penzler. And finally, for generous, thorough and brilliant editorial assistance far beyond the call of friendship or professional duty, I am indebted beyond words to Dori Gores.

Bibliography

All photographs are courtesy of the State Historical Society of North Dakota, North Dakota Heritage Center, Bismarck

PUBLICATIONS:

Bartz, David C., Editor, *The Bad Lands Cow Boy.* (Historical articles in newspaper form.) Various issues. Beach, North Dakota, 1985. (See also Packard, Arthur T.)

Brooks, Chester L., and Ray H. Mattison, *Theodore Roosevelt and the Dakota Badlands.* Washington: National Park Service, 1958 and 1962; Reprinted, with revisions, at Medora, North Dakota, by the Theodore Roosevelt Nature and History Association, 1983.

Burdick, Usher L., *Marquis De Morès at War in the Badlands.* Fargo, N.D.: publisher unidentified; circa 1929.

Deming, William Chapin, *Roosevelt in the Bunk House: Visits of the Great Rough Rider to Wyoming in 1903 and 1910.* Laramie, Wyoming: Press of the Wyoming Tribune-Leader, c. 1920.

Dresdan, Donald, *The Marquis De Morès, Emperor of the Bad Lands.* Norman, Okla.: University of Oklahoma Press, 1970.

Easterwood, Thomas Jefferson, *The Lights and Shadows of the Rocky Mountains*. New York: Appleton, 1888.

Goplen, Arnold O., *The Career of Marquis De Morès in the Bad Lands of North Dakota*. Bismarck: State Historical Society of North Dakota. Written 1938; first published as a journal article in 1946; pamphlet version published 1960.

Hagedorn, Herman, *Roosevelt in the Badlands*. Boston and New York: Houghton Mifflin Co., 1921.

Johnston, William Davison, *TR: Champion of the Strenuous Life*. New York: Theodore Roosevelt Association, 1958.

Kingsbury, George W., *History of Dakota Territory*. Chicago: The S.J. Clarke Publishing Co., 1915. Three volumes.

Lang, Lincoln A., *Ranching with Roosevelt*. Philadelphia: J.B. Lippincott Co., 1926.

Mattison, Ray H., "Life at Roosevelt's Elkhorn Ranch—The Letters of William W. and Mary Sewall." *North Dakota History*, Vol. 27, Nos. 3 and 4 (Summer and Fall, 1960).

———, "Ranching in the Dakota Badlands." *North Dakota History*, Vol. 19, Nos. 2 and 3 (April and July 1952).

———, "Roosevelt and the Stockmen's Association." *North Dakota History*, Vol. 17, Nos. 2 and 3 (April and July 1950). Reprinted as a pamphlet at Medora, North Dakota, by Theodore Roosevelt Nature and History Association, 1969.

McCullough, David, *Mornings on Horseback*. New York: Simon & Schuster, Inc., 1981.

Morison, Elting, *Letters of Theodore Roosevelt*. Cambridge: Harvard University Press, 1951. Volumes I and II (covering years 1868–1900).

Morris, Edmund, *The Rise of Theodore Roosevelt*. New York: Coward, McCann & Geoghegan, Inc., 1979.

Packard, Arthur T., *The Bad Lands Cow Boy*. (Newspaper.) Medora, Dakota Territory; various issues, 1884–1885.

Petty, Warren James, "History of Theodore Roosevelt National Memorial Park." *North Dakota History*, Vol. 35, No. 2 (Spring, 1968).

Pringle, Henry F., *Theodore Roosevelt, A Biography*. New York: Harcourt, Brace & Co., 1931.

Putnam, Carleton, *Theodore Roosevelt: Vol. I: The Formative Years, 1858–1886*. New York: Scribner's, 1958.

Riis, Jacob A., *Theodore Roosevelt the Citizen*. New York: The Outlook Co., 1903.

Roosevelt, Theodore, *Hunting Trips of a Ranchman*. New York: G.P. Putnam's Sons, 1922.

———, *Ranch Life and the Hunting Trail*. With numerous illustrations by Frederic Remington. New York: Century Company, 1888, 1899, 1901. A trade paperback edition, reprinted from the first 1888 edition but somewhat reduced in size, was published at Lincoln, Nebraska by the University of Nebraska Press in 1983.

———, *Theodore Roosevelt, An Autobiography*. New York: Charles Scribner's Sons, 1920.

Schoch, Henry A., *Theodore Roosevelt: The Story Behind the Scenery*. Las Vegas, Nev.: KC Publications, 1974, 1979.

Sewall, William Wingate, *Bill Sewall's Story of T.R.* (With an Introduction by Herman Hagedorn.) New York: Harper & Brothers, 1919.

Trinka, Z'dena, *Medora*. First published in New York 1940, as *Medora: The Secret of the Bad Lands*. Reprinted in hardcover, Lidgerwood, N.D.: First Award Books. 1960.

Tweton, D. Jerome, *The Marquis De Morès: Dakota Capitalist, French Nationalist*. Fargo, N.D.: North Dakota Institute for Regional Studies, 1972, 1974.

Wister, Owen, *Roosevelt: The Story of a Friendship—1880–1919*. New York: The Macmillan Co., 1930.